Anthea Halliwell was born in Ceylon, where her father was a tea planter. She returned to Britain in the 1930s and later worked in journalism, teaching, as an actress and photographer. She lives in North Wales.

THE CUCKOO'S PARTING CRY

Anthea Halliwell

BLACK SWAN

THE CUCKOO'S PARTING CRY
A BLACK SWAN BOOK : 0 552 99774 9

First publication in Great Britain

PRINTING HISTORY
Black Swan edition published 1998

Copyright © Anthea Halliwell 1998

The right of Anthea Halliwell to be identified as the author of this
work has been asserted in accordance with sections 77 and 78
of the Copyright Designs and Patents Act 1988.

All the characters in this book are fictitious,
and any resemblance to actual persons, living or dead,
is purely coincidental.

Condition of Sale
This book is sold subject to the condition that it shall not,
by way of trade or otherwise, be lent, re-sold, hired out or
otherwise circulated in any form of binding or cover other than that
in which it is published and without a similar condition including
this condition being imposed on the subsequent purchaser.

Set in 11/13pt Linotype Melior by
County Typesetters, Margate, Kent

Black Swan Books are published by Transworld Publishers Ltd,
61–63 Uxbridge Road, London W5 5SA,
in Australia by Transworld Publishers (Australia) Pty Ltd,
15–25 Helles Avenue, Moorebank, NSW 2170
and in New Zealand by Transworld Publishers (NZ) Ltd,
3 William Pickering Drive, Albany, Auckland.

Reproduced, printed and bound in Great Britain by
Cox & Wyman Ltd, Reading, Berks.

For Averil Ashfield,
lynx-eyed editor and guide

Ac i bobl Y Bermo, 1932–1962

ACKNOWLEDGEMENTS

To Paul Gould for his practical help, generously given.

And to Mary Irvine, my agent, for her professional expertise.

So have I heard the cuckoo's parting cry . . .
'The bloom is gone, and with the bloom go I.'

'Thyrsis' – Matthew Arnold

1

That August was hot, and here on this side of the estuary, quiet; the air too languid to carry the shrieks of holidaymakers from the beaches a mile away.

And this afternoon was hotter than ever. All morning the river had pursued the tide out until the water lay now, sleek and exhausted, at low ebb.

No birds sing in August. The hot silence was broken only by the drone of a bumble-bee hurrying to inspect me, lurching away again, drunk with nectar. For days now, there had been no breeze to sway the jungle of bracken on the marshes, and the foxgloves stood tall, untouched by any lifting of the air. Only the water moved, sifting idly through the gravel at its edge.

I was sitting on a rock, feet dangling in the water, trying not to watch the road. On the sandbars out in the river the oyster-catchers dozed in the drowsy stillness of the afternoon. Even the seagulls were silent, waiting for the turn of the tide.

I was waiting too, listening, half-hoping that they'd come back and say *Ha, ha! We were only joking,* but knowing that they wouldn't. They were probably miles away by now, the wind in their faces, intoxicated by the thrill of the ride in Eric's car.

It was an outrage. I had tried a few experimental sobs but they were unconvincing. Used as I was to Fiff's playful mockery – or what seemed to her to be playful – this time she had gone too far. So instead I scowled down at my feet, swirling them apart and

11

together again under the water. The soles were a spectral blue-white like the bellies of dead fish; the tops, tanned in the pattern of my sandal straps, were a faded grey, the summer gold shabby under the water.

A train trailing a snow-white plume of steam started its rumbling journey over the bridge, train and steam and bridge mirrored in the still water below.

The afternoon stretched emptily ahead. I had come racing home just in time – I was *certain* I was in time because I was hungry – but they'd gone, and now I couldn't think of anything to do but sit here angry and disconsolate, as they must have known I would. I knew what Fiff would say if I complained. I could hear her saying it. *If you'd really wanted to come with us, Fidgie, you'd have come home in time.* And Cly's voice saying *It's no use talking to her, Mamma, she doesn't listen. She prefers the company of her dirty little cronies . . .* Cly enjoyed reminding me of the time when Tom and I had come home from school with nits in our hair.

Even Pipsy was missing: Cly must have taken her too. They might be gone till bedtime, too thrilled with the car ride to return in time for tea. I pictured them driving along, licking sliders, laughing. The picture was so clear I could taste the ice-cream, feel its icy bite on my tongue, nibble the melting wafers either side of it.

Hunger lurched through me, adding to my gloom. I thought about the birthday cake with its luscious pink and white icing waiting on the marble slab in the pantry, and bade it an angry goodbye. They could eat that too. I would refuse to touch a crumb of it.

Planning revenge was some comfort, but not much, because I knew it wouldn't work: I'd never dare to act on it; and nothing could make up for missing the ride in the dicky of Eric's car. That was a treat never experienced until he'd come to stay a week ago. And once or twice he'd allowed Tom and me to ride on the running-boards, an experience even more exhilarating than the dicky.

There were footsteps approaching through the grass on the river bank behind me but I took no notice even when I heard someone jump down on to the sand nearby. Whoever it was would have to speak first, and even then I wasn't sure I'd bother to answer.

But nobody spoke, and after a while curiosity got the better of my fury, and I turned my head. But it wasn't Tom. The faint, wild hope that he hadn't deserted me, that he too had been left behind, died. This was a boy I'd never seen before. The dismissive glance I gave him told me that he was about my own age, maybe a bit older, fair-haired and skinny like Tom and me. He was leaning against a rock pretending not to see me. Presently, out of the corner of my eye, I saw him bend down and select a flat pebble. At last he came closer and tried to skim it over the water. It sank. I sighed elaborately.

'You can't play ducks and drakes when there aren't any waves,' I said, hoping for a quarrel. 'Everybody knows that.'

'There's nothing else to do around here,' he said, finding another pebble and sending it after the first, with the same result.

This was promising. His remark was a deliberate provocation and my hackles rose deliciously. 'There's lots to do,' I said loftily. 'But not for *trippers*.' This was the deadliest insult I could think of. Everyone here knew from infancy – and we had learned from them – that trippers were the lowest of the low. They weren't even proper holidaymakers. They came for the day in charabancs and left a mess of broken bottles and discarded fish-and-chip papers on the beach. Often they got so drunk they sicked up on the street. But I felt sure that this stranger wouldn't know that: I could insult him with impunity and enjoy the satisfaction of knowing that I'd wreaked revenge on *someone*, even though the real targets of my wrath – Fiff and Cly – were, as always, out of reach.

But he seemed to know what I meant. 'I'm not a tripper,' he said, finding a third pebble and preparing to throw it. 'I live here.'

I didn't believe him, but it might just be true, so I said warily, 'I've never seen you before.'

'I've seen *you*,' he countered. 'You live in those houses over there.' He nodded towards the row of houses further downstream and flung his pebble.

Until this moment I'd never given those houses a second thought. Now, suddenly, without being able to put it into words, it struck me that there was something odd about them: they were completely out of place in this wild landscape, as if they had once been part of a town now mysteriously vanished. The river flowed where the houses opposite should have been, and where there should have been a suburban street a wide stretch of gravel separated the front gardens from the river wall. Behind the houses a rocky knoll rose, high as a hill, sheltering their back gardens.

They were the only houses visible, one of them detached – Miss Wragg's – the other two semi-detached, as if the builder had run out of bricks and had been forced to cram the last two together to save building an extra wall.

There were other houses here somewhere, but they were far apart and hidden, buried in trees or withdrawn behind other rocky outcrops. One of them, a bungalow bearing a sign reading FOR SALE OR TO LET, crowned the top of the hillock behind our house. Rather grandly, it bore the name Hill Top House. I'd been up to explore it once, hoping to find children to play with, but it was empty. Some people had taken it for a month last spring – *Honeymooners,* Fiff had said, making a moue, *so we shan't be seeing much of them.* And she'd added, with gloomy certainty, *Poor girl! She'll find out* . . . Clearly honeymooners were no use, but I hadn't yet given up hope that someone interesting, even exciting, might come to live there one day.

Most of the other houses around here were so secluded that we had no idea who lived in them, or even if they were lived in at all. In one of them, the biggest one of all, about a mile up-river and hidden from here, it was rumoured that a mad old man, a hideously ugly one-eyed ogre, lived with a giant dog, a killer trained (Jacko said) to tear the throats out of anyone reckless enough to go near that house. The two of them, the old man and his dog, dragged the bodies into the cellar, where they roasted and ate them. It was a desperate temptation to put our courage to the test, to sneak up to the front door, ring the bell and run away, but none of us had quite plucked up the nerve to do that yet. None of us would have accepted a dare, not even me, not even on Hallowe'en. *Especially* not on Hallowe'en . . .

But I wasn't going to tell this boy any of that. He wasn't one of us. Which made it all the harder to digest the unwelcome news that he, a total stranger, knew more about me than I knew about him. It gave him an advantage. Either I had to counter by pretending that I knew where *he* lived – in which case he might call my bluff – or I could ignore it and find out by devious means later. I decided on that. Meanwhile it would be a good idea – and fascinating too – to find out just how much he did know about us.

'You know my brother and sister too?'

The water had begun to move, sending miniature

wavelets ashore. The boy bent sideways, took aim, and threw a fourth pebble. This time, surprisingly, it managed one skip before it sank. 'I've seen you with them.'

This was unlikely. Cly was years older than Tom and I. She attended a private boarding school and made sure we knew that she belonged to an altogether higher caste: a Brahmin to our Untouchables. She took care never to be seen in our company, ragamuffins that we were, and we for our part avoided her as far as we could. Still, it was just possible that he had seen us together. I had to make the questions trickier. Tom and I went to school in Moravon, two miles away and on the other side of the river. Surely he couldn't know that?

'Bet you don't know what school we go to,' I said, scenting triumph.

There was no hesitation. 'The council school in Moravon,' he said. 'I've seen you in the playground.' Another pebble flew, skipping twice.

His coolness, his grasp of our affairs, was infuriating. 'Do they teach you how to spy on people in your school?' I said acidly. 'I suppose you know everything about everybody around here.'

There was no denting his conceit. 'Why, what do you want to know?' he asked, and I suspected a grin in his voice. 'As a matter of fact, I think I'll probably be a spy when I grow up. Finding things out is interesting.'

I scowled and turned back to swirling my feet in the water. Tom could be just as infuriating when he chose. Were all boys as aggravating as this? I had no choice but to play their games – when they would let me – or play alone. Apart from Cly, who didn't count, there were no other girls around here. Crossing the river to Moravon to play with the girls from school meant paying the ferryman a penny, which was more than I

16

could afford. It was half my week's pocket money. And walking over the bridge took time: it was nearly a mile long, apart from the distance we had to walk to reach the start of it from here.

And even the bridge wasn't free, or wasn't supposed to be: you had to pay a penny toll to walk over it, though sometimes the toll-house keeper would let us through free, if he was in a good mood. If he wasn't – and if he wasn't looking – we could crawl, flat on our stomachs, under the turnstile. The sand and dust our clothes collected in this manoeuvre was easily brushed off, though it did leave a tell-tale ghost of grime.

I had been fishing from the bridge with a crab-line, a birthday present from Tom, when I'd suddenly remembered the trip in Eric's car. I supposed I could go back and start again where I'd left off, but the pleasure had gone out of it. And as if all that wasn't depressing enough, here was this boy, forcing his company on me as if he had the right to, which was cheek.

Worst of all, he was obviously a show-off, because, for one thing, he was wearing a wrist-watch. None of the boys I knew had a wrist-watch. Why should anyone want to know the time? It was outlandish to put on such swank; almost as embarrassing as the plus-fours Eric had once appeared in. He was getting on my nerves. Somehow I had to get rid of him, but he seemed to think he had a right to be here, and it wasn't going to be easy. Outright rudeness seemed to be the only way to dislodge him.

'Can't you think of anything better to do than throwing stones?' I asked, using my Cly voice. Coming from Cly, it never failed to flatten me. I wanted him to know that I'd had enough of him, that I required to be left alone. Anyone with any sense would have taken the hint by now. But not this boy.

'Let's go swimming,' he said.

'I've *been* swimming,' I said ungraciously. Swimming meant going to Moravon because Fiff had strictly forbidden swimming in the river – the currents were too dangerous, she said – and I wasn't going to admit that I couldn't afford the ferry. Quite apart from the wrist-watch, it was obvious from his clothes – which were much the same as Tom's even down to the elasticated red-and-navy belt with the snake clasp, but not nearly as shabby – that his parents were rich. Fiff wasn't poor, exactly. It was just that we couldn't afford things, and anyway my clothes always seemed to look as though I'd been dragged through a hedge backwards. At least, that's what Cly always said, and Fiff never contradicted her. Every now and then I made great efforts to be tidier, but somehow they never seemed to work for long. That was why I was being extra specially careful with the shorts I was wearing today: they had box pleats back and front, like a short skirt, and I'd been longing for a pair for ages, and now I'd got them I was intensely proud of them and felt inclined to swank a bit. None of the other girls had shorts. The only drawback – which I was determined to ignore – was that they were a birthday present from Eric. Eric was our cousin, much older even than Cly; a grown-up. I didn't like him much and he didn't like me at all. I knew he'd only given me the present to show Fiff how generous he was.

The boy suddenly threw a whole handful of pebbles into the water and smacked the sand off his hands. 'OK, then,' he said. '*You* suggest something.'

'Why?' I asked. 'I don't want to do anything.' Even if he hadn't been so pushy, I had no interest in fair-haired boys: they were too ordinary. Now, if he had been dark and handsome and unapproachable like Dougie Parrish, it would have been different. But then, Dougie

Parrish would never have asked me to go anywhere with him. He was as old as Cly – almost a grown-up – and because of that he lived in a completely different, half-mysterious world, a world in which they learned unheard-of things like history and geography and mathematics; a world I felt sure I could never enter. I could only gaze at him from afar.

'You're just going to sit there all day twiddling your toes in the water,' he said, and added, scoffing, 'I thought you said there was plenty to do around here.'

This was unanswerable, and when I didn't say anything, he seemed to accept defeat.

'OK, I'm off,' he said, and jumped back onto the bank.

Now that he was going I wanted him to stay, but it was beneath my dignity to say so. I watched him walk away. He was heading for a grassy knoll overgrown with scrub oak. It gave me an idea.

I watched him climb the stile and take the path which would lead him round the back of the knoll, and as soon as I was certain he wouldn't look back, I scrambled off the rock and crammed my feet into my sandals. Then my long training as an Indian scout in all the Tom Mix films I'd seen came into play. My name was White Feather and, swift and sinuous and silent as a snake, I swarmed up the knoll and down the other side, where I waited, hiding behind a tree. He came, walking slowly, scuffing a stone here and there on the path. I waited until he drew level and then, uttering my most blood-curdling war cry, I drew my bow and let fly. The arrow went straight through his heart.

He did all the right things: he reeled about, groaning and clutching his chest, and collapsed onto the grass beside the path, his arms spread-eagled.

'I got you! I got you!' I yelled in triumph and jumped

19

down, hooting with laughter. I expected him to get up at once and chase me to exact revenge. That's what Tom or any of the other boys would have done. But he went on lying there with his eyes open, but quite dead, staring at the sky without seeing it, until I began to get worried.

'Oh come on!' I said. 'Joke over. Stop pretending!' Then when there was still no response, I decided to try ridicule. It was the most potent weapon in our armoury, one that had never been known to fail.

'If you could only see yourself!' I scoffed, trying not to sound anxious. 'You look a perfect fool lying there with your mouth open!'

It was only when this failed to work that I began to get alarmed. Perhaps he really was dead? If he was, then somehow I must have killed him. Could a pretend arrow really kill? Even the shadows of the leaves above his face lay still, unmoving in the silent heat. A horsefly landed on his hand and I saw it curtsey, stinging him, but still he didn't move. Soon there would be bluebottles, glittering and malevolent, laying eggs that would turn into maggots and eat into his flesh like the ones I'd seen on the dead lamb last spring.

My first thought was to run away and keep quiet about it, be seen somewhere else, let somebody else find him; but I knew I'd never be able to carry it off. I'd have to tell Tom, and he might even decide that I'd better tell Fiff. And Fiff, who was very strict about these things, would tell the police, and then they'd come to arrest me. I'd be hanged for murder. Cly would gloat. The other kids would sing mocking songs about me like the one we sang about Dr Buck Ruxton. The terrifying scenes unrolled in an instant before my eyes.

Horribly, inexorably, I faced the truth. Somehow I'd

killed him and I'd have to own up. And quickly. But how? There was no-one in at home . . .

I had just decided to run and tell Mrs Bellamy in the house next door when his eyes seemed to come back to life. His eyelids flickered and he gazed vaguely up at the sky. I was so relieved I just stared at him wide-eyed, hardly daring to believe in my reprieve, half-convinced that I was imagining it. Then suppressed fright took over and I stood up and stepped away from him as he sat up. A disturbing thought had come to me. If it were true, it would explain his sudden appearance, his claim to live here, his strange behaviour.

'You're from that funny hospital, aren't you?' I said flatly.

'What funny hospital?' His voice sounded as if he had just woken up. He shook his head as though denying something and rubbed the back of his hand across his forehead.

'The one on the road to Dolgarran,' I said. 'Where all those queer people are.' I started to back away.

He put a hand up to feel the back of his head. When he withdrew it, there was blood on his fingers. 'Must have banged my head on a rock,' he said.

My fears began to subside, but not very far. He'd knocked himself out, that was all, but all the same, that close brush with the hangman had made me wary.

'I've got to go home now,' I said, taking another step backward.

'Why?' he asked. The dazed look had almost cleared from his face but he still spoke drowsily. 'There's no one in, is there? They've all gone off in the car.'

I had forgotten that for the moment, and the reminder silenced me. Even if he didn't come from the hospital – and where else could he have come from? – I still didn't trust him.

21

He drew his knees up, hanging his arms over them and dropping his head, and suddenly I felt a bit of a sneak going off and leaving him like this. After all, he *had* been joining in my game. Besides – and here another shrivelling thought assailed me – what if he went home and told his mother that I'd nearly killed him? It would be a sissy thing to do, but he might. You never knew. The ensuing icy exchange between his mother and mine didn't bear thinking about. It would be almost worse than the gallows: Fiff would never forgive me for disgracing her like that. I'd never be allowed to forget it.

'Are you OK?' I asked. 'You can come home with me if you like.' The invitation was not heartfelt. I wouldn't have dared to make the offer at all if Fiff had been in. She didn't like Tom and me to bring our friends home. 'I could put some iodine on that cut.'

He looked up, squinting through the leaves at the sky as if to bring it into focus. 'It doesn't matter.' He got to his feet, a bit shakily I thought, watching him uneasily. 'I'm OK now.'

'But your head,' I said. 'What will you tell your mother when she sees that cut?' I knew that if *I* came home with blood on my head, Fiff would demand a full explanation, and if she didn't like what she heard, there would be punishment – I'd be sent to bed early at the very least, or worse still, forbidden to play again with whoever I'd been playing with.

'I haven't got – I mean my mother's not here,' he said.

'Your father, then. Won't he mind?'

When he didn't reply, I gave up trying. It was well understood among us that we didn't have to give explanations if we didn't want to. Interrogations were what we had to put up with at home. Out here we were free.

He set off again the way he had been heading originally, on the path which led up-river. I followed, running and skipping to catch up. The blood on the back of his head was still shockingly red and wet.

'I didn't *really* shoot you,' I said. It was important that he understood this before he got home. 'I was only pretending.'

He mumbled something without turning round. It sounded like 'Don't be stupid, kid,' a devastating double insult which threw me into a rage.

'You're only a kid yourself,' I shouted, hoping I wasn't going to burst into tears. It had been a horrible afternoon and I'd never forgive him if I started to cry right here in front of him. The thought of it made me spiteful. 'And at least I'm not stupid enough to cut my head on a rock,' I said. 'Don't blame me if you get lockjaw and die.'

He probably knew as well as I did that you only got lockjaw if you cut yourself on the loose skin between your thumb and forefinger, but I was trying to frighten him, to pay him out for the fright he'd given me.

But I found that I was talking to myself. He had stopped suddenly and turned, listening, to face the way we had come. I stopped too, watching him, puzzled. 'What is it?'

'Car coming,' he said. 'Come on,' and he grabbed my wrist and drew me with him into the bracken. 'Get down.'

We threw ourselves onto the grass between the stalks and lay there waiting. Hidden in this green jungle all I could hear – apart from the ticking of some insect in the grass and the chirring of grasshoppers – was a train beginning its rumbling journey over the timbers of the bridge; and on this side of the river, faint as a distant bumble-bee, the sound of a car coming from the direction of Moravon Junction, where some

23

trains came from inland and others went down the coast.

'Who are we hiding from?' I asked, enjoying this new game. I loved hiding and I was good at it. I had learned years ago that it was wise to hide from Boko as much as possible.

'My tutor,' he said tersely. 'I think that's him in the car, coming back from London. He went down there for an interview, 'cos he'll be leaving here when I go back to school.'

I waited for him to explain further, but he didn't seem to think it needed any explanation. I puzzled over it for a while until curiosity got the better of me and forced me to swallow my pride.

'What's a tutor?' I asked.

'A teacher, sort of.'

Hiding from a teacher was understandable. I thought that I too would probably hide if I saw one of *my* teachers – especially Mr Hughes, the headmaster – during the holidays. Mr Hughes was the only teacher who ever caned me, bringing the ruler down painfully across my outstretched palm.

'Does he cane you?' I asked interestedly.

'Cane me? Of course not. My uncle – my *great*-uncle – would sack him if he did.'

'Can he do that?' I asked in amazement. I was pretty sure that Fiff could not sack Mr Hughes. I rather doubted if she'd even try. Fiff had drummed obedience into us. She kept a leather strap which she didn't hesitate to use on Tom and me if we disobeyed the fixed command to be home before sunset. She didn't land many strokes – we ran round the room too fast for that, and she might not even have tried very hard – but it scared us and the few which did connect convinced us that she meant what she said. Mr Hughes though was different. He went purple, his face swelling with rage. We got our revenge by singing a rude song about him behind his back.

'You've never had the cane?' I persisted. 'Nearly all the boys in my form have, and so have I. You must be an awful sissy.'

I don't know why I said it: it was a terrible insult. I think I was still trying to provoke him. Or maybe it was because the flies were driving me mad. There were swarms of them under the bracken, and it seemed even hotter in here than out in the sun. Bracken smells funny anyway, like squashed mosquitoes.

The boy had begun scratching furiously at the place on his hand where the horsefly had bitten him. I was sorry now that I hadn't swatted the thing when I saw it land on him. If I'd known that he was still alive, I would have. As it was, the itching was going to drive him mad for the rest of the day and tomorrow too, probably.

The humidity here under the bracken was making me irritable. 'Can't we go and hide somewhere else?' I complained. There was a big house nearby, set high on a rocky outcrop above the river, its grounds surrounded by a new plantation of young cypresses. They were very densely packed but it was possible, just, for children to squeeze through. 'We can go and hide in those trees below Holly Hill. That car's going so slowly it won't catch us if we run.'

We could hear it more clearly now, picking its way joltingly along the stony track in low gear, but it was probably still hidden behind the knoll.

The boy stuck his head up through the bracken to check. 'OK,' he said. 'There's something I want to see at Holly Hill anyway. Come on.' He got up and I followed. 'Stay in the bracken and keep your head down,' he ordered.

We ran, crashing through the jungle. The stalks were so tall that we hardly needed to bend our heads to keep out of sight, but anyone watching could have followed our progress by the frantic thrashing of the fronds above us. When we reached the track, which we would have to cross to reach the cypress hedge, the car had still not emerged from behind the knoll and we made a mad dash across the open space and squeezed between the thin trunks just in time, laughing wildly with the excitement of the chase. I was Maid Marian, and the boy was one of the Merry Men – Will Scarlet perhaps – and we had only *just* escaped with our lives, safe now in Sherwood Forest.

Peering out carefully from inside the cypress hedge, we watched the car – a big American Hudson – go by, driven by a chauffeur. There was a man in the back seat, and I focused on him keenly, expecting to see an evil face with a black beard and pointed teeth, but this man didn't look like the Sheriff of Nottingham at all. He was only middle-aged – about twenty-three perhaps – with horn-rimmed glasses and a disappointingly mild expression.

'Is that your teacher?' I asked.

'Tutor, yes.'

A thought occurred to me. 'Don't you get any holidays?' I asked curiously. 'We don't have to go back to school for *weeks* yet.' It was less than a fortnight, actually, but I could never resist the temptation to swank. Besides, this boy was obviously rich, so it was satisfying to feel that I had something he didn't have.

'Of course I get holidays,' he said with annoyance. 'I'm on holiday *now*. Well, sort of. I only have to work in the mornings. But I have to go back to school – to boarding school – in a couple of weeks, when term starts again.'

'But why do you have to go back there, if you've got a teacher all to yourself?' I asked. 'Why can't you stay here?'

He sighed the way Tom sighed when he began to get exasperated by my questions. 'Because Mr Caster can only teach me maths and Latin and history; stuff like that.' He paused as if knowing that this explanation was inadequate, but reluctant to explain further. Finally, he made up his mind and added, 'I missed a term because of an accident, if you must know, and I had to catch up on school work. I was in hospital for a time. Satisfied?'

I wasn't, but I was quelled by his tone of voice, and I was afraid that if I asked him about the accident he'd lose his temper and walk away, just when I had begun to rely on his company.

'Come on,' he said, turning and pushing further into the hedge, 'there's something I want to see.'

It was deliciously aromatic and cool among the cypresses, their resinous scent disturbed by our passage. We pushed further into them until we emerged on the other side into a paddock full of overgrown grass and buttercups and ox-eye daises.

I still wanted to know about the accident, but clearly it wasn't safe to pry any further; so instead I said, 'What about the people in this house? Won't they be angry when they see us playing in their garden?' I could just imagine what Fiff's reaction would be, if I were hauled up in front of her, accused of trespass by some furious old lady. Even though I had only seen Mr and Mrs Guest, who were quite young really, I supposed, I was sure that the house would contain, like so many of the houses round here, some glowering crone who disapproved of children. I thought nervously of old Mrs van Gelderen up at the Hall, who kept a spyglass in her drawing-room window for the sole purpose, it seemed to us, of spying on us and reporting any bad behaviour to our parents. None of us had ever seen her – though we imagined we had – but at least she was human, in a nasty sort of way, unlike the monster at Llwyn-yr-eos, who was something between a vampire and a werewolf, wholly inhuman and terrifying and invisible. Because Mrs van Gelderen lived most of a mile away, on the hill above the village, we tended to forget about her until it was too late. The Hall was clearly visible from here. Was she watching us now? The thought made me want to drive back into the cover of the hedge.

'There's no one in,' he said. 'They may have gone away. I was scouting around here this morning.'

'But how do you know they haven't come back since then?' I pointed out.

He didn't answer. I had begun to notice this trick he had of not answering when he didn't want to. It made him seem enviably self-contained and impregnable. I wondered if I could do it: it would annoy Cly no end. But on second thoughts I decided that annoying Cly was too risky. I wasn't as brave as I pretended to be, and Cly had a whole repertoire of elegant small tortures – like Chinese fire – which she used on me whenever I annoyed her.

There was an enormous shed at one end of the paddock, and he was heading towards it. I followed, stumbling once over an anthill hidden under a tussock of grass. When I picked myself up, I had a bright green grass stain down the front of my shorts, a disaster I didn't notice until later.

The shed was locked, and anyway the doors were so big that we'd never have been able to pull them open. We tried peering through cracks, but they weren't wide enough to show anything inside, and besides, the smell of creosote, intensified by the heat, was scraping the inside of my nose like sandpaper, so we gave up and tried jumping up at the windows. I had no success at this, but the boy was taller and he managed to cling on to the window-sill for a few moments before he had to let go.

'Wow!' he exclaimed with awe. 'Wow! It's true!'

'What is? What is?' I begged, frantic with curiosity.

'Here, have a look,' he said, bending down with his back to the wall and cupping his hands. I put one foot into this stirrup and jumped up to the window. All I could see was a weird machine which took up most of the space inside. It looked like one of the things Tom built with his Meccano set, only made of metal tubes, and huge, too, like a gigantic dragonfly.

'It's an autogyro!' he explained excitedly. 'Isn't it marvellous? Mr Guest is building it, using an aeroplane engine he designed himself. My uncle told me about it, but I thought he was fooling. Imagine it! Building an *autogyro*!'

'But what is it supposed to do?' I asked, disappointed but still hoping to be as enthralled as he was.

'Fly, of course,' he said impatiently.

'That thing?' I scoffed. 'How can it fly? It's got no wings.'

'It's a new idea,' he said, entranced as a saint by the momentary glimpse he'd had of this mystery. 'Well, fairly new, anyway. It doesn't need wings. Those propellers on top whizz round and keep it up in the air. They're called rotor blades.'

'Oh,' I said, losing interest. I thought it was a stupid idea anyway to expect something to fly without wings, though it would be exciting if Mr Guest tried to fly it one day and fell out of the sky and got killed, especially if he did it right outside our house. We'd be the envy of all the other kids. I still felt deprived because I'd missed the aeroplane accident on Moravon beach the year before we came. The others had all seen it, or pretended they had, and the story got more gruesome and thrilling every time I heard it.

'I'm going up to the house,' he said. 'To ask Mr Guest if I can see it properly. He might let me help him build it.'

'You said they'd gone out,' I reminded him, alarmed.

He gave a yelp of laughter. 'I made that up,' he said sunnily.

I was outraged. 'We could get into *awful* trouble,' I stormed.

He was infuriatingly sure of himself. 'Stop worrying,' he said, 'it'll be all right. I know them.'

'Well I don't,' I grumbled. 'I've hardly ever seen them.'

'That's because they only live here in the summer,' he said. 'Mr Guest has a factory up north, near Manchester, making parts for aeroplane engines.' His voice took on a note of happy awe. 'He knows how to fly a plane, too, and he says he'll teach me when I'm old enough.' He spread his arms like wings and began to weave about the paddock. 'I'm going to be a pilot in the next war.'

'There isn't going to be a next war,' I said. 'Is there?'

'Oh, I expect so,' he said contentedly. 'Bound to be, somewhere or other.'

To catch him out, I said, 'I thought you said you were going to be a spy.'

'Nothing to stop me doing both,' he said with a triumphant grin. 'Especially in an autogyro.'

I fell silent. He was the sort of annoying boy who has an answer for everything. We began climbing some rough steps made of blue slate slabs. Above us, the top storey of the house, surrounded by a verandah, appeared above a jungle of wild rhododendrons. Flowerless now and darkly green, they had been a mass of mauve blossom in early summer.

'Anyway, they probably *are* out,' he went on, 'and we had to hide somewhere, remember.'

'*You* had to,' I pointed out balefully. 'It wasn't *my* tutor we were hiding from.'

That was when he said what I didn't want to hear. 'You don't have to come with me if you don't want to. Girls are stupid about engineering anyway.'

'And you know everything about it,' I sneered, feeling depressed. He was going to abandon me now that he'd found something more interesting to do. I hoped Mr Guest would be out, or better still, that he'd be the sort of grown-up who had no time for children and shooed them away, roaring and shaking his fist like some of the old farmers up in the hills around here. I only knew him by sight, from a distance, not to talk to, and he didn't look like the sort of man who would behave like that, but with grown-ups you never knew. In our world, we avoided adults as far as possible. They were usually disapproving and always unpredictable.

But this boy had no doubts about his welcome. 'Mr Guest's pretty decent. You'll see. He's an engineer and I'm going to read engineering, too,' he said, and added with absolute certainty, 'when I get to Cambridge.'

Trying to think of something to hold his interest, I made my second mistake. 'I'm going to *Oxford*,' I lied valiantly. I always backed Oxford in the Boat Race, but only because Tom wouldn't let me have Cambridge.

'Oxford,' he scoffed. 'Huh!'

We toiled on up the rise in silence after that, following a path through the rhododendrons. There was an open-fronted summer-house at the top, just visible through the foliage. We had almost reached it when he stopped so suddenly that I crashed into him. He whipped round on me before I could speak and clapped his hand over my mouth.

'Ssh!' he breathed almost soundlessly and pushed me back among the bushes so unexpectedly that I fell over and he collapsed on top of me. In the silence I could hear strange moans and gasps and strangled cries coming from the direction of the summer-house.

'What's the matter?' I hissed, offended by the indignity of being manhandled like this, but still obeying his call for secrecy.

He picked himself up and dragged me upright beside him. 'We'd better clear off,' he whispered. 'Mrs Guest is in there . . . with some man . . .'

'So what?' I asked, missing the point. 'You said it would be all right. You said you knew them.'

He clapped his hand over my mouth again and hissed, 'I know Mr *Guest*, and this isn't him. It's a man who lives across the river, and they're . . .' he broke off and turned away, whispering urgently, 'Come *on*. We've got to get away from here.'

If there was something interesting going on, I wanted to see it. Especially if it was something I wasn't supposed to see. I took a further step up the path, craning my neck, only to have my arm grabbed and to be yanked sideways back into the shrubbery. I found myself gazing into his furious face. Without another word he started back down the path, moving with exaggerated stealth, and I followed reluctantly, puzzled and annoyed. He had prevented me from seeing something I wanted to see, a feeling that was hard to bear. We were halfway down the slate steps before the reason for our precipitate flight began to dawn on me.

'Do you mean they were *having a spin*?' I asked, thrilled. I always felt these words must be whispered. It was Ellen's phrase, and I had a pretty good idea what it meant, even though I'd never seen it happen, except when Mrs Bellamy's cockerel did it to the hens; but that couldn't be the same. I had missed my chance to find out: Jacko had offered me a pear if I'd go up the mountain with him, but I didn't like pears much and I'd turned the offer down.

'You're not to tell Mr Guest,' he said earnestly. 'Promise me you won't.'

I was longing to sneak back and take a peep, but I was afraid he would disappear and leave me here if I did. All the same, I couldn't resist one protest.

'It's not fair,' I grumbled. 'Why wouldn't you let me *see*?' But I didn't expect a reply and I didn't get one, so I brought out my favourite word. 'It's *disgrumptious*!' I said. I wasn't sure if this was a real word or if I had made it up, but I liked the sound of it.

He didn't answer.

I felt deprived. There was a knot of girls who gathered together in the girls' playground at school and did a lot of giggling and whispering, some of which I'd overheard, dawdling about on the fringe of the group; but I didn't know whether to believe what they said: it sounded so unlikely and so *rude*. But even so, I was sure that there was more to this business between men and women than kissing, and kissing was bad enough. Fiff never kissed anyone, not even us, for which I was grateful. Kissing was sloppy and wet and embarrassing.

The boy didn't even pause to take another look at his beloved autogyro through the window of the shed, but kept going until we had both pushed our way through the cypress hedge again, where another shock awaited us. We burst out to find ourselves face to face with Mr Guest, on his way back home with a shotgun over one arm and a poacher's bag slung over his shoulder. He must have seen the commotion in the hedge and now stood waiting to see what was causing it. His greeting did nothing to lessen my embarrassment, even though he was looking at the boy, not me, when he spoke.

'Oh, it's you. What on earth are you doing wrecking

33

my hedge? Small wonder you both look so guilty.'

While the boy apologized, I folded my arms tightly behind my back and stared at the man beseechingly. A jumble of excuses, none of them very convincing, tumbled through my mind. My only comfort was that he didn't look as angry as I was expecting him to be. He had caught two children pushing through his boundary hedge and he could hardly have failed to be annoyed, if only mildly; but we both looked so shamefaced that he had begun to be amused by our discomfiture, unaware that we had other reasons besides trespass for our shifty behaviour.

He addressed the boy. 'So, Chaz, I suppose you've discovered my secret? I've been expecting you, though not through the hedge.'

So this boy's name was Chaz. What sort of stupid name was that? It was almost as outlandish as mine. I watched him while he apologized again and explained that he'd heard about the autogyro and wanted to see it (though I noticed that he left out the bit about hiding from his tutor) but I wasn't really listening. I was happy to distance myself from the two of them and bask in the blissful realization that, for once, I wasn't in trouble.

I was so lost in that pleasure that I was startled when the boy half-turned to me and said to Mr Guest, 'And this is Fidgie Jacques.'

'Fidgie?' Mr Guest said. 'Is that a nickname?'

They both looked at me. I wriggled my toes inside my sandals and stared at the ground. I never told anyone my name if I could help it: it was too unheard-of . . . too disgrumptious. Besides which, I couldn't pronounce it.

Chaz spoke for me. 'It's short,' he said with a snort of laughter I could have killed him for, 'for Iphigenia.'

I was furious. How could he have found out?

2

Mr Guest didn't believe him.

'Stop teasing her, Chaz,' he said with mild disapproval, winning my instant devotion. I gazed at the
man with astonishment. He'd stood up for me! I
thought that all grown-ups, in the mysterious cabal of
adulthood, could tell just by looking that I was the
black sheep of the family, in permanent disgrace,
condemned for my fatal inability to behave myself. I
decided that I must somehow prevent him from finding out. Perhaps I could turn over a new leaf here and
now and suddenly become as ladylike as Cly? It didn't
seem likely. I sighed inwardly, feeling wistful but
resigned: I knew I could never aspire to be the sort of
shining example Cly was, well-behaved, well-groomed,
sophisticated, basking in Fiff's approval. In *everyone's*
approval . . . Mr Hughes would never have *dreamed* of
caning Cly. But then, it was impossible to imagine Cly
getting the giggles in class or making up cheeky chants
and acting the fool in the playground, as I did.

Mr Guest began moving again towards Holly Hill
and we drifted along with him, Chaz sometimes
walking backwards in front of him, waving his hands
when he wanted to make a special point or ask an
important question and be sure of Mr Guest's attention; and I skipping along beside him, not really
listening. But I noticed that Chaz kept stopping in front
of Mr Guest, forcing him to stop too, and I suddenly
realized that he was trying to delay Mr Guest's return

home. I racked my brain to think of something I could do to help, but my mind had gone blank, and nothing occurred to me. There seemed to be an awful inevitability to our progress. Mr Guest would get home and discover what we had discovered, and we were powerless to prevent it.

I looked up at him curiously, studying him, wondering why his wife had gone off him. He seemed nice-looking to me, in fact more than nice-looking. Not as beautiful as Dougie Parrish, of course, but then, nobody was, not even the Prince of Wales. I decided I liked the colour of his hair, a dark red, darker than a chestnut. It couldn't be that. His eyes, though, were a disappointment. They were a pale grey, ghostly, like fishes glimpsed at the bottom of a stream. Perhaps his wife was put off by the colour of his eyes.

He was telling Chaz something about a Spaniard who'd invented rotor blades when he suddenly broke off to say sharply, 'What have you done to your head, Chaz? Your hair's all matted with blood.'

'It's nothing much,' Chaz said. 'I fell.'

Mr Guest said, 'Fell?' and a sudden small silence descended, almost palpable in its uneasiness. I looked first at him, then at Chaz, and waited.

'We were playing,' Chaz said quickly. 'Acting the fool. I tripped over.'

There was something about the way he rushed into this explanation, and the way he stuck his hands into his pockets and tried too hard to look nonchalant which sent question marks zigzagging through my head. I could see no reason for his embarrassment, but I sensed that he was willing Mr Guest not to persist with his questioning. I couldn't understand what was going on, but I rushed in anyway to back him up; normal procedure when any of us was under attack from adults.

'Oh, look!' I said pointing off towards the reed beds on the marshes. 'I think I saw a heron.'

'Unlikely,' Mr Guest said. 'The tide's out. They only fish there when the pools are full.'

I said to Chaz, 'I'm sure I saw one. Let's go and sneak up on it and see how close we can get before it sees us.'

But Mr Guest was implacable, in the way grown-ups always are. 'You can do that afterwards,' he said. 'First I think it would be a good idea to come with me to Holly Hill and let my wife clean up that cut for you. It may need stitches.'

The mention of Mrs Guest electrified us both and threw us into disarray. Our eyes met wildly and we both spoke together.

'No, I'm OK, thanks—'

'He can come home with me—'

To Mr Guest we were a pair of kids who thought medical attention a boring interruption of playtime. He said firmly, 'No arguments, you two. You'll do as you're told. Come on, the sooner we get it done, the sooner you can go and look for your heron,' and he moved off briskly towards Holly Hill.

We had no choice but to go with him, but we avoided looking at each other because of the summer-house. By now I had convinced myself that I had seen what Chaz had seen in there, and I knew very well that what Mrs Guest was doing was something she should only be doing with her husband, and I was angry with her. Mr Guest had stood up for me, and I didn't want him made to look a fool. Somehow Chaz and I had to make sure he didn't find out. I knew what would happen as soon as we got to the house: he would call for his wife and when she didn't answer, he would go and look for her. What excuse could I make to stop him if he decided to go and look in the summer-house? The problem occupied me all the way along the track and I still had no answer when we reached the house, but as we entered the big double gates my worries were submerged by curiosity.

Holly Hill was much bigger than the house we lived in, Fiff and Tom and I, and much handsomer too. If I leaned out far enough and craned my neck I could see its white walls and shallow roofs from my bedroom at River Cottage. I liked looking at it. It had roofs at different heights and angles, the sort of exciting house, I thought, which would have lots of hiding places. But most of all I liked the verandah which ran round the upper storey, and I had decided that when I was grown-up I was going to live there and have a bed-room opening on to that verandah, so that I could sleep there on summer nights. Houses had fascinated me from as far back as I could remember – we had lived in so many – and this one looked more interesting than any I had seen so far. For a start, it was new, and modern, and I found that enchanting, like all new things. In fact, by the time we had walked through the garden, crunched across the sweep of gravel wide enough for a big car to turn round in, and climbed the steps to the front door, Mrs Guest had slipped my mind completely in the sheer pleasure of knowing that I was actually going to be allowed to enter Holly Hill and perhaps even explore it.

What I had thought to be the front door turned out to be the back, because we found ourselves in a corridor which ran straight into the hall and through it to the wide-open front door. All the doors and windows had been flung open to catch any breath of air stirring, and the front door framed a hazy blue view of the mountains across the river.

Mr Guest turned aside into a small bare room containing only outdoor coats, wellingtons, sports equipment, a washbasin and the door to a lavatory – a disappointing start to my exploration of Holly Hill. He unslung his bag from his shoulder and hung it on a hook.

'Did you get anything, sir?' Chaz asked him.

'No, not a thing,' Mr Guest said. 'The rabbits have all gone to ground: too hot for them, I expect. And anyway, I'm not a very good shot.'

This was a startling admission. I'd thought grownups were good at everything. I watched as he took the cartridges out of the gun before he snapped it shut and propped it on a rack above the coats. Chaz eyed it longingly.

'Can I clean the gun for you, sir?' he asked eagerly.

'No, I'll do that later,' Mr Guest said, while the fleeting hope died in Chaz's face. 'I'd rather do it myself.'

We waited while he washed his hands, then, moving into the hall, he called, 'Gillian?'

'Up here.'

To my surprise the voice came from upstairs. I threw an accusing look at Chaz, but he shrugged one shoulder and stared me out. All that fuss for nothing! Mrs Guest had been upstairs all the time: she'd never been in the summer-house at all.

'You made it up,' I muttered, glowering at him, but he frowned back ferociously to silence me and didn't answer.

We watched her come down the stairs. Mrs Guest had never struck me as the sort of woman who would tend to children's cuts and bruises. I'd only ever seen her once or twice before, always in the car, usually at a distance and looking straight ahead, bored and remote; seeing her now, close up, I was ravished. She was wearing beach pyjamas with a halter neck, made of some kind of lissom silk which clung to her slender

39

hips and floated round her ankles. The material was vividly splashed with big scarlet poppies on a white ground and her lipstick exactly matched the red of the poppies. All this appeared to me gradually from her sandalled feet up as she came downstairs slowly, moving with languid grace and reluctantly. I think my mouth was probably hanging open while I stood wide-eyed, taking it all in. Her hair – coal black and shining and straight – was cut as short as mine, but in a bob, unlike my hated shingle, and with the same fringe; but unlike mine which tended to part at one side, hers lay in a perfect line across her forehead. I thought she was the most beautiful woman I'd ever seen.

I didn't like her.

'Darling, you've been out for ages,' she said. 'Teddy arrived more than an hour ago.' She spoke in the voice grown-ups use when they are annoyed and pretending not to be. And that *Darling* made me squirm. Nobody I knew used that word in public: it was a very private word.

'I didn't see his car,' Mr Guest said. He had gone to the foot of the stairs and was standing with his hand on the newel post, and because she had stopped halfway down as if posing for a photograph, he was forced to look up at her like a worshipper transfixed by a vision. She was carrying a long-handled bamboo fan which she raised now to dismiss the stifling air from her face. I caught the faint drift of a delicious scent.

'He came by boat,' she said, bored. 'It's his latest toy. I expect he's down there now. He's absolutely dying to show it off. You know what a fool he is.'

She gave no sign of noticing Chaz and me politely effacing ourselves behind Mr Guest. He drew attention to us.

'Chaz has a cut on his head which ought to be seen to,' he said. 'Could you do something about it?'

Her gaze flicked over us without interest and she sighed impatiently. 'Oh God! Couldn't you have said so before I came down?' she asked. 'I can't mess about with blood and bandages and all that sort of thing without changing my clothes. And it's too hot to keep racing up and down stairs.' She began to turn as if to retrace her steps, martyred.

'Don't worry about it,' Mr Guest said quickly. 'I'll attend to it,' and he turned back to us.

'It's quite all right, Mr Guest,' Chaz cut in hurriedly, embarrassed. 'Honestly, it doesn't matter—'

But Mr Guest was already shepherding us back down the corridor. 'We'll use the downstairs cloak-room,' he said, leading us back to the small room where he had stowed his bag and gun.

I felt like an unwanted stray, turned away from a kitchen door where I'd hoped for scraps, and some-how Mr Guest too seemed to be included in this rejection. We were all three of us in disgrace. I hoped Fiff would never find out and decide that I'd made a nuisance of myself in someone else's house. Presently, when I had time to think, I would have to start making up excuses, just in case.

Chaz was trying to apologize, though I couldn't see why he should. 'I'm afraid I've inconvenienced you, sir,' he said stiffly. It sounded very grown-up to me and I flicked him a look of respect, though I resolved that never as long as I lived would I ever call any man sir, except in school where I had to. Calling people sir was craven.

Mr Guest seemed unconcerned about his wife's dismissal. 'Oh, rubbish,' he said easily.

He made short, efficient work of the first aid, mopping gently at the matted blood with wads of cotton wool while Chaz bent over the washbasin and I watched interestedly by his side. The cut, when it was revealed, was nothing much, not very deep and only half an inch long, but Chaz drew a sharp breath when the iodine was applied. I think the sting took him by surprise, even though Mr Guest warned him beforehand. Iodine does that, so I didn't blame him.

'Now,' Mr Guest said when he'd finished, 'I suppose I'm expected to go down and look at this boat. You coming?'

'You bet!' said Chaz with enthusiasm.

I didn't know if I was included in the invitation, but I went along anyway: it was something to do, though the boats in Moravon were not really worth inspecting: they were mostly open fishing boats with putt-putting engines, used in the summer for trips round the bay or up the river. Their shallow draught allowed them to negotiate the channels in the estuary even when the tide was out.

The zigzag path down the garden was only wide enough for two people to walk side by side through the forest of wild rhododendrons, and I trailed behind Chaz and Mr Guest, keeping quiet, hoping that he wouldn't turn round and discover me and send me home.

Halfway down the hill where the ground levelled out, there was a surprise. The bushes had been cleared to make room for a swimming-pool. It wasn't as glamorous as the pools in Hollywood musicals, but a real swimming-pool all the same, cool and blue; and there were Lilos and a table with a sun umbrella stuck through a hole in the middle.

I forgot my strategy of silence. 'Oh, Mr Guest!' I breathed, entranced. *'A swimming-pool!'*

He turned round and his face lit up with amusement when he saw my enraptured gaze. 'Didn't Chaz tell you?' he asked. 'He comes here to swim most days. You can both come together if you like.'

'But,' I ventured, 'will Mrs Guest mind?'

'Of course not,' he said blithely, as if the very idea astonished him. I wasn't so sure, but I thanked him as politely as I knew how, and gave him my sunniest smile. I wanted him to know how much I liked him.

'H'lo, Johnny,' a voice said behind us, and we turned to see a man climbing the path towards us. He was tall and dark and ought to have been good-looking, but he had a pencil moustache like all the smoothest and nastiest gangsters in all the films I'd ever seen, and I disliked him at once. He couldn't have been wearing a black, pinstriped suit with a black shirt and a white tie and co-respondent shoes on a hot summer's day, but that was how I saw him and I couldn't shake the image off.

''Lo, Teddy,' Mr Guest said without enthusiasm. 'Gillian says you have a new toy. We were just on our way down to see it.' His voice was matter-of-fact, but I was standing close beside him and I sensed something, I don't know what – a tremor on the air perhaps – which made me glance up at him quickly: he didn't like this Teddy any more than I did. We followed him down the wandering path through the rhododendrons.

Chaz was in a different world, where only machines are interesting. 'She's a beauty,' he assured Mr Guest, and to Mr Ransom he went on with a rush of enthusiasm, 'I saw her when she arrived yesterday. What sort of engine has she got? She kicked up a heck of a wake. The waves spread right across the river to our place.'

I stopped listening. I had just caught sight of the boat-house at the bottom of the path. It looked like a tiny whitewashed cottage, and I slid instantly into a dream. There was no time now, but tonight, in bed, I would move into that cottage and lock the door and live there all alone, safe from Cly and Mr Hughes and everyone else, especially Boko – though we were fairly safe from him now – with only the swans, the coots, and the otters for company. I sighed with longing. It was only when I heard Chaz call out, 'Fidgie! Are you coming or not?' that I realized I had been standing still for ages, staring at the little house, day-dreaming, while everyone else had boarded the boat.

Things had changed in the time since I'd been sitting on the rock. The tide had turned. It was racing in now at an astonishing speed. It only ever moved as fast as that at high springs, and I remembered that there had been a brilliant full moon the last few nights. Even as I watched, the sandbars out in the estuary were disappearing as water reclaimed them, overwhelming them swiftly and silently. Awakened from their siesta, the seagulls were greeting the returning tide with screams of excitement; and flocks of oyster-catchers wheeled overhead, piping. The somnolent hiatus of afternoon was over.

I ran and skipped down to the slipway, caught hold of a stanchion on the deck of Mr Ransom's boat, and swung myself aboard, feeling as light as thistledown. I always enjoyed proving to myself that I could do things like that every bit as well as Tarzan did. Mr Guest had bent down to help me up, and I grinned up at him, expecting to see an answering smile, but he had been looking at Teddy and the expression on his face was so grim that I wondered if I'd done something wrong.

Seeing my face fall, he put an arm round my shoulders, gave me a brief hug, and said bracingly, 'Clever girl. We'll have you in the Olympics yet,' which sounded good, even though I had no idea what the Olympics were; but I guessed that he was trying to be jolly while feeling anything but light-hearted himself, and I blamed Teddy. Somehow Teddy's arrival had driven a nail through the afternoon, splintering its smooth surface. A sudden uncomfortable thought assailed me – surely Mr Guest couldn't possibly know about the summer-house?

Chaz, completely wrapped up in specifications and unaware of any shift in the mood, was asking, 'How much water does she draw?'

'Only about three feet,' Teddy said. 'The water in the channels is probably deep enough already to take us. D'you feel like a spin? We can take her out and put her through her paces.'

I glanced wildly at Teddy. Didn't he know what a rude word *spin* was? I expected to see a grin cross Chaz's face, but he couldn't have noticed. 'Great!' he exclaimed, his face alight. 'Can Fidgie come too?'

'Of course,' Teddy said. 'I meant everyone.'

'Some other time,' Mr Guest said. 'I've got to catch the post.'

Chaz, deaf to anything but the prospect of getting under way, said to Mr Ransom, 'If you show me where to find the plumb line, I'll take soundings.'

The channel below Holly Hill opened out into a big, black, sinister pool. One of the boys – Jacko, I think – had told me that it was bottomless. *Bottomless!* The thought filled me with awe and dread. If you fell into it, I supposed that you would be sucked right down into the centre of the earth and never be seen again. It was a frightening thought. I turned to tell Chaz about it, but one look at his rapt face warned me that he wouldn't listen if I did.

So, still Tarzan – or perhaps Cheetah – I went below to explore, swinging apelike down the companionway and landing in the saloon. This, I found, was another little house: it might even be better than the boat-house. Moored well offshore, no one could come battering at the door, demanding admittance. If Cly came, I could fend her off with the boat-hook – without fear of reprisals for once – and make a dash for America.

I had wandered around looking at the galley and the heads, and I was trying out one of the bunks in the forward cabin when the engine started, a strong purposeful rumble vibrating up through the decking. I clambered hurriedly back into the cockpit to find Chaz there, holding the boat-hook ready to fend the stern off the slipway in case Teddy made a hash of pulling away.

Mr Guest was still standing there with his hands in his pockets, watching, an unreadable look on his face, and I suspected that he was making sure Teddy left, that he would watch until we were well on our way to Moravon. Teddy probably thought that Mr Guest was lost in admiration or racked with envy. I waved and got a preoccupied smile and a half-raised hand in return. It was more than I expected because I was suddenly sure, watching his face, that he was thinking about Teddy in the same sort of way I sometimes thought about Cly and Mrs van Gelderen, only worse. It made me uneasy. I glanced up at the wheel-house. Since boarding, Teddy had adopted a yachting cap which he sported now at an insouciant angle. I couldn't help thinking of him as Teddy. There was something about him – a lack of dignity perhaps, or maybe knowing that he'd been doing rude things to Mrs Guest in the summer-house – which lowered my respect and prevented me from thinking of him as Mr Ransom, as I ought to have done. He had his back to me, and now that I couldn't see that moustache, I thought he looked rather handsome. Of course he wasn't wearing a gangster's outfit: he was wearing a navy blue blazer with white flannels and white deck shoes and a yellow paisley-patterned cravat. I wondered how he could bear to wear all those clothes on such a hot day, and he must have thought so too, because as soon as we were well away from Holly Hill, almost opposite River Cottage, he called Chaz from the bows where he had begun taking soundings.

'Can I trust you to take the wheel for a minute while I go below and change?' he asked.

Chaz was insulted. "Course you can,' he answered scornfully, 'I've had a boat of my own since I was *seven*.' He spoke as if that had been twenty years ago. 'Fidgie can take over the soundings.'

I was back in the saloon by then, looking up into the wheel-house, and as Teddy spoke, he began to wrench off first his blazer and then his cravat, revealing a momentary glimpse of red blotches on his neck and chest. Two of the buttons had been torn off his shirt.

As I passed Chaz on the few inches of deck beside the cabin housing, I lowered my voice and said confidentially, 'I wouldn't go too near him if I were you. I think he's got measles or chicken-pox or something.'

But Chaz wasn't listening. All he said was, 'Get for'ard, quick, and start taking soundings.' He was ordering me about in the same way Tom did, and I obeyed without question as I did with Tom, except when I felt like quarrelling.

He had to explain how to do it, of course, shouting through the window of the wheel-house until Teddy reappeared, clad now in a short-sleeved Aertex shirt like the one I was wearing, but with the cravat replaced to hide his measles. By that time we had reached the bridge, were cruising under it, and Chaz had pointed the bows towards the open sea, intending to bypass the harbour.

Moravon was not a fashionable resort – far from it –

47

and there were only two other pleasure craft, both motor cruisers, though not as big as Teddy's, at anchor in the roads. We were hailed from one of them.

'Ahoy, there, *Love Nest*! Coo-ee!'

It was a woman's voice. She was lying on one elbow, sunbathing on the deck of the nearest boat, and waving a sun-hat at us. Or rather, at Teddy, who had taken over the wheel again. His reaction was instant. He throttled down until we were doing little more than holding our own against the current.

'Daphne!' he exclaimed with extravagant delight, and added cautiously, 'Where's Stan?'

I had the feeling that this simple question concealed a different one which Chaz and I were not supposed to understand.

'Gone back to Brum,' she said and smiled broadly, lifting her eyebrows like twin question marks.

Teddy turned to us. 'Look, kids,' he said, 'I'd forgotten that I promised to spend the afternoon with friends. Sorry, but I'll have to put you ashore. We'll do the trip another time. OK?'

I was used to this kind of let-down by grown-ups. It was understandable, I supposed – though often a blow to one's self-esteem – that they should prefer the company of their own kind. After all, I preferred the company of other children. Being with adults for any length of time was a strain: ladylike behaviour required more prolonged concentration than I could give it. At any moment I might start jumping about, or pointing, or giggling, or even – worst of all – shouting.

Chaz, though, must have shown his disappointment at being forced to forgo his cruise, because Teddy reached into his hip pocket and pulled out his wallet.

'Ten bob,' he said, extracting the familiar brown-and-orange note. 'Buy yourself and your little friend some treats.'

I hated being called a little friend as if I were some mangy stray which had attached itself to Chaz, but ten shillings was a very handsome bribe, and I lusted after it. I had rarely seen so much money as close as this before, and certainly never handled it, so I was appalled when Chaz tried to refuse it.

'That's not necessary, sir—' he began stiffly, standing on his dignity. When Teddy glanced over at Daphne for a moment, to hold her attention during this hiatus, I gave him a sharp dig in the ribs.

'Nonsense,' Teddy said. 'Your uncle would have my hide if he heard I'd sent you home penniless. Not another word.' And to my great relief, Chaz took my hint and gave in.

Teddy landed us at the seaweed-covered stone steps which the ferrymen used. Hidden among the swirling crowds of holidaymakers on the quay, we watched as he made a beeline back to Daphne's boat, and saw her climb awkwardly aboard *Love Nest,* holding on to Teddy's hand and trying to look as slinky as Jean Harlow. No one else followed her from her boat.

'Huh,' Chaz said in disgust, 'so much for friends, plural.'

'I didn't like him anyway,' I said.

Chaz said nothing. I thought about that ten-bob note in his pocket and said, 'Couldn't we have something to eat with that money he gave you? I'm starving.'

We found a chip shop open, and because we were rich, or perhaps because Chaz was too well brought up or too snooty to eat chips out of a greaseproof bag wrapped in newspaper, he led the way inside and we sat down at a table. The waitress looked as if she didn't believe we could pay, I could tell that; but Chaz's bearing, his confident manner, subdued her. She brought our order, though with scant ceremony, slamming the plates down on the table in front of us so that the chips jumped, to show her disapproval of being forced to wait on kids.

We ate in silence at first. The fish was juicy and delicious, the batter crisp, and I began to feel cheerful for the first time since I found that Fiff and the others had left me behind. But I could tell that Chaz was still gloomy about missing his boat trip. He said morosely, 'Stupid name for a boat, anyway.'

I said, 'Why were you so keen to go on Mr Ransom's boat, if you've got one of your own?'

'Because mine's only a dinghy, really; a conversion, decked-in for'ard to make a bit of a cabin. It's clinker-built and rather old. Teddy's is the newest design, twin-skinned, with those terrific raked bows. He had it brought all the way from Poole in Dorset. That engine can do nearly thirty knots . . .'

Thinking about it seemed to bring him close to tears and I wished I hadn't brought the subject up, but I couldn't think of anything else to talk about, until I suddenly remembered Mr Guest's swimming-pool.

'Can we go swimming at Holly Hill tomorrow?' I asked.

'If you come out early,' he said. 'But we'll have to make ourselves scarce before ten o'clock. After that Mrs Guest might come down, and she doesn't like kids roaming around.'

'Mr Guest said she wouldn't mind,' I said.

'Just take it from me,' Chaz said, 'she would. So don't go there after breakfast time unless you like getting your head bitten off.'

I puzzled about this in silence. Had Mr Guest told a fib, or didn't he know what his wife was really like? This last seemed quite possible when I compared Mrs Guest with Cly. Nobody knew what Cly was really like except Tom and me, and there was no point in telling anyone, because they wouldn't believe us; they'd only think we were trying to get Cly into trouble, out of spite.

Something else occurred to me, something that had been gnawing at me for hours. 'How did you find out my name, anyway?' I asked. 'Nobody's supposed to know.'

I felt crotchety about it: it was so *rude* to nose around, digging out secrets the way he did.

'Oh, that,' he said casually. 'I was spying out the land on the hillock behind your house the other day, and I overheard your mother talking to Mrs Bellamy in the garden. Sound carries upwards, you know . . . and I'd just been reading up on Greek mythology . . .'

That silenced me. I had never heard of Greek mythology.

To my surprise, when he paid for the food Chaz did not produce Teddy's note. He pulled a handful of coins – shillings and half-crowns and florins – out of his pocket and left a threepenny bit under his plate for the waitress, who didn't, I thought, deserve it.

As if he'd read my mind, he pulled the ten-shilling note out of his other pocket when we got outside and held it out to me. 'Here, you have it,' he said. 'You wanted it; I didn't.'

Put like that, the money seemed less desirable. And how would I explain it when I got home? I wouldn't be able to hide it, or not for long: I'd be sure to let it fall out of my pocket sooner or later, and then Fiff would demand an explanation which she almost certainly wouldn't believe. Or if Cly found it first she would make my life a misery until I handed it over, and then she'd probably tear it up or burn it over the candle while I watched, heartbroken. No, the money had to be spent, and it would be better if Chaz did the spending.

Inspiration suddenly came to me: a good reason for

splashing out. 'He told you to spend it on treats,' I said. 'And it's my birthday today.'

Startled, Chaz said, 'Why didn't you say so before?' and after a moment's thought, he added, 'How old are you anyway?'

'Eight,' I said, pleased that he'd asked. I was intensely proud of being eight, and relieved too. I had been seven for such a long time that I'd begun to think I was stuck, that I'd have to go on being seven for ever. But now I was well on my way to being a grown-up. Perhaps when I was nine I'd find the courage to stand up to Cly.

'Well,' he said, 'if you like, we could go to the pictures.'

'Oh Chaz!' I breathed. Going to the pictures on a Friday as well as our usual Saturday matinée was an unheard-of luxury. I almost threw my arms round him, but I remembered in time that boys hate even being *seen* with girls, let alone being hugged by them. Or not at our school, anyway, Tom's and mine. Such behaviour would bring a chorus of jeers and catcalls down on our heads. Tom even refused to be seen walking to school with me. Boys who allowed themselves to be seen in the company of girls were sissies.

I drew back to protect him from this fatal accusation, but I couldn't hide my excitement. '*The Murders in the Room Org* is on at the Pavilion,' I said. 'Do you think they'd let us in?' I'd heard this film was very frightening and I yearned to see it. I loved terrifying stories, or at least I did until I blew my candle out at night.

'We can try,' Chaz said. 'The usherettes usually let me in, even to films only grown-ups are supposed to see.'

I bet they do, I thought, looking at him with envy. Chaz seemed to be able to do anything he wanted. It was quite exciting being with someone who could twist adults round his fingers. It was a truly enviable accomplishment. I knew I'd never be able to do it.

'Is there anything else you'd like?' Chaz asked. 'As a birthday present, I mean.'

I felt shifty. We were strictly forbidden to ask for presents, but surely if I answered his question it wouldn't exactly be asking? My mind had flown instantly to the pair of dancing-slippers I'd seen in a shoe shop I passed on my way to school. I'd been to visit them every day since they'd first appeared in the window, praying that they'd still be there, that nobody had bought them. They were ankle-straps, a ravishing shade of bronze with rosettes of bronze silk on the toes. I knew that even if they were mine I'd never be able to wear them, because I never went to any parties, but they were beautiful and I loved them desperately.

I mentioned them tentatively to Chaz, expecting a yelp of scornful laughter, but all he said was, 'Well, if that's what you want, go ahead and get them.'

'Come with me,' I begged, suddenly unnerved. I'd never been into a shoe shop on my own before. Shoes were things grown-ups bought. I couldn't remember when I last had a new pair. Normally I wore Cly's old ones, passed down when she grew out of them.

Chaz shrugged. 'OK,' he said and followed me into the shop, hands in pockets, unruffled.

The shoes were ten and six, an awful price, more than twice what Fiff had paid for my best dress from Paris House; and sixpence more than Teddy had given us. I looked at Chaz with alarm when the assistant told me, but he showed no sign of outrage. Afterwards, carrying the white shoebox out of the shop, I felt both guilty and triumphant, and for the moment I put off the problem of how I would explain them to Fiff. I felt uneasily sure that she wouldn't be pleased, and might even – a searing thought – demand that I return them. I decided that it would be a good idea to hide them until I could think of a reasonable excuse for having them. To say that a boy I hardly knew, a boy not much older than me, had bought them for me, would not go down well; of that I was sure.

'I'll pay you back,' I told Chaz recklessly, and then, realizing the folly of such a promise, I added quickly, 'The extra sixpence, I mean.'

'Don't be silly, kid,' he said, and for once I didn't resent this piece of cheek: I was too ecstatic.

And as he'd promised, we got into the cinema without difficulty. Chaz paid, and the usherettes smiled on us and held back the heavy chenille curtain to let us through. No one seemed to notice that we were too young to be allowed to see a horror film.

When we came out, still wreathed in mists of fantasy, the sun was setting. Already the lighthouse was flashing from its island on the tip of the peninsula, far out across the bay. The sky above the sea was a brilliant gold, shading upwards through orange and pink into turquoise, and higher up into deeper blue. The sun was poised on the brim of the horizon, and I had been staring, awed by the brilliance of the colours, for some moments before the significance of the scene burst in on me. When it did, I let out a yelp of fright.

'I've got to go,' I said in alarm. I threw a wild look over my shoulder at the setting sun and started to run, the shoebox clutched awkwardly under one arm. 'I've got to get home.'

'What's the matter?' Chaz asked, catching up with me. 'What's the rush?'

'I've got to get home before the sun sets,' I panted. 'Or I'll be in *awful* trouble.'

Chaz was keeping pace with me. 'Don't be a fool,' he said. 'You'll never do it. It must be at least two miles.'

I already knew that, so I kept running and didn't answer.

Chaz ran ahead of me and turned, jogging backwards. 'We could take a taxi,' he said, stunning me with the outlandishness of this suggestion. To get back to River Cottage by road required a detour of nearly seven miles up-river to the toll-bridge, and another seven miles back again down the other side.

Anxiety was ruining my temper. I could see the leather strap coiled up and waiting like a cobra on the top of Fiff's wardrobe. 'There's only Mr Jones,' I said irritably. 'And he only drives at five miles an hour. We wouldn't get back till Christmas. Or even *Easter*.'

'Ring your mother up, then, and explain why you're late.'

'I *can't*,' I wailed. 'We haven't got a telephone. Shut up and run if you're coming with me.'

'Stop panicking,' he said. 'And stop running. I'll telephone my uncle and he'll send the car. He can tell Henderson to go to your mother's place first, and tell her you're OK.'

I stopped so suddenly I nearly fell over. The sheer beauty of this idea, its cunning and simplicity, were breathtaking. And arriving home in such style was bound to placate Fiff. I was saved.

'Would he do that?' I asked in awe.

'I'll be amazed if he refuses,' Chaz said calmly and made for the telephone kiosk outside the funfair. When he came out, he said, 'Right, that's fixed. We may as well start walking to meet the car, unless you want something to eat.'

I didn't. He had bought packets of crisps, which we had eaten in the cinema; and when the usherette came round with ices in the interval, he had bought us each a choc-ice too. In fact, what with all that and the fright I had just had, I was feeling a little sick.

We had almost reached the Clock House on the estuary road before I dared to ask the question which had been puzzling me.

'How can you have a telephone when there isn't any electricity on our side of the river?'

'Batteries,' he said succinctly.

I digested this for a while before asking tentatively, 'Like in a torch?'

'No, fathead. Accumulators. Like the ones I expect you use in your wireless.' I might have known he'd think me a fool, but I still wanted to be sure.

'Big square glass things full of acid?' I asked, expecting another rebuke, but he cut across it.

'And anyway, we *have* got electricity,' he said. 'We use a generator. Mr Guest has one too.'

I remembered then how brilliantly lit Holly Hill sometimes was at night, and felt squashed. I wondered what it would be like to be so rich that you could afford to have a machine to make your own electricity, so rich that you didn't have to walk miles carrying gallon cans of paraffin, or batteries full of acid which sometimes slopped on your clothes and burnt holes in them however careful you were. I hoped that when I grew up I should be able to marry a man as rich as that, but it didn't seem likely. The only rich men I knew were married already, like Mr Guest, and like him, so old that – at the rate I was growing – they would be dead, probably, by the time that I was old enough to get married.

Walking along the estuary road in the warm darkness was almost the best part of the day. Ahead of us the eastern clouds were rosy with light reflected from the dying sunset, though night was drawing a dark veil over them. Curlews were calling somewhere out over the marshes, their liquid calls bubbling up like water in a mountain spring. Only one car – an open-topped sports car – passed us as we walked, and it came far too early to be the car we were expecting. It roared past with a rich snarl and Chaz turned and looked after it admiringly till it disappeared round a bend.

'Mrs Guest,' he said with a touch of envy. 'I'll have a car like that when I'm old enough. Uncle Hil's cars aren't sporty enough. But it would be no use asking *her* to let me drive it.'

'Stop pretending,' I scoffed. 'You can't drive. You're not old enough.'

'Of course I can drive,' he said, as if surprised that I should doubt it. 'I've been driving since I was seven. So long as you keep off the main roads, who's to stop you?'

It was only later, much later, just before I fell asleep that night, that it occurred to me that I knew very little more about Chaz now, after spending all those hours in his company, than I'd known when he first appeared. I still didn't know where he lived. I had even forgotten to find out his surname.

And I might never see him again.

3

I'd been right – though only partly right – about Fiff. She wasn't as angry as she would have been if I'd come home in the dark and alone, but even so, she was worryingly tight-lipped. I had, after all, been missing when she and the others returned from their trip; I had spent the day in the company of strangers; and the fact that Chaz had a chauffeur-driven car at his command did not alter the fact that I had wandered off without leaving word with anyone where I was going.

Because I had been afraid that Fiff might lecture him about keeping me out after dark, I'd refused to let Chaz come with me to the house. It was enough, I thought, that she should hear the car arrive and see me get out of it.

The front door was open, as it always was until bedtime in the summer. I raced in and headed for the stairs to hide my secret shoes in my bedroom, but Fiff came out of the drawing-room and waylaid me as I was halfway up. The hall was only dimly lit by two oil lamps, the larger one on the hall chest, and a tiny one more like a night-light on the window-sill halfway up the stairs, but I knew that even in this low light the white shoebox could not be hidden. I thought about putting it behind my back, but decided that that would only make it more obvious. Fiff, though, didn't seem to notice it.

'So, my girl,' she said coldly, 'you've decided to come home at last.'

'I'm sorry, Mummy,' I said guiltily, 'I forgot the time.'

I was always forgetting the time. Fiff shook her head, resigned to the lame excuse. 'You really are the most feather-brained kid!' she said. Her gaze focused on my clothes, and she heaved a sigh heavy with exasperation. 'And you come home looking like a tramp's lurcher. I see you've already managed to ruin your new shorts. You'd better get them off before Eric sees the way you've treated his present.'

That was when I looked down and discovered the grass stain.

She went on implacably, 'And who are these people who brought you home by car? Do I know them?'

'It was just a boy,' I said. I was uncomfortably aware that, somewhere out of sight, Cly would be listening and revelling in my discomfiture. 'We went to Moravon.'

'So I gather,' she said grimly. 'But I shall want a proper explanation, and it had better be a good one. I won't have you wandering about the countryside in the company of strangers. Really, Fidgie, have you no more sense?' I hung my head, mortified. When I didn't answer, she relented. 'Well, hurry up and come down. Supper's on the table.'

Relief flooded through me: she wasn't really angry, and either she hadn't noticed the shoebox, or she thought it unimportant. The strap would stay in its suitcase on top of the wardrobe. Chaz had saved me, and I gave him humble and hearty thanks as I fled upstairs.

There was no light in my bedroom but I didn't need one. I could have found my way around in the dark, as I often did, but the full moon rising gave me enough light to see what I was doing, and I slipped my precious shoebox under the bed, out of sight.

But when I stood up and turned round again, I felt

myself go icy with fright: Cly was standing in the doorway, and even in the faint moonlight I could see the look of malicious triumph on her face.

'Pigface has a boyfriend! Pigface has a boyfriend!' she chanted, but not loudly enough to be heard downstairs. 'Who is it, Pigface? He must be blind as well as stupid if he fancies *you*.'

I longed to hit her, but I didn't dare. I felt myself blushing so furiously that I thought it must be obvious even in the semi-darkness. I was outraged too, on Chaz's behalf, but I had learned long since not to cross swords with Cly: she always won. And besides, I was too frozen with fright and too worried about the shoes to think of anything to say.

Telling an unseen confidant, she went on gleefully, 'He's given her a present, and she's hidden it under the bed.'

Driven into a corner, I said the first thing that came into my head, disastrously.

'It's only some shells we found on the beach,' I said wildly.

'Bring them down and show them to Ma, then,' she said, impaling me on my own lie with unerring accuracy. 'You ought to show her what your rich boyfriend has given you. We'll all want to see.'

I was at bay. If I walked past her, she would dig under my bed and find the shoebox. And if she took it downstairs and showed it to Fiff, what could I say? I hadn't yet had time to think of an excuse to explain the shoes. Yet I couldn't very well just stay there waiting for Cly to go. I knew she would out-wait me.

I took the only course I could think of. Quaking at the risk I was taking, I shrugged. 'If you don't believe me,' I said, 'go and look for yourself.'

It worked. Cly tossed her head. 'Keep your stupid box, then. No one's interested in your babyish rubbish,' she said, 'or your stupid ugly boyfriend.' She disappeared. A moment later, I heard her going downstairs, somehow managing to convey contempt with every step. I started to breathe again.

Heart thumping, and fumbling with frantic haste because it would be just like Cly to sneak back upstairs and catch me, I retrieved the shoebox, snatched the shoes out with their tissue paper and thrust them under the clothes in one of the drawers. Then I pushed the empty box back under the bed and followed Cly down, twitching from the narrowness of my escape. And I was still uneasy about the shoes. I'd have to find a better hiding-place for them in case Cly had heard me close the drawer. And if I could just find some shells to put in the empty shoebox . . . I cursed myself for telling that stupid lie about the shells. Why hadn't I just said the box was empty, that I'd found it and brought it home to keep things in?

Everyone except Eric was sitting round the table in the dining-room – which was also the sitting-room – and the others were already eating, the meal already begun, the savoury smell of toasted cheese scenting the air. All of a sudden, I was hungry again.

'Has Eric gone home?' I asked, slipping into my chair and trying not to sound hopeful.

'He's gone to see *Murders in the Rue Morgue*,' Fiff said. 'We could all have gone with him if you'd come home when you were supposed to.'

I just stopped myself in time. I might get Chaz into trouble if I admitted that he'd taken me to see a horror film. Fiff might never allow me to see him again.

'It's a horror film,' Tom said, spoiling the effect of Fiff's rebuke. 'They might not have allowed us in.'

'Of course they would,' Fiff said, contradicting him briskly. 'That little cinema needs every penny it can get.'

To me, Tom said, 'You missed a great ride. We went all the way to Bardsey – well, nearly – and had a swim. It's fifty miles at least—'

'Not quite that far,' Fiff put in. She was a stickler for accuracy.

'—and the water's *freezing* there.'

Cly was cutting her toast into fingers and offering bits to Pipsy while Fiff wasn't looking. Feeding the dog at table was strictly against the rules, but Fiff never seemed to notice when Cly did it.

'We've saved a slice of birthday cake for you,' Fiff said. 'Do you want it now?'

'No, thank you,' I said. It hurt to say it, but I had to keep my afternoon vow.

Fiff was annoyed. 'You'll have to eat it tomorrow, then,' she said. 'And it will be dry by then.'

I didn't care: I'd give it to Pipsy.

Tom said, 'I'll eat it if you like.'

'No, you won't,' Fiff said quellingly.

Silence fell. I was bursting to tell Tom about Chaz, but not while Cly was there. It wasn't safe to let her know anything, especially about something I valued, and I valued my new-found friendship with Chaz.

Fiff sent Tom and me off to bed as soon as supper was over. We were usually allowed to listen to the wireless for a while in the evening, but the accumulator had run low and the programme was too faint to be heard properly. It was disappointing, but it happened so often that we knew we had no choice but to accept it. I didn't mind all that much because I was hugging to myself the secret of my new shoes, and I could hardly wait to try them on again. But Tom was disgruntled.

'I bet Cly did it,' he muttered as we climbed the stairs. 'The wireless was all right at lunchtime. It would have been just like her to leave it switched on all afternoon while we were out, to run the accumulator down. Just for spite. She knows we like to listen to the wireless before we go to bed.'

Quite suddenly, while I was brushing my teeth, I decided that I wouldn't tell Tom about Chaz after all, or no more than the bare minimum. I had no idea why I didn't want to share him; I just didn't. I told myself that Tom had plenty of friends without Chaz, and he hadn't asked anyway. So serve him right.

To justify this meanness I reminded myself of all the times that he and Harry, Jacko and Dick and the other boys had refused to let me play football with them, even when I offered to play in goal, a position nobody else wanted.

I was drying my face when Tom called from his bedroom.

'Fidgie!'

'What?'

'Here a moment. I've got something for you.'

I fell for it, and went. The moment I opened the door, a pillow hit me with some force.

'That's for landing me with sly Cly all afternoon,' he snarled, keeping his voice low.

I snatched a pillow from the other bed – Eric's – and hit him with it.

'And that's for going off without me, you sneak,' I hissed, equally furious.

We enjoyed fighting, but our fights had to be conducted in silence, or as near silence as we could manage, because Fiff disapproved of horseplay. After my initial squeal of outrage, swiftly stifled, we attacked each other with muffled grunts and squeaks until Tom tripped over a chair and fell with a heavy crash. That was the signal to scatter, and I reached my room just as Fiff's voice came up from the foot of the stairs.

'What on earth are you two doing? You'll bring the

ceiling down! Get into bed at once, both of you. Say your prayers and go to sleep.'

I always took a flying leap into bed, even when I wasn't in a hurry. There was a huge python curled up in the dark under the bed, lying in wait to grab me by the ankles; so I was in bed, the candle blown out, before Fiff had even finished speaking. But if she had come to check, this hasty stratagem would have been betrayed by the smell of hot candlewax and the wraith of smoke, easily visible in the moonlight, curling up from the candle's wick.

As soon as I decided it was safe, I got up again, closed my door, and retrieved my new shoes. Even by moonlight they were beautiful. I revelled in them, inhaling the scent of newness, feeling the glossy leather not yet creased or scuffed; the soles magically smooth and unworn, the perfect contours not buckled to the shape of Cly's foot. I put them on and danced around the moonlit room on tiptoe, in silence, until my steps drew me to the window. It had been wide open all day and I leant through it looking out along the ghostly river to Holly Hill, whose front windows were golden with light. And somewhere up-river beyond Holly Hill, Chaz lived. Tomorrow, perhaps, I'd find out where.

Mrs Bellamy's hens crooned sleepily to themselves in their coop, safe from prowling foxes. On silent wings in the moonlight a barn owl sailed over the garden like a great white moth.

I sighed with contentment. Even without the birth-day cake or the ride in the dicky, it was the best birthday I could ever remember, and I was pretty sure I could remember at least three; perhaps four.

Something – a door slamming perhaps, though it sounded as sharp as a gunshot – woke me some time later. The moon had moved round towards the west and my bedroom was no longer as brightly lit as before. I was pretty sure that the great dark shape looming just inside the door was my dressing-gown hanging on a peg, but it *could* be a huge gorilla, come to get me like the girl in the film. It took a while to raise the courage to get up and go to investigate it.

My mouth had gone dry with fright by then, and I went into the bathroom for a drink of water, but the tumbler had disappeared, taken probably by Cly when she had come up to bed. I was slopping water into my mouth with one hand when I remembered the crate of fizzy drinks Fiff had bought from the Corona delivery lorry. It was strictly forbidden to eat or drink anything but water after we'd cleaned our teeth, but the more I thought of Ice-Cream Soda and Dandelion & Burdock – my favourites – the more I longed for them. Driven by this lust, I began to sneak downstairs, making sure I trod on the outside edges of the stairs where they didn't creak, and keeping a wary eye on Cly's bedroom door.

I'd thought it was so late that everyone must be in bed and asleep, but halfway down I heard the sound of Eric's voice in the sitting-room, and paused in alarm, wondering if I dared go on; but it was Fiff's reply to whatever it was Eric had said which finally cleared the sleep from my head and jolted me awake.

'How *can* I divorce him? For one thing, I couldn't possibly afford it, and for another, a divorce would cause such an appalling scandal. Imagine what your Aunt Gertie would say.'

'She wouldn't need to know. Nobody need know.'

'The children would know. One of them would be sure to let it out. You know what a scatterbrain Fidgie is.'

Eric's grunt of assent was followed by a silence

before Fiff went on, 'You don't know what it's been like. Believe me, you don't know the half of it. I'd cheerfully *murder* that man if I thought I could get away with it.' There was suppressed desperation in her voice.

Probably embarrassed by this show of emotion, Eric said with a heavy attempt at humour, 'Well, maybe he'll crash that big car of his and do himself in.'

Fiff said gloomily, 'He did that once, in Ceylon – went over the *khud* – a ravine. Anyone else would have been killed, but not Thorp. He got out without a scratch. He leads a charmed life.'

There was a moment or two of silence, during which Eric must have been thinking, because at last he said, rather reluctantly I thought, 'If you like, Aunt Fran, I can make an excuse to go and call on him when I get home. It should be easy enough to tell whether this woman is really his housekeeper or not. If she isn't, if it's obvious they're living tally, you've got your ammunition.' After another pause, he added with a touch of sarcasm, '*If* you can bring yourself to use it.'

They were talking about Boko and the conversation fascinated me, especially when they began to talk about a woman he was living with. It was clear that she was doing something she shouldn't, like Mrs Guest in the summer-house, and I was agog to hear the details. But it was dangerous to stay where I was. Cly was probably reading her secret love magazines in bed, but at any moment, alerted by her sixth sense, she might come out of her bedroom and find me there, eaves-dropping. Creeping back upstairs even more quietly than I'd gone down, I lay awake for a long time thinking.

I knew what divorce was: I'd heard women lowering their voices to talk about it; whispering when they got to the most interesting bits, a device which never failed to alert me. They'd thought that if they spelled it out – D-I-V-O-R-C-E – I wouldn't understand, and I had always pretended not to, out of good manners, while listening with pricked ears.

It would be a relief to know that, if only Fiff could divorce him, I should never have to see Boko again, never again have to stand, quaking, in his menacing presence. Once in a while he would descend on us in high good humour, carrying bags of sweets, and giving Tom and me sixpence each, a fortune.

But the good mood never lasted, and the sweets and sixpences didn't make up for the sudden terrifying rages, the pain of the beatings, the sick dread and the misery.

I had already said my prayers once, before I'd gone to sleep, but I decided to say them again, this time kneeling beside the bed, nervously defying the python to prove my earnestness and give my pleas more weight. This time I rattled through the prayers Fiff had taught us, anxious to get to the bit at the end where, duty done, special requests were allowed.

'Please, *please* give Fiff the money for a divorce,' I begged the mysterious old man in the sky. He probably wasn't even listening, but it was worth a try. I redoubled my fervour. 'And I promise faithfully I'll never *ever* breathe a word to *anyone*. Word of honour.'

4

Mrs Bellamy's cockerel woke me, triumphantly claiming the day. Even as early as this, it was scarcely any cooler. The air smelled of sunbaked earth and parched grass turning to hay. The stunted oaks on the hillock behind the houses clung grimly to the thin soil, their wizened roots grasping the rock like arthritic fingers, their leaves dark green and thirsty, beginning to curl up at the edges.

From my window I watched Mr James's van arrive. He hauled a milk churn out of the back and struggled with it through the side gate. Yesterday's milk would be sour by now, in spite of all Fiff's efforts to keep it cool. Using the measuring dips hooked over the rim of the churn, Mr James ladled three pints into the jugs Fiff had left out for him in the meat safe, and clanked away out of sight to deliver to Mrs Bellamy and Miss Wragg. I often wondered why he didn't use the yoke I'd seen other farmers using to carry milk churns. Perhaps he couldn't afford one.

Chaz had said we could use the swimming-pool at Holly Hill before breakfast-time. I had no idea what time it was now, but it felt early, and it was certainly before *my* breakfast-time. Fiff had banned swimming for two hours after a meal, so if I didn't go now, before breakfast, I couldn't go at all. The problem was to get out of the house without being seen and questioned. I felt inexplicably shifty about Holly Hill, perhaps because of Teddy and Mrs Guest.

My bathing costume and towel had been hanging over the window-sill to dry ever since yesterday and I shook the dried sand out of them both before putting my costume on and adding a dress on top. The bathing costume had a small hole in it, but the hole was round the back where I couldn't see it, so it didn't matter. I would have liked to wear my shorts again, but I knew that Fiff would never let me go out in them now that she had seen the grass stain.

Before I'd got into bed last night, I had hidden the shoes on top of the wardrobe, out of sight behind the pediment, and it was satisfying to see in daylight that they were not visible from any angle directly below. But when I turned at the top of the stairs and looked back down the landing, I felt sure I could see the top of the ankle straps just showing. Even that much wasn't safe from Cly, so I returned, closed my door stealthily and, clambering up on my chair, moved them further away. At last, satisfied that they were completely hidden, I crept carefully downstairs carrying my towel, hoping that nobody would be up yet, so that I could sneak out unheard.

I reasoned that if Fiff were up, she would most likely be at the back, in the kitchen, so I made for the front door. But I might have known that escape wouldn't be as easy as that, because Tom came clattering down the stairs even before I'd turned the handle. I turned and put my finger up to my lips to signal silence, but too late.

'Hey, Fidge,' he called, loudly enough to be heard all over the house, 'Where you off to?' And sure enough, the kitchen door opened and Fiff looked round it.

'You're neither of you going anywhere until you've had breakfast,' she said, and disappeared again.

'I'm going to *kill* you,' I hissed at him. 'Now I won't be able to go at all.'

'Go where?'

I realized I'd said too much, and didn't answer. If Tom knew that I was going to Holly Hill to bathe, he'd want to come too. And what excuse could I make to stop him? I was afraid that if Tom knew about Chaz, Chaz too would be sucked away into the boys' gang, and I'd be on my own again.

'Go *where*?' he insisted.

'Mind your own business,' I mumbled sulkily. 'I don't ask *you* where you're going.'

'Oh yes, you do,' he countered. 'You're always trying to follow me about.'

That stung, partly because it was true, but mostly because he was saying that he didn't want me around. 'All right,' I snapped, 'from now on, go where you dratted well like. *I* don't care.' It was a measure of my fury that I dared to swear at him like that. Auntie Gertie had once sent me to bed for saying 'drat'.

'Stop that, you two,' came from the kitchen, together with a delicious smell of bacon frying.

Eric was sitting at the dining-table in his pyjamas and dressing gown, reading a book, which meant that we were supposed to keep quiet and not disturb him. I felt sure that he had grabbed the book on purpose when he heard us in the hall, because he was still sitting sideways on his chair. The front of his pyjama trousers was slightly agape, and I got a glimpse of a patch of dark, wiry hair before he swung his legs back under the table. I averted my eyes and pretended I hadn't seen, though it was deeply interesting and I wished I had the nerve to stare. If only Eric hadn't been such an enemy . . . I wasn't sure where this thought was leading me, so I stopped thinking it.

Grown-ups eat some horrible things. Eric was munching his way morosely through a bowlful of Grape-Nuts, and there was a packet of Force on the table too. I had tried Grape-Nuts once and hated them: it felt like chewing coffee grounds. There was no sign of Shredded Wheat on the table, my favourite.

I went into the kitchen and asked, 'Haven't we got any loofahs?'

Fiff was turning bacon in the frying pan. 'In the sideboard, where they always are,' she said vaguely. We were so used to it now that we never noticed the smell of the paraffin stove. In any case, it didn't smell much at all when the wicks were clean, as now, and not turned up too high, as sometimes happened.

Cly came in with Pipsy at her heels as I was pouring milk on my loofahs. Pipsy was supposed to sleep in her basket in the kitchen; we weren't supposed to know that she slept on Cly's bed.

'Greedy guts,' Cly said, watching me, and 'Ma! She's using half the milk on her Shredded Wheat.'

From the kitchen, Fiff said mildly, 'Leave some for the others, Fidgie.'

Eric looked up from his book and studied my bowl where I was sprinkling sugar liberally. My hand faltered.

'You're old enough now to understand that food costs money,' he said coldly. 'Money your mother can ill afford.'

I stared down at the sugar-coated, milk-flooded cereal in my bowl. It had never occurred to me before that I might be eating more than Fiff could afford, and I was mortified beyond words. I couldn't eat it now, with everybody watching and condemning every spoonful I put in my mouth. Just sitting there with Eric glowering at me across the table and Cly secretly gleeful was unbearable. Even Tom was looking at my plate. I slid off my chair and fled towards the front door.

Cly's voice, richly gratified, followed me. 'Take no

71

notice. She just wanted an excuse to get out.' She raised her voice to be sure I heard. 'Serve her right if she's starving by lunchtime.' And Eric's snort of laughter followed me too. He always admired the things Cly said.

I wrenched the door open and flew down the path. Nobody tried to stop me and I didn't slow down until I'd reached the knoll and buried myself in the trees, determined not to give Cly the added satisfaction of seeing me burst into tears. I felt sick. Fiff had left it to Eric, an outsider, to point out that I was eating more than she could afford. Coming from him, it was unbearable, a betrayal.

The tears didn't last long. There was something friendly and calming about the trees even though they were so stunted, or perhaps because of it. There was nothing grandiose about them, nothing awe-inspiring. Their trunks were so undernourished that I could put my arms round them easily. I made straight for my favourite, where I had hidden my valuables – coloured pebbles, a swan's feather, a mermaid's purse and a pink shell – in a hole under the roots. It was comforting to put my arms round it and hug it and feel its rough bark against my cheek. After a while, when I felt better, I sat down on the moss beneath it and thought fiercely about murder. Cly would be the first to go, obviously, then Eric, though I hated them all, even Tom, who had been too craven to stand up for me.

But then, looking into a future which held only Pipsy and me, I decided perhaps to let Fiff live, and maybe Tom too. Without Cly to spy on us and carry tales, Fiff might not be so strict with us.

Casting a spell might work the trick. I gathered some twigs, and muttering *abracadabra*, laid them in a saltire – which seemed more magical than an ordinary cross – at the foot of the tree, and placed four pebbles between the arms. It didn't really seem adequate, so I invented a dance, sidling round the tree with mystic hand-weaving and humming and the most intricate steps I could devise. Finally, to round it off, I made several passes over it with my hands, intoning, 'Open Sesame!'

Nothing happened, but then I hadn't really expected anything to happen immediately, like having Cly's corpse come crashing down through the trees to land at my feet, though that would have been deeply satisfying. The spell would probably take time to work. Cly would die horribly, perhaps next Hallowe'en, of some disease the doctors had never heard of.

This was the same hillock where I'd stalked Chaz yesterday afternoon. It was probably too late now to swim in the pool at Holly Hill, but at least I could keep watch for Chaz from the far end of the hillock, to catch him when he came out of the gates.

I made my way along the crest swinging from branch to branch, just above the ground and as silently as possible, partly because I had just broken out of Sing Sing and the bloodhounds were closing in on me, baying for my blood; and partly because, if my feet touched the ground before I'd counted up to a hundred, the spell on Cly wouldn't work.

So I was hanging from a tree when I saw Mr Guest. I had only reached eighty-something, but seeing him was so unexpected that I forgot how far I had got. He was sitting at the foot of a tree with his back to me, the gun on the moss by his side. His hands were hanging limp over his knees and his head was bent. He might have been asleep, but if he wasn't, he looked as unhappy as I had been half an hour ago before my tree cheered me up, and my heart went out to him. I dropped the few inches to the ground as quietly as

I could in case he was asleep, and approached him diffidently.

'Are you all right, Mr Guest?' I asked. I had spoken quietly, but he was as startled as if I had shouted. For a moment I was frightened by the look on his face, but then his expression softened.

'Oh, it's you, er . . . Fidgie,' he said, and put his hands up to rub his face as if he had just woken up. 'Yes, I'm OK. Just tired. Didn't get to bed last night.' The fact that he had remembered my name, even though only just, confirmed me in my good opinion of him.

'You've been hunting all *night*?' This was yet more evidence of the strangeness of grown-ups, the lawless lives they led, the enviable way they could do anything they wanted, things forbidden to us, like staying up all night. Unlike us, they had no rules to obey. But how could anyone stay awake *all night?* It was impressive.

'Well, not exactly hunting,' he said. The idea seemed to amuse him, in a sombre sort of way. 'Thinking, mostly.'

The gun was lying across his legs with its barrels pointing towards him. It looked dangerous to me, leaving it like that. There was a white gash across the trunk of the tree behind him, just below his ear. I said earnestly, 'You shouldn't let that gun point at you like that. It might go off and shoot you.'

I was trying to be helpful, but to my chagrin he laughed suddenly, a harsh, sardonic, worrying sound. 'Yes, I suppose it might,' he said. 'In fact, it very nearly did. But it's harder to shoot yourself than you think.' He sounded tired now, resigned almost.

'I think you should go home to bed,' I said severely. I was still offended – and puzzled too – by his laughter, or I would never have dared speak to a grown-up like that.

'You're right,' he said. 'It was a waste of a good night's sleep.'

He got up, dusted the twigs and bits of moss off his trousers, and picked up the gun. He looked at it vaguely as if he'd forgotten how it worked, then turned it round, broke it open, and took a spent cartridge out of one of the barrels. The other barrel was empty.

'To hell with everything,' he said obscurely. Then suddenly, he drew in a deep breath, flexing his shoulders and stretching his spine before he breathed out again in a huge sigh. 'Well, that's that,' he said, and looked at me as if noticing me fully for the first time. 'You're up early. Have you had breakfast yet?'

I shook my head.

He looked at his watch and seemed surprised by what he saw there. 'It's gone eight o'clock. Come on, we'll go and find something to eat.'

I slipped my hand into his and, forgoing the temptation to show off, allowed him to help me jump down the last three feet onto the track as we set off towards Holly Hill.

Asking personal questions was bad manners, I knew, and heavily frowned on by Fiff, but it was such an interesting pursuit that to suppress the urge to do it, as I'd forced myself to do with Chaz yesterday, was a painful self-denial. I saw no reason to bite back my curiosity now, so I asked him, 'Have you lived here long?'

In my experience, nobody ever lived anywhere for long, and my next question was going to be, 'Where did you live before?'

But, 'Actually, I live near Manchester most of the time,' he said. 'That's where I work. Holly Hill's my holiday home. I had it built specially a few years ago.'

This was a new and startling idea. I had never heard of anyone having a house built specially. If I'd ever thought about it at all, I think I must have supposed that houses just existed, waiting for people to move in and out of them, like fishes darting in and out of pools. I wanted to ask, 'Do you have to be very rich to build your own house?' but I knew that if he ever told Fiff I'd asked him if he was rich, I'd be in deep disgrace. Fiff never forgot bad behaviour or lapses of good manners, and she was apt to remind me of them long after I had forgotten. *I haven't forgotten the time you tore Mrs Fenn's mosquito netting . . . I seem to remember a certain Easter when you ate Clytie's Easter egg . . .* I was pretty sure that she didn't know the Guests, but that didn't mean she never would. I was treading on dangerous ground and it was exciting and scary, like accepting a dare, though I was fairly sure that Mr Guest wouldn't report me deliberately. Not like old Mrs van Gelderen anyway.

So I decided to risk it.

'You must be very rich,' I said.

After a moment, he said, 'Yes, I suppose I am.'

I sighed with longing. 'I expect you can afford anything.'

'Within reason,' he said gravely. 'Why, is there something you want?'

I suddenly remembered the conversation I'd over-heard last night. 'Does a divorce cost a lot of money?' I asked.

He stopped dead and turned to stare at me, frowning alarmingly. This time I knew I'd gone too far. But why? What had I said? Was divorce something rude, then? Fiff had said it would cause a scandal, and she and Eric had been speaking in lowered voices even though they were alone. I quaked. In this impenetrable world of adults, how was it possible to know what was permissible and what was not?

'Why do you ask?' His face and voice were both

suddenly unfriendly. I had to redeem myself somehow, but I couldn't betray Fiff. I wasn't at all sure that God would give her the money, as I'd asked – in fact I was dismally sure that he hadn't been listening – but he just might have been. He might be considering it, waiting to see if I'd break my promise, so it wasn't wise to take the risk. Luckily, it was easy to fool grown-ups – the nice ones, anyway. I just had to be a little vague and he'd never guess I was talking about Fiff.

'Someone I know would like one,' I mumbled, staring down at my feet and kicking at a stone embedded in the path. 'But sh— but they don't think they can afford one.'

I glanced up at him, and to my great relief saw his expression relax, but he went on staring at me in a strange way until I began to worry. Seeing my discomfort and mistaking the reason for it, he put an arm round my shoulder and gave me a light hug.

'I see,' was all he said, but I was still worried.

'Is it something bad, then?' I asked. 'I thought it just meant that married people don't have to live together any more.'

He sighed. 'Yes, that's all it means,' he said.

'So why do people always whisper about it?'

'Because they think it's shocking. People who get married are supposed to stay married for good,' he said. 'No matter what.'

'Even when they don't want to?'

'Even if they hate the sight of each other,' he said. 'Unfortunately.'

'But why?'

He shrugged. 'That's just the way it is.'

'In that case,' I said with determination, 'I'm *never* going to get married.'

He laughed sceptically. 'Tell me that again when you're seventeen and all the boys are chasing you.'

It seemed unlikely that I would ever be seventeen. Even Cly wasn't that old. We started walking again, idling along the track in the growing heat, and he began musing in disjointed sentences, talking to no one in particular, thinking aloud, not really expecting me to understand.

'I read somewhere that there was a time, not all that long ago, when you could only get a divorce by an Act of Parliament . . . Amazing, really. Only the very grandest people did it. It's easier now, but . . . it still carries a stigma . . . Divorced women are looked on as social outcasts . . . All the other women cut them . . .'

I still didn't understand why people should make such a fuss about it, but I was afraid to go on questioning him in case he lost patience with me. And I enjoyed being spoken to as if I were a grown-up. If I interrupted his flow of thought, he'd realize he was only talking to a kid, and stop. We had reached the gates of Holly Hill by this time. He opened one of them and held it open for me. That was when I suddenly remembered Mrs Guest and began to wish I had not accepted his invitation. I knew I wouldn't be welcome and began to hang back, but he didn't seem to notice and led the way indoors. I followed, hoping Chaz was right when he said that Mrs Guest didn't get up for breakfast.

Mr Guest opened the kitchen door while I stayed nervously in the corridor, keeping a wary eye on the stairs.

'Two of us for breakfast, Mrs Evans,' he said. 'I have a guest.'

Delicious smells of coffee and bacon and freshly baked bread came out of the kitchen, and this last, especially, sent me into an ecstasy. Fiff hardly ever baked bread herself. Sometimes she freshened up a stale loaf by steaming it in the oven, but that wasn't the same.

Mr Guest had crossed the passage to the cloakroom where he had tended to Chaz's head. Behind me, the kitchen door opened again and a maid in blue and white striped morning uniform emerged carrying a breakfast tray. I watched her as she disappeared upstairs, her starched pinafore rustling.

'Is someone ill in bed?' I asked Mr Guest, keeping my fingers crossed and trying not to sound hopeful.

'Ill?'

'The maid just took a tray upstairs.'

'Oh, that,' he said, turning off the tap in the washbasin and beginning to dry his hands. 'No, my wife always has breakfast in bed.'

He must have seen the worry dissolve from my face because he laughed suddenly, a merriment in his face I'd never seen before, the tiredness instantly, if temporarily, wiped out. Relieved and charmed, I laughed too, and decided that I liked his eyes after all.

'Come on,' he said, 'let's get breakfast over. After that I'll have to leave you. I need a bath.'

'Wouldn't a swim do?' I asked, hoping to be invited to join him in the swimming-pool. I had left my towel behind in my flight from home, but that didn't matter: I often let my bathing costume dry on me.

'No,' he said. 'No. Today I feel I need a good scrub.'

The remark was addressed to someone else, not me; to a grown-up who would understand the underlying meaning. People think that kids don't understand anything, so it doesn't matter what they say in our hearing. But I had seen him sitting under that tree and I guessed that he was saying something about his sleepless night. Still, perhaps he just meant that spiders and woodlice and beetles had been crawling over him all night and he felt itchy.

The corridor opened out into the hall and I followed him through it and into the dining-room. It overlooked the river, and because at this hour the sun was still behind the house, everything – the walls, the ceiling, the air itself was bright with cool light reflected off the water far below. He went to the sideboard and lifted the lids off two or three of the silver dishes on it.

'What would you like to eat?' he asked. 'I'm usually alone for breakfast, so there's not much choice. Mrs Evans only cooks the things she knows I like. But if you'd rather have a boiled egg or . . .'

'I'd like whatever you're having,' I said politely, hoping it wasn't Grape-Nuts.

I was glad when he dismissed the maid after she had brought in the coffee. I had long forgotten what it was like to be waited on at table, forgotten even that I ever *had* been waited on, and her presence unnerved me.

He helped me to bacon and sausage and mushrooms. I had only recently acquired a taste for mushrooms, and I was mad about them. I was the only one in the family who liked them – except Boko, and he was mad about them too – but I stuffed that thought hastily into the back of my mind: I didn't want to think about Boko. I refused to admit that he and I had anything in common. I swung my thoughts quickly back to Mr Guest.

I liked him. I liked his house too: the rooms were spacious and full of light, unlike the rooms at River Cottage which tended to be dark even in summer because of the hillock rising steeply at the far end of the garden. In here, wreaths of light reflecting off the river below – or perhaps the swimming-pool – twinkled and danced across the ceiling as if we were in the cabin of a boat. The furniture – pale wood inlaid with darker wood – looked as if it had all been bought at the same time, unlike our furniture at River Cottage. Most of that had arrived, a piece at a time, after one or other of Fiff's sorties to the auction rooms, while other pieces – like the Chinese silk carpet in the drawing-room, the Benares brass trays, the exquisite ivory carvings in the curio cabinet, and the elephant's foot wastepaper basket – were all that was left to remind us of our life in Ceylon.

But in spite of the luxury of Holly Hill I decided that I rather preferred the comfortable muddle of River Cottage. For all its ordered beauty, or perhaps because of it, there was something lifeless about the house. It seemed to be waiting for someone to shout, to sing and dance and play the gramophone; to stop polishing the furniture and straightening the cushions; anything to shatter its cool calm and force its still heart to start beating.

'I suppose you won't be seeing much of Chaz now that his tutor's come back,' Mr Guest said as we sat down. 'He'll have to keep his nose to the grindstone from now on if he's to catch up with his school-work. You know he spent a time in hospital?'

'He said he had an accident. I don't think he wants to talk about it.'

'I'm not surprised.' He sighed. 'If I tell you what happened, will you promise to keep it to yourself, until he feels able to tell you himself?'

Secrets are always thrilling. I could feel my eyes widening with pleasure, but then I saw that he was serious, and forced myself to look solemn. 'Cross my heart,' I said earnestly, doing it, 'and hope to die.'

'Because Chaz has enough to put up with,' he said. 'Both his parents were killed in that accident, and Chaz himself nearly died.'

'Oh,' I said, shocked into silence for once.

'It left him with a . . . a slight disability.'

The subject seemed to embarrass him. I was puzzled. To me a disability meant a limp or a stammer, and Chaz did neither of those things.

'What sort of disability?' I asked tentatively, knowing that grown-ups don't like explaining things. If they were in a good mood, they fobbed us off with nonsense; if they were in a bad mood they got irritable.

'Oh . . . nothing much, really . . .' Mr Guest became vague. He broke off a piece of bread and prepared to put it in his mouth. 'It's called *petit mal*, I believe. He tends to lose consciousness now and then . . .'

I remembered the way Chaz had passed out yesterday, when he was pretending that I had shot him.

He went on, 'So don't talk to him about it unless he brings the subject up himself.'

'Is that why he's living with his uncle?' I asked.

'Great-uncle, yes.'

I supposed that 'great-uncle' must be some kind of courtesy title. Boko's business friends had always encouraged us to call them uncle. I wouldn't have liked to have to live with any of them, even though they all had houses much grander than River Cottage; houses almost as beautiful as Holly Hill.

'Poor Chaz,' I said faintly. 'How awful. Wouldn't they let him go on living in his own house?'

He poured coffee and passed me a cup. 'His parents didn't have a home in this country. They were on leave. His father was in government service in Ceylon.'

I was startled. 'We came from Ceylon too,' I said excitedly.

We still grieved over our forced exile from our birthplace. I couldn't understand why we'd had to leave. Fiff said vaguely that it was considered bad form for children born there to stay there after the age of twelve. I had to accept that, but I still couldn't see why. Even Cly, who liked nothing and nobody as far as Tom and I could see, said that when she grew up she intended to be a stewardess on a ship so that she could go back to Ceylon.

'Then your parents may have known his parents,' he said. 'Vivian and Joan Channing.'

'I think my parents only knew other planters,' I said doubtfully. 'But I'll ask.'

He had been speaking without any real interest. His voice flat with tiredness. I guessed that he was only really making polite conversation with me; had probably regretted inviting me to breakfast and wanted only to go to bed to sleep. We finished the meal mostly in silence. From the way he staggered slightly when we got up it was obvious that he was half-asleep already, and I knew that I had better leave.

'Please, please don't have a bath first,' I urged him earnestly. 'You'll fall asleep and drown.' I knew I ought not to have spoken to a grown-up like that: it was cheek, and Fiff would have been annoyed if she'd heard, but Mr Guest wasn't aloof and intimidating like most adults. He was more like us.

He produced a smile. 'I think I'd better take your advice,' he said.

I thanked him for breakfast and added, 'I can see myself out.' It was something I'd heard grown-ups say.

We parted at the foot of the stairs and I scampered out through the back door as fast as dignity would allow, afraid that Mrs Guest might appear at any moment and kill us both with the same chilling distaste she had shown yesterday.

Once outside the gates I slowed down and began to dawdle, trying to decide what to do next. It was Saturday, a day of joyous freedom in term-time, a magic day even in the holidays because Saturday was the day we went to the pictures. It was also the day we got our pocket money. I thought sympathetically of Chaz. From what Mr Guest had said, Chaz probably had to work on Saturdays, buried in books indoors.

I decided to go to Moravon and spend the morning

swimming. If I was careful, I could get past River Cottage without being seen and hauled up before Fiff – and worse, Eric – to explain my behaviour at breakfast.

The decision to keep out of the way cheered me up. By lunchtime, with luck, Fiff would have forgotten or be too busy to care.

Also I could take the opportunity to collect some shells to put in the shoebox under my bed, to fool Cly if she ever did decide to snoop inside it.

I'd have to sneak under the toll-gate, of course . . .

I began to run and skip, singing my favourite song. *'Oh, the object of my affection . . .'*

It was only later, when I was crossing the bridge, that I realized I'd missed the chance to ask Mr Guest where Chaz lived.

5

In Moravon I made a half-hearted search for friends to play with, not really expecting to find any. Dilys and Ruthie, I knew, had to stay at home and look after the younger children while their mothers worked in hotel kitchens somewhere. Ellen, my best friend, lived with her mother and brother in a dark basement under a row of shops. The door was open and I stood on the threshold and looked in. The tablecloth of soiled newspapers was covered with the usual array of cracked and broken cups. I had never seen any plates.

What little light penetrated the grimy window was blocked by the newspapers Mrs Morris had hung as curtains. It was so dark in there that I had never seen beyond that kitchen table, and I didn't try. It was obvious that there was no one in, so after knocking and calling Ellen's name twice with no response, I gave up and went to the beach alone.

All morning, in between building sandcastles, and swimming whenever the heat became too much to bear, I kept an eye open for discarded pop bottles, as we always did when we were broke, because there were pennies to be earned by returning them. The Corona bottles, their ceramic tops held down with a rubber washer and a wire clip, were the best. They were worth thruppence, so just one of those would have bought me a ha'penny bag of chips and a Lyons Cup Cake – which cost tuppence – leaving a ha'penny over for sweets – a farthing bag of sherbet dabs and a liquorice bootlace, maybe – but Corona bottles were a rare and exotic find, abandoned only by the very richest or most careless people; and my luck was out.

When the tide got low enough, I waded across to the island at the mouth of the harbour and continued my search, more desperately now because just thinking about the fizz of sherbet sparkling on my tongue made my mouth water. The island was a good place to find things because people went there at night, especially in the summer, to hide in the sandhills where nobody could see them, and they often lost things or left them behind in the dark. It could be a treasure trove so long as you were careful not to pick up one of those rubber things which were full of something wet and rude.

But this time, all I could find was a brass brooch inset with sparkly glass, probably won from the crane machine at the funfair. It was quite useless: nobody would have given me anything for it, but apart from the fact that the pin was slightly bent, it was prettier and much less tinpot than the usual funfair trinkets, so I straightened out the pin as best I could and fastened the brooch to my dress.

An hour later, sandy and salty and sunny, but still penniless and now starving, I left the beach and began to head for home along the promenade and through the harbour, the quickest way to reach the bridge. The church clock high on the hill chimed the half-hour and I glanced up at it. Its face told me nothing except that its small hand was pointing straight up and the big hand straight down, but I felt sure that it must be lunchtime. I'd heard the clock striking the hour some time ago but I'd been too busy to count the strokes. I could remember only that there'd been a lot of them. A small breeze had got up, no more than a warm breath, but it was the first lifting of the air for days, and it carried occasional faint, famishing fragrances from the bakeries and fish-and-chip shops in the town.

We called the holidaymakers 'the people from away' and the harbour was crowded with them, some waiting for the ferry, most just ambling about or standing at the quayside staring down at the activities on the fishing boats, ignored by the fishermen who went on unloading their catches or mending their nets apparently unaware of the surveillance.

To me, the harbour was the most interesting part of Moravon: the quayside was piled high with lobster pots, and smelled saltily of seaweed and shellfish and reminiscently of tarred ropes and oil, reminding me of our voyage home from Ceylon.

I was weaving and dodging through the crowds when I caught sight of Mrs Guest. She was standing near the railing at the edge of the quay, and there was something so concentrated in her face that I followed her line of sight and saw Teddy and a woman I'd never seen before, coming up the slipway where Teddy had moored his boat. They were walking with their arms round each other's waists and gazing at each other in the sort of way which would have sent Ellen into a fit of the giggles, but Mrs Guest was anything but amused. I saw her take a step away from the rail as if to confront them.

I hesitated. It would have been fun to hang around and see if they would all have a terrible row, but it might take ages and I was ravenous. And just as I was trying to decide between fun or food the decision was made for me. Teddy and his girlfriend parted at the top of the slipway, waving and blowing kisses, and Mrs Guest turned her back and slipped out of sight behind a boat-shed, her whole body taut with fury. Clearly nothing exciting was going to happen after all.

Disappointed, I gave up and set off home at a jog-trot. Ten minutes later when I was halfway across the bridge, Teddy's boat emerged from under it, heading upstream on the falling tide.

A footpath ran beside the railway on the bridge, and as I ran skipping and dancing along it, the brooch suddenly flew off, which explained why I had found it in the first place. I caught it in mid-air just as it sailed towards the railing, and after that I took care to hold it tightly in my hand so that it wouldn't get a chance to fall off again and disappear over the edge into the river.

Just as I reached the end of the bridge and turned off towards home I saw Mr Guest's car pull gingerly out of the gate of Holly Hill and begin the jolting journey along the track which led past the small knoll before turning inland and disappearing behind the big knoll, the one which sheltered River Cottage and the other two houses. I broke into a run so as to be near enough to wave to him before the car vanished from sight, and to my pleasure he saw me coming and stopped.

'Where are you going?' I asked breathlessly, knowing perfectly well that questioning an adult like that was bad manners. 'If you aren't going far, can I have a ride on the running-board? I'll open the railway gates for you.'

His face, which had been sombre, relaxed into a smile. 'Another time,' he said. 'I'm going to Manchester and I want to make good time. A problem's come up at the works and the sooner I get there, the sooner I can get back.'

'Oh.' My face must have showed my disappointment. 'How long do you think it will take?'

'With luck I'll be back on Monday evening. Would you like me to bring you anything?'

I shook my head, oddly dismayed by the question, and stepped back. He waved, put the car in gear, and drove away. I watched, feeling some emotion I couldn't define, until he disappeared behind the big knoll. I didn't want him to go away, even for two days.

I'd wanted to say, 'Come back soon' but didn't quite dare, in case he thought it cheek.

When I got home, my dress still damp because I'd pulled it on over a wet bathing-costume, I found that there was more, and worse, to explain than my departure without permission from the breakfast table. The attack came unexpectedly, just when, entering the hall, I was pinning the brooch back on my dress, safe from loss now that I was home.

I had found several other children, strangers, to play with on the beach at Moravon, and but for the disappointment over Mr Guest's departure, I had come home carefree, the scene at breakfast completely forgotten.

So I was unprepared when Fiff – who should have been, usually was, in the kitchen at this hour – opened the drawing-room door as I entered and said coldly, alarmingly, 'Fidgie! In here. I want a word with you, young woman.' Being called *young woman* was always an ominous sign.

I followed her in and she closed the door behind me. I knew then that I was in deep trouble or she would have said whatever she had to say in front of the others. I ran a quick, panicky review of my behaviour over the last few days, but I couldn't remember doing anything really bad.

She stood in the centre of the room and said, 'Now then. Where have you been?'

Startled and apprehensive, I said, 'In Moravon. Swimming. I've been there all mor—' That was when I remembered I hadn't exactly been there *all* morning. I could see from Fiff's face that I must have done something really shocking, but surely, leaving the table without first asking permission wasn't all that terrible?

'You were seen coming out of the woods hand in hand with a young man,' Fiff said.

I was stunned. A young man? I didn't *know* any young men. And then I remembered. She must mean Mr Guest. 'It wasn't a young man! He's quite old!' I cried indignantly. I thought of old Mrs van Gelderen and added her to my list of people who deserved to die horribly, preferably hit over the head with her dratted telescope.

'And he put his arm round you and hugged you.'

'He didn't!' I shouted, outraged. And then I remembered that Mr Guest had indeed hugged me. My face fell. 'Well, not like that,' I finished lamely. I could feel myself beginning to writhe. I knew now what lay behind Fiff's anger. She thought that Mr Guest was one of those funny men who did things people weren't supposed to see. We all knew men like that; had seen what they did, had refused invitations from them, knowing that they wanted us to do something rude. They knew where to find us, those men; knew that we were watching, and didn't seem to care that we were bursting with suppressed giggles, obscurely excited by the knowledge that we were watching something forbidden; daring each other to approach them.

But Mr Guest was not like that at all. I shuddered involuntarily. It was a terrible insult to him even to *think* it. But how could I explain this? I knew I looked shifty.

'He's not like that at all,' I repeated inadequately.

But Fiff was relentless. Without raising her voice, she said, 'Who was he?'

I didn't want to tell her. What if she went up to Holly Hill and told Mrs Guest? I'd never dare show my face again. I would have to hide for ever. I would *die*.

'We were only talking,' I pleaded. 'And I *didn't* walk hand in hand with him.'

'*Who was he?*'

Looking into my mother's implacable face, I admitted defeat and hung my head.

'It was only Mr Guest,' I mumbled reluctantly.

'Guest? Of Holly Hill?' It was Fiff's turn to be startled. 'Since when have you known the Guests?'

It seemed a good idea to lie about this. To admit that I had been hugged by a man I'd only met yesterday would only make things worse.

'Oh, since ages,' I said vaguely, and quaked. I knew I was not a convincing liar.

'Hm,' Fiff said, softening slightly. I knew she wanted to believe me, but if I gave her time, she might think of a reason not to, so I threw in a plea to distract her.

'Oh please, Mummy, don't make a row about it. He's such a nice man, and he'll never speak to me again if you do . . . or let me use the swimming-pool . . .' She was listening, so I babbled on. 'He'd been hunting and he was going home to breakfast and he invited me too . . . and it's such a beautiful house . . . and we had mushrooms . . .'

I could tell that she was almost won over, but she was thinking hard. In the end, she said, 'From what I hear, Mrs Guest is not the sort of woman I'd want a daughter of mine to associate with.'

This was astonishing. Criticizing grown-ups was not allowed and I had never before heard Fiff disapprove of anyone older than me, let alone a grown-up.

'I don't like her much, anyway,' I said quickly, remembering the summer-house. 'I keep out of her way.'

'All the same,' she said, 'I won't have you running in and out of that house as if the Guests were friends of ours. In fact, I don't want you to hobnob with them at all. Do you understand?'

The storm seemed to be over and I had survived it, but only just. 'Yes, Mummy,' I agreed meekly, hiding my rebellion. I couldn't, wouldn't, be parted from Holly Hill now, whatever anybody said. I didn't see why I should. And Fiff didn't seem to realize that she had only asked me if I understood. She hadn't actually asked me to promise *not to go* to Holly Hill again. I began to breathe again: this *must* be the end of the interview.

But Fiff hadn't finished yet. 'Very well . . . *Now*!' She paused with chilling effect, 'If Mr Guest is such a nice man, and you don't like Mrs Guest, who gave you that expensive brooch?'

I had forgotten the brooch. I gasped and clutched at it guiltily. 'No one did. I found it,' I protested. 'On the beach.'

'Give it to me.'

I obeyed, fumbling at the catch.

'If you really found it, why didn't you hand it in at the police station?'

'I didn't know I was supposed to,' I mumbled, handing it over. 'I thought someone had thrown it away.'

Fiff sighed with exasperation. 'Really, Fidgie! Surely you're old enough to know that people don't throw away diamond brooches?'

'Diamonds!' I gasped. '*Real diamonds?* Oh Mummy, just think! If we sold it, we'd be rich! You could afford a div—' I stopped myself just in time, and covered up quickly. 'You could afford all sorts of things! *Please* don't give it to the police.'

Unexpectedly, Fiff started to laugh. I couldn't see the joke and felt affronted. It seemed a perfectly good idea to me. Everybody said *Finders keepers*.

'Oh, go upstairs and get washed. And hurry up: lunch is ready.' But as I reached the door she added menacingly, 'And don't ever let me hear that you've been speaking to strange men, young woman, or you'll get a lot worse than a flea in your ear.'

Cly was coming downstairs as we emerged into the hall. I knew very well that she had been eavesdropping, had probably raced silently upstairs when she heard the interview coming to an end, and was now coming down again, looking innocent; and I could tell by the tight look on her face that she had been hoping to hear me get a good hiding and was furious that I had been let off. Knowing that she had been thwarted was no comfort to me because I knew from past experience that she would find her own way to take revenge for Fiff's failure to punish me.

Upstairs, I emptied the shells out of the pockets of my dress into the shoebox before hastily washing my hands and running downstairs again, feeling satisfactorily devious. Just so long as Cly hadn't looked in the box already . . .

A ravishing scent of curry was drifting out of the kitchen and I ran to meet it. Even the prospect of having to face Eric across the table could not spoil so voluptuous a pleasure.

As soon as Tom and I had done the washing-up and put the dishes away, Fiff gave us our pocket money. There was threepence for the pictures and tuppence to spend. Tom got an extra penny because he was older and because he was a boy. A waste, I thought, because Tom didn't *enjoy* money, as I did. He saved it until he had half a crown – an awe-inspiring sum – and then he put it in his Post Office Savings book where it disappeared for ever and gave nobody any pleasure. I couldn't understand how he could bear to throw money away like that.

'What do you two plan to do this afternoon?' Fiff

asked Tom and me. 'Where are you going to be?'

Tom and I both spoke together.

'At Dick's father's farm,' Tom said. 'The sheepdog trials.'

'Moravon,' I said. 'I'm going to enter the sandcastle competition.' I'd seen it advertised on the beach that morning. The first prize for girls was a skipping rope, a special one with ball-bearings in the handles, much better than the ordinary ones we were used to. If I could win it, I should be the envy of all the other girls in the playground; everyone would want to borrow it; I'd feel rich and successful and generous. I could already feel one of the painted handles in my hand, see Ellen holding the other, hear the chant *Salt, pepper, mustard, vinegar,* as the others danced dextrously in and out, over and under the whirling rope.

'You *are* an old meanie,' I complained to Tom as soon as we were alone. 'Why can't you come and help me build a sandcastle?'

'Why should I?' he countered. 'That's kids' stuff.'

'The boy's prize is a cricket bat.'

'I've got a cricket bat.'

'Only a titchy little old one. And anyway,' I said, referring back, 'you *are* a kid.'

'I'm a year older than you,' he pointed out witheringly. 'More than.'

I wanted to point out that we were in the same class at school, but I knew that the reminder would hurt his pride and annoy him, so I gave in and resigned myself to going to Moravon alone. 'You *will* be back in time for the pictures?' I asked anxiously. 'I shan't be able to get in if you're not there.' I was considered too hare-brained to be trusted not to lose my ticket-money. It was true, too: I *did* lose things and forget things. So Tom was put in charge of both his ticket-money and mine.

94

'Oh, here, take it,' he said, digging in his pocket and detaching a silver threepenny bit from among the pennies. 'Just don't tell Fiff that I gave it to you. And if you lose it, don't expect me to pay for you. I can't afford to.'

I wrapped it carefully in my handkerchief and put it in my pocket, and to make absolutely sure that the pocket would not gape open, I went upstairs to look for a safety pin.

Through the open window of my bedroom I saw two women emerging from the gate of Holly Hill, and as they got nearer I realized that they were the cook and housemaid I'd met this morning, released for the afternoon and almost unrecognizable in their going-out clothes. Behind them, on the river, a small motor cruiser was nosing down the channel below Holly Hill, a big black dog lying couchant on the cabin roof. After I'd pinned up my pocket I watched it idly for a moment, leaning on the window-sill and wishing we had a boat, until I suddenly realized that I knew the slight figure at the wheel.

'Chaz!' I yelled, leaning out of the window and waving wildly, knowing that this was bad behaviour, and not caring. Finding Chaz again, just when I had resigned myself to an afternoon on my own, was more important than ladylike behaviour. When he didn't hear – he was looking back over his shoulder – I cupped my hands round my mouth and yelled again. This time he waved back and turned the craft towards the landing-stage at the bottom of the garden, and I left the window and clattered joyfully down the stairs and out of the house.

I reached the landing-stage a few minutes before the boat arrived. It was not in the same class as Teddy's sleek motor cruiser, I could see that, but to have a boat at all was impressive.

95

Chaz brought the squat little craft alongside the landing-stage without bumping against it and I jumped aboard, grinning happily. It was only then that I saw that he was not alone. An old man – he seemed enormously old to me, thin, with a mane of white hair and a white imperial – was sitting, his head bent over a box of fishing tackle, on the slatted seat which ringed three sides of the cockpit. He was wearing the same sort of thing Boko had always worn in Ceylon: bush jacket and shorts. Lean tanned legs emerged from pale, washed-out khaki and ended, surprisingly, in bare brown feet. I was speechless with envy: Fiff never allowed *me* to go barefoot. My ayah always let me go as barefoot as she herself did when we were out walking – at least until we were back in sight of the house – but Fiff insisted on shoes. I had no idea why, but I obeyed because she set so much store by it.

The old man was smoking a pipe and working on one of the fishing rods propped up against his knee. He kept his head down, but I could see that he had a black silk patch over one eye. My face had fallen on sight of him because I wanted to tell Chaz about the diamond brooch. He might even enjoy hearing about my encounter with Mrs Guest and the other woman and Teddy, though that was unlikely: boys were inexplicably bored by that sort of thing. But I could only tell him in private, certainly not in front of a grown-up.

I was so taken aback by the old man's unexpected presence that I hardly heard Chaz's formal introduction, aware only that this must be the great-uncle Mr Guest had told me about. I wondered if Fiff would expect me to drop him a curtsey, but I considered curtseying old-fashioned, so I restrained the impulse. Most old people were censorious and disapproving, but except for his age and that fierce beard, he didn't look particularly intimidating, especially since he kept his face turned away from me; but after I'd murmured a polite 'How do you do, Mr Channing?' I took refuge in silence, just to be on the safe side.

He took the pipe out of his mouth, glanced up at me, nodded, and said, 'Fidgie,' by way of acknowledgement, and that was when I saw the jagged scar running from his temple and down his cheek under the eye patch. The puckered white skin of the scar stood out against the leathery tan of the rest of his face. It was so unexpected and so unnerving that it took me a moment to gather my wits before I managed a small, quick smile, and turned away, afraid he would think I was staring. I was annoyed with myself for recoiling. His face wasn't anything like as horrifying as poor Miss Wragg's, after all, and I had taught myself to look into her painful eyes without flinching when I spoke to her, though it was an effort.

To Chaz, he said, 'Better get going, Charles, before we're stranded. This part of the channel gets very low at slack water.'

I had to turn my back on the old man to speak to Chaz at the wheel. 'Where are we going?' I asked him.

'Nowhere in particular,' he said. 'We're just going to drop lines in the bay, see what comes up; maybe go as far as Shell Island.'

The big dog had lumbered to his feet to examine me and I raised a hand to stroke its head, though it was high above me on the cabin roof, but Chaz said amiably, 'Clear off, Jenkins, I can't see where we're going,' and the dog returned to his post and subsided with a disgruntled groan.

I stood beside Chaz, leaning my arms on the decking of the cabin and screwing up my eyes against the brilliant light blazing up from the water. The breeze had increased since lunchtime, but it was still a warm wind and did little to ease the heat. The heat itself no longer had the hard, searing quality of the past weeks: there was something uneasy and oppressive about it now, perhaps because of the rising wind. The sky was bleached white by the heat as it had been for weeks, but for the first time clouds had appeared behind the veil of haze, towering white castles looming over the peninsula to the northwest.

'Go for'ard,' Chaz ordered me, 'and check we don't get too close to the sandbanks.'

I climbed over the cabin, stepped carefully over the dog, and did as I was told, feeling useful and important, a vital member of the crew: our safety was in my hands.

When the tide was out, the river water was dark brown and peaty, and the sandbanks loomed up dimly, sinister shapes emerging gradually through shades of burnt umber in the gloomiest depths to a silvery beige in the shallows.

I sat on the deck at the bow, my legs tucked up beside me, propping myself up on one hand and peering over into the water. We had almost reached the deeper water under the bridge when things started to go wrong. Instead of rounding a spit of sand, I saw that we were heading straight for it, and shouted a warning. Nothing happened: Chaz took no notice. I jumped to my feet and shrieked, *'Chaz!'* only to see him staring ahead, his face slack, his eyes blank. At almost the same moment his uncle, moving with surprising agility, leapt to his feet and swung the wheel, taking us clear of the sandbank and into the main channel. Chaz was still standing beside him, empty-eyed and vacant as a corpse, an ugly, sinister stranger, the face I'd seen in every horror film I could remember.

It scared me. I scrambled back to the cockpit, stumbling between Jenkins's legs. 'What's the matter,

Chaz?' I asked urgently, wanting to shake his arm but afraid to touch him. There was no response. Although his mouth stayed shut, his jaw moved as if he were chewing a wad of toffee. He looked ridiculous and frightening at the same time. Even the dog looked puzzled, leaning his head first to one side and then the other, and whiffling anxiously.

'It's all right, Fidgie,' his great-uncle said. 'This happens from time to time. Nothing to worry about: he'll come out of it in a moment.'

I wasn't comforted. I had seen the face I knew and liked turn, nightmarishly, from the familiar into the grotesque, and I was afraid of him. Who knew what someone like that might do? I avoided looking at him and backed as far away from him as the small cockpit would allow.

Mr Channing must have known, even though he had his back to me. 'It's bound to worry you the first time you see it,' he said without turning from the wheel. 'But it's only an occasional loss of consciousness and it only lasts a few seconds. It's the result of the accident.' He glanced round at me. 'You know about that?'

I nodded, but for me the sun had gone in and a shadow had fallen over the day. To dispel it, I reminded myself of Chaz's generosity to me yesterday, how he'd got me out of trouble at the end, and what a good companion he had been. None of it seemed to count now, and I was afraid I was going to cry. Everything had been spoiled.

His uncle went on, 'They never last long, these things, and when he comes round, I want you to pretend you didn't notice anything. Will you do that for him?'

'But oughtn't we to go back home?' I asked. 'Shouldn't he lie down, or something?'

He took his pipe out of his mouth and stared at me

over his shoulder. 'He wouldn't thank us for making a fool of him,' he said coldly. 'He'll be all right presently.'

And even while he was speaking, Chaz took a deep breath and regained consciousness, looking as if he had just woken up in a strange room. And then I remembered yesterday afternoon, and Chaz pretending he'd been knocked out when he fell. After a while, he'd recovered completely, my suspicions had subsided, and the day had rolled on seamlessly. Perhaps today would be the same.

But still shaken by the strangeness of it, and chastened by his uncle's rebuke, I grabbed Chaz's arm and said a little wildly, 'Did you see that seal?'

'Seal?' Chaz spoke distantly, still not fully connected. 'There aren't any seals here.'

'I *saw* one,' I insisted, pointing behind him. 'Over there.' And when he turned slowly round, I added, 'It's gone now. You missed it. Serves you right for daydreaming.'

Mr Channing emitted a sound somewhere between a snort and a grunt. To cover it, he said matter-of-factly, 'Get the bait out, Charles.'

From out here at sea, Moravon's seafront row of boarding houses, so tall and imposing at close range, was reduced to the size and shape of bathing huts. Behind the town, the mountains had become little more than hills, a rumpled brown eiderdown untidily patched with yellow gorse and purple heather. The cleft of the estuary showed to the south, but from here the mile-long railway bridge was hidden by the houses crowding the harbour.

A plume of smoke rose behind the hills where a summer fire had broken out in the parched grasses. Below the promenade the beaches were swarming with people, and I could make out the banner announcing the sandcastle competition. In spite of the burbling of the engine and the slapping of the waves around us, the shrieks of the bathers reached us clearly over the water. It felt godlike to be so detached from the rest of the world, watching it yet apart from it.

It didn't seem likely that we would get back in time for the matinée, but I didn't really care: I preferred being where I was. I had never been out in the bay before, and now that I was here, I was in thrall to the beauty and strangeness of the sea, and soothed by the lulling of the boat.

We moved placidly along the coastline, still heading into deeper water, lilting through waves urged into long rollers by the wind. There was only one other boat to be seen in all the wide sweep of the bay. It looked like Teddy's, but it was too far away – almost on the horizon – to be clearly identified. It had emerged from the harbour mouth, moving fast, when we were already far out at sea, and surely only Teddy's boat could move at that speed? Chaz and his great-uncle, concentrating on where we were heading, had not noticed it. Since emerging from behind the island, it had hurtled westwards, throwing up smooth curved bow-waves, until it had all but disappeared into the blazing path of the sun.

'He must be going to America,' I said, shading my eyes and squinting against the glare.

'Who?' Chaz asked vaguely, more interested in plying his line. Like all boys, he had a way of making me feel I'd said something stupid, so I didn't answer.

Just as he had yesterday, Chaz had recovered completely, and once we had cleared the harbour, Mr Channing had handed the steering back to him. Warily at first, but then with growing confidence, I had spoken to him as if nothing had happened, and gradually the shadow had lifted and the day had righted itself. Jenkins too had relaxed and was lying flat on his side basking, his flanks glossy in the sunshine.

Chaz said suddenly, 'You didn't come swimming this morning.'

'I couldn't find you,' I said. 'And Mr Guest said you had lessons, so I went to Moravon.'

Mr Channing had a line trailing over the stern. His presence had acted on me like a strait-jacket at first, as the presence of all adults did, especially relatives. But since Chaz's blackout he had shown no sign of being aware of my existence. He sat relaxed on the seat in the cockpit, smoking contentedly, so absorbed in his fishing that he might as well have been absent or deaf. Once I was sure that he wasn't secretly watching and listening, ready to pounce on any lapse, I abandoned caution and told Chaz about finding the brooch, though I left out the bit about looking for bottles. Chaz was so rich he'd despise me for that.

'Where did you find it?' he asked.

'In the sandhills,' I said. 'On the island. People go there . . .' I glanced over my shoulder. Mr Channing still wasn't listening, but I lowered my voice all the same to say the rude words, '. . . *for a spin*. You know? At night, when no one can see them.'

He didn't answer at first, then he said, 'What did it look like, this brooch?'

'It was shaped like a leopard pouncing,' I said, adding with relish, 'and it had emerald eyes.' I didn't know if they really were emeralds, but it sounded more impressive than 'green'.

He said quietly, 'Mrs Guest has a brooch like that.'

As soon as he said it, I had a glimpse of Mrs Guest's

102

car passing us in the dark on the estuary road last night.

'Whew,' I breathed. 'You don't think . . . do you?'

We fell silent for a moment, both of us probably thinking the same thing, then I told him with dramatic flourishes about seeing Teddy and the other woman and Mrs Guest on my way home this morning. 'She looked,' I finished gleefully, 'as if she was going to *murder* him.'

But Chaz wasn't really listening.

'Where is it now? The brooch, I mean.'

I sighed. 'I had to give it to my mother,' I said regretfully. 'She's going to hand it in at the police station. She always goes in to Moravon on Saturdays, so she's probably there this very minute.'

'Pity,' he said. 'I had an idea.'

'What?'

'We could have left it at the swimming-pool. On one of the chairs. She'd have found it there.'

I was alarmed. 'But what if it isn't hers?' Fiff had told me that if nobody claimed it, the police would give it back to me, and I had convinced myself that I only had to wait – perhaps until Christmas, though that was a lifetime away – and the brooch would be mine again, for keeps.

'It's not very likely that anyone else around here would have a brooch like that,' Chaz pointed out with relentless logic. 'Most people around here – even the holidaymakers – are too poor.'

I recognized the truth of this and my heart sank. That beautiful leopard – which had grown even more beautiful since I discovered that it was *real* – would never be mine. It would crouch once again on the shoulder of a woman who couldn't be bothered to look after it.

I could have wept. 'My mother said I could have it back if no one claimed it,' I said mulishly.

103

'Don't worry, Fidgie,' he said airily. 'I expect you'll get it back. Mrs Guest is far too snooty to go and ask the police if anyone handed it in. She might think they'd ask questions about where she lost it. They probably would, too.'

'But if you're sure it's hers,' I said, 'we could get it back from the police and just give it back to her.' I began to warm to the idea. If I couldn't have the brooch – and I'd never really believed I would – at least I could earn applause for having found it. 'And then she'll be so grateful, she'll let us use the swimming-pool all day long,' I finished, looking into a bright future.

But Chaz squashed that, too. 'Huh,' he said scornfully, 'I wouldn't count on that. She's bound to have a good idea where you found it, and if she thinks you might tell, you won't be popular. If anyone gets murdered, it's more likely to be you than Teddy Ransom. That's why it would be a good idea to give it back secretly.'

I thought about the rubber things, and fell silent.

Chaz seemed able to read my mind. 'That place,' he said without bothering to lower his voice, 'is knee-deep in French letters.' And he let out a yelp of laughter.

I glanced over my shoulder in trepidation, expecting the heavens to fall, but Mr Channing couldn't have heard because he showed no interest at all, let alone outrage, over the discovery that we should possess this forbidden knowledge. He had caught a skate, a strange-looking, triangular thing with a long spike for a tail, and was busy reeling it in.

He seemed to me to be a very odd sort of adult. I didn't know what to make of a grown-up who didn't hand out constant warnings, threats, injunctions and reprimands.

I lowered my voice just in case Mr Channing wasn't deaf, and said to Chaz, 'Doesn't your uncle ever tell you off for *anything*?' and was immediately mortified to hear Mr Channing let out a snort of laughter.

6

After the skate, Mr Channing let Chaz and me take our turn at fishing while he took over the wheel, and for the rest of the afternoon we idled along a couple of miles offshore, mostly drifting but sometimes under way, so intent on our lines that we failed to notice that the sun had gone in and the day was cooling, or that sudden cat's paws of wind were stroking the surface of the sea, brushing the nap here and there like a giant broom.

After about an hour, to great applause from Mr Channing and Jenkins and me, Chaz had landed a big sea bass, but the only thing I caught was a fish so small I felt sorry for it.

'Is it all right if I put it back?' I asked Mr Channing. I knew better than to do anything without permission when grown-ups were around, and even though he *seemed* not to care, it was always wiser to tread warily. He couldn't – he just *couldn't* – be as easygoing as he seemed, especially looking as fierce as he did.

But all he said was, 'Of course you can. Why do you ask?' so I put it back carefully into the water.

I went on hanging over the side, entranced by the fluid patterns of the water out here beyond the waves, by its salty, seaweedy smell, and by the way its colour changed from blue to a green as clear as glass in the shadow of the boat. Through this window I could see frilly strands of brown seaweed; pale, almost transparent jellyfish crowned with violet horseshoes;

egg-cases like handfuls of white bubbles, and other nameless sea things all suspended in a translucent green world. Because I was afraid of it, of its depth and danger, of its almost irresistible summons, I would never have dared to slip in, sliding headfirst down the side of the boat, though I longed to. Its smiling surface masked green terrors only glimpsed in nightmares.

Once, looking up, I thought I saw a shark's fin cut the surface. It worried me because I thought I'd left sharks behind in the Indian Ocean. I was just going to ask Mr Channing about it when he rose suddenly and started the engine with an urgency in sharp contrast to his former quiet abstraction.

'We'd better get back,' he said, putting the wheel over. 'There's a storm on the way.'

Chaz and I looked up to see that the sky on the horizon had turned an ominous shade of khaki and seemed to be bearing down on us like an advancing army, shooting fitful shafts of sunlight ahead as if using a searchlight to find its way.

'Better not get caught out here in a thunderstorm,' Mr Channing said, and even as he spoke a raindrop landed on the floor of the cockpit with a splash as big as a half-crown.

The shower stopped again after a scatter of raindrops, but the sky grew even darker and small wisps of cool air began to curl round us. In the livid light, colours deepened to a strange intensity. There were fewer people on the shore up here, but we could see them scampering to collect their buckets and spades and towels, and making a dash for cover, and Mr Channing kept the boat's bow pointed towards Moravon. Jenkins was standing up now at the bow, ears pricked, long legs splayed, swaying with the movement of the boat and looking like a figurehead so loosely fixed it might come adrift at any moment.

I didn't want to go home. The house would be empty on a Saturday afternoon and there would be nothing to do. I thought about it as we hurried back to harbour, wondering what I could find to do in an empty house with no wireless to listen to, and rain pouring down outside. I sometimes danced to the gramophone, but we only had four gramophone records, two of them comic recitations which I knew by heart; and anyway, all the gramophone needles were blunt, and no one could afford to buy a new tinful. The book I'd had for Christmas had been read long since, and Fiff's books in their dark bindings looked too gloomy and impenetrable for my liking. All Cly had was the stack of love magazines which she hid under her bed. I'd borrowed one once, from the middle of the pile, thinking she wouldn't notice, but she did, and applied Chinese fire until I gave in and owned up. I'd heard rumours that Cly was fast, but I found it hard to believe. Surely she was far too snooty to let a boy even kiss her, let alone do any of the other things – the shockingly, deliciously rude things – I'd heard some of the girls giggling about in the playground?

And what if Cly hadn't gone out, and I found myself alone with her?

'Please could you land me at the quay?' I asked Mr Channing. 'There won't be anyone in at home. I think I'll go to the pictures.'

'We went to the pictures yesterday,' Chaz pointed out. 'Why don't you come home with us? She can, can't she, Uncle Hil?'

'Of course, if she'd like to.' He sounded preoccupied. I glanced up at him and realized that he was genuinely worried that we would get caught out here by the thunderstorm, so I began to worry too.

'*Could* we get struck by lightning?' I asked Chaz,

who was tidying up the fishing tackle.

'Of course,' he said dismissively. 'Lightning always takes the shortest route to earth, and out here, we're it. We stick out like a sore thumb.'

I started looking over my shoulder, half-scared, half-excited, at the pursuing storm. Ragged grey curtains of rain were hanging from the sky behind us, blanking out the end of the peninsula, and as I watched, a jagged streak of lightning flashed from the murk down to the sea. I had only counted up to six before a grumbling snarl of thunder followed the lightning. I was cold now, too, and beginning to shiver. We seemed to be very little nearer Moravon than we had been when we started.

'The storm's only six miles away,' I told no one in particular. 'Can't we go any faster?'

Neither of them answered, but Mr Channing, following a different train of thought, suddenly muttered to himself, 'What the hell does he think he's doing?'

'Who?' Chaz and I said together.

'Ransom.'

We followed his line of sight and saw Teddy's boat – unmistakable now that it was closer – broadside on to the waves and wallowing in the peaks and troughs. Like us, he must have been returning from his trip out to sea, because now he was almost as close to Moravon as we were, on a converging line.

'Engine trouble?' Chaz suggested. I could tell by the thinly veiled contempt in his voice that he hadn't forgiven Teddy for yesterday's broken promise. Teddy was now a fool, capable of any ineptitude. 'Maybe he's run out of petrol,' he finished cheerfully.

'We'll have to lend a hand,' Mr Channing said, though I could tell from his voice that he was reluctant. Thunder rumbled again, nearer now, and I guessed what he was thinking: he wanted to get us to safety, and Teddy – who ought to have been able to look after himself – stood in the way.

It took nearly ten minutes to reach Teddy's boat, and by then the rain had begun again, tentatively at first, then in a drenching downpour, and the wind had risen. I knew I could have gone down into the cabin to shelter, but I couldn't bear the thought of being left out, of not being able to see what was happening. From half a mile away we had all been trying to raise Teddy with shouts of *Ransom!* and *Hoy, Love Nest!* but there had been no response, and now that we were nearer it was clear that there was no one in the wheelhouse.

The sea had begun to get choppy now, the boats bucking; and boarding Teddy's boat was not going to be easy.

'Let me board her, Uncle Hil,' Chaz said as we struggled to hold the two cockpits alongside each other, our hands slippery in the pouring rain.

'No. You and Fidgie stay here,' Mr Channing said firmly. 'Something's badly wrong. Ransom may be injured.'

He climbed aboard awkwardly because of the seesawing of the two boats, and disappeared into the saloon pursued by Jenkins, his claws clattering and slipping on the wet deck, while Chaz held on to the coaming of Teddy's boat, and I stood back clasping my arms and shivering in the rain. Chaz's hair was slicked wetly down his forehead, rain running down his face and dripping from his chin, as it was from mine.

It was only when a streak of lightning ripped out of the sky behind us that I realized how dark it had become. The crack of thunder that followed the flash sounded as if the sky was splitting. Watching the drama of a thunderstorm from inside the safety of a house was exhilarating, but exposed out here it was frightening: a raging monster was stalking us: it meant to kill us and there was nowhere to hide. Through teeth beginning to chatter I could hear myself whispering *Oh hurry up, Mr Channing. Please hurry up!* And like an answer to prayer, Mr Channing reappeared.

'Get over here, both of you,' he shouted. 'Get below and don't touch any metal. *Hurry.*'

I tumbled aboard Teddy's boat with such haste I didn't even notice when I cut my knee on something. Chaz jumped after me clutching the painter and made it fast to a cleat on the stern. Mr Channing had said nothing about Teddy, but by that time I didn't care; it was such a relief to be able to hide. Summer was still trapped in the saloon of Teddy's boat: it was warm and dark and seemed as safe as the inside of a house.

Jenkins was running about, his nose to the floor, a concentrated frown on his forehead, investigating. He had shaken himself vigorously in the saloon, and drops of rain from his coat had flown everywhere.

'No sign of anyone aboard,' Mr Channing said, and to Chaz, 'Get into the wheel-house and take the wheel. I'm going to make *Sea Slug* fast to the stern. We'll tow her.'

'But what if he's only gone for a swim?' I asked uneasily.

He fixed me with his good eye and said drily, 'In a thunderstorm? Leaving his boat to drift? Unlikely, Fidgie,' which made me realize how stupid my question had been.

Abashed, I said, 'I meant . . .' and stopped. It seemed rude to point out that we were taking Teddy's boat without his permission. He'd be sure to be furious. I pictured him swimming around looking for it.

I tried again. 'Do you think he got struck by lightning?' It happened in cartoons all the time: the

111

baddy got struck by lightning and *poof!* he disappeared.

Unlike most grown-ups, Mr Channing considered what I'd said. 'I suppose anything's possible,' he said, frowning. Then, noticing that I was hugging myself and shivering, he said, 'There should be some towels aboard. Go for'ard and see if you can find us some.'

He went back to the cockpit to check that *Sea Slug* was secure while I went in search of towels, climbing up into the wheel-house where Chaz was examining the controls, and down again past the galley and into the cabin. The scent which had haunted me in the saloon was stronger in here. I recognized it as Evening in Paris because Cly had some. I had taken several guilty and blissful sniffs of it the day I borrowed the copy of *Lucky Star.* I felt it ought to remind me of Mrs Guest, but it didn't.

There were big beach towels in a locker above one of the bunks. As I collected them the engine came to life with a powerful roar and the floor vibrated underfoot.

Once we were under way, Chaz asked his uncle, 'What do you suppose has happened to Mr Ransom?' He had to shout to make himself heard over the drumming of the rain on the wheel-house roof, the noise of the engine, and the thunderstorm. A giant was rolling barrels around in the attic overhead and every so often one of them fell about our ears and split with a deafening crash.

'No telling. He must have fallen overboard. We'll have to alert the authorities. Probably the lifeboat will start a search for him.' His gaze pinpointed my knees. 'Where did you get that cut?' he asked.

I looked down and saw a trickle of blood making its way down my shin. Illuminated by a flash of lightning, it looked black.

I shook my head and shouted back, 'I must have cut

it on something when I got on board,' adding hastily, 'It doesn't matter,' in case he thought me a nuisance.

I could hardly hear his answer above the next crash of thunder, but it sounded like, '. . . been yours, then,' which made no sense to me.

7

As soon as we had tied up at the slipway, Mr Channing leapt out, retrieved a pair of canvas shoes – now soaking wet – from *Sea Slug*, and with an oilskin held over his head, shouted to Chaz, 'Get Fidgie up to the doctor and have that knee seen to: it may need stitches.' He threw another oilskin to Chaz. 'Then go and wait in the Anchor. I'll send for the car.' And he vanished up the slipway on to the quay with Jenkins racing ahead.

'I don't need to go to the doctor,' I said to Chaz. 'It's only a cut.' I knew Fiff couldn't afford the doctor, especially for something that only needed a dab of iodine and a bandage, but I wasn't going to say so to someone like Chaz. Besides, I was cold and wet and the rain was coming down so hard that the rain-drops were bouncing back upwards again as they struck the ground: it would be like walking through a waterfall.

'If Uncle Hil says you've got to go, then you've got to go,' Chaz said implacably. 'Come on.'

Then, when I still hung back, he seemed to guess the reason and added, embarrassingly, 'Don't worry, Uncle Hil will pay the bill.'

We waited until the next flash of lightning had passed and then we made a dash for it, each holding a lapel of the oilskin overhead with one hand while clutching the beach towels round our shoulders with the other. Awkwardly because of our mismatched strides, we ran until we reached the safety of buildings and could slow down. Even then I had to keep putting in extra steps to avoid being left behind.

Apart from a few bedraggled holidaymakers taking shelter in the doorways of shops, the streets were deserted, swept by gusts of rain; but the cafés were crowded, faces dimly seen through steamy windows.

The doctor Chaz took me to see was not our own family doctor. I knew him, of course, from a distance, and I didn't like him. He was an old man with a thin ascetic face and I knew at once that he disapproved of me and, but for Chaz, would probably have refused to treat me, would have sent me to my own doctor whose surgery was much further away. Cravenly, because she had never been a friend of mine, I tried to curry favour with him by telling him that I had been in kindergarten with his daughter – a distant, unsmiling, wraithlike girl – but he didn't seem to hear. I think he didn't care to be reminded that she had ever been forced into the company of people like me, ragamuffins who now went to the council school. As he dealt with me his nostrils seemed to twitch in distaste and close like the nostrils of a camel in a sandstorm. I was sure that I couldn't be dirty because I'd spent most of the morning swimming. The stitches hurt, too, but I gritted my teeth and pretended not to notice.

Half an hour later, limping exaggeratedly, partly to impress the Watchers – those entities who mostly lived under the sideboard in the sitting-room, noting everything I said and did – and partly because the bandage really did make my knee stiff, I followed Chaz as he inserted himself through the crowd sheltering in the doorway of the Crown and Anchor. It was not yet opening time and the bars were closed, the interior dark and smelling of stale beer and cigarette smoke. We made our way to a window to watch out for Henderson.

The storm was easing a little, the periods between thunderclaps longer, and the rain had settled to a steadier, less ferocious beat. Rivers of water rushed along the gutters and small lakes formed round the drains.

'What do you suppose has happened to Mr Ransom?' I asked Chaz.

'Who knows?' he replied, without interest. 'Maybe you're right and he went for a swim. Perhaps he didn't know how to berth the boat so he abandoned it and swam ashore.'

This didn't seem likely to me, and I knew that he didn't believe it either: he didn't care what had happened to Teddy: whatever it was would turn out to be something stupid.

I went away to find the lavatory. As I struggled to get out of my wet dress and the damp bathing costume under it, it occurred to me that Chaz was as envious of Teddy's boat as I was of Mrs Guest's diamond brooch. It was pleasing to know that Chaz – all-knowing, self-sufficient, capable Chaz – had a weak spot. Since the strange episode this afternoon there had been a change in my attitude to him: from liking tinged with respect for his apparently effortless superiority, I had begun to have a fellow feeling for him. He was more human now, more on a level with me.

'If Teddy *has* got drowned,' I said to comfort him when I got back, 'they might let you have his boat.' I wasn't sure who I meant by 'they'.

'Huh,' he said scornfully, 'fat chance.' But he cheered up noticeably after that, though he added cautiously as if to placate some Watchers of his own, 'Anyway, he's sure to turn up.'

Mr Channing was already installed in the front of the car when Henderson arrived to pick us up, and Chaz and I, still clutching the damp towels, piled thankfully into the back where Jenkins rose courteously from the floor to make room for us before flopping down again at our feet, expelling a sigh like a cushion.

It was the same big car which had carried us home from Moravon yesterday evening, with pull-down seats folded away in the upholstery behind the front seats, and a window, now open, between us and the driver. I had been in a car like this before: it had belonged to our only rich uncle, and riding in it made me feel very wealthy and important, like a film star. I was pretty sure that it was a Rolls-Royce, and I asked Chaz to confirm it so that I could tell Tom. Tom was besotted with cars: he soaked up data about them like a sponge.

'A Rolls Phantom III,' Chaz said, taking the same sort of pleasure in the information as Tom would. 'The latest model. Why?'

But I didn't want to share him with Tom. Tom had enough friends already, friends he was reluctant to share with me because I was only a girl. So I simply shrugged. 'Just wondered,' I said.

The car flowed effortlessly along the streaming road, climbing the hill out of the town to drop down again beside the river, the only sound the swish of the tyres as we drove through floods. I leaned back and luxuriated, only half-listening to the discussion, which was desultory anyway, of Teddy's disappearance and the moves Mr Channing had made to institute a search for him.

All that was of only marginal interest: riding in this regal car occupied all my attention. I was wearing a sleek white satin ball-gown trimmed with white fur – or maybe swansdown – the one I'd seen Carole Lombard wearing in *Picturegoer*. My hair was platinum blond, permed in tight waves with fat curls at the neck so that when I lifted my chin I could feel them brushing my shoulders. I wore long white gloves, and a wide diamond bracelet flashed fire on my wrist. Surrounded by a cloud of Evening in Paris and deliciously conscious of my overwhelming beauty, my irresistible sex appeal, my adoring public, I lay back blissfully against the seat, only sorry that no one – especially Cly, who would die of rage, and serve her right – could see me thus starrily caparisoned and elegantly borne.

We had nearly reached the turning to the rickety wooden toll-bridge where the car could cross the river when Chaz broke into my dream, leaning towards me and pointing through the rain-streaked window. Heavy clouds were sagging down the mountains like dark grey sacks full of water, and because of them and the rain they disgorged, it had already begun to grow dark at least an hour too early.

'That's where Mr Ransom lives.'

There was nothing to see but tall wooden gates, firmly closed, and behind them a jumble of wet roofs and chimneys almost hidden by dark pines. A flash of lightning lit the scene momentarily, making it look deeply sinister.

'It looks creepy,' I said, screwing round on the seat to keep the scene in view as we passed, 'Like in that film *The Old Dark House*.'

I thought he'd agree, but he seemed to feel an urge to defend the house. 'Only because it's getting dark. And because of the trees. Actually, it looks quite decent in daylight. It's almost opposite Uncle Hil's house, across the river, so we can see the front of it.'

Even then, the truth didn't dawn on me. I knew of course that he lived on the other side of the river, but I still didn't know where. Instead, absorbed in the house and its occupants, I asked, 'Does he live there all alone?' Loneliness and Teddy didn't seem to go together.

'He's got two sisters, a lot older,' Chaz said vaguely. He was losing interest, or perhaps he didn't know any more, and I decided not to persist, though I was endlessly curious about houses, their gardens, and most of all their interiors. Old houses like this always had infinite possibilities for games of hide-and-seek, not to mention Murder and Sardines and Smee. I longed to see inside it, but only if I had other people with me.

I knew that there was no real likelihood of persuading Mr Channing to go back because by now Henderson had slowed almost to a stop to take the turning to the bridge, but I tried anyway.

'Oughtn't we to go and tell them that he's got lost?' I asked hopefully.

'I think not,' Mr Channing said. 'No point in alarming his sisters unnecessarily. We don't even know for certain that Ransom had been aboard that boat in the first place. Unlikely as it seems, it's just possible that someone else had taken it out. Then again, Fidgie may be right: he may have jumped or fallen overboard and swum ashore to the Point. If he did, it would take him hours to make his way back, even if he'd suffered nothing worse than a soaking . . .'

From this speech, spoken slowly with pauses for thought, it was obvious that he had been debating the question with himself before I spoke, and had still not reached a conclusion.

The car bowled across the flat floor of the valley heading for the toll-bridge. Once, ages and ages ago, Chaz said, the river had covered all this. I tried, and failed, to imagine what it must have looked like then, reduced as it was now to little more than a stream winding through all this vast expanse of turf and clumps of sedge and pools. On sunny days the pools were blue, reflecting the sky. They were grey now and pockmarked with rain.

Crossing the toll-bridge cost sixpence. That was the return fare, and since Henderson had come through it once, he didn't need to stop again. The toll-keeper waved us through and Henderson, lofty as only the chauffeur of such a lordly car can be, swept past him without acknowledgement. I felt ashamed of this behaviour and turned round to wave to the toll-keeper through the small back window, but the apology was wasted because he had already disappeared back into the shelter of the tollbooth, indifferent.

We swept through a granite village bleak even on sunny days, gloomy and sodden now with rain, and headed back towards the coast again, to the railway junction where we could cross the track and wind our way across the marshes to the river and home; but unexpectedly Henderson turned right quite soon, down a steeply sloping lane darkened by dripping sycamore and beech trees. This diversion was worrying because the lane led, I knew, through the woods to the vast house where the mad old man lived with his nightmare dog.

I wondered if I ought to warn them. It seemed wise in view of their apparent ignorance of our danger. I began cautiously, lowering my voice.

'Do you know the people who live down here?' I asked Chaz. There must be other houses I had not previously known of at the bottom of this lane.

'People?' Chaz said, clearly nonplussed. 'Nobody lives here but us. This is the drive to Uncle Hil's house.'

'But . . .' I said, and stopped. The answer had suddenly dawned on me: the mad old man must have gone away, died perhaps or vanished like Teddy, his house bought by Mr Channing. He couldn't have been arrested for murdering and eating people because, as we all knew, no one, not even the police, dared go near the place.

8

Mr Channing's house looked deserted, as if nobody had lived in it for years; but that was probably because, having only recently moved in after the disappearance of the mad old man, he had not had time to put up curtains or cut the grass, which stuck out everywhere in dried blond tufts in the forecourt and from the base of the masonry. Perhaps fortunately, the rain had come too late to save that errant grass: it had died of drought long since, or by now it would be waist-high. What had once been a garden was now – and had been for years by the look of it – a jungle of overgrown shrubs whose intertwining unkempt branches seemed bent on strangling each other in their desperate quest for light. Only the forecourt, a rough circle of hard-packed earth which had once probably been covered with gravel long since ground into the surface, remained clear of encroachment.

And it was a huge house too, so perhaps Mr Channing couldn't afford a lawnmower or fresh gravel; and certainly not curtain material for all those windows. I could understand that. After all, Fiff had had to cut up my sari to make curtains for my bedroom, and Tom and I had to take turns to cut our grass with shears whenever Fiff decided it should be done; but all the same it was disappointing to find that Mr Channing was as broke as we were. Because of the car, I had expected him to be rich.

'Is it haunted?' I asked Chaz nervously as we drew

up outside the front door. A stupid question: *of course* it was haunted. How could it not be? It was probably full of spiders too. But Chaz was scornful.

'Haunted? Why should it be?' he asked, turning a face full of bright mockery towards me. 'Honestly, Fidgie!'

Quelled by his scorn, I decided not to tell him. After all, he was new here and he had probably never been down to the cellar where, as Jacko had described in a voice resonant with awe, the ancient ogre had cut up the bodies, throwing an occasional blood-soaked haunch to his slavering dog; and I was quite determined that nobody would persuade *me* to go down there either. Upstairs was probably, though not certainly, safe from the fearful miasma which must pervade the place. I envied these two their sturdy insouciance. Men, clearly, were impervious to fright. Or perhaps they just didn't know what had gone on in this house before Mr Channing bought it.

My courage was not put to the test. When the car came to a halt, Mr Channing turned to me and said, 'Henderson will take you home, Fidgie. You'll have to get out of those wet clothes, and we have nothing here suitable for a girl to wear.' He got out, and cowering a little under the rain, leant back in to add, 'Convey my compliments to your mother, and ask her permission to come and visit us. If she gives it, come to luncheon tomorrow. Mrs Henderson will be your chaperone.'

All Chaz said was, 'If you're coming swimming tomorrow morning, meet me outside Holly Hill first thing.' And then he was gone, disappearing with his uncle and Jenkins into the dark maw beyond the huge front door before I had a chance to tell him that I was forbidden to go to Holly Hill.

Henderson didn't return to the main road as I was expecting him to, but followed the drive round until it

123

emerged through the dripping shrubbery on to the same track which ran past Holly Hill, the track where, a mile away, Chaz and I had hidden in the bracken yesterday as his tutor passed.

Relief at having escaped from that awful house was giving way to glee at the prospect of being able to boast to Tom and the others about it. No need to let on that the monster had gone: they wouldn't know that, or that the house was occupied now by a perfectly sane if rather eccentric old man. *Word of honour,* I would say casually, *I rang the bell and ran away. The dog chased me for miles with blood dripping from its fangs, but I ran like the wind and got away.*

Dick and Jacko and the others would be sceptical, they wouldn't want to believe that a girl, a mere *kid* of a girl at that, could do something nobody else had ever dared to do. They would probably sneer and scoff, but the bandage on my knee could be shown as proof of my narrow escape. I doubted though that I could keep up the pretence with Tom, or not for long anyway, but I could swear him to secrecy.

Silent as ever, the car stopped outside River Cottage and I got out without realizing that I was supposed to wait until Henderson opened the door for me. I waved from the garden gate to thank him but he was already busy reversing the car and didn't notice.

Even though Eric's car was parked outside the house, the front door was locked. This was unusual and meant that everyone was out. It was so rare for everyone to be out at the same time except when we went to the pictures together that Fiff had never made any arrangement for hiding a key in the garden.

The back door too was locked, and except for the wash-house across the yard there was no shelter from the rain, which was still falling steadily. The wash-house with its concrete floor was too cheerless to shelter in for long. It held nothing but the bricked-in boiler in one corner, the dolly-tub with its posser beside it, the big old mangle with its massive wooden rollers standing against one wall; and in the corner behind the door, the cardboard box full of torn blankets where poor Pipsy was forced to sleep when she was on heat.

But luckily my bedroom window was still open, the curtains sucked out by the wind, their hems clinging wetly to the window-ledge. Getting up there was a fairly simple matter of climbing onto the wash-house roof where it met the rising ground behind, slithering down the other side until my feet found a purchase on the guttering, then teetering like a tightrope walker along the top of the wall which enclosed our back yard, and scrambling up the slope of the porch above the back door; though it would have been easier if the slates had been dry, and a lot easier without the bandage – now soaking wet and dirty – impeding my knee. Mrs Bellamy's cat was sheltering on the kitchen window-sill, her paws tucked up under her chest, watching me with wary green eyes. I put my finger up to my lips and breathed 'Ssh!' to her, to warn her not to let out a yowl and give the game away. Fiff didn't know I could get in this way and I hoped that Mrs Bellamy didn't either: she was nice but she would almost certainly feel it her duty to tell Fiff if she saw me – grown-ups were always so certain that we were going to break our necks – and any combination of different punishments would ensue. Or none at all, depending on how seriously Fiff viewed it – she was quite capable of bursting out laughing – but I was pretty sure that she wouldn't overlook such hoydenish behaviour altogether. All the same, I felt a glow of triumph when I finally pulled myself through my bedroom window.

Halfway up the roof of the back porch I had begun to think about food. Prompted probably because this roof was above the kitchen, I suddenly remembered the last slice of my birthday cake. Even if Fiff hadn't thrown it out for the birds, the sponge was very likely stale now, the cream turning sour, the icing hardening, but even so, I could hardly wait to get downstairs and pounce on it. I kicked my wet sandals off and made for the bathroom to get a towel, padding silently along the landing.

That was when I heard excited giggling coming from Cly's room. It stopped me in my tracks for a moment, my worst fears realized: I was alone in the house with Cly. And yet, if she was giggling, surely she must have someone with her? If she had, I was safe: she would never show herself up in front of a friend. But she chose her friends well: always girls who were willing to fall in with her plans to subjugate me. I wasn't willing to be subjugated, but I had never yet managed to think out a way to prevent it.

And then I heard a boy's voice and panic seized me. If Cly caught me listening, the consequences didn't bear thinking of. Hastily I slipped back into my room and finished changing.

Too hastily. I took care not to close my bedroom door completely, knowing that it was impossible to do it without a loud click, but I had forgotten that my wardrobe door gave a screech when it was opened.

I froze and listened, but all seemed to be well: no sound came from the far end of the landing and I began to creep quietly towards the head of the stairs. I had just reached them when Cly's door flew open and she stood there on guard, probably expecting to see Fiff. When she saw me her face closed darkly with rage the same way Boko's did, and almost as alarmingly.

'I might have known it was *you* sneaking about,' she snarled.

126

'I *wasn't* sneaking,' I protested, although it was clear that I was.

'And now you're going to split on us to Ma,' she said, speaking in a babyish sing-song meant to sound like me.

'No, Cly, honestly . . .' I began, though a small part of my mind noted with interest that I had stumbled on something Cly – the flawless, invulnerable Cly – wished to keep secret.

She cut me short. 'Turn round,' she ordered, advancing on me. 'It's time someone taught you a lesson.'

I obeyed weakly, knowing that something unpleasant was going to happen. As I did so, she seized my arm and wrenched it up behind my back. I squealed with pain and fright.

'This is just the beginning,' she hissed into my ear. 'If you breathe so much as a word to anyone . . .'

Being scared of Cly was humiliating. To salvage some dignity I summoned up enough courage to cheek her. 'How can I?' I managed to gasp. 'I don't know what you were doing. If you tell me, I'll know what I'm not supposed to tell.'

This insubordination brought another vicious tweak on my arm.

It wasn't wise to betray pain to Cly, but I couldn't hold out any longer.

'Please, Cly, you're hurting.'

'Not half as much as I will if you blab, you little snitch. And don't think I won't know if you do. I'll know if you even *think* of it.'

I believed her. She gave my arm a final agonizing wrench before she let go. 'Now get out of my sight, and stay out,' she said.

Even though I knew full well that refusing to be cowed would only infuriate her more, I skipped downstairs as if nothing had happened and made for

127

the kitchen, singing 'Happy days are here again . . .' to show her I didn't care, and was rewarded by a click of the tongue and a snort of fury from upstairs. I knew perfectly well that giving Cly lip like this was one of the things which gave me a bad name in the family, but I couldn't think of any other way of keeping my end up.

I kept it up all the way down the hall, but once in the kitchen, I dropped the act and clasped my painful shoulder, waiting until I heard footsteps coming downstairs. Although I told myself that I didn't care *who* had been in Cly's bedroom – I only wished it had been the gorilla from the Room Org, now carrying Cly's lifeless body out – the temptation to peep through the crack between the hinges of the kitchen door was irresistible. It was, anyway, my only available form of revenge.

But my heart dropped like a stone, almost stopped, when Cly's secret was revealed. *Dougie Parrish?*

Dougie, darkly brooding, mysterious, distant and glamorous as a star, so far removed from ordinary boys that he must belong to a different race! How *could* someone as marvellous as Dougie like someone as horrible as Cly? And like her enough to do rude things to her in her bedroom? Because I was sure that that was what they had been doing. I'd never even seen him smile. Now he had been doing things to Cly that made her titter in that queer, excited way. That he should so carelessly, so disastrously cast himself off the pedestal I had placed him on was a sort of betrayal. I went off him straightaway and felt a fool.

Even the birthday cake was no comfort, and I cut my thumb with the bread knife when, still hungry, I sawed a slice of bread off the loaf, scattering drops of blood all over the marble table-top in the pantry. They were such a beautiful crimson against the white stone that it seemed a shame to wipe them up.

The cut hurt; but the deicide of Dougie, the inglorious puncture and collapse of the myth I'd cherished, hurt much more.

The rain had stopped by the time Fiff and Eric came home on the train. Laughing together and looking perfectly dry, they walked the half mile from the junction through the golden light of a gorgeous sunset which had followed, like a handsome apology, after the rage of the storm. Fiff was wearing a beige dress with white polka dots the size of pennies and the dark brown amber necklace she had bought in Marseilles, the one Tom and I called her seaweed beads because of the strands of something, probably grass, trapped in the amber. She had put on one of her special rings, the milky blue star sapphire set in a tracery of gold.

Eric was carrying two bulging brown-paper carrier bags, the string handles biting into his fingers; and Fiff, holding it well away from her dress as if carrying something that might bite her, clasped the handle of a square package heavily padded with newspaper: an accumulator, freshly charged. Eric went into the sitting-room to insert it in the wireless and try it out. Because the volume had been turned up as high as it would go as the battery faded, the strains of a dance band playing *South American Joe* exploded from the room like a bomb until he hastily turned the volume down.

Carrying a slender wax taper from one wick to the next, Fiff set about lighting lamps to dispel the gathering gloom in the house. Fiff hated housework; its never-ending monotony bored her, and it was only when visitors were expected that she applied herself to it seriously. Then everything was turned upside down and Tom and I were called on to help. Before Eric came, I had been sent up the stairs with a hot flat-iron and a sheet of blotting-paper to melt the candlewax out of the stair carpet, and Tom had trimmed the wicks of the lamps and washed their chimneys till they gleamed. I was deeply impressed that he had managed to wash all that delicate glass without breaking a single one, not even the big, unwieldy one on the Aladdin. Now, as the glass heated up, they gave off a comfortable smell of clean, warm oil.

'Where is everyone?' Fiff asked when she realized that the house was empty except for me. 'And why are you wearing that dirty rag on your knee?'

'It's a bandage,' I explained proudly.

'I don't care what it is: get it off at once. I won't have a child of mine walking round looking like a tramp. Really, Fidgie! Why can't you stay clean and tidy? If Clytie can do it, so can you.'

Abashed, I began to explain how I'd got the bandage dirty, forgetting that I must not mention the roofs, but Fiff, who was tying an apron round her waist and not really listening, interrupted before I managed to incriminate myself.

'Where were you, anyway? You weren't in the cinema. I looked for you.'

'I went fishing,' I said. 'With Chaz. On his boat. We went right out in the bay.'

This claimed her attention: she was horrified. 'You and this boy? Right out at sea? Has he no sense at all?'

'His uncle . . . his *great*-uncle . . . was there too,' I hastened to say. 'Mr Channing.'

Fiff had begun whisking eggs, preparatory to coating the cod steaks she had taken out of one of the carrier bags. She put the bowl down abruptly and turned to me, her impatience suddenly gone.

'Channing?' she said, staring at me; and then, to

herself, 'Good God, that explains the Rolls-Royce.'

Uncertain whether this meant approval or not, and urgent to persuade her of the Channings' credentials, I went on, 'Mr Channing's very nice, Mummy, honestly, but very old and' – apologetically because I felt sure that Fiff disapproved of poverty – 'I think he's very poor.'

'Poor?' Fiff gasped. '*Poor*? You silly child, he's *enormously* rich! What on earth gave you the idea that he's poor?'

I writhed and looked down at my feet, conscious of having made yet another inexplicable mistake. 'He hasn't got any curtains,' I said.

Fiff burst out laughing, a harsh half-hysterical sound that made me realize I'd said something *really* stupid this time. 'That isn't very surprising in a bachelor establishment,' she said, and returned to preparing the meal; but another thought struck her and she asked in the sort of voice which filled me with foreboding, 'Does that mean that you've been *in his house*?'

'Not inside,' I said hastily. 'I didn't get out of the car.' The muddled explanation I began was interrupted by Tom's arrival, breathless, panting from the effort of getting home before the sun set.

'Where's Clytie?' she asked him.

'Search me,' he said sturdily. 'She's probably still up on the knoll with Dougie Parrish. I saw them going up there when I was crossing the bridge.'

I began to let out a gleeful snigger and quickly clapped a hand over my mouth when I realized that Tom's careless revelation would be the death of me. If Fiff questioned her about it, Cly would take it for granted I'd blabbed, and the consequences would be, as she had promised, painful. In this emergency my wits deserted me: I couldn't think of any way of contradicting him or distracting Fiff's attention.

We were sent out to pick runner beans in the lingering afterglow of the sunset – now that the peas were over we had beans with everything – and when we came back Cly had returned wearing a look as smug as the picture I'd seen of the Mona Lisa; and the subject of my afternoon didn't arise again until the meal was nearly over.

While we ate I wondered if I dared tell Fiff that Mr Channing had invited me to lunch tomorrow. It was only this afternoon, after all, that she had forbidden me to go to Holly Hill. It seemed a good idea to leave this problem for the time being.

The others had been swapping stories about the thunderstorm. Cly, it seemed, had seen the storm coming and had been making her way home over the bridge when she had been overtaken by a boy she knew only by sight and didn't much like. And when the storm broke she had been forced, much against her will because he was a boy from school and rather common, to offer him refuge in the house. She hoped Fiff didn't mind. Fiff didn't, but craftily she asked where the boy lived that he couldn't go to his own home to shelter.

'Oh,' Cly said vaguely, 'over there somewhere, I think.' She waved a hand indifferently in the direction of the knoll. 'In the village.' The village was most of a mile away across the marshes. I gazed at her open-mouthed, wondering if I could ever learn to be as smooth as that; expecting closer interrogation; but Fiff nodded, satisfied, and turned to me.

'And were you still out at sea?'

My story of Teddy and the drifting yacht was received without the fascination I thought it deserved, and it became clear to me that I wasn't believed; I had made it all up, or most of it, to draw attention to myself. Eric eyed me acidly across the table until I

132

dropped my eyes and trailed to a stop, mortified.

'Trust *her* to show off,' Cly said to no one in particular. 'She probably saw a drifting dinghy and invented the rest.'

But Tom was enthusiastic. He said, 'I say! It may be on the nine o'clock news: Mystery surrounds the disappearance of a yachtsman this afternoon in a thunderstorm in Cardigan Bay . . .'

Cheered by his support, I asked Fiff, 'What does chaperone mean?'

Fiff explained crisply and asked, 'Why do you want to know?'

This was difficult, verging as it did on the invitation to lunch. I decided to smear over it. 'Mr Channing said . . .' I closed my eyes to summon up exact memory, 'to convey his compliments to you and ask if I could have your permission to visit them. He said Mrs Henderson would be my chaperone.'

When I opened my eyes I could see that Fiff was pleased. Cly was not, and Eric was eating with elaborate indifference.

'Well,' Fiff said, 'just don't disgrace me. No racing around shouting like a ruffian and getting your clothes dirty as you usually do, or you'll very soon find that you're no longer welcome there.'

Tom and I were allowed to stay up till nine-thirty on a Saturday night, but there was no mention of Teddy on the news. It was mostly boring stuff about the Nazis in Germany. It usually was. I couldn't understand why we were expected to worry about them. Germany was miles away – miles and miles, I knew that – much too far away to be interesting.

When we were sent off to bed, Tom raced ahead yelling, 'Baggy me the bathroom!'

Following him reluctantly up the stairs, lingering on each tread, I heard Cly say to Fiff, 'You're not going to let her go visiting people like the Channings, are you? She has no idea how to behave. She's sure to make an exhibition of herself. She'll only disgrace us.'

I turned with a hand on the banister, just in time to see Fiff, through the partly open door, put a warning finger to her lips to silence Cly. Then she crossed the room and closed the door, and I knew with dismal certainty that they were going to discuss my failings.

The first thing I noticed when, candlestick in hand, I entered my bedroom, was the white gleam of the shoebox under the fringe of my counterpane. I knew I'd pushed it much further under the bed. Someone – and who else but Cly? – had pulled it out and failed to push it under again out of sight, as I'd left it. Something icy ran up my spine. Leaving it like that wasn't just carelessness on her part: she wanted me to know that she was on my trail and also to remind me to keep quiet about Dougie Parrish. In some telepathic way she knew that I too had something to hide.

Closing the door firmly, I pulled the chair up to the wardrobe and climbed on it, holding my breath in trepidation.

But they were still there, my beautiful dancing shoes, their soft bronze leather ravishing to see and to touch. I held them up to my face, one to each cheek, and closed my eyes to savour their softness and breathe in the lovely smell of newness. The relief of finding them still there, still safe, still mine, was enormous.

But it had to be short-lived. Cly – or anyone – might come in at any moment. I put the shoes hastily back in their hiding place and climbed down, worrying. Somehow I must think of somewhere safer to hide them, just in case the shells had not convinced her.

Tom was still in the bathroom, cleaning his teeth as noisily as possible to underline his triumphant capture of the room. To pay him out, I went into his bedroom and threw myself on his bed, knowing perfectly well that it would cause a fight, and it did.

And I might have won too, if Tom hadn't knocked one of my teeth out in the struggle. The tooth wouldn't have mattered – it had been loose for days and it wasn't a front tooth – but I could have got sixpence for it if I hadn't swallowed it by mistake.

9

I didn't like Sundays.

No trains or buses ran. People wore black and walked to chapel. I had never been to chapel or church but I was sure I wouldn't like it if I did. The people who went looked the same as I did when Mr Hughes swished his cane and said *Hold your hand out, girl!*

Without the trains and the buses, an eerie silence fell over the day, the only sound the wind, or the trees rustling. The world stopped, perhaps never to start again. Even the cheerful dogs had fallen silent in the distant village. It was useless looking for friends to play with: they weren't allowed to play on Sundays, not even Ellen, who didn't care much about anything on weekdays, and didn't seem the sort who went to church.

Even Fiff, who never went to church either – who had long since given up hearing our bedtime prayers – even she dared not cross the mysterious line which marked Sunday off from any other day. She never dared to hang so much as a handkerchief on the clothes line in the back yard, or be seen in the garden with a trowel in her hand. Slugs and dandelions, against which she waged relentless war all week, lived on, hated but happy, till Monday.

But this Sunday was going to be different. Not only was I going to spend it with Chaz, well away from Cly and hidden by folds in the hills from Mrs van Gelderen's prying lens, but Eric was supposed to be going home today, and I hoped that when I returned he would already be gone. I would forget to say goodbye.

I had won a small victory. Fiff was in a completely different mood today, playful and indulgent, and I felt it safe to confess my invitation to stay to lunch with the Channings. When she heard this, she made me have my bath early. That was bad enough, because the bath-water was little more than lukewarm; but then she tried to make me wear my party dress, the grey silk one patterned with small strawberries, a present from Auntie Louie. But I hated it: it was old-fashioned, its waist round my hips. Fiff, who made no secret of detesting Auntie Louie, did not insist. So we compromised, or she did, and I was wearing the dress she had made me for the summer holidays. She'd had enough material left over to make a pair of knickers to match, with pockets on the front big enough to hold a handkerchief, and I was very proud of them. I had shown them to Ellen, whose only comment had been a disappointingly terse 'Huh!' but I couldn't very well show them to Chaz – unless I could think of some way of doing it accidentally – because it was rude to show your knickers to boys. It was a pretty dress – of white cotton sprinkled with buttercups and cornflowers – but it would be almost impossible to keep clean because I had every intention of exploring the jungle at Mr Channing's house – so long as Chaz was with me, in case we found any dead bodies left over when the mad old man disappeared.

The temperature had dropped since the storm, the sunshine coming and going as clouds loitered over the sun, plunging the valley floor into cool gloom from time to time, and dragging their blue shadows languorously over the distant mountains.

I was in no hurry to meet Chaz. I loved the heady scent of brand new cotton rising from my dress; the morning, like the cotton, was crisp and clean and fresh, and the day stretched endlessly and blissfully before me to do with as I pleased. First I climbed the knoll to see if my tree looked better, less parched, after the rain. There was a subtle difference, but I was dismayed to see that the ground below the trunk looked every bit as dry as it had before the thunderstorm.

'Never mind,' I said, patting its trunk to comfort it, 'it was better than nothing, wasn't it?'

I thought about the possibility of hiding my shoes in the hole between the roots, but now that I knew that Cly came up here with boys — with Dougie Parrish, anyway — my secret would clearly be no safer here than it was at the top of the wardrobe. And the ground might not always be dry.

Today I was carrying my bathing costume rolled in a beach wrap and stored in the embroidery bag Fiff had lent me, emptying it of its coloured silks and wools for the occasion. It was easy to carry by its wooden handles, even when I found a loose pebble and used it to play imaginary hopscotch along the path. Fiff had replaced the bandage on my knee with a sticking-plaster which made the skin feel tight, but it was tidier and less of a nuisance than the bandage. Sticking-plaster, though, lacks drama, and I'd parted with the bandage only under protest.

The track here between the knoll and Holly Hill — and most of the way to Mr Channing's house — was open to view in all directions, but even if Mrs van Gelderen reported me for playing on a Sunday I didn't think Fiff would care much. I thought of sticking my thumbs in my ears, putting my tongue out and waggling my fingers in Mrs van Gelderen's direction the way Ellen would have, but I knew that this would be going too far.

Playing hopscotch needs concentration: you have to

keep your eyes on your feet and on the ground in front of you, to make sure you don't kick the pebble too far ahead, and I didn't see Chaz until I had almost passed him. He was sitting on a boulder outside Holly Hill, his knees up to his chin, his swimming costume rolled in a towel beside him.

'I was beginning to think you weren't coming,' he said, collecting his swimming things and jumping down.

Fiff had prevented me from leaving until she was sure I was, as she said, presentable, and had eaten a good breakfast. *I won't have you eating like a starving horse the minute you get there,* she had said. But I couldn't tell Chaz this: it didn't do to tell boys that you had gone to some trouble preparing to meet them.

'I can't go swimming,' I said. 'Not for two hours anyway. I've just had breakfast.'

'You should have waited or got up earlier,' he said with the sort of mild annoyance boys use when confronted with the inexplicable silliness of girls. 'I had breakfast an hour ago. You'll just have to sit and watch while I swim. Come on.' And he headed for the cypress hedge guarding the grounds of Holly Hill. It ran all the way from the track down to the rocks above the water.

I sighed. 'I'm not allowed to go to Holly Hill either,' I said mournfully.

He was annoyed. 'For pity's sake, why not?'

'My mother doesn't like Mrs Guest.'

'So what? We aren't going to see Mrs Guest. She stays in bed half the morning anyway.'

I hesitated. I longed to throw caution away and follow him.

'Anyway,' he said, 'who's going to know?'

I threw a nervous glance over the marshes to the big house a mile away, high on the hill above the village.

'Mrs van Gelderen,' I said. 'Didn't you know? She watches everybody. Through a spyglass. She reported me yesterday for talking to Mr Guest, made him sound awful, and my mother made me promise not to go to Holly Hill again.' I explained that Mrs van Gelderen was an invalid and though never seen in public herself except dimly as a face at the big bay window of her drawing-room, sent her daughter down to the village to carry her messages of reproof.

'I've a good mind to take my pants off and wave them at her,' Chaz said, his hands moving up to his belt, starting to undo the buckle.

'Oh no, don't! *Please*!' I begged in a panic. 'She'll tell on us, and I'll never be allowed to play with you again.'

He burst out laughing. I was not amused at first: he had given me too much of a fright; but suddenly I got a picture of old Mrs van Gelderen fainting with horror, spread-eagled in her great armchair, and Miss van Gelderen fanning her frantically with a tablecloth, and I got the giggles. We both yelled with laughter, reeling about in an ecstasy.

'She'll probably report us for laughing on a Sunday,' I said, still laughing and not caring.

'Oh well,' he said when the gale subsided at last, 'if we can't teach the nosy old girl a lesson and we can't go to Holly Hill, let's go down to the river. We can paddle upstream and look for treasure. Maybe we'll find some nuggets washed down from one of the gold mines.'

He must have known that this was unlikely, since both of the gold mines were on the other side of the river – and one of them miles away upstream – but we went just the same, following the line of the cypress hedge until we reached the rocks and could climb down to the water. We stuffed Chaz's bathing things

140

into my bag to make climbing easier, swapping it between us as we swarmed over the rocks.

'I'm not going near that big black pool,' I warned him. 'The one below Holly Hill. They say it's bottomless.'

'That's absolute cock,' he said scathingly. 'Nothing's bottomless.'

I wanted to say *Sez you* as loftily as possible because I was annoyed that he should treat this cherished piece of local lore with such disdain, but I was afraid that he was right and would prove it; and I wanted to go on believing it. So instead I said, 'Why didn't you bring Jenkins with you?'

'He wouldn't have come,' he said. 'He's Uncle Hil's dog.'

It was impossible to get past Holly Hill without crossing some part of its land, and we climbed up again from water-level past the boat-house and descended along the slipway until we reached more rocks and clambered over them. Looking up from down below here we could see only the eaves of the house, which meant that we couldn't be seen by anyone in the house or – which was more important – by Mrs van Gelderen.

It was while we were still on the slipway that I asked him, 'Did Mr Ransom come home in the end?'

'No,' he said. 'He's still missing. So he *must* have had an accident. Maybe you were right and he got struck by lightning.'

'Perhaps he went home and didn't tell anyone.'

'He couldn't have. Uncle Hil phoned his sisters after we got home yesterday to tell them what had happened. They promised to let him know if Mr Ransom came home.'

Teddy's sisters, he explained, were elderly, a lot older than he was, and spoiled him – here Chaz's voice had an edge of sturdy contempt – as if Teddy were still a small kid.

Somebody had been making a mess there on the slipway, wrenching stones out of the raw earth of the bank opposite the boat-house, leaving holes in the soil and scattering earth on the concrete. They'd thrown the chain away too, and a rusty smudge marked where it had lain. Whoever it was had not bothered to clear up properly: there were scuff marks where someone had swept the soil off the edge into the water with a foot. There was something both angry and indifferent about it, as if whoever had done it had said *Who cares?* and left it for somebody else to clean up. It was disquieting that whoever it was should treat my boat-house – my lovely little doll's house – so uncaringly, and if I had been alone I would have stopped and cleaned up the mess.

We lost track of time while we scrabbled about among the rocks, searching the shingle for hidden treasure, digging in the sandy mud, popping the bladders on dried seaweed and drawing our names in the sand with bits of wood found at the tideline.

The tide stopped flowing upstream and paused as if waiting to gather strength to begin its rush back to the sea, but it was still full and we had to climb high along the rocks above the water-line to get from cove to cove. In each, the high-tide mark was drawn by a line of detritus made up mostly of dried seaweed and mussel shells and driftwood brought from the sea by the tide. All we had found so far was the rotting carcass of a seabird, a waterlogged paper cigarette packet which had once held five Woodbines, and a green glass float torn from a fishing net. We carried the glass float with us, bulging out from the top of Fiff's embroidery bag.

'We'll try the next cove,' Chaz said, 'and if we don't find anything interesting we'll give up.'

Clutching the embroidery bag whose handles would hardly close now over the green glass float, he led the way, jumping down onto the shingle with the sort of crunching crash only small pebbles can make. I was just gathering myself to follow him when something deep down in the water caught my eye. It was round and white, barely moving on the current, and at first I thought it was a jellyfish swept upstream by the tide, but it was too round and too white.

Pointing, I said to Chaz, 'There's something funny floating down there.'

From where he was, just above water-level, he couldn't see it and I had to keep pointing, my arm out like a signpost. He untangled a long slim branch of driftwood from the seaweed at the tideline, and following my directions, fished in the water until he managed to draw it out. It took quite a long time, our prize bobbing and dodging away from Chaz's fishing pole, and at one point he threatened to wade in and dive for it, and probably would have if he'd had his swimming trunks on, but the idea scared me and I begged him not to.

'It's *miles* deep,' I wailed. 'You mustn't!' And to clinch it, I added the worst threat any of us could think of. 'I'll never *speak* to you again if you do.'

And after all that, disappointingly, the mysterious object was only a yachting cap.

Examining it, Chaz said, 'It's Mr Ransom's. It must be.'

I joined him, jumping down into the cove. 'You mean,' I breathed, awestruck, 'he's down there, in that awful pool?'

'No, of course not. How can he be? Honestly, Fidgie, you are a dope!' he said. 'We found his boat right out at sea, remember? This must have come up on the tide.'

'Oh yes, of course,' I said, quelled. But even though I

143

didn't like Teddy I didn't want him to be dead, so I went on arguing.

'But what if it isn't his? It might belong to someone else.'

'Oh, wake up,' he said. 'How many other people have you seen wearing yachting caps around here?'

I couldn't think of anyone, and when I didn't answer, he went on, 'Anyway, Uncle Hil will know what to do about it. It's probably not important. It may just have fallen overboard.' And he hoisted it on top of the branch he had used to fish it out, and spun it like a juggler's plate, drops of water flying off it.

But for all his insouciance, the finding of the cap – so very probably and ominously Teddy's – had replaced the interest of our treasure hunt with a new and macabre fascination, and we abandoned the game by unspoken consent, climbing out of the cove and making our way to Mr Channing's house. My steps got slower and slower as we neared Llwyn-yr-eos: we were Roman soldiers, the last remaining of a whole army slaughtered on the battlefield, the doom-laden bringers of bad news to the emperor who would fly into a rage and order our immediate execution, and we would be dragged off, pleading in vain for our lives . . .

'Oh, come on, slowcoach!' Chaz's voice startled me out of my absorption. The sun had gone behind one of the vast clouds standing perfectly still high overhead, and in its shadow the breeze had turned chill, rustling through the gorse and riding roughshod over the bracken.

'Bet I can beat you to the gate,' I said, and started running before I'd finished speaking, to give myself an advantage.

It didn't work: he caught me up and passed me some yards before we reached the tall stone columns. And what was even more maddening was that he still had the yachting cap safely hooked on the end of the branch. I had been hoping that he would drop it and have to turn back.

I knew the house was very old. Its name, half-obscured by ivy and overhung by the branches of laurel and sycamore, was carved into the top of the granite columns, each column surmounted by a stone ball.

'Do you understand Welsh?' he asked, indicating the name.

''Course I do,' I said boastfully and not very truthfully. Mr Griffith, our teacher in Standard Two, was pleased with me, but in fact I understood only the simple Welsh I had learned in the past three terms.

'So what does it mean?' he asked.

I had noticed the name yesterday, and Tom had helped me translate it, but it was such a triumph to be able to tell Chaz something he didn't already know that I pretended I was translating it then and there.

'Plas,' I intoned knowledgeably, 'means Hall, sort of, and Llwyn-yr-eos means The Little Wood of the Nightingale.'

'Grove,' he said, spoiling my triumph, 'Nightingale Grove Hall. My tutor tells me off if I translate too literally.'

'It doesn't sound the same, somehow,' I grumbled.

Suddenly, startlingly, so close beside us that I jumped and threw up a hand to ward off attack, a bird screamed and fled clattering through the overgrown bushes. A moment later I gasped with terror and stood rooted to the spot as a huge black thing emerged silently through the bushes and swivelled its eyeless head towards us. All my fears of this place returned redoubled. I grabbed Chaz's arm and hung on, too paralysed even to squeal.

The monster must have seen my terror, because it

reached up and, removing a head-dress of black net, became Mr Channing.

'It's all right, Fidgie,' he said, amused. 'This is what I have to wear when I'm dealing with my bees.'

Chaz, unaware of my terror or dismissing it, offered the cap on the end of the branch. 'We found this, sir,' he said. 'Brought up on the tide, I expect.'

The amusement left Mr Channing's face at once. 'Ransom's?' he said.

'Must be.'

'Where did you find it?'

Chaz explained as we followed his uncle up the drive. As soon as the house came into view I could see Jenkins at one of the windows standing with his front paws on the window-sill, anxiously staring down the drive towards us. When he saw us he jumped down and vanished, to reappear in the hall, whiffling with pleasure and relief as soon as we entered the door. He had tucked his top lip up above his teeth, which made him look ridiculous, as if he were wearing a sentimental smile as he gazed up at Mr Channing. I tried to attract his attention by patting my thigh and making kissing noises, but though he acknowledged me with a glance, he refused to leave his master's side. Mr Channing pulled the dog's silken ears absentmindedly as we crossed the hall. I quite forgot that I had ever been scared of this house.

But it was as brown and bare inside as it was grey and bare outside, the only furniture a grandfather clock against one wall and an oak chair against another. The walls were panelled in oak and an oak staircase rose from the rear, branching from a landing halfway up. No rugs softened the bleak expanse of wooden floor and our rubber-soled sandals squeaked on its polished surface, a sound I found curiously satisfying. The pungent scents of floor polish and beeswax mingled with the smell of antiquity in a way which would have been pleasant if the rooms had not been so empty, so bleak. It reminded me of school. The classrooms must look like this in holiday time, but at least they had desks, and there were nature study drawings to brighten up the walls.

We followed Mr Channing through a door near the foot of the staircase. Inside the room, chaos reigned. Books and papers were stacked everywhere, overflowing the shelves and bookcases and piling up into heaps on the floor. A grey cat was curled into a ball on the leather chair behind the desk. It gave no sign of being aware of our entrance until Jenkins approached it, when it hissed, got up and stretched, and jumped down. But perhaps because its sleep had been disturbed, or simply to make a point, the cat suddenly stood up and boxed Jenkins's ears. Then, ignoring the dog with an hauteur even Cly could not have bettered, it stalked to the door and waited with the dignity of a duchess until Chaz let it out. I made up my mind then and there to ask Fiff if we could have a cat.

Mr Channing hung the hat with the black veil on it on a hook behind the door, set the black tin he was carrying on top of a cupboard, and tossed the yachting cap onto the mantelpiece, where it began to drip into the hearth.

'That will have to be handed in to the police, of course, and if Ransom still hasn't turned up, they will want to know exactly where you found it.'

'I realize that, sir,' Chaz said. Perhaps because he felt that the finding of Teddy's cap was much more important, more sinister, than he had been pretending, or because the house oppressed him, he had suddenly become very formal.

'In that case,' Mr Channing said, picking up the phone, 'we'll hand it in at the police station on our way

147

to collect the *Slug*. Go and find something to do, but stay within earshot.'

'Couldn't we go for the *Slug* now, Uncle? The tide has already begun to turn.'

'I've got things to do first,' Mr Channing said. 'Make yourselves scarce for a bit.'

As soon as he had closed the study door behind us Chaz leaned close to my ear and breathed, 'Don't make a sound. My tutor's around somewhere, and I still haven't done the Latin prep he set before he went away.'

The house seemed unnaturally silent, so silent that the ticking of the grandfather clock sounded almost as loud as a gong. Chaz crossed the hall lightly and I followed with exaggerated stealth until we were safely through the door opposite. Inside was the biggest room I'd ever seen except in the big hotel in Colombo. Tall windows, uncurtained, took up most of the long wall opposite, and like the hall it was almost bare of furniture. A few spindly chairs were drawn up against the walls between the windows, and a tall cupboard, polished to the colour and gloss of a chestnut, stood in one corner, its brass key-plates glinting like gold; but the whole room – the whole house – looked as if it had been sold, cleared of furniture and abandoned, its occupants planning to leave as soon as the last few things were packed. But Mr Channing had only just arrived: that probably explained it.

'It'll look nice when the rest of the furniture arrives,' I told Chaz, to reassure him.

'What furniture?' he asked, surprised. 'We've got all the furniture we need.'

'But you can't have!' I cried, shocked. 'There's nothing here. It's awful.'

Chaz looked around, genuinely puzzled. 'What's wrong with it?'

'It's empty. There aren't even any carpets.' I knew I was being extremely rude, but I couldn't help it: I was obscurely annoyed that anyone who could afford luxury should choose to live the cold life of a cave-dweller. Unless Fiff was wrong. Maybe Mr Channing was as broke as we were. If he were, then I had committed a truly shocking gaffe, and if Chaz told his uncle what I'd said I wouldn't be asked again.

But Chaz wasn't abashed. 'Huh!' he said. 'Trust a woman to make a fuss about nothing.'

I refused to back down. 'It must be *freezing* in the winter.'

He pointed to the long back wall. It was only then that I noticed the fat cast-iron radiators all round the room. 'Ever heard of central heating?' he asked in the manner of one ending an argument conclusively. 'Uncle Hil spent most of his life in Africa, living rough mostly, prospecting. So long as the place is warm, he doesn't care what it looks like.'

I couldn't think of the answer to this, though I was sure there was one. He took my silence for surrender and his small triumph made him generous.

'Look,' he said, 'if you swear faithfully not to tell, I'll show you something. But you must swear never to breathe a word to anyone as long as you live.'

Instantly agog, I said earnestly, 'Cross my heart and hope to die. Honestly and truly.'

He studied me for a moment with his fists thrust into his trouser pockets before finally making up his mind. 'OK,' he said. 'Turn round and close your eyes. And don't open them until I tell you.'

I obeyed. We were standing near the tall cupboard in the corner, and partly because I was slightly miffed that he didn't trust me enough to let me watch, and partly because his injunction had sharpened my curiosity, I listened with acute interest.

So I heard him cross the room, pick up a chair, come back and climb onto it. Then, after some scrabbling, I heard him get down, put a key into a lock, and open one of the cupboard doors.

'I'm not supposed to know about this myself,' he said. 'That's why you have to keep it secret too.'

I heard a drawer being pulled open, and after a moment's silence, closed again.

'You can look now,' he said.

I turned and looked. He was holding a shapeless grey lump of something which might once have been glass in the palm of his hand and there was a look of wonder, almost of reverence in his face.

'Know what this is?'

'A piece of glass,' I said, wondering what could possibly be exciting about the sort of sand-scoured, cloudy glass you could see any time among the pebbles in the shingle.

Laughter came into his face. 'Fooled you,' he said, delighted with my mistake. 'It's a diamond.'

I was annoyed that he should think me fool enough to believe him. 'Don't be stupid!' I snapped. 'How can it be? Diamonds *sparkle*.'

'Only after they've been cut,' he said. 'They mostly look like this when you first dig them up. See the shape? It's what's called an octahedron.'

I took it out of his palm and stared at it, disappointed and puzzled.

'Touch it with the tip of your tongue,' he urged, and when I did, he asked, 'Well?'

'It's cold,' I said. 'Icy cold.'

'That's how you tell the difference,' he said, 'between glass and diamond.'

I didn't know whether to believe him or not. I thought about it later while we ran, skipping over the shaggy tussocks of what had once been a lawn, and decided against it as we neared the river. I was fairly sure that he had played a joke on me, and I was beginning to feel grumpy about it. He had made me turn my back and close my eyes again when he replaced the piece of rock, a precaution I thought unnecessary for so dubious a secret.

'I don't believe *anyone* would keep a diamond in a cupboard,' I began.

'That's because you don't know Great-Uncle Hil. And anyway, that one's badly flawed: it's full of crystals of zircon, so it's pretty well worthless, but he keeps it as a . . .' he searched for the word he wanted, '. . . a memento.' And just when I was beginning to marvel at his grasp of this arcane knowledge, he finished, 'It says so on the label.'

We had arrived at a stand of beech trees. Behind them there was a low building set at an acute angle to the river. A concrete ramp ran from wide doors down into the water: a boat-shed. The house now was far away across acres of meadow. It had been standing dark-eyed and secretive in deep shade, but as I watched the shadow began creeping away pursued by brilliant sunshine, and the long grass glittered in the sudden incandescence. A breeze rippled sensuously over the meadow which had once been lawns. The earth still smelled thirsty and hot.

Chaz swung round and pointed to a house across the river, an elegant building with a wrought-iron verandah. 'That's the Ransoms' house,' he said. 'You see? It's not at all creepy when you see it in daylight.'

The verandah reminded me. I asked, 'Whereabouts did you live in Ceylon?'

'I didn't,' he said tersely. 'I was at boarding school in London. I only saw my parents when they came home on leave.'

This was a disappointment. I'd been looking forward

to comparing experiences with him. If I couldn't be in Ceylon, talking about it was the next best thing. I sighed and resigned myself.

Chaz threw himself down at the foot of a tree, and after nursing my disappointment for a moment I flopped down on my knees close by, picked a long blade of grass, and held it on edge between my thumbs. When I blew through the narrow aperture, it emitted a hoarse squawk. I kept on trying until I managed to produce a note that was almost musical. After a while Chaz took it up too, and together we produced a raucous cacophony of shrieks and groans from our makeshift pipes.

But ever since seeing the inside of that empty house I'd been thinking, and now I couldn't hold my curiosity in any longer. 'Why doesn't your uncle have a wife?'

Surprised, Chaz said, 'He doesn't need one.'

This seemed a wholly novel idea to me: I thought all grown-ups wanted to get married – except, of course, people like poor Miss Wragg – but I knew it was pointless to argue with boys: they were always so certain they were right. I began picking daisies to make a daisy chain, but I'd bitten my nails so hard that it was difficult to make the necessary slits in the delicate furry stalks. I concentrated on it.

'Anyway,' Chaz went on, throwing his blade of grass away and picking another, 'he did have a wife once. Long ago when he was out in India.' He began to bite the juicy end of the stalk. 'She had a baby but they both died. Lots of women died having babies in those days. But you've got to swear you won't mention any of this in front of him. I'm not supposed to know it myself. I only found out because I overheard my parents talking about it. Swear you'll keep quiet or I won't tell you anything else.'

'I *swear*,' I said earnestly. 'Word of honour.' This secret was much more interesting than the diamond. I thought about it for a while before asking, 'Was he a planter?'

'Of course not. He was in the Army.'

'You said he'd spent most of his life in Africa.' I was trying to catch him out, but he had an answer for that, too.

'He did. The Army sent his regiment to the Sudan. That's how he got that sabre-cut across his face – at a place called Omdurman.' He leapt to his feet and made slashing movements and swishing noises to illustrate his story. Then he clapped one hand to his face and staggered about, wounded.

'Oh don't, *don't*!' I shouted, scrambling to my feet and holding my face. I could almost feel the wound as the sabre cut into the flesh and bone. 'How can you make fun of him? You're *hateful*.'

I was sorry as soon as I'd said it, because his face fell and I felt as if I'd hit him.

'I *wasn't* making fun,' he protested, startled, but he dropped his hand and became serious. 'Anyway, he had only one eye after that, so he had to leave the Army. And when he got better, he stayed in Africa and trekked south. That's when he found the diamonds.'

'You mean,' I said, awed and dazzled, 'there were *lots* of them?'

'Millions,' he said, losing interest. 'Millions and billions and *trillions*. Come on, I bet you can't climb this tree.'

10

Climbing was awkward because I was hanging away from the tree, trying to keep a space between the bark and my new dress. Because of this I had been forced to abandon any idea of trying to compete with Chaz, and he was well above me, climbing easily. From about ten feet up he called down, 'Hey! We could make a platform here, and build a tree house.'

'What with?' I asked, not sure if I liked the idea. I already had a house in the reeds on the marsh, made by tying the tops of the reeds together. It got very wet when it rained, especially underfoot, and the leaves cut like razor blades; but at least it was safely on the ground, not halfway up in the air.

'There are planks in the boat-shed,' Chaz said. 'Come on.'

We found a ladder in the boat-shed too, and once we began we became absorbed in the project and forgot everything else. Time vanished while we scrambled up and down the tree, awkwardly carrying the planks between us, tying them to the branches with lengths of old rope found in the boat-shed. The platform began to take shape, but even to me it looked a bit ramshackle.

'It would be better if I drove some nails into the tree,' Chaz said.

'Oh no!' I said quickly. 'You mustn't.'

'Why not? It would make the platform much safer.'

I didn't know how to explain. 'It would hurt the tree,' I managed in the end.

'That's stupid. The tree won't feel it.'

'It would,' I said. 'How would you like it if someone stuck nails in you?'

'That's different. I'm not made of wood.'

'All the same.'

We were sitting among the breeze-blown leaves, looking at our handiwork and arguing, when a bugle sounded distantly from the house.

'That's the Recall,' Chaz said and began climbing down. 'Come on, we're going to fetch the *Slug*.'

We clambered down and raced across the shaggy lawn back to the house. Mr Channing was waiting for us with the Hudson on the shabby forecourt outside the front door. I climbed into the back seat because I knew that boys always claimed the front seat as of right, and I had given up arguing about it. Besides, with Fiff's last injunction but one still reverberating in my head, I was on my best behaviour.

Fiff thought I took no notice of anything she said, but I did. Earlier, when we had been climbing over the rocks, I had started to tell Chaz about my missing tooth so that he could mourn with me over the sixpence lost for ever; and then I remembered Fiff's very last exhortation, made as I was running down the garden path . . . *And don't cadge . . . !* I'd bitten off the story at once, but the thought of how close I'd come to cadging made me wince.

I stared at the back of their heads as they settled into their seats and wished that I didn't have to behave myself in Mr Channing's presence now that I knew that he was rich and important; or be careful not to cadge from Chaz. Things had been different yesterday when Mr Channing had been just an old man who fished barefoot and left us alone; and Chaz just someone new to play with. Even his strange affliction didn't *really* count, so long as he didn't do it too often.

The car climbed up the lane through the tunnel of trees until we reached the main road and turned towards Dolgarran. Jenkins was sitting like a rajah on the seat beside me, staring as fixedly ahead as if he were driving the car. I would have liked to throw my arm amicably round his shoulders, but the stiffness of his posture made it clear that he would not welcome familiarities, totally concentrated as he was on his master, and indifferent to everything else.

A few minutes later as we swept past the turning to the toll-bridge we had crossed in the Rolls the day before, Chaz asked in alarm, 'Where are we going? Aren't we going to Moravon to collect the *Slug*?'

'Presently,' Mr Channing said. 'But first I have to hand this yachting cap to the police in Dolgarran. Had you forgotten?'

'Oh,' Chaz said, and subsided. 'But why Dolgarran?'

'It's the county town.' And when Chaz said no more, he added, 'That's where they'll be running the inquiry into Teddy Ransom's disappearance, if he doesn't turn up soon. They've already started a search for him.'

Dolgarran lay huddled in its narrow valley under the mountains, its granite houses seeming greyer even than Moravon's, its streets even narrower and more twisting.

'You may as well stay in the car, Fidgie,' Mr Channing said when he pulled up outside the police station. 'The place will be crowded if we all go in.'

I wanted to protest that it was I who had spotted the floating cap, that Chaz had only fished it out; but long experience had taught me that arguing with grown-ups was not only forbidden but likely to bring unpleasant consequences; so I stayed in the car and suppressed a disgruntled groan till they had gone, carrying the be-draggled cap with them and accompanied by Jenkins who had leapt over the front seat as soon as the door was opened.

After they had gone I wound down the window, hoping to see or hear something to relieve the boredom of waiting, but only the ivy leaves riffled by the occasional gusts of wind disturbed the somnolent quiet and there were only the usual sights and sounds of Sunday to occupy me, until the sudden blare of an organ from a nearby chapel split the silence. It seemed to startle the surrounding cottages into activity, and after the hymn had died away I listened to the clatter of dishes from kitchens all around. That, and the smells of roasting meat and boiling cabbage began to excite me into luscious thoughts of lunch.

Half-hidden among the outcrops of red valerian bursting exuberantly from crannies between the stones of the wall, a black and white cat lay, its paws tucked up under its chest, its eyes closing on the tedium of Sunday. I thought about cats for a while, and wondered if they caught spiders.

Just when I had begun to think I couldn't bear the boredom any more, that I would have to get out of the car and risk being asked by someone – possibly even the police – why I wasn't in chapel, Chaz and Mr Channing reappeared, closing the door behind them.

'Has Mr Ransom come back yet?' I asked them.

'Not so far,' Chaz said with no sign of regret. 'Looks as if he's a goner all right.'

'Were they pleased we found the hat?' As usual I was longing for approbation.

'Sort of. They thought it had probably been washed up-river by the tide. Just like I said.'

Mr Channing started the car and began to weave it through lanes so narrow I was surprised we didn't run over the doorsteps of the cottage on either side. Instead of crossing the square when we came to it, he turned down another narrow lane. There was a big hotel facing us at the far end of it, its front covered with a Virginia creeper whose leaves were just beginning to change into their autumnal shades of crimson.

'Aren't we going to Moravon to fetch the *Slug*?' Chaz asked anxiously when his uncle drew up on the cobbles outside the hotel.

'She'll keep,' Mr Channing said. 'First we'll have lunch.'

'But the tide must have turned *hours* ago.'

'So let's not waste time arguing. I'm hungry if you aren't, and I'm sure Fidgie is too.'

Chastened by the reminder that he had a guest, Chaz capitulated. Crossing the cobbled courtyard, Mr Channing explained unapologetically, 'I'd forgotten when I invited Fidgie to take luncheon with us that today is the Hendersons' day off.'

We followed Mr Channing through the swing doors. Inside, the coffee lounge was crowded and eyes turned in mild curiosity at our entrance, only to fix on Mr Channing's face and widen with shock. The horror was quickly disguised but the eyes still stared fascinated, and all of a sudden I flew into a temper. I wanted to shout at them, 'How would *you* like it if people stared at *you*?'

Instead I slipped my hand into Mr Channing's so that he would know that I was on his side against these horrible people, and I scowled back at their children as rudely as I knew how.

The dining-room was crowded, and full of delicious smells and of the sounds of cutlery and muted conversation. I noticed that Mr Channing chose a chair with its back to the rest of the room, and I didn't blame him. I knew that *I* couldn't have borne being stared at, the way people stared at him.

We were halfway through our roast beef, Chaz

lagging behind because he had asked for an extra helping of Yorkshire pudding, when Mrs Guest appeared in the doorway and paused to survey the room. I didn't recognize her for a moment because of the dark sun-glasses and the hat she wore, but she wasn't the sort of woman who can pass unnoticed for long, even in dark clothes. She was dressed in navy blue chiffon with a wide-brimmed leghorn hat half-hiding her face; and she was with a man I'd never seen before. Taking no notice of anyone, she drifted through the room like a dark swan.

I kicked Chaz conspiratorially under the table. 'There's Mrs Guest,' I said innocently, taking care to sound matter of fact so that Mr Channing wouldn't realize I was passing a message.

Chaz looked round, glanced at Mrs Guest's elegantly swaying back, and said in the same flat tone I'd used, 'I haven't seen Mr Guest since Friday, have you?'

'He's gone to Manchester,' I said.

'Who says?'

'*I* say.' I told him about my chance meeting with Mr Guest on my way home to lunch yesterday. 'He said he was in a hurry,' I finished.

'Lunchtime?' Chaz said. 'You mean one o'clock?'

'Earlier, I think,' I said warily. I still couldn't tell the time, a failure which drew yelps of derisive laughter from Tom, who had been able to read a clock for years; so I always took care to be vague about it. The best I could do was to blow the fuzz off a dandelion clock, and count how many puffs it took, but I was pretty sure the method was unreliable.

'That's funny,' Chaz said. 'I saw his car going towards Fairhurst yesterday about that time. And Fairhurst is in the wrong direction if you're going to Manchester. He turned into the drive of that big house on the marshes.'

'It can't have been him, then,' I said stoutly, concealing

the shock I felt. I didn't want to believe that Mr Guest had told me a fib.

'Or maybe,' Mr Channing put in, making one of his rare interventions in our conversations, 'he had to call on someone first before he set out for Manchester.'

'The house is empty,' Chaz said with the sort of suppressed satisfaction Tom used when he huffed three of my kings in one move. 'It's been up for sale for years.'

'Then it may have been someone else; someone who was thinking of buying the house,' Mr Channing said.

'Well . . .' Chaz said. 'The car was a long way away, but I'm pretty sure it was Mr Guest's Humber. He's got the only Snipe around here.' But Mr Channing appeared to have lost interest in the subject, and Chaz, taking his cue from his uncle's pointed silence, said no more.

I was suddenly certain that Chaz was right, and I felt betrayed. Mr Guest hadn't been in such a hurry after all. He *could* have given me a ride on the running-board. My liking for him wavered for a moment until the thought occurred to me that perhaps Mr Channing was right and Chaz, for all his eagle-eyed vigilance, *could* have been mistaken. After all, it was quite a long way from the road to the house on the marshes. And, though cars were rare, especially on our side of the river, it *might* have been somebody else's; some holidaymaker's, some house-hunter's. The thought cheered me up and when the waiter came I asked Mr Channing if I could have a Knickerbocker Glory.

'Have whatever you like,' he said with the faint, lopsided smile which was all the scar allowed him.

I could hardly believe my luck. Up to now, I'd only ever seen pictures of this magical thing in the window of the ice-cream parlour in Moravon, and now I was really, thrillingly, going to taste one.

When it came I ate it in a slow sweet ecstasy,

relishing, separately and together, the flavours of cream and ice cream, nuts, fruit, and strawberry sauce. It seemed to me that I had never been so ravished in my life, and probably never would be again; and I had Mr Channing to thank for it.

I took his hand again when we came out. It was a hard, cool, bony hand, and it held mine loosely, as if Mr Channing had never been in the habit of holding hands with anyone.

Jenkins was sitting waiting in the car. He had tucked his top lip up above his gums again, but this time, his teeth were showing dangerously white and long as if he had just snarled at someone, and far from looking sentimental his eyes glared out maniacally from behind the window. He looked capable of tearing us to shreds – until he saw Mr Channing. It occurred to me that he couldn't have looked more frightening if he had been the mad old man's evil familiar. A startling question suddenly leapt up at the back of my mind, but I dismissed it at once with a shudder. Lots of old men had dogs. It was just too silly to compare Mr Channing and Jenkins with the two murderous monsters who had lived at Llwyn-yr-eos before them. Mr Channing and Jenkins just happened to have moved into the same house, that was all.

When I opened the car door to return to the back seat, Mr Channing said, 'You can sit in the front with us, you know. There's room for all of us. Unless you *prefer* the back seat.'

It was only then that I noticed that the big American car's front seat ran the whole width of the car, like a sofa.

'Oh yes, please,' I said happily and climbed into the front seat beside Chaz.

We drove up the stone bridge which spanned the

railway and the river, and began the winding journey down the other side of the valley, back to the coast, the sun now in our eyes. We got glimpses of the river, a dazzling silver snake, as the road wound in and out between trees and hillocks, and Chaz began to worry about the tide again.

'The *Slug* will probably be aground by the time we get there,' he mourned.

But Mr Channing was unmoved. 'The tide's half an hour later today than it was yesterday, don't forget,' he pointed out tranquilly. 'And we managed to negotiate the channels yesterday without going aground.'

When we got to Moravon, *Love Nest* and *Sea Slug* were still where we had left them, tied up below the slipway, and the quayside was as crowded with holiday-makers as it had been before the thunderstorm. What I most envied about these people from away was that none of them seemed to care that it was Sunday: they were dressed as casually and they behaved as freely – laughing and shouting to each other, licking ice-creams and eating chips – as if it had been a weekday.

We escaped from the heat of the car into the gusting breeze as if released from prison. Jenkins raced down and leapt aboard without waiting for the rest of us to catch up.

'What happened to the fish we caught?' I asked, seeing the cockpit empty.

'Took them home with us, of course,' Chaz said. 'In the boot. Had the bass for supper. You don't think we'd have left them to rot after all that, do you?' And to his uncle he said, 'I can take the *Slug* home, Uncle Hil, if you don't want to leave the car here.'

'Henderson can fetch her back tomorrow,' Mr Channing said, climbing into the cockpit. He set about unhitching *Sea Slug*'s mooring rope from one of the iron rings in the harbour wall.

Chaz tried to argue. 'It's only a couple of miles, Uncle Hil. I can do that with my eyes shut.'

Mr Channing paused with the painter in his hands and turned to Chaz. A gust of wind whipped his white mane across his face. 'Did you remember to take your phenobarb?' he asked meaningfully.

Chaz hesitated a moment too long. 'I think so,' he said, and looked downcast.

I couldn't understand this exchange, and looked from one to the other, hoping for an explanation, but none came.

'So you see,' Mr Channing said, as though we all understood, 'it's better if we all go back together. Cast off at the stern, Charles.'

Away from the shelter of the harbour wall the water was choppy under the breeze, the wavelets glittering in the sun. Watched by the crowds on the quayside (we were setting out into mortal danger, perhaps to our doom, while the watching crowd paid silent tribute to our cool courage), we threaded our way between the sandbanks left by the retreating tide, and headed across the harbour towards the channel which ran along the far side – our side – of the river.

Chaz had been silent, still dejected, since the exchange with his great-uncle, but as we drew abreast of the Point his spirits began to revive. He was standing at the wheel and I was beside him, leaning my forearms on the deck above the cabin.

'Why don't we go back to the place where we found Mr Ransom's boat, and see if there's any sign of him?' he asked his uncle. 'There might be other bits of his clothes washed up on the beach, or he might be lying in the sandhills on the Point somewhere.'

I liked this idea; it sounded exciting, like hide-and-seek or Hunt the Slipper. Clearly Chaz didn't want to go home, and neither did I: we both wanted to stay out here on the water, with the sunny waves slapping at the prow, the boat dipping and rocking through them, and the breeze combing our hair. Occasionally, at the whim of the cloud-hunting sun, the heat of the day vanished abruptly and we were plunged into chilly shadow, but the warmth always came blissfully back once the cloud-shadow had slipped over us. I looked over my shoulder at the sandy spit we called the Point, a barren stretch of sand dunes and marram grass. Perhaps in those dunes, using my tracker's skill, I could find Teddy Ransom . . . I became a national heroine, the girl who found the world-famous yachtsman half-drowned in the sandhills, and revived him with the magic potion the Red Indians had given me . . . I was just beginning to enjoy my fame when Chaz spoke again.

'What do you think, Uncle Hil?' he asked. 'Can't we try?'

We looked round at Mr Channing, but he barely paused over the pipe he was filling, tamping the tobacco down with the corner of his matchbox; and without looking up, he said, 'The police have already searched the place. It's unlikely they could have overlooked a decent-sized pebble, let alone a full-grown man.'

We were approaching the bridge. Under its span I could see River Cottage, and from an upstairs window a big, brightly coloured beach towel hung, idly rippling in the wind. I groaned.

'I'll have to go home anyway,' I said resignedly. 'My mother wants me back.'

Chaz was puzzled. 'How do you know?' he asked. 'Did she tell you to be back by a certain time?'

Fiff did not allow pointing – it was bad manners – so I shrugged and tipped my head towards the house. 'She always hangs that big beach towel out of her bedroom window when she wants us back,' I explained. 'I 'spec some visitors have arrived.'

I meant that I *hoped* some visitors had arrived, but I could see Eric's car still there, parked at the garden gate with his suitcases stowed in the dicky, and I had a pretty good idea that Fiff was only summoning me home to say goodbye to him. She was a stickler for the courtesies, and Eric had, after all, given me an expensive birthday present. Fiff probably thought, too, that I had spent quite long enough on my visit to the Channings. *Don't overstay your welcome* was always her strictest instruction whenever we were invited anywhere.

We chugged unhurriedly up the channel, and presently Chaz guided the boat to the foot of the stone steps. 'Are you coming out again later?' he asked as I clambered out.

'If I can,' I said gloomily. 'I expect I'll have to stay until my cousin leaves, and he may not go for ages.' The thought depressed me: Eric's company, even for a short while, required more good behaviour than I was really capable of.

To Mr Channing, I said, 'Thank you very much for inviting me. I'll never ever forget the Knickerbocker Glory. It was—' I searched for a word to describe it, 'it was *heavenly*,' I finished, proud to have found such a sophisticated word. It was the sort of word Mrs Guest would have used.

'It was a pleasure to have you, Fidgie,' he said, equally formally. 'You must come again.' I knew very well that grown-ups said things like that without really meaning them: I had done nothing to give him any pleasure, so obviously it couldn't be true, but it made me glow with pride all the same. I just wished Cly had been there to hear it; though, on second thoughts, it would only have infuriated her, and Cly in a rage was something to avoid at all costs.

'See you sometime then,' Chaz said breezily, and revved up the engine.

I watched from the top of the steps as they drew away from the landing-place, ready to wave if they looked round, but neither of them did, so I made my way across the road and up the garden path. The front door was standing open as always on summer days, and a warm smell of baking, drifting from the kitchen, lingered in the hall.

Fiff was in the pantry making sandwiches, cutting the bread as thin as lace. She looked round when I entered and sighed.

'I see you've come home looking like a scarecrow as usual,' she said resignedly. 'You've managed to ruin your new dress.' I looked down at my dress and noticed the grey smears on bodice and skirt, probably acquired when Chaz and I were building the tree house. Ineffectually, I caught up two handfuls of material and began rubbing them together, but then her next words electrocuted me.

'And what have you done with my embroidery bag? You *did* remember to bring it back with you, I hope?'

I froze. What had I done with it? I stared back the way I had come, in the wild hope that it might be following me like some faithful, forgotten hound. I had no idea when I'd seen it last. Had I left it in the cove where we'd found Mr Ransom's cap?

'I think I left it at Mr Channing's house,' I said, hoping it was true, though I had uncomfortable visions of Fiff's bag licked off the shingle by the tide and floating down the river, to sink into the bottomless pool, never to be seen again. I tried not to look as alarmed as I felt.

'Oh, for goodness' sake!' Fiff exclaimed in exasperation. 'I might have known. I never knew a child with a head so full of jollyrobins. Well, you'll just have to go back and find it.'

I started back towards the front door, but she stopped me.

'*Not now!* We're having tea early so that Eric can get home before dark. Wash your hands and then see if you can find the lace doilies.'

I obeyed hurriedly, hoping to make up in helpfulness for my latest lapse, though I knew that only the safe return of Fiff's embroidery bag would restore me to favour, and even then she wouldn't forget the initial gaffe, and I would be reminded of my irresponsibility for ever after. I could hardly bear to wait until I was free to go and look for it. While I scurried about I prayed silently and fervently *Please, tide, please don't come in yet.*

When the sandwiches had been made and the lemon cheese tarts, the sponge cake and maids of honour set out on plates, I followed Fiff out through the kitchen door, across the yard and up the steps into the garden, carrying the smaller of the trays, the one with the teapot and hot-water jug and sugar bowl. They were only electro-plated nickel silver – it said so on the bottom – and very plain, so it wouldn't matter much if I dropped them, or not as much as it would if it had been the *real* silver tea service; but that was only taken out into the garden if somebody frightful came, like Auntie Gertrude. We all knew that Auntie Gertrude, who was Fiff's eldest sister, must be prevented at all costs from getting a bad impression of us; must not be allowed to think that we lived like gypsies. Even Fiff was scared of Auntie Gertie, though she pretended not to be.

The garden, like the interior of the house, was a cheerful muddle, a ragbag of hydrangeas and horse-radish, peas and parsley, potatoes, carrots and poppies, lavender and marguerites and montbretias, all planted wherever Fiff had found a spare niche, or wherever they had seeded themselves, though some effort had been made to separate the vegetables from the flowers and shrubs. At the far end of the garden, where bare rock emerged taller than a wall at the base of the big knoll, the row of runner beans stood, still bearing its generous offerings of scarlet flowers and pendant pods.

Cly and Eric were sitting sunbathing in the faded deck-chairs round the table, and Pipsy was lying panting in the shade under it. Tom and I had helped Fiff make the table out of spare bricks we'd found in the rubble left over from the building of the houses. Across the top of the two short pillars we'd built with the bricks, Fiff had laid the white marble top of an old-fashioned washstand. There was just room between the pillars to push the lawnmower through, if we ever got a lawnmower. I considered the result very handsome.

'Tom not back yet?' Fiff asked, putting the tray down.

Eric pushed his panama back from his forehead and said, 'No sign of him.' His hair, newly brilliantined, shone like a black mirror. Smoke from his cigarette drifted idly down his nostrils. Nowadays he wore Oxford bags, but I could never really trust him not to turn up in those plus-fours again.

'He went off with that fat boy from the farm,' Cly said with distaste. 'And that monkey-faced little squirt from the smithy.' She was rewarded with a burst of laughter from Eric and Fiff.

I saw an opportunity to get away and look for the embroidery bag before it was too late. 'Shall I go and bring Tom back?' I volunteered.

'You stay where you are,' Fiff said, subsiding into a deck-chair near the teapot. 'You can pass things round.'

'He'll come back when he's hungry,' Eric said.

Something about the smug way he said it got my goat. How dare he talk about Tom like that, as if he owned him, knew what he would do? Before I could stop myself I started arguing. 'Not if he has tea with Dick at the farm,' I said, courting displeasure. Fiff had told me off hundreds of times for contradicting. When Eric's face began to crease into a scowl, I added hastily, 'But he'll come back for a ride on the running-board.'

I wasn't hungry really, and anyway I wanted my tongue to go on remembering the Knickerbocker Glory, but Fiff's maids of honour were irresistible. For once, she had placed the pastry crosses neatly over the crust of ground almonds. Usually she didn't care whether they were straight or not. She caught my hand as I reached out for one.

'Behave yourself, child,' she said mildly. 'You know you're not allowed to eat cake first.'

Dutifully I took a sandwich instead. It was filled with potted meat, savoury and succulent, and if I'd been hungry I'd have wolfed it. As it was, after the first mouthful I felt I couldn't manage any more. Pipsy seemed to know it. She squirmed round under the table and looked up at me hopefully. I sneaked a quick look round at the others. Nobody was watching: they were idly discussing the route Eric would take on his journey home, and Fiff began reminding him of messages to take to Auntie Meg, his mother.

I broke off a corner of the sandwich and slipped it to Pipsy under cover of the table.

Cly said, 'Ma, she's giving that sandwich to the dog.'

Everyone broke off and stared at me. 'No, I wasn't,' I lied, mortified. 'A bit fell off.'

'I *saw* you!' Cly persisted, 'you handed it to her deliberately.'

'Only after it fell off,' I insisted. I could hear my voice

rising with desperation. Accusations always did that to me, especially if they were true. Soon I would be shouting, and then Fiff would be annoyed and I would probably be sent to bed for bad behaviour.

Tom saved me. He burst through the side gate with a whoop. 'Hooray!' he yelled when he saw Eric. 'I thought you might have gone. You haven't forgotten you promised me a ride?'

'Only as far as the railway crossing.'

'That's a *swizz*!' Tom exclaimed, outraged. 'You said as far as the main road.'

'Now Tom, don't pester,' Fiff said, 'or Eric won't want to take you anywhere.' But she sounded tired and the rebuke was only half-hearted.

The sandwich and Pipsy and I were forgotten while Eric and Tom struck a deal. They finally agreed on the main road, on condition that Tom open and close the crossing gates to let the car through. I was so busy wondering if I could wheedle my way into Eric's good books far enough to get a ride on the other running-board, that I lowered the sandwich to my lap and hardly noticed when Pipsy gently relieved me of the rest of it.

I could feel Cly's basilisk glare drilling into me as I reached for a maid of honour, but I took good care not to look at her.

I had to walk back alone from the main road. Ungraciously as usual, Eric had allowed me a ride on the other running-board, and to show my gratitude, I had opened and closed both the railway gates, though I made Tom help me close the second one, in case Eric drove off while I was closing it: it was the sort of thing he did. But when we got to the main road and jumped down and Eric drove away, Tom sped off to the village to resume his interrupted play with Dick and Jacko.

I started after him, yelling, 'Tom! Wait for me!' But he only turned round, jogging backwards, to yell back, 'Push off, Fidge. We don't want girls.'

Furious, I shouted after him, 'I bet you're doing something you shouldn't. You wait till Fiff finds out!'

'We're collecting conkers. So there!'

I knew this couldn't be true because it was too early for conkers – they weren't ripe enough to fall yet – but there was nothing for it but to swallow the lie and go back home. He knew very well that I wouldn't tell Fiff, because I never did.

But before he could disappear round the bend in the road, I made a last desperate attempt to hold him. 'I've got something to *tell* you,' I shrieked, hoping I'd be able to think of something if he took the bait, but he refused it.

His reply came back distantly as he finally disappeared, 'Tell me after.'

I set off back down the track we called Blackberry Lane. The hedges on either side of it were tall and sprawling and laced with convolvulus and wild rose – over now – and brambles. The blackberries were still red, nowhere near ripe, but I plucked one and bit into it, hoping its bitterness would take my mind off Tom's desertion. There had been a time, before we came here, when Tom and I had been inseparable. It had been Tom's idea to give our parents secret names – Fiff and Boko – names that only he and I would know. I missed him badly, but though I still tried not to believe it, it became increasingly clear that I had lost him the moment we started going to school. In Ceylon, Fiff had taught us and we were always together. We had even run away from home together once, when Fiff, to our deep disgruntlement, moved us on from the two-times to the three-times table. It dawned on us that there might even be a four-times table, and we decided that the time had come to make a stand.

But that was long ago when I was young – four, or maybe five – and the jungle, which we were used to, held fewer terrors for us than the impenetrable tangles of arithmetic Fiff was forcing us to struggle through.

Sometime, unnoticed, the breeze had dropped. The air was still, not merely because the high hedges sheltered the lane from the wind: their shaggy tops, which should have been thrashing wildly in the gusts, stood motionless. The vast white clouds had slipped down the dome of the sky, and now lay crushed into creamy folds above the distant mountains, discarded banners of a retreating army. The day was settling into a quiet, golden evening.

A butterfly – a peacock – exhausted by the gale or stupefied by the day's nectar, landed on my arm, but before I had time to study it, it flew away again to land on a tangle of honeysuckle in the hedge.

Where the lane forked, one branch leading to the railway junction, I bore right, over the crossing, the way we had come, and clambered over the railway gates without bothering to open them.

The hedges came to an end at the first of the gates as if the railway lines had sheared them off; after the second, the marshes began. Sheep scattered into the clumps of sedge as I jumped down and began to make my way back along the track towards the two knolls half a mile away. To the east, the distant hills appeared to meet at the head of the valley. Like the clouds, they too seemed to have folded themselves up and retreated, still multi-coloured with sunshine and shadow, still jewel clear, but with a quiet contemplative tranquillity about them, as if preparing not just for the end of day, but for the end of summer too.

But perhaps, I thought, trying to think of something to look forward to, perhaps now that Eric was gone, now that we had the house to ourselves again, Fiff could be persuaded – as she sometimes was, for a treat – to play us to bed with *The Robin's Return* on the old upright piano in the drawing-room.

I was still a long way off the knolls, dragging my feet and trying to think of something else to do till suppertime, when Chaz swung down from a branch of one of the oaks and stood waving his arms like a semaphore, signalling to me to come quickly. Until that moment, the embroidery bag had completely vanished from my mind, but now it came back with a new and even more chilling urgency, and I began to run towards him.

'Chaz!' I gasped as soon as he was within earshot, 'I lost my mother's bag. Have you seen it? The one with the—'

'Calm down,' he said. 'You left it in Uncle Hil's study. It's OK: I brought it back.'

I stared at him open-mouthed, hardly daring to believe that salvation had been so easy. 'Then where is it?'

'There didn't seem to be anyone in at your place—'

'They're out in the garden, at the back—'

'—so I left it on the chest in the hall.'

'Oh Chaz—!' I clapped my hand to my heart, rolled my eyes, and reeled about in a pantomime of relief. 'You've saved my life. You can't think—'

But he cut my thanks short. 'That's OK; forget it,' he said impatiently. 'There's something interesting going on, down on the river. I saw them when I was bringing your bag back and I hung around in case you turned up. Come and see.'

As he spoke he set off again up the knoll. I toiled after him, demanding, 'See who ... what?'

But he ignored this. 'We'd better keep out of sight, just in case.'

'In case of *what*?'

'In case they see us, of course. The police. They've got a boat and long poles and grappling hooks and things, and they've been poking about in the water all the way down the river. It must be because we found Mr Ransom's cap. I don't know how far up they started, but they're almost as far as Holly Hill now. Come on, but keep out of sight. If they see us watching, they're sure to chase us off.'

We knew perfectly well that the police were unlikely to find any more of Mr Ransom's clothes, because he had disappeared out at sea, but it didn't matter: this was the best fun we'd had all day. We worked our way down off the knoll, keeping low by running doubled up through the bracken and dashing across the track until we reached the cypress plantation. There, we flattened ourselves and wormed our way forward on our elbows until we could see the river, but the view was partly obscured by the branches, which grew densely right down to the ground, and we were still a good distance from the men in the boat.

'Keep your voice down,' Chaz warned. 'Sound carries over water.'

Even though nothing much happened for ages, it was fun lying there spying, whispering conspiratorially and suppressing giggles when we tried, with increasing inventiveness, to guess what the police might find. The giggles got more delicious as the jokes got wilder and ruder.

After a while, when we were both exhausted with laughter, I began to wish we had something to eat, to pass the time, and Chaz, who never seemed to be at a loss, produced a bar of nut milk chocolate from his shirt pocket and shared it with me. It was warm and slightly limp from being pressed against the warmth of his chest, but it melted all the better for that.

While we were eating it, the policemen had reached the part of the bottomless pool directly under Holly Hill and continued their patient probing, but it was all taking too long and nothing much was happening, and once the chocolate was finished, I began to get restless. Besides, I had to keep brushing woodlice and earwigs and tiny spiders off my arms.

'I'm fed up,' I said. 'They aren't going to find anything, and even if they do, it won't be interesting. Let's do something else.'

'Like what?' Chaz said. 'It's too late to go anywhere. The sun will be setting before long, and you'll have to be home before it does.'

'It won't set for hours yet,' I said, grumpy because of this reminder. I didn't *want* the sun to set.

While we were debating it, the sound of the men's voices changed from the routine and businesslike to a sudden alertness, and their activity increased.

'They've found something,' Chaz said with sharpened interest.

The branches made it difficult to see much. And then, almost as if they knew we were watching, as if they wanted to prevent us from seeing whatever it was they had found, the men swung the boat round so that its bows were pointing towards us while they manhandled their find over the stern, their bodies completely blocking our view. Perhaps our giggles and suppressed shrieks of laughter had been heard in spite of the care we'd taken to clap our hands over our mouths.

And after all that, the only thing they'd managed to dredge up, as far as I could see, was something bound with a heavy chain.

It looked like a dripping bundle of old clothes, except that it seemed to have a foot, white as marble, sticking out of it.

11

I thought at first that it must be a guy left over from last Guy Fawkes' Night, but that was unlikely because who would go to the trouble of making a guy only to deny themselves the thrill of burning it? Burning the guy on top of the bonfire was the *highlight* of Bonfire Night. Besides, the policemen were clearly satisfied with their find: they were packing up all their gear and making preparations to leave. Perhaps Mr Ransom had thrown *all* his clothes overboard, not just his cap. It seemed a strange thing to do, puzzling; but then, rich people were always doing things like that, throwing away stuff they'd hardly used.

'What do you suppose it was?' I asked, and when Chaz didn't reply, I looked over my shoulder at him.

The look on his face alarmed me. All his earlier laughter had drained out of it and he looked sick.

'Let's get out of here,' was all he said.

'Don't you feel well?' I asked nervously. I was afraid that he was going to have another of his strange blackouts, and I didn't want to see it.

'I'm OK,' he said tersely, turning and beginning to squirm his way out of the hedge. 'Let's go home.'

It was easier to pull ourselves along on our stomachs than to try to stand up, but at least we didn't need to worm our way the whole length of the hedge as we'd done when we first arrived, and moments later we were out in the open again and brushing the twigs off our clothes.

'I'm going home,' Chaz said. 'I've got to tell Uncle Hil.'

'Tell him what?'

'That they've found Mr Ransom.'

'But they haven't. They only found some old clothes.'

'You can't have been looking,' Chaz said furiously. For some inexplicable reason he was angry with me. 'Didn't you see the trouble they had getting it into the boat? It was *heavy*! That wasn't just some old clothes. That was Mr Ransom's body.'

'Oh!' I said, shocked into silence for once. Then, remembering Teddy's boat drifting out at sea, I tried to argue. 'But how could he be here, when his boat was right out past the Point?'

'I think,' he said bleakly, 'I think someone killed him.'

I remembered Mrs Guest's face as I'd seen it yesterday, watching Teddy with that other woman; and an image of Mr Guest's shotgun raced through my mind. I saw it all: Teddy, the two-timing lover, arriving in his boat, and Mrs Guest waiting for him, stepping out from the boat-house with the shotgun in her hands, her face wild with jealousy: it was just like a scene from a film.

'You mean Mrs Guest *shot* him?' I exclaimed excitedly.

But Chaz had already turned towards home. 'How do I know? Maybe someone hit him on the head with a rock,' he said irritably, and broke into a run.

His sudden departure left me at a loss for a moment, but I didn't mind too much because now I really did have something interesting to tell Tom, and I began to relish the prospect of having his undivided attention at last.

I stared after Chaz for a while before turning to go home, but as I did, I caught my breath and stopped

177

dead. All thought of Teddy Ransom went out of my head. There was a big, dark red car, a Studebaker, parked outside River Cottage: Boko's car. Boko always arrived like this, suddenly and unexpectedly.

For a wild moment I thought of running after Chaz and begging him to let me hide at Llwyn-yr-eos, but the thought died almost as soon as it was born. Chaz wouldn't understand, would think me mad, and Fiff would be angry with me for betraying family secrets to outsiders. I climbed down over boulders to the river bed and went to hide behind an outcrop of rock while I thought what to do. I hadn't bitten my nails so much in the days since I'd been with Chaz, but they came in useful again now, as an aid to concentration. I could cope with Cly because I had to, and I did it mostly by keeping out of her way, but Boko was different. If I hid from him, he would demand to see me, and if I didn't appear, Fiff would get the blame.

The tide was running strongly, and out beyond the bridge, beyond the sand dunes of the Point, the sun was low in the sky, making its way steadily down towards a bank of grey cloud lying in wait just above the horizon. I dared not put off my return much longer.

At last, when the tide began to lap my sandals, I emerged and walked slowly home. Perhaps this time things would be better; perhaps this time Boko would be different, miraculously changed . . . and anyway, he never stayed long. This last thought cheered me.

I heard his voice as soon as I entered the hall, and to my intense relief he didn't sound at all angry. But then, he was nearly always in a good mood when he first arrived. He had probably brought sweets and cream cakes. All the same, I moved down the hall cautiously. Somehow I always managed to do something to annoy him, and it was better to delay being seen as long as possible.

He and Fiff were in the drawing-room, talking, and the door stood slightly ajar. I listened anxiously, but there were none of the ugly, familiar sounds I dreaded so much: the shouting, the thud of a fist into flesh, the crash of a body hurled against furniture, the suppressed cries of pain. Yet even though there seemed to be nothing to worry about, it wasn't worth taking any risks. Judging by his voice, Boko was standing over by the window, probably with his back to it, which would explain why he hadn't seen me entering the house. Either that, or he was more interested in his conversation with Fiff, and that suited me; but if he were standing by the window, it meant that he would be more likely to see me and call me in if I were to pass that half-open door, so I hovered indecisively. I was caught in a snare: likely to be seen whether I went forward or back, certain to be in even worse trouble if I were caught standing here eavesdropping. I was so busy worrying about passing that gap that it took me some time to notice what was being said, but the tone of Fiff's voice suddenly alerted me.

She was saying, 'You haven't paid back the last two loans yet, and I have these children to bring up. I *can't* lend you any more, Thorp. I've nothing *left* to lend.' She sounded desperate but determined.

'You've no business to have money of your own. I'm your husband: your money should be mine by rights, Missis.' Boko seemed to know that the coarseness of this address intimidated Fiff, offended her, reminding her that he despised the polite society she had once belonged to.

'You *know* I can't touch the capital—'

Boko made a sound in his throat which sounded halfway between a grunt and a snarl. 'You bought this house against my wishes. If you wanted to buy a house, you could just as well have bought one in a civilized place. But no, you had to buy one in this God-forsaken dump, miles from anywhere. You did it deliberately. To defy me.'

This was frightening: the worst thing any of us could do was to defy Boko. His voice was getting louder, taking on that hard edge which came before the full force of his rage broke, and sick tremors of apprehension started in my stomach. Now that I was alert, I could sense the tension inside the room even out here in the hall, and I bit hard on my thumbnail.

In a small voice as if she didn't expect to be believed, didn't really believe it herself, Fiff said, 'I bought it because it was so cheap. I couldn't have afforded to buy a house anywhere else.'

Judging by the snort he gave, Boko dismissed this, but when he spoke again his voice was lower, almost jolly, as if Fiff's explanation had mollified him. He said, 'Anyway, now you've got it, you can borrow on the deeds. Or better still, hand them over, and I'll borrow on them.'

Fiff said in a voice of barely controlled alarm, 'I can't. They're at the solicitor's.'

'Then get them out.'

'I can't. He'd want to know why.'

After a long moment of heavy silence, Boko said in a voice which seemed to clinch the argument, 'Louie and Frank are still willing to adopt Tom. You can't give him the sort of education a son of mine should have, and they can.'

Standing up to Boko was foolhardiness of the worst kind, and when Fiff began to say something which sounded like 'Tom's not for sale . . .' he raised his voice to a frightening roar and cut across her, silencing her. The noise was terrifying.

'He's my son, and I've every right to take him whether you like it or not. Get that into your head.' An ominous silence fell, lasting for what seemed an age before he went on, 'So he'll be coming back with me. You savvy?' I could imagine, because I'd seen it so often, that he had backed her up against the wall, his face pushed into hers. At last, satisfied that the thunderous roaring had had the desired effect of cowing her, he went on, 'I'm not having my son turned into a sissy, growing up in a houseful of women. And since you make out you're so poor, you ought to be grateful to Louie and Frank for taking him off your hands.'

I had understood nothing so far, except that some sort of threat hung over us, but this I understood all too well: I was going to lose Tom altogether and I had to warn him. Fear of losing him, my only ally, was worse than my fear of getting caught eavesdropping and I made a dash past the door on tiptoe and out through the kitchen and the yard to the back gate, determined to catch him on his way home and warn him.

I was just in time. Tom, cheerfully dishevelled, appeared at the gate as I reached it.

'Don't go in!' I gasped. 'He's going to take you away.'

'Who is? What are you talking about?'

'Boko,' I hissed. 'He's here and he's going to take you away to live with Uncle Frank and Auntie Louie.'

His reaction was not what I expected. I thought that he would be as horrified as I, that he would join with me in planning to escape, to run away and hide until Boko had gone away. But instead of the dismay I thought this news would bring, his face lit up, and he said, 'Really? That's great! Yippee! Good old Boko!' and leapt over the gate in sheer delight.

His treachery stunned me. Miserably, I said, 'I thought you liked it here.'

'It's OK,' he said, shrugging. 'But if I lived with Uncle Frank I could have all sorts of things . . . a bicycle even, and a *whole* Hornby train set, not just bits . . . and I could buy a Dinky car *every* week!' The list of luxuries came out so pat that it was clear he must have thought about it often, the way I dreamed about my secret house.

As he rushed past me, eager to hear Boko confirm the joyful news, I caught his sleeve and begged, 'Don't tell him I told you! Pretend you don't know!' but he paused only long enough to say dismissively, 'Oh, OK,' before he disappeared into the kitchen.

I climbed the steps into the garden. The deck-chairs were still there but the tea things had been cleared away, and the shadows were lengthening over the lawn. I sat on my hands on the marble tabletop and wondered if I dared take my secret route over the wash-house roof to hide in my bedroom. There was always the risk that I'd be caught doing it, but I'd been lucky so far. I stood up, but even as I made for the roof of the wash-house, I heard Mr Bellamy's voice in the yard next door, and presently I heard Mrs Bellamy, unseen behind the high hedge, come into her garden to round up the chickens and shoo them into their coop for the night.

'Come along, girls,' she was saying affectionately, 'Beddy-byes.'

The shadow of the hedge had reached the table. The heat of the past few weeks had gone, the settled weather broken by the thunderstorm. It was getting cold and a shiver ran through me. There was nothing for it but to give in and go back into the house.

Fiff was in the kitchen, stooping to light one of the wicks of the oil stove.

'Your father's here,' she said, glancing up. And then, taking in my dishevelled state, she straightened up and added in an urgent half-whisper, 'For heaven's sake, child, you look as if you've just slept the night in a ditch. He'll be annoyed if he sees you looking like that. Upstairs at once! Get washed and change your frock. Quickly, before he sees you. And comb those twigs out of your hair while you're about it.'

Taking my cue from her, I lowered my voice and asked, 'Is he going to take Tom away?'

She didn't ask me how I knew. She bent again to adjust the wick and replace the enamelled chimney. Her hands were shaking – the chimney clattered as she tried to replace it and she had difficulty reseating it – but her voice was as controlled as ever, and that was reassuring. Nothing bad had happened.

'Only for a holiday,' she said without looking at me. 'Now go and do as you're told.'

I fled upstairs as quietly as possible, scaring myself at every step with the thought that Boko might emerge downstairs and call me back to face him before I'd had a chance to tidy myself up.

Cly was coming from the direction of my bedroom – or perhaps Fiff's – as I reached the top step. She took in my dishevelment at a glance, and as I passed her she drew back with elaborate distaste and held her nose.

'You dirty little tick,' she remarked with satisfaction as I dived into the bathroom. 'I doubt if *you*'ll ever be invited to the Channings' again.'

'Well, I *am* invited again,' I muttered to the wash-basin as I turned the taps. 'So there!'

But was it true? Perhaps Mr Channing and Chaz secretly despised me for my slatternliness but had been too polite to say so. Perhaps Cly was right, and I never would be invited again, in spite of Mr Channing's parting words. I remembered how Chaz had pulled my chair out for me in the hotel dining-room, and how, when we walked up a street together, he always made a point of moving to the outside of the pavement. I'd found his formal good manners confusing

183

at first, embarrassing too, because I felt sure he knew they were wasted on an urchin like me: he was just showing me that he was used to more polished companions.

I dawdled through my washing and changing. We weren't really supposed to use Fiff's purple soap – it was too expensive and special – but there were times when I couldn't resist it: it turned the water a fascinating shade of pale mauve, and its scent was entrancing.

From the landing, as I made for my bedroom, I could hear the voices of the others downstairs. Tom, especially, sounded happy and excited, probably because of the visit to Auntie Louie and Uncle Frank; but even Fiff's and Cly's voices were the same as always. The normality of it all was reassuring, and my spirits began to rise. Perhaps I had only imagined that there was a threat hanging over us. After all, Boko had only been *talking*, he had hardly shouted at all. And perhaps this time he would be pleased with me; maybe this time I could manage not to annoy him. Presently, as I was pulling a clean dress over my head, Cly called upstairs, 'Fidgie! You're to come downstairs and make yourself useful,' and because by this time I had convinced myself that if I behaved myself, nothing could go wrong between now and bedtime, especially now that I was clean and tidy, I stopped dawdling and ran downstairs.

Tom had gone outside with Boko to the car: I could hear their voices through the open front door, and I was grateful for Tom's obsession with cars: it meant that I was safe from Boko's notice for a little while longer. From the clink of cutlery, I guessed that Cly – who usually stayed in her bedroom with Pipsy until a meal was ready – was laying the table in the dining-room. As I passed the open door, she said, 'This is your job. I wouldn't have had to do it if you hadn't spent so long trying to turn yourself into a fashion plate.'

When I didn't answer, she shouted after me, 'You were wasting your time, Pig Face.'

I longed to make a crushing reply, but all I could think of was *Pig Face yourself*. It wasn't as witty or as withering as I would have liked, and besides, it was obviously untrue – Cly was the acknowledged beauty of the family – but I muttered it anyway under my breath.

The kitchen was very warm. Fiff had lit the kitchen range that morning as she always did on Sundays, to roast the joint and heat the water for baths. The fire in the kitchen range was dying down now, and Fiff was cooking on the paraffin stove, frying tomatoes in butter.

'Make the toast, child,' she said when I entered. 'You'll find the slices ready cut in the pantry. Two for your father.'

I held the bread to the embers glowing behind the bars at the front of the range, turning the toasting fork to make sure the toast didn't brown in stripes, another thing Boko wouldn't have liked. Halfway through, he returned with Tom from the car.

Boko was a big man: to me he seemed huge. The kitchen, which I'd always thought spacious, shrank around him until we all seemed to be standing in a huddle in the middle, much too close to him, boxed in by the walls.

'Well, Fidgie!' he said jovially when he saw me. He seemed to have a secret source of satisfaction; and whatever it was, he was in high good humour about it.

'Hallo, Daddy,' I said, and added with careful politeness, 'Did you have a good journey?' Boko liked to be asked about his journeys.

'First rate,' he said jovially. 'Absolutely top hole. No traffic even driving through Manchester. Made good time.' He and Tom both carried handfuls of paper bags: the sweets – brightly coloured fondants and candies – he usually brought with him.

'And some cream cakes especially for your mother,' he said, holding out a shallow white box. 'Your mother will do anything for a cream cake, won't you, Fran?'

Fiff didn't look and didn't thank him. 'Put them in the pantry,' she said without enthusiasm. 'The cream will go sour in here.'

I was afraid that his good mood would evaporate with this rebuff, but her response seemed to amuse him hugely. He gave the box to Tom and rubbed his hands together with tremendous satisfaction.

'Are you going to be here long?' I asked – craftily, I thought – and this amused him even more. He roared with laughter.

'Trying to get rid of me already?' he asked.

Caught out and appalled, I hastened to deny it. 'No, Daddy. I only meant . . . I meant you don't usually stay long.'

'Well, you'll be pleased to hear I'll be off again tomorrow. Your mother and I had some business to attend to, and now that's settled, I'm off back. Tom will be coming with me. He's going to stay with your Auntie Louie and Uncle Frank.'

I didn't much like Auntie Louie, who was Boko's sister, but she and Uncle were so rich that they could do anything they liked, an ability I envied and hoped I too might acquire when I grew up. They even went to the theatre and knew all the stars of the musical comedies. It was exciting to be so close to wealth, so wreathed in scented luxury, and I said, 'Could I come too?'

'You'll have to wait till you're invited,' Boko said.

'They can't do with two of you.' Then he added, 'Tom's a boy, and boys are more important than girls, remember. They have to make their way in the world. Girls only get married.'

I was forced to admit the truth of this, even though I knew that I would never get married, because I couldn't imagine that anyone would ask me. But it seemed surprising to me that Auntie and Uncle couldn't do with two of us, considering the big house they lived in and all their servants, but I didn't dare to argue. Instead, I decided to give Tom a good thump as soon as we were sent to bed, to pay him out for being a boy, and for deserting us so enthusiastically.

Because enthusiastic he was, and he said now, 'Come on, Dad, let's go and play the new records you brought,' and as they disappeared down the corridor, I heard him add, 'Did you remember to bring a new tin of needles?'

When the tomatoes were browned, Fiff spooned four halves on to each slice of toast, and together we carried the plates into the dining-room. If I hadn't been in the kitchen helping Fiff, I would have taken the chair nearest to hers at table, because I always took care to put as much distance as possible between myself and Boko, but now Cly had taken that place and I was forced to sit at the corner nearest to him, with Cly beside me and Tom opposite.

When Fiff placed Boko's plate in front of him, he stared down at it and asked with disgust, 'Is this all we're getting?'

'I didn't know you were coming,' Fiff said. 'There's nothing else in the house.'

I thought of the tins of tongue and ham and chicken breasts in the pantry, kept for special occasions, special guests; and said nothing. The tomatoes, which had smelled so delicious, suddenly looked stingy and foolish, squalid even; and I felt ashamed of the meal.

'Well, it's a poor do,' Boko said with contempt. 'No wonder Tom looks half-starved, if this is the sort of meal you dish up. I can see that Louie's going to have her work cut out putting some muscle on him.'

Even I could tell that this was meant as an insult, and I didn't dare to look at Fiff.

The atmosphere was fragile: it could splinter at any moment. I had to be on my very best behaviour, passing Boko the salt without being asked; hurrying to get the sugar bowl instead, because I had forgotten that he preferred to put sugar rather than salt on his fried tomatoes; and generally taking every step I could think of, including keeping quiet and not looking at him, to make sure I gave him no cause for displeasure; because with Boko, you never could tell. Storms of staggering force often struck with terrifying speed and ferocity – with almost no preliminary darkenings or rumblings – out of a placid sky. Even in apparently relaxed moods he seemed to be on the verge of erupting. I could feel the anger coiled inside him whenever I was close to him – it almost made the air vibrate – an anger which could explode suddenly into unimaginable fury.

Luckily Tom held his attention through most of the meal. While Fiff and Cly exchanged occasional, muted sentences, Tom eagerly buried himself and Boko first in a description of the latest model he was building in Meccano, then in the details of his attempt to fix a telephone link from his bedroom to the hall, and finally he occupied Boko with questions about the Studebaker's performance.

'A tinny American thing,' Boko said with contempt. 'I'm going to change it for a Frazer Nash BMW. You can't beat the Germans for engineering. And now that they've got this new chap, Hitler, there'll be no holding them . . .' Addressing Tom as though he were a grown-up, he launched into a boring lecture about the Nazis. They were doing marvellous things in Germany. Best of all, they were going to get rid of the Jews. I had never heard of the Jews before and I didn't understand why they had to be got rid of, or why getting rid of them should give him so much satisfaction. But I couldn't spare the time to worry about it: any lapse in concentration could bring dire consequences, and I was just glad of any subject which prolonged his good mood. I stared at Tom, willing him to hold Boko's interest until the meal was over and we could all safely escape.

It was only when I slid off my chair to help clear the plates that Boko's attention fell on me, and it fell disastrously.

'Well, Fidgie, my girl,' he said as I lifted his plate, 'how are you getting on at school? Have you learned to tell the time yet?'

He couldn't have asked a more difficult question. Startled by this unexpected thrust, I said evasively, 'A little,' and hoped that he would accept it. He had never been much interested in my educational progress. But now, it seemed, he was.

'So what's the time now?'

I stared at the clock on the mantelpiece and thought fast, fright fuelling my brain. I remembered hearing it strike seven as I was carrying the plates to the table, but how long could it have been since then?

'It's after seven,' I said, hoping that would satisfy him, but it didn't.

'How *long* after seven?'

I stared desperately at the clock's uncommunicative face, willing it to tell me. Its hands made a tent shape. 'Um . . .' And then I caught sight of Tom, who had turned, like everyone else, to look at the clock. Turning back, he was mouthing *'twenty-two minutes'* at me.

'Twenty-two minutes,' I said, with enormous relief.

Cly said, 'Tom told her that, Dad. I saw him.'

'No, he didn't,' I said quickly, afraid for Tom.

'All right,' Boko said, rising. 'We'll see.' He crossed to the clock, and standing in front of it so that its face was hidden, he opened its glass door and turned the hands. When he stood back, they had assumed quite a different shape, and I was lost.

I stared at it fixedly, but it was no use. My eyes flicked beseechingly to Tom, but having been caught out once, he was staring down at his plate. Silence fell while everybody waited, transfixed.

'I don't know,' I admitted.

Boko's face had been darkening during the silence. Now it became thunderous. His eyebrows snaked down above his nose like twin cobras striking, as they always did when his rage approached its climax. 'Of course you know!' he shouted. 'Are you trying to defy me? *What's the time?'*

This was the danger signal. I went on staring at the clock hopelessly, half paralysed and sick with fear, trying desperately to force myself to understand the mysterious figures, trying to force the clock to tell me the time. But it was no use. I shook my head guiltily. My heart had stopped beating.

One stride brought him to my side. He towered over me and thrust his face into mine. *'What's the time?'* he roared, lifting his hand high across his chest. I knew what was going to happen, and it did. His hand struck me so hard that I fell sideways, dropping his plate and clutching at the table to avoid falling into Cly's lap.

Fiff half rose. 'Thorp!' she protested, even though she must have known it wasn't safe to interfere.

He took no notice and brought the back of his hand down again with full force as I tried to rise, and this time the tablecloth came with me and several plates fell and splintered, scattering cutlery and crumbs and greasy tomato skins as I fell against the table and collapsed in an undignified heap on the floor.

Tom rescued me. 'Aw, Dad,' he said, his clear voice penetrating the armour of Boko's rage, 'She can't help being stupid. She's only a girl.'

It worked. Boko drew back, his face still contorted with fury. 'Get out of my sight, and stay out,' he roared at me, and to Fiff, as I picked myself up out of the debris and scrambled dizzily to my feet, he shouted, 'This is all your fault!'

I had made up my mind years ago never to cry when he hit me, never to give him that satisfaction, however much the beating hurt. I left the room without looking at anyone and climbed the stairs, shaken but glad to have got off so lightly: Boko didn't usually give up so easily, and I suspected that his capture of Tom had sweetened his temper. Judging by the faint clinking, somebody – probably Fiff – had begun to clear up the mess, because I heard Boko roar, 'Did I give you permission to do that?' and afterwards there was silence.

Fiff had told me once that both Cly and Tom had felt the weight of Boko's fist in the past. I found that difficult to believe, because it had been my turn – and Fiff's – for as far back as I could remember.

It was peaceful upstairs. Dusk was gathering, but I didn't light my candle: it felt safer to hide in the dark, curled up on my bed against the wall, even though I knew no one would come near me now that I was in disgrace. Fiff must have closed the window sometime during the day, leaving only a small gap at the bottom, an opening through which a faint breeze, risen again, reached the curtains, making them shiver. Presently a thin rain began to prickle against the windows. From downstairs after a while I heard the sound of music from the drawing-room and guessed that Tom and Boko were playing the new gramophone records. The strains of *The Wedding of the Painted Doll* drifted upstairs.

Various parts of me hurt, some more than others, and my head ached where it had struck the table, but it was a small price to pay for my escape. I was only sorry that my failure to unravel the mystery of the clock-face had got Fiff into trouble. I had not realized until now that telling the time was so important. Somehow I was going to have to find someone who could show me how. Tom refused to, saying that I ought to be able to find out for myself, as he had; but perhaps, if I could swallow my pride and ask him, Chaz could do it?

With the thought of Chaz came the cheering reminder of my adorable dancing shoes. Just seeing them again would be a comfort. It occurred to me that if I got ready for bed I could get them down and hide them under the covers with me. To spin out the pleasure of seeing them and holding them again, I took my time cleaning my teeth and pulling on my pyjamas, and it was only then, when I was ready to fetch them down from their secret hiding place, that I noticed that my chair had been moved. It was standing askew beside my dressing-table as if someone had used it and replaced it carelessly.

That was when I suddenly remembered the expression of gleeful satisfaction, of delicious triumph, Cly had worn when we'd met on the landing before supper, and a dreadful foreboding hit my stomach like a fist. I stood and stared at the chair, afraid now of what it might reveal once I carried it to the wardrobe and stood on it. But surely she wouldn't have thought of looking on top of the *wardrobe*? This thought gave me the courage to carry the chair across the room and climb on it. As I straightened up, I kept my eyes tightly closed until the last moment in an agony of prayer.

Please, please, let my shoes be all right, I prayed, *and I'll never do anything wrong again as long as I live.*

But it was no use: I'd known all along that something was wrong. The shoes had gone.

12

The pain of that loss, the bereavement, put everything else – even Boko – out of my mind.

My head was aching. As the headache grew worse, it occurred to me that if I took care not to think about my shoes, if I never climbed on the chair again and looked, my beautiful shoes would still be there, ready to be worn again whenever I needed them. Tomorrow I would start to search for them, but I knew I'd never find them again unless Cly relented and left them somewhere where I *could* find them. Bitterest of all to bear was the thought that I had only myself to blame: I had forgotten to find a safer place to hide them.

Fiercely, but without much conviction, I began to plan revenge. As soon as she'd gone back to school, I'd raid her top drawer and take all her bottles of scent: the Phul-nana, the 4711 cologne Auntie Meg had left behind, and the Evening in Paris in its dark blue bottle; and then I'd hold them to ransom. *Give me my shoes back, and I'll give you your smelly old perfume back.* I'd never dare to do it, of course, but it was a comforting thought that I *might*.

Fiff, risking Boko's wrath, came to see me after about an hour, bringing me a glass of Ice-Cream Soda and two maids of honour. I felt too sick to eat them, but I was so grateful to her for her courage that I decided to own up.

'I'm sorry, Mummy,' I said, careless now of consequences, 'I used your soap. Your purple Erasmic.'

'It doesn't matter,' Fiff said, taking the maids of honour out of her dress pocket and putting them, with trembling hands, on the nightstand by my bed. 'Don't let your father see these. If you hear him coming, hide them.'

She brought me an aspirin and sat down on the bed while I swallowed it with a gulp of pop. I felt safe while she was there and I wanted her to stay, but I knew that she couldn't. She was taking an enormous risk by coming to see me at all. Presently she squeezed my hand and got up.

'He's leaving after breakfast.' She said it quietly, conspiratorially, as though we were both in hiding. 'Just keep out of his way until then.'

I noticed that she flushed the dubby before going downstairs again, just in case Boko was listening.

After she'd gone I got up again and hid the maids of honour in the chest of drawers. Perhaps tomorrow I'd be able to eat them. At the moment, just the thought of the jam and the ratafia-flavoured ground almonds made me feel sick.

Once back in bed, I went to live in Mr Guest's boat-house. It was quiet and safe in there with the door shut and the river outside and no one else around, and I made a point of installing an electricity-making machine like the ones Chaz had told me about. I had acquired the magical ability to tame the birds, and the swans allowed me to ride on their backs as they sailed majestically out to sea. Returning from such a voyage, I was in the middle of hanging the curtains – midnight-blue silk velvet, I thought, like one of the evening dresses Fiff still kept, packed away in tissue paper in a steel trunk in the attic – when I fell asleep.

To go downstairs for breakfast next morning seemed a risk not worth taking. Boko was always morose at

195

breakfast, and even at the best of times it was wise to tread warily then. It was very early – even I could tell that – so I dressed quickly and quietly, took the maids of honour out of their hiding place, stowed them in the pocket of my dress, and made my escape downstairs and through the kitchen.

It had been raining and the air was chill, but there was a pearly autumnal sky over the mountains above Moravon, and to the south-east, the sun, barely risen over the mountains on this side of the river, promised warmth later. Hidden among the branches up on the knoll I ate the small sweet pies and felt more cheerful. The ground was still dry under the trees in spite of the rain, and I found a cushion of dry moss to sit on. From here I could keep an eye on the track leading to the railway crossing, even though it was far too early for Boko to leave, or – and here a happy thought struck me – for Mr Guest to come home. Just the thought of seeing Mr Guest again lifted my spirits.

It was quite a long time before I noticed the mushrooms, but once I did, I saw that the ground was covered with them, some of them beautiful – rose pink, or brown like buns, or scarlet with white spots. I knew that these scarlet ones were toadstools and not safe to eat, because of the painting of them in *Alice in Wonderland*, with the Caterpillar sitting on top, smoking a hookah. I was nervous of puff-balls too, because they gave out a puff of blackish smoke if you kicked them, and someone – Ruthie or Dilys – had told me that if you got that smoke in your eyes, you went blind. But there were some white ones too which must be mushrooms. Their stems were much more spindly than those of the mushrooms Fiff sometimes bought for a treat, and they were white underneath instead of brown, but that must be because they got no sunlight, growing here in the shade of the trees.

It occurred to me that to bring such a luxury home for breakfast might appease Boko and restore me to favour with Fiff, and I set about gathering them industriously, holding out my skirt as a receptacle in place of a basket. While I was doing it, Mr James's milk van rattled up the lane, and I could hear Mrs Bellamy letting out her hens for the day, which meant that I had to hurry because Fiff would soon be cooking breakfast. Mr James had filled our jugs and disappeared round the front of the houses to Mrs Bellamy's back yard by the time I climbed down the knoll and made for home, carrying my harvest.

The back door was still unlocked as I had left it, but there was no one in the kitchen. That didn't matter because the mushrooms were meant to be a surprise, but while I was emptying them out of my skirt onto the wooden draining-board, I heard Boko's voice in the hall. Tossing out the last ones hurriedly, I fled outside again. It would only be safe to approach him after he had eaten them and was in a good mood. *Then* I might even be praised, might bask in rare approval.

The police car passed just as I came out of the yard gate again, and it was only then that I remembered what had seemed so enthralling yesterday evening – the search for Teddy Ransom. I jogged after the car, following it round the knoll until I saw it turn into the gates at Holly Hill.

I was still standing looking after it when I heard Mr James's milk van returning from delivering to Mrs Bellamy and Miss Wragg. It ground along the track in low gear, its churns clanking as it headed for Holly Hill. When he got near me I stood aside to let him pass, but he stopped beside me and said, 'What's going on at Holly Hill, girl? Have you heard? There's all sorts of rumours flying around . . .'

I had no idea, but I said importantly, 'A police car

just went there. I think they're going to arrest some-body.'

Mr James pushed his hat back, allowing a shock of curly black hair to escape from under the brim. He leaned on the steering wheel while he considered the problem. 'Well,' he said, 'I expect they'll still want their milk delivered.' He put the van into gear and added obscurely, 'If anyone's still there.' Then, on a sudden generous impulse, or because he guessed that I was as curious about the police car as he was, he said, 'If you want a lift, girl, hop in quick.'

He dismissed his sheepdog into the back with the churns, and I obeyed with enthusiasm. A ride was always a treat even though the van was full of dried mud and wisps of straw, and smelt of milk and hay and animals and hot engine oil. Until now I had had no clear idea of what I was going to do next, apart from hanging around waiting to see if anyone got arrested; but in Mr James's van I might even see it happen, and the prospect of being able to swank about it when I got back to school was an unexpected piece of luck: I'd be the centre of attention in the playground, especially if Teddy Ransom really had been murdered, and not simply fallen off his boat. If I dared, I might even boast that I'd seen it happen, though telling lies took a lot more nerve than I pretended to have; and anyway the truth was easier to remember.

Mr James gave me a quizzical look as I got in, and said, 'What have you done to your ears, '*eneth i*? Been painting them blue?'

I had noticed this strange phenomenon earlier, when I combed my hair before the looking-glass on my dressing-table. I hardly ever looked properly in a looking-glass. I didn't dare to, for fear that what Cly said was true, that I really did have a face like a pig; and this morning I'd merely glanced at my reflection until I'd seen the blue ears, and then I'd stared, astonished. There was no way to explain it to Mr James, so I brushed it aside and said, 'I think I must have got ink on them.'

Mr James seemed to accept this explanation readily – his son Dick, after all, had never been seen clean and tidy – but to make sure he asked no further questions, I began telling him about finding Teddy's boat drifting out in the bay, and about the bundle of clothes in the bottomless pool; and he proved a much more satisfactory audience than I'd had at home. Telling a grown-up something he was willing to hear was a novel experience, and I was beginning to enjoy a heady sense of importance when we turned in at the gates of Holly Hill and pulled up on the forecourt behind the police car.

There, though, my pleasure at the prospect of seeing something exciting happen dimmed considerably when Chaz appeared round the far corner of the house with his bathing towel over his shoulders and his hair damp and tousled. I had been secretly revelling in the thought of being able to tell him something he didn't know. I had been storing it all up, every detail and every word, ready to tell him. Now, thanks to his nosiness, his infuriating gift for always being in the right place, my prize was wrenched from my grasp, and I felt deflated. Besides, I was envious of his freedom to use the swimming-pool when I was forbidden even to enter the house. I looked off to the right and pretended not to see him.

The housemaid at Holly Hill must have been waiting jug in hand just inside the door, because she flung it open and flew, bursting with news, down the steps almost before the van had stopped. While Mr James ladled two quarts of milk – in slow motion – into her jug, I twisted round in the seat and tried hard to follow the hushed conversation taking place in Welsh at the back of the van. My grasp of the language, so far, was limited and Mr James had left the engine running, as he always did, to save himself the trouble of cranking the starting handle after every stop, so it wasn't easy to hear; but as far as I could make out, he was telling her that someone called Sarah Mary – whoever she was – had been spreading a tale round the village that a madman had broken into Holly Hill and murdered everyone with an axe.

The housemaid was scornful. 'Oh, trust *her*!' she said scathingly in English, but after that their Welsh became too fast and too complicated for me. The name *Mrs Guest*, though, needed no translation.

I was concentrating so hard that I yelped with fright when Chaz spoke right beside me. 'What are you doing in the milk van?'

I scowled at him. 'You gave me an awful fright,' I said angrily. 'Sneaking up on me like that. I thought it was the madman with the axe.'

It was only when he said, 'What madman? And what's this about an axe?' that I realized I had been lost in Sarah Mary's fantasy.

'Oh, nothing,' I said, sulky with embarrassment. 'Anyway, why are *you* here? I thought you were supposed to be doing lessons.'

'Not till nine o'clock,' he said, and grinned. 'Don't be stupid. And why have you painted your ears blue?'

'Mind your own business,' I snapped. 'I can have *green* ears if I want to.' Suddenly I felt like bursting into tears. My blue ears, which I'd hoped were not noticeable, were attracting everyone's attention, and I hated it. It reminded me painfully of the force of Boko's hand striking my head, the ugliness of his rage; and it was all Fiff's fault for making me wear my hair so short. If I'd had a bob like Cly's and all the other girls, no one would have been able to see my ears.

His face clouded as he realized he'd said something that touched a nerve. He had probably been taught, as I had, that making personal remarks was bad manners, and he made haste to repair the damage. 'Cheer up, Fidgie,' he said, climbing onto the running-board, 'I expect it's only ink.'

By now, Mr James was closing the back doors of the van and the housemaid was retreating up the steps carrying the now heavy jug of milk with both hands.

'You were right, by the way,' Chaz said. 'Mr Ransom *was* shot, and Mr Guest's gun has disappeared. They're hunting for it.'

'Who told you?'

'I'm a spy, remember?' He made a face which was meant to be sly and sinister. 'Ve heff vays of finding out.'

Mr James wrenched the driver's door open and said gloomily as he climbed in, ' '*W annwyl dad!* Looks like Mrs Guest's in trouble up to her neck.'

'What's happened?' Chaz and I spoke together, but Mr James didn't seem to hear, and all he would add was, 'Hell of a shame too, beautiful woman like that!'

He put his hand out to the gear lever, but before he'd had time to engage it, the door of the house opened and, flanked by two policemen, Mrs Guest emerged wearing a creamy shantung coat and looking haughtier than ever. Taking no notice of us, she strolled to the police car and waited imperiously until the door was opened for her before she got in. In the sunshine she was dazzling.

We watched, all of us, transfixed. I wondered if I would ever be able to behave as regally as that, even if I could somehow manage to marry the Prince of Wales, that golden god.

Respectfully, as if we were watching a funeral cortège, Mr James waited until the police car had made the sweep of the forecourt and disappeared through the gates before he set the van in motion. Only then did we feel free to speak.

'*Crr . . . ikey!*' I breathed in awe. 'Did you see that? Do you think they're going to hang her?'

Chaz was annoyed with me. 'Of course not!' he said. 'They're only going to question her.' But on second thoughts, he added with a grin, 'Or try to. Mrs Guest never speaks to anyone if she can help it. I wish I could be there to listen.'

Mr James stopped at the gates and we watched the police car going back the way it had come. Then, before he turned towards Llwyn-yr-eos, he seemed to notice that Chaz was still riding on the running-board and holding on to the open window beside me.

'Hold on tight now, *machgen i*, if you're coming with us,' he said. 'We don't want no more dead bodies.'

The old van picked its way gingerly along the track between the green walls of bracken while Chaz told Mr James the bit of the story I'd forgotten: the finding of Mr Ransom's yachting cap. When we entered the gates of Llwyn-yr-eos, he said, 'Thanks for the lift, Mr James. Be seeing you, Fidgie,' and jumped down running, without waiting for Mr James to stop.

I longed to jump out and go with him, and only the knowledge that he was going home to do lessons stopped me. Knowing Chaz, I suspected that something – a sense of duty to his great-uncle perhaps, or even a genuine pleasure in learning – would prevent him from playing truant, whatever diversions I might suggest.

So, since there seemed to be nothing else to do, I stayed and helped Mr James with his milk round. After

Llwyn-yr-eos, where the jugs had been left out in a meat safe in the courtyard and the back door remained shut, we turned towards Dolgarran and called at the gloomy stone terrace above the toll-bridge, its long roof still untouched by the rays of the sun even this late in the morning. Absorbed in this new game, I ran up the steep gardens to collect the jugs left out for the milk, and toiled carefully up again to return them after Mr James had filled them.

The round must have taken much longer than usual because, as he doled out milk into jugs, Mr James delivered the news of Mrs Guest's arrest to the scattered houses along the main road, and the ensuing discussions took time. In some magical way, as if by jungle drums, the news had spread ahead of us, so that by the time we arrived back in our own village, where the cottage doors opened directly onto the road, people were standing on their doorsteps relishing the story with their neighbours.

I opened the van door and climbed down, knowing I'd have to make my way home on foot from here, and as I did so, Boko's Studebaker swept past. I just had time to catch sight of him with Tom beside him before they vanished round the next bend in the road. I raised my hand to wave, but too late, and suddenly I felt disconsolate. Tom had gone, perhaps for good, and I might never see him again. So I reminded myself that I was not friends with Tom. He had come into my bedroom last night on his way to bed and said, 'It's your own fault, you know, Fidgie. You keep doing things to annoy him.'

It had been the last straw. 'I hate you,' I'd said bitterly. 'You're a sneak, and I'm *glad* you're going away. I hope you never come back.' I'd meant it, too, at the time, though I wasn't so sure now.

But at least it was safe to go home now that Boko had

gone, especially since I was pretty sure that I'd seen the back of Cly's head too, through the car's back window.

I ran and skipped through the village to cheer myself up. When I turned off down the lane towards the railway crossing, I sang and whistled too, hidden between the twin palisades of bramble bushes. I found that the higher I jumped and the louder I sang, the easier it was to hold at bay the thought of never seeing Tom again. In the end I was shouting. It seemed to do the trick.

Away from the mountains which still cloaked the village and the main road in shadow, the day was bright and getting warm. When I got home, Fiff was in the kitchen, washing clothes in the sink. It was only then, looking at the draining-board, that I remembered the mushrooms. There was no sign of them anywhere, and all of a sudden I yearned to taste them. Under the smell of soap suds there was a delicious smell of cooking in the kitchen. Fiff only ever made a cooked breakfast when there was a man in the house. Men were special: they had to keep their strength up.

'Did you eat *all* the mushrooms?' I asked wistfully.

Fiff kept her back turned. She picked up the packet of Oxydol, sprinkled it on the clothes, and plunged her arms into the washing almost up to the ivory bangle she wore above her elbow.

'What mushrooms?' she asked without interest.

13

I couldn't seem to convince her that I'd brought some mushrooms home and left them on the draining-board. She didn't seem to care. I don't think she was really listening.

'There weren't any here when I came down to cook breakfast,' was all she said. From the clipped way she spoke I sensed that, with Tom gone, perhaps for ever, she was in no mood to talk about mushrooms or anything else, so I retired to the dining-room to eat loofahs and try to decide what to do for the rest of the day.

But apart from a half-formed and rather unsatisfactory idea of going to Moravon to look for Ellen, I had still reached no decision by the time I took my plate back to the kitchen. There I found that Fiff had shaken off her earlier preoccupation and become brisk. Clearly, she was having one of her efficiency days. Tomorrow, or the day after, she would lapse back into her more familiar – and more comfortable – hit-or-miss routine. Until she did, it was as well to be on my best behaviour.

'Take the basket and go round to Mrs Bellamy,' she said, 'and ask if she can spare any eggs. If she can, ask her if she would like some runner beans, and then come back and pick a good bunch for her. And when you've done that,' she finished, becoming stern, 'you can clean your room. The floor is knee-deep in sand.'

I took the basket from its hook behind the pantry

door, and asked carefully, 'Has Cly gone too? To stay with Auntie Louie?'

'No,' Fiff said. 'She's gone to buy a new gym slip and blazer for the autumn term, and then she'll be staying with a friend in Dolgarran for the night. She'll be back tomorrow.'

It was disappointing but better than nothing. Pipsy, banished from the kitchen, was mooching disconsolately about the yard, sniffing, in the hope of finding something interesting to pursue. I called her and she followed me gladly now that Cly had abandoned her.

I liked going to see Mrs Bellamy. She had no children and she never seemed to get impatient, as Fiff did. She was quite nice-looking too, in a comfortable sort of way – Fiff, who was quite tall, called her 'a bonny little woman' – and she had once knitted a pink dress for the floppy toy monkey I shared with Tom. Tom, though, scornfully refused to let the monkey wear the dress, and I had never dared to tell Mrs Bellamy, in case she asked me to give it back. I couldn't risk that because we'd torn big holes in it, snatching it back and forth in the fights we'd had over it.

There was a warm wet smell of soapsuds coming from the wash-house in Mrs Bellamy's back yard, and she was in the garden hanging out washing when I got there. She greeted me as delightedly as if she hadn't seen me for months, and I climbed up the steps into the garden and hung around watching till she'd finished.

'I see your father came down over the weekend,' she said, pegging up a tablecloth.

'Mm,' I mumbled, looking away down the garden to where her Rhode Island Reds scratched and pecked industriously behind their chicken-netting. Boko was the last person I wanted to talk about.

'You don't sound very enthusiastic,' she said with

mild surprise. 'You're very lucky, you know. Your father is such a charming man, and so handsome too. Such a shame his work takes him away so much.'

I wanted to say *He's taken Tom away and I don't think he's going to bring him back,* but I was afraid that she might repeat this to Fiff, and I was pretty sure that Fiff would consider such a remark came under the heading of Discussing Our Family Affairs with Outsiders, which was strictly forbidden. Besides, I wanted Mrs Bellamy to go on thinking that Boko was handsome and charming. I had never heard anyone describe him like that before and I marvelled at it: it made him sound just like the father I wished I had. People would despise us if they knew what he was really like.

So instead I said, 'The police have arrested Mrs Guest. They think she murdered Mr Ransom.'

Mrs Bellamy was satisfactorily shocked, but for the wrong reason. She must have thought that I was making it up because she said, 'Honestly, Fidgie, you really ought not to say things like that. What on earth have you been reading? You could get into awful trouble if people heard you.'

'But it's *true,*' I insisted. 'I *saw* them. They think she killed Mr Ransom.' And to impress her with the drama of it, its lurid possibilities, I added, 'I think they're probably going to hang her.'

This time she believed me, but reluctantly. 'I still think you're too young to be talking about such things,' she said, and then, to distract me – and perhaps herself too – from the news that something so shocking, so *improper,* had happened so close by, she added, 'If you like, you can go and look in the nesting boxes and see if there are any eggs. I saw Dolly and Daisy go in some time ago. They've come out now.'

I found a warm brown egg in each of the nesting

boxes. I had been nervous of eggs ever since Ellen had told me that you can get warts from touching their shells. I wasn't sure whether to believe her or not, but I dared not take the risk of *dis*believing her.

I'd left the basket on Mrs Bellamy's kitchen table, so, to be on the safe side, I used my skirt as a basket to carry the eggs back to the kitchen, where Mrs Bellamy was emerging from the pantry with others in a bowl. There didn't seem to be more than eight; ten with the two I had brought in.

'Tell your mother that the hens have almost stopped laying now,' she said, putting six of them carefully into the bottom of my basket. 'I doubt if there'll be many more after this till next spring.'

Later, when I was upstairs in my bedroom, I heard Fiff and Mrs Bellamy discussing my news across the hedge which separated the two gardens. I was kneeling down sweeping the linoleum with the dustpan and brush, so they couldn't see me and had probably forgotten I was there. Besides, they were quite a distance away down the garden, but even so they were speaking in lowered voices, and there was no mistaking the bitterness, the contempt, in Fiff's. She said that any woman who was kept in the lap of luxury, as Mrs Guest so clearly was, ought to stick to her husband even if he couldn't perform.

'Oh, but it couldn't be *that*,' Mrs Bellamy put in, in the sort of voice which made me think that she was probably blushing. 'He must be still in his *twenties*! No, from what I hear, she must be a nympho.'

After that, they lowered their voices even further. That meant that they must be talking about rude things, mysterious and exciting things, things only grown-ups were allowed to know. I stretched my ears in an effort to hear, but I could only catch a few disconnected words.

When I went downstairs Fiff was in the wash-house, wreathed in clouds of steam, lifting sheets from the copper. Before going to help her I went to empty the dustpan on the rubbish tip behind the wash-house, and made a discovery. The rubbish tip was hidden behind luxuriant hydrangeas and it was lucky that I hadn't tossed the sand from my dustpan over the bushes without looking, because there, thrown on top of the broken plates from last night's supper, was the white cake box Boko had brought. I picked it up and lifted a corner of the lid wistfully, expecting to find it empty, its marvellous contents marked only by ghostly whorls of grease. But unbelievably the cakes were still in there, all of them, a little squashed from being thrown down, but untouched. I picked out a cream horn and stared at it for a long moment, trying to make myself put it back, but it forced its way irresistibly into my mouth, pursued by the chocolate éclair, my very favourite.

I shouldn't have done it, I knew that. Fiff, who loved cream cakes, had meant them to be thrown away, a gesture of angry contempt; by eating them I had rendered her sacrifice worthless.

I got hiccups.

Closing the lid reluctantly on the temptation of the cream heart and the meringue still left in the box, I put it back on the rubbish tip and fled with the dustpan.

Fiff was too busy in the wash-house to do more than glance my way as she heard me enter, or she would have known at once from the look on my face that I was guilty of treason. The copper, bricked-in in one corner, was still steaming, but the fire under it was dying down. The air was hot and humid and filled with the pungent scent of washing soap.

Fiff was pumping the posser energetically up and down on the washing in one of the dolly tubs. She must have been lost in memories of Ceylon, living in a past as real to her as the present, because, feeding the corner of a sheet into the mangle, she said, 'The *dhobi* used to beat our sheets against a rock in the river. He could ruin them as fast as I could buy them.' After a moment she added drily, 'Boiling them and grinding them between wooden rollers is probably not much better.'

Turning the handle on the big old mangle while Fiff fed the sheets and towels into it was my favourite job. It was curiously satisfying too, to see all the water squeezed out, full of soapsuds to begin with, then cloudy from the rinsing, and finally a clear blue. The cogs of the big wheel were well greased and I was using both hands on the handle, but even so it took quite a lot of strength to turn the rollers if the sheets bunched up as they went through, and sometimes Fiff had to take over.

'Oh child,' she said suddenly as we worked, 'don't ever get married.'

The idea that I might one day get married was startling. It was too remote, too far-fetched even to consider. 'I'm not going to,' I assured her.

She heaved a heavy sigh. 'That's what you say *now*,' she said resignedly. 'But I daresay you'll make the same mistake as the rest of us when you grow up.'

The washing took all the rest of the morning. I was laying the table for lunch when I noticed that Fiff had left her cigarettes on the small table beside her armchair and wondered if she'd notice if I took one. They were only small, cheap ones – Ardath – but smoking a cigarette would be sure to impress Chaz, and I could offer to share it with him. But as I reached out for the packet I noticed Fiff's dictionary on the shelf below, and forgot about the cigarettes: finding out what Fiff and Mrs Bellamy had been talking about

210

was much more interesting. I took the book out and looked up 'nimfo' and then 'nimffo', but I couldn't find either of them: it must be a word so rude that even the dictionary refused to print it. So I looked up 'perform', which must, I thought, mean something quite different from what I had always supposed. It must mean something that men were supposed to do for their wives; but 'perform' proved disappointing too. It said 'to carry out an act, to take part in a play, to play a musical instrument, usually in public.' It was puzzling. Even if Mr Guest *couldn't* play the piano, why should that be a reason for Mrs Guest to go around with other men and shoot Teddy Ransom? I had no one to ask, now that Tom was gone; and I had a sneaking feeling that it was something I couldn't ask anyone else, even Chaz. Ellen, though, would be sure to know. I'd ask her the minute I saw her again.

We were to have cold lamb – the remains of yesterday's hot roast – for lunch, with tomatoes and creamed potatoes; the sort of scrap meal we always had on wash-day. While Fiff was mashing milk and a generous knob of butter into the potatoes, I fetched the joint from the meat safe, where it had stood under its net umbrella since lunchtime yesterday; and Fiff took her glasses off and examined it minutely for fly-blows before she carved into it.

She and I had worked together companionably in the wash-house, but as soon as we sat down at the table it was clear that she had not forgotten her conversation with Mrs Bellamy.

'I have a bone to pick with you, young woman,' she began as she picked up her knife and fork. 'I hope you haven't been hanging around Holly Hill again. You were told to stay away from that house. The more I hear of those people the less I like what I hear.'

'I was only helping Mr James deliver the milk,' I

protested. 'We went round everywhere, not just Holly Hill. And Mr Guest is *nice*, Mummy. *Honestly*.' I felt I had to defend him at all costs.

'Not if he's mixed up with the police,' Fiff said flatly.

I was outraged. 'But he *isn't*!' In desperation, my voice was becoming shrill. 'He went away on Saturday, Mummy. I saw him. He told me he was going to Manchester. He wasn't here when Mr Ransom got shot.'

But Fiff wasn't listening. 'No woman of any breeding would behave as that woman does,' she said angrily, and I could tell that she hadn't heard a word I'd said. 'I've no time for women who don't know when they're well off.' And as an afterthought, she added, 'And I've no patience with a man who allows his wife to make a fool of him. He should have put his foot down and called a halt to all her shenanigans.'

'But that's not fair,' I protested. 'I don't see how he could, when he wasn't here.'

'I meant, long before it got to this.'

I began to feel surly. 'I still don't think it's his fault,' I grumbled, uneasily aware that I was getting close to the limit of her patience but risking it anyway, for Mr Guest's sake. He'd stood up for me, after all, when Chaz had teased me.

Fiff didn't answer at once. I had the feeling that she agreed with me but wouldn't say so. 'Oh do stop *contradicting*, Fidgie,' she said tiredly at last. 'You really are the most argumentative kid.'

'Well . . . !' I said, writhing in frustration. I wanted to go on standing up for Mr Guest until I had convinced her, but I didn't dare. I couldn't understand why she had turned against him now, after taking his side when she was talking to Mrs Bellamy. Grown-ups always seemed to be changing their minds. It was maddening. It made me want to scream and stamp my feet when people – I meant Fiff – changed sides like this. I bunched my toes up inside my sandals and squeezed them hard enough to hurt. It was the only way I could force my tongue to keep still.

We finished off the apple pie and the cold custard left over from yesterday, and while we were clearing the dishes away, Fiff said, 'If you're going out to play this afternoon, you'd better wear a cardigan. You don't want people to see that bruise on your arm.'

14

Obeying Fiff's parting instructions, I went to call on Miss Wragg. Left to myself, I would never have gone voluntarily. I felt desperately sorry for Miss Wragg, but trying to look into her hideously burnt face without flinching, trying to pretend I saw nothing wrong with it, was a strain. And besides, she often pretended to be out when I knew very well she was in.

So, when there was no answer to my ring at the front door, I was tempted to accept my dismissal with relief and run away as fast as I could. Miss Wragg's front door, unlike ours, was at the side of the house and always seemed to be in chill shadow. Goose pimples rose on my arms as I stood there, in spite of the cardigan, and I longed to get back to the golden warmth of the sunshine I had left outside the garden gate. Fiff, who suspected that Miss Wragg was even less able to afford things than we were, had given me copies of the *Strand Magazine* and *Argosy* to pass on to her, and I pushed them through the letter-box and turned to make my escape. But Fiff had also commanded me to ask if Miss Wragg needed anything from Moravon, a command I felt honour bound to carry out, so I went doggedly round to the back door and tried again. *Poor Miss Wragg,* Fiff had said, *Going out in the summer with all those strangers gawping at her must be agonizing. It would take more courage than I have . . .* This time, I heard a faint clink – probably accidental – from inside the kitchen, and renewed my efforts.

'It's only me, Miss Wragg,' I called. 'My mother sent me to ask if there's anything you'd like me to get from the shops.'

This time the bolt was withdrawn and the door, scraping on the tiled floor, lurched open while I waited on the doorstep and steeled myself to smile into the terrible ruin of her face. It was a face from a nightmare. Everything about it – what was left of the eyelids, the nose, the shiny, puckered skin – looked like wax solidified suddenly halfway through the process of melting. The wig she wore, ugly and improbably black though it was, salvaged what little was left to her of a human face. Jacko's mother had told me – though I often wondered if she had made it up – that when she was sixteen, Miss Wragg had fainted and fallen face down in the nursery fire. This conjured up a picture so horrific that I recoiled from it. Her skin was so reptilian that it was impossible to imagine she had ever been a young girl.

Diffidently she asked, 'Could you wait while I cut some flowers from the garden? And then deliver them to St John's? Mrs Henderson should be there: it's her turn to do the flower arrangement this week.'

Going on errands, or what Ellen called 'running messages' was fun, and I brightened up and waited, chattering idly, while Miss Wragg cut roses and dahlias and marguerites from her garden. It was easier to talk to her when her back was turned and I didn't have to look into her red-rimmed, painfully weeping eyes; but I said nothing about the topic which most interested me: the business of Teddy Ransom and Mrs Guest. Without being able to put the thought into words, I felt that she had already suffered so terrible a catastrophe that she must be shielded from further brutalities. In any case, she spent most of her time in church, so completely detached from the crude excitements which fascinated the rest of us that it would have seemed bad manners – cruel, even – to drag her down to earth with talk of murder and drowned bodies and guns.

But Teddy and Mrs Guest sprang back into the forefront of my mind a few minutes after leaving Miss Wragg. Carrying my armful of flowers, I had made my way along the narrow path to the bridge and clambered up the embankment to join the walkway beside the railway line, when I heard a car engine in the distance behind me, and glancing back across the water, I was just in time to see Mr Guest's car emerge from between the two knolls and head towards Holly Hill, returning at last from Manchester. Overjoyed, I waved wildly to him, but I doubt if he saw me because there was no response, not even a pip from the horn, and my spirits fell when I realized that he had more serious things to attend to than waving to a kid he hardly knew. It was a blow to my self-esteem, but I comforted myself with the thought that he might not have been able to see me: I was, after all, quite a distance away – at least half a mile, perhaps more – and half-hidden behind the railing of the bridge and the bunch of flowers. And even if he'd seen me, he might not have recognized me or realized that I was waving at *him*. In summer, the children who came here always waved at everything, at passing cars, at trains, at people in boats. It was part of being on holiday.

The tide had been ebbing for an hour or more. I kept stopping at intervals to hang over the wooden railing, fascinated by the small whirlpools, no more than dimples in the water, swirling round the barnacled piers of the bridge and sliding away to sea, to be replaced by others. From the bridge it was possible to see not only the harbour – Mr Channing's car still stood on the quayside where he had left it yesterday afternoon – but also the big church I was heading for, high on the hill above the town. As I neared Moravon, I began to have doubts about going into the church. I had never been in a church in my life as far as I knew – though I had been in Hindu and Buddhist temples – and I was afraid that there might be someone frightening inside who would recognize me as a heathen and shoo me away in a rage; so I went to find Ellen, whose insouciance I secretly relied on.

I liked Ellen a lot because of her lawlessness, or what seemed to me to be lawlessness because she did things Fiff would have frowned on, and did them airily. She was usually wearing a washed-out dress at least one size too large, but always freshly laundered, her dark hair drawn across her forehead and held back with kirby-grips, her manner unconcerned. Her nonchalance fascinated me: it was a quality I longed to possess, and I did my best to copy it, to feel unshackled and free. When grown-ups frowned at our behaviour, we giggled and ran away.

This time I found her by accident. As I was passing the fish-and-chip shop where Chaz had taken me to eat the day we met, I glanced inside and saw her at the counter, collecting a ha'penny bag of chips. She was already wolfing them hungrily, dipping into the bag with greasy fingers, as she emerged onto the pavement. I eyed the package in its newspaper wrapping with longing. The exquisitely mingled scents of salt and vinegar were driving me wild, the memory of cold roast lamb and apple pie fading into insignificance.

'I hope you wasn't expecting me to give you any,' she said, with the sort of bluntness I admired. 'I'm too hungry to share. So you'll just have to watch.'

'I've just had my lunch,' I said loftily. 'You can keep your greasy old chips. So there.'

We ambled along the High Street together, weaving among the shoppers and holidaymakers on the pavement, stopping sometimes to admire the colourful array of buckets and spades and beach balls, and bickering amicably over the relative beauty of yellow sandshoes and red sandshoes while Ellen ate from her greaseproof bag. When at last she had finished and licked the last delicious vestiges of flavour from her fingers, she wiped her hands on the newspaper, screwed it up and stepped aside to plant it in the dustbin of a hotel we were passing. I admired the casual way she did this. I felt sure that if I'd done it, the proprietor would have rushed out and made me take it out again, but Ellen could always get away with things like that.

She said suddenly, 'Who was that boy you was with, Saturday? You got a pash on him?'

'What boy?' I asked, pretending ignorance.

'That boy you was with in a boat. Stop pretending. I bet you got a pash on him.'

'Don't be stupid,' I said, annoyed by her persistence. 'I haven't got a pash on anyone.' The idea of having a pash on Chaz made me uneasy, and in my haste to dispel the idea, I betrayed myself. 'I used to have a pash on Dougie Parrish, if you must know, but I've gone off him now.'

'Ha, ha. Sez you,' she said, but to my relief she dropped the subject.

On the pavement outside the Auction Rooms a sandwich-board announced that the usual Wednesday auction of household goods would not take place this week. Instead, a sale of the contents of Garth Hall, Fairhurst, would be held from Monday till Friday, by order of the Executors. I wondered if Fiff knew. If she didn't, I could get into her good books by telling her of it.

'Where you going, anyway, with all them flowers?' Ellen asked.

'I've got to take them to the church,' I said, and added, begging, 'Come with me, Ellen. I've never been in that church before.' I didn't like to admit I'd never been in *any* church before.

She looked at me. 'You won't be allowed in anyway,' she said. 'You have to wear a hat to go into church. All us ladies have to.'

This was a facer. 'But why?'

Ellen shrugged thin shoulders. 'Don't know. I just know that ladies have to cover their hair.' When I said nothing, pondering this strange prohibition, she added, 'Well, never mind. I'll think of something. You got a handkerchief?'

I felt in my pocket. 'Yes,' I said.

'Well, there you are then. Put it on your head before you go in.' When it came to church, it seemed that even Ellen dared not flout the rules.

As we toiled up the steep hill to the church, I told Ellen about Teddy and Mrs Guest. In some mysterious way, details of the murder had spread almost as soon as the police had found the body, and Ellen was agog, though she pretended indifference, skipping ahead or stopping to pluck a stem of valerian from a wall. But if I stopped talking, she turned and said impatiently, 'Well, go on!'

Bathed in the splendour of being an eye-witness – well, as good as, anyway – I was enjoying my advantage so much that by the time we arrived at the church steps I had very nearly reached the point of pretending I had actually seen Mrs Guest shoot Teddy, but the hugely impressive church door silenced me, and I quailed at the thought of the lie I had very nearly told, a sin which would have ensured some terrible retribution once inside. We paused to spread our handkerchiefs solemnly on our heads before entering.

Remembering the Buddhist temple, I said, 'Don't we have to take our shoes off?' but Ellen seemed not to hear, and I was too nervous to press the question. I remembered with shame how Boko had blustered when the monks had insisted we remove our shoes.

The church seemed to me to be vast, and every bit as intimidating as I had feared. Inside, there was a breathing silence, a silence so all-encompassing that I felt as if I'd suddenly gone deaf. The busy sounds from the town, the distant shrieking of holidaymakers on the beaches, all ended abruptly the moment we closed the heavy door, which swung shut with a worryingly loud and hollow boom. Inside, the church seemed very bare to me, but I didn't dare say so. There were no shadowy gods wreathed in aromatic smoke, no perfumed joss-sticks, none of the darkness and strangeness and mystery of a Hindu temple. Sunlight flooded in from tall windows facing the sea, but the far end of the church was twilit and secret, despite the massive stained-glass window towering over the altar. My gaze flickered from the red light burning distantly on that shadowy table to the railed-off enclosure nearby which protected a stone angel kneeling on one knee and holding a huge scallop shell on the other. Ellen followed my gaze.

'That's the font,' she whispered. In the silence her whisper was as disturbing as a shout. It seemed to penetrate to the most secret recesses of this vast space, where somebody or something terrifying was listening, and might pounce. It was worse than my Watchers, who at least were fairly friendly. 'It's where they bring babies to be christened. Come on, we'd better go to the vestry. That's where they do the flowers.'

But as I took a step forward to go down the centre aisle, she caught my arm and hissed sternly, 'You're not supposed to go in front of the altar. If you do, you have to curtsey. Honestly, Fidgie, ha'n't you never been inside a church before?'

Chastened and feeling foolish, I followed her down a side aisle. The smells of beeswax and Brasso and old prayer books mingled strangely, hauntingly, with the faint scent of flowers, and the rubber soles of our sandals barely whispered on the woodblock flooring.

As if she had guessed my first impressions, Ellen said in an exaggerated whisper, 'It'll be Harvest Festival in a couple of weeks, and you should see it then. It's all going to be decorated: sheaves of wheat, baskets of fruit, bread baked real beautiful shapes, flowers, all sorts of stuff. I'll bring you to see it if you like.' She spoke like someone explaining to a foreigner, a believer in some exotic Eastern cult, and I wondered sheepishly if she had seen through my pretence and guessed that I had never entered a church before.

As we neared the door at the far end of the aisle, it became clear that the silence was not as complete or the church as empty as I'd thought. The door was ajar and the sound of someone drawing water from a tap could be heard clearly through the opening. Ellen knocked and pushed it further open. Inside, surrounded by flowers, a tall woman in dark brown was standing at the sink holding a brass vase under the tap.

'We've brung you some more flowers, Mrs Henderson,' Ellen said, taking charge of the situation. I was so uneasy in these surroundings that I was happy to let her do the talking.

'They're from Miss Wragg,' I put in hastily, cutting across Mrs Henderson's routine thanks in my anxiety to get the errand over and escape back into the safety of the open air. It had begun to dawn on me that her name was familiar, but she seemed so stately that I hesitated to ask her the question which had begun to gnaw at me. The answer, anyway, was less important than getting out of here. I couldn't wait to shed the oppressive weight of awe the church imposed on me. I felt a panicky urge to assure someone that I *did* – sometimes anyway – say my prayers.

It had been so hot climbing the hill to the church that I had stopped halfway up and taken my cardigan off, passing the bunch of flowers awkwardly from one arm to the other as I struggled out of it. I had forgotten about the bruise and Ellen had made no comment, but now Mrs Henderson took hold of my arm and said, 'Good heavens, child, what on earth have you done to yourself?'

I felt as if I had been caught doing something I had been told not to. 'I fell down,' I said, embarrassed. It was true, but it felt like a lie. 'Last night. I hit my arm against the table.'

Her eyes travelled up to my face. 'And I suppose that's ink you've got on your ears?'

Ellen had begun to stare at me, adding to my mortification. 'I forgot to wash it off,' I said. It was humiliating to be quizzed like this by a stranger. It brought back sickening memories of the scene at the supper table last night, and the black rage in Boko's face. Somehow she must have guessed. I backed towards the door. 'We've got to go now.'

'Speak for yourself,' Ellen said sniffily, but she followed me, and as soon as we had closed the vestry door behind us, I stopped and pulled my cardigan on again. It was cold in the church anyway.

The answer to the question I had not dared to ask Mrs Henderson came unexpectedly as we closed the church door behind us. Mr Channing's car, its windscreen glinting in the sun, pulled up as we descended the steps from the church door, and Mr Henderson got out. When he saw me he saluted me briefly, a finger touching the brim of his cap.

'Miss Fidgie,' he murmured as he passed us.

The moment he was safely inside the church, Ellen picked up her skirt as if to curtsey, and said mockingly, 'Ooh, la la! *Miss* Fidgie!' and began to dance away from me, swinging her hips, a parody of swank.

'Oh, shut up!' I shouted furiously, stung by her mockery. 'It's not my fault. They *live* near us.'

'*Miss* Fidgie! *Miss* Fidgie!' Ellen went on, baiting me until I ran after her and gave her a push which made her stumble, but instead of retaliating, she burst into a fit of the giggles.

Furious, I shouted, *'Paid a gwneud fel diawl gwirion!'* hoping that it meant 'stop acting the fool', but Ellen drew a sharp breath in horror, and said piously, '*Ooh . . . !* You'll go straight to hell, you will, Fidgie Jacques, swearing like that right outside the church!'

Quelled by the shame of making such a gaffe, I said sulkily, 'I was going to ask you something, but I won't now. So there.'

This stopped her, but all she said was, 'See if I care,' and skipped away.

'*Don't care was made to care, don't care was hung,'* I chanted furiously. '*Don't care was put in a pot and boiled till he was done!* You probably don't know the answer anyway.'

'You won't know if you don't ask me, will you?' Ellen answered craftily.

'That's disgrumptious,' I said, playing for time while I tried to think of a way of framing the questions I wanted to ask about 'perform' and 'nimffo'; but before I could, something happened which put the problem out of my mind, and afterwards I made up my mind never to talk about rude things ever again.

A car was climbing the hill, and when it turned the

corner by the church hall we saw that it was a hearse. Through its engraved windows we could see that it carried a small coffin. We stood back against the wall even though the road here was wide, and watched it go past.

'That's that little girl from down by the harbour,' Ellen said. 'They'll be leaving her in the church till tomorrow.'

I didn't know that children could die. It seemed bizarre to me. 'What did she die of?' I asked.

Ellen, who always seemed to know everything, said, 'Diphtheria. So you better not go near her coffin, or you'll catch it.'

I would have argued about that, though I knew nothing about it, but I felt suddenly as if something from the church, from the hearse, had reached out and touched me with an icy finger and I wanted to get away as fast as possible, so instead of arguing I said, 'Come on, let's run down the hill.'

We didn't stop running until we reached the High Street where we had to pause until there was a gap between the charabancs and cars; and after that, breathless, we slowed to a jog along the station thoroughfare. By then I had shaken off the feeling of being pursued by the hearse, and we ambled over the railway crossing and down to the promenade. The tide was ebbing and the beaches, as always in August, were crowded with people, all of them strangers as far as I could see.

'Let's go to the island,' I said. We could usually play in peace on the island where hardly anyone ever came in daylight because of having to wade out to it. People didn't like taking off their shoes and stockings or getting their holiday clothes wet, but all we had to do was to bunch up our skirts and stuff them into our knickers before wading across, holding our sandals, thigh-deep through the water.

The sand on the island was silky, sensual, dribbling warmly, deliciously between our bare toes. We chose one of the valleys among the sandhills and spent the rest of the afternoon – or what seemed like the rest of the afternoon – absorbed in building houses in the warm sand, decorating the rooms with shells and pebbles and pieces of coloured glass, bits of bottles broken, no doubt, by those holiday drunks, the trippers from the charabancs. Once our houses were as perfect, as elegantly appointed, as we could make them, we played May Queens, our favourite game. Sometimes I carried Ellen's train and sometimes she carried mine, walking behind each other in solemn procession to our coronations. Ellen's train was quilted red satin edged with golden tassels, like the curtains in the Royal Hotel, and mine was white velvet trimmed with swansdown. I wasn't really sure what swans-down was, whether feathers or fluff, but it sounded gorgeous and I refused to be moved from my choice even though Ellen thought it wishy-washy. We both agreed about our crowns, though: they sparkled with every jewel we could think of; and we carved the throne out of the sand between two clumps of marram grass.

I don't know why we suddenly noticed when the church clock struck six – we hadn't noticed it striking four or even five – but just as I was placing the crown on her head Ellen suddenly jumped up with a squeal of alarm and gasped, 'We got to go!'

Somewhere in the back of my mind for some time now I had been aware of the sound of water, the chuckling sounds it made when the tide began to turn, to flood in; and now, alerted by the panic in Ellen's voice, realization came, and I swarmed up to the top of the nearest sandhill and looked over. As soon as I saw the water I knew we were in trouble. The placid surface we had waded through was gone, replaced by a roiling flood hurling itself against the island and across the beach to the promenade. In the centre of the channel a sinister current raced past like a savage army invading by stealth. Ellen climbed up beside me and let out a wail.

'My Mam's going to *kill* me,' she said.

'We'll have to swim,' I said, but without conviction. It seemed unlikely that even a grown-up could battle against that seething race.

'I can't swim,' Ellen said. 'Don't be stupid. Even Johnny *Weissmuller* couldn't swim through that.'

We sat back to think about our plight.

'We've got to do *something*,' I said. 'Or we'll have to stay here until the tide goes out again.'

'That won't be till three o'clock in the morning,' Ellen pointed out. 'Or even four.'

I hadn't thought of that. Sneaking home to face Fiff's wrath in the middle of the night didn't bear thinking about. 'Someone's sure to see us before long,' I said hopefully, and even as I spoke I saw the ferry nosing out from the Point and heading across the harbour. 'Quick, run!' I yelled, jumping up and tumbling untidily down the side of the sandhill onto what was left of the island's beach.

We ran, waving and yelling, towards the tip of the island, but the ferry was too far away, and the noise of its engine must have drowned our cries. Standing at the stern, holding the tiller, the ferryman barely glanced at us. The passengers, seeing two children jumping about and waving, wild with the excitement of being on holiday, waved back, cheerfully indulging us.

When the ferry had disappeared behind the stone jetty, Ellen threw herself down on the sand. 'I'm not playing with you no more,' she said, made waspish by

226

disappointment. 'I'll have a terrible row off my Mam when I get home.'

A picture of the strap coiled up on top of Fiff's wardrobe leapt into my mind, but I dismissed it hastily: sunset was hours away yet.

'*I* know!' I said, struck by a brilliant idea. 'We could gather white pebbles and make an SOS with them in the sand.'

'By the time we get enough, there won't *be* any sand,' Ellen pointed out crossly. It was true: the tide was already swirling round our feet, forcing us to edge back up the slope of the sandhills.

I wasn't prepared to give up yet. Anything was better than facing Fiff and the strap. 'Well, I'm going to look for some anyway,' I said, clambering back over the dunes. Ellen followed me silently, dragging her feet as we ploughed through the deep sand in the centre of the island. I knew that she was angry with me, knew that I deserved it because I had got us both into this fix, and I began to fear that she was right: we would have to spend the night here and face our angry parents – or even the police – in the morning. Her determination to expect the worst was catching, so that even while I collected what few white pebbles I could find, I began to see that the idea was silly, and after a while I dropped them again. By the time we were climbing the sandhills on the other side of the island I had given up hope of being rescued, so that when I saw the *Sea Slug* moored off the Point I wasn't sure if I was imagining it, or if it was some other boat whose passengers, like those on the ferry, would assume we were just having fun; but at the same moment Chaz, wearing only bathing trunks, emerged from the sandhills. I let out a yell of joy and screamed his name, determined to be heard this time. He looked across the channel and waved, gathering up his mooring line.

'You see?' I said triumphantly to Ellen, pretending that I had personally produced this miracle. 'I told you someone would see us. So there!'

The channel on this side of the island was wider and the current at the edges less turbulent, but boarding *Sea Slug* was difficult and very nearly disastrous. Chaz had to drag each of us aboard clinging to the painter, the boat's small engine barely able to hold her against the racing tide. But we weren't completely soaked: I had had the bright idea of taking off my dress and throwing it in a bundle to Chaz, and I made Ellen do the same, but we were both shivering, mostly with excitement and fright, by the time we had pulled our dresses on again in *Sea Slug*'s cockpit.

'Don't you never *dare* tell nobody I took my dress off,' Ellen hissed at me, 'in front of a boy, too. My Mam'll kill me. And I'll never speak to you again.'

'Oh Ellen, for goodness sake!' I snapped, losing my temper. 'You're dry, aren't you? And we're safe now.'

We were heading for the harbour by then, and presently Chaz brought the boat up against the steps and Ellen, still shaken and not saying anything, climbed out. I shouted something after her to mollify her, but she ran off without answering and without looking back. Chaz, noting this, said cheerfully, 'Don't worry. She'll get over it.'

I wasn't so sure, but I was so annoyed with her for running off like that without a word that I decided I didn't care. Secretly I knew it was all my fault. I had got us both into the pickle in the first place, and the burden of guilt did not improve my temper. I decided that it would serve her right if I never spoke to her again.

'She might at least have thanked you,' I said sulkily, forgetting that in all the confusion I hadn't thanked him either.

I had tried to squeeze the water out of my knickers, but it wasn't easy without taking them off – which was unthinkable – and they were still dripping wet. I began to shiver as Chaz pulled away from the shelter of the jetty. He didn't seem to feel the cold. I'd noticed before, with envy and puzzlement, that boys never seemed to feel cold. The sunshine had faded, dying out unnoticed while we were on the island, and the wind was cold out here on the water. The sky was covered now by small clouds huddling together like the hummocks on an eiderdown, and small spiteful waves began slapping the *Slug*'s prow as we swept upstream on the current. Now that the tide was rising, Chaz had no need to pick his way from channel to channel like someone winding his way through a maze. The sun was long gone, and it was obvious that it had no intention of coming back. We had almost reached the bridge before it occurred to me to say, 'What are you doing here anyway? I thought you were having lessons.'

'That was this morning,' he said. 'I only work with Mr Caster until lunchtime anyway.'

'I wish *we* only got school in the morning,' I said enviously. 'It must be heavenly to be able to play all afternoon.'

'I haven't been out of hospital long,' he said defensively, 'and I'm supposed to be taking it easy. This afternoon I ought to be swotting up on the Repeal of the Corn Laws, but all that stuff in Parliament is boring ... So after lunch I brought Henderson in to collect the car, and I've been mooching around since then.'

I didn't know what repeal meant, and I had never heard of the Corn Laws, and was grateful that I'd never need to. They sounded grim. 'We only have to learn English and Welsh and sums, and do mental arithmetic,' I said smugly. It sounded boastful, so I added quickly, 'and sometimes Nature Study, but not

229

much. Nature Study's silly anyway. All we do is bring in leaves and twigs and put them in jam jars.'

He fell silent; speechless with envy, I thought, that we didn't have to learn about the Corn Laws; so I took pity on him.

'You wouldn't have to learn all that stuff if you went to school here,' I pointed out. 'Couldn't you ask your uncle to let you stay here? You could come with us to our school.'

'Nothing doing,' he said. 'Uncle Hil would laugh if I even suggested it.'

'But why?'

'Because the schools here aren't good enough. Have you ever heard of anyone from here going to *any* university?' And he added crushingly, 'Let alone Cambridge.'

I fell silent, thinking about it. When he spoke again, he had changed the subject completely. 'I got fed up with Moravon, so I decided to go out to the place where we found Mr Ransom's boat and scout around to see if I could find any more clues. Something might have been washed up on the Point.'

'But why bother?' I asked, irritated by his niggling away at a crime already solved. 'The police know Mrs Guest did it.'

'Because,' he said as if explaining to a baby, 'if Mr Ransom got shot at Holly Hill, then somebody else must have taken his boat out there, to make it look as if he'd fallen overboard. So maybe they left clues.'

'Well, all right,' I said impatiently. 'Mrs Guest drove the boat out there. What difference does it make? Honestly, Chaz, you really are an awful snoop.'

He shrugged, and then added sarcastically, 'You think Mrs Guest abandoned the boat, swam ashore, walked over the Point, and then swam up the river all the way back to Holly Hill?'

I refused to be browbeaten by his mockery. 'She might have. Or she might have walked over the marshes and round the back, behind the knoll. Who cares? She's a horrible woman anyway. I hope they keep her in jail for ever . . . Or at least until February.'

'Why February?'

I shrugged and didn't answer. Fiff had told me that I could have the dimaond brooch back in February if no one had claimed it by then, but I couldn't very well admit this to Chaz. I didn't want him to know how much I longed to possess it, even though I knew it was Mrs Guest's: he'd think it the same as stealing.

Chaz was silent for a moment, and then he said, 'If you promise you won't tell anyone – anyone at all – I'll tell you something I found out. But you must swear first.'

'OK,' I said, instantly intrigued. 'I swear. Cross my heart and hope to die.'

'Because if you peach, it could get someone into trouble.'

'I won't breathe a word. God's honour.'

But in spite of my protestations, he seemed reluctant to begin. The *Slug* had puttered under the bridge before he said, 'That *was* Mr Guest's car I saw at that empty house, the day he told you he was going to Manchester. I'm sure of it. And there's a path across the marshes to the back gate. I went along there to check. And somebody's been there recently, too: the grass has been flattened where someone pushed the back gate open. You can still see the trail they left, heading over the railway towards the sandhills. That's where I'd been when you hailed me.'

Instantly, without any further explanation, I understood what he was saying, and set up a wail. 'Oh no, Chaz. You mustn't! You mustn't tell anyone. You'll get Mr Guest into *awful* trouble!'

'I'm not going to tell anyone,' Chaz said, astonished

by my vehemence and annoyed by the implied accusation. 'What do you take me for? I *like* Mr Guest. I was just sleuthing. Out of interest.'

We didn't speak again until he drew up alongside the steps below River Cottage, and then all I said was, 'I don't believe Mr Guest did it, and even if he did, I don't care. So there. And you're not to go spying on him again.' But then, because this sounded dangerously like Cly, I added quickly, 'Please, Chaz, promise me.'

But Chaz only grinned infuriatingly and said, 'I'll think about it,' before he pulled the *Slug* away from the steps, leaving me in suspense.

It was more than I could bear. 'I'll never speak to you again if you tell!' I shrieked after his departing back, but I couldn't be sure he heard the threat, because he only waved without turning round and surged away, leaving the small waves of his wake splashing up the steps on to my feet, so that I had to jump out of the way.

It was impossible to tell from the look on his face whether he had been serious or only teasing. What if, having thought about it, he decided that he was honour bound to tell someone what he'd seen at the empty house? I was so worried about it that I was only dimly aware that my feet hurt as I picked my way gingerly across the gravel from the river wall to the front gate. It was only when Fiff, coming downstairs as I entered the front door, asked ominously, 'What have you done with your sandals, child?' that I looked down and saw with a shock of dismay that I was barefoot. And before I had time to recover from that, she added, 'And weren't you wearing a cardigan, too, when you went out?'

15

The eiderdown sky had smoothed into a grey quilt and a faint drizzle had begun to fall. Indoors, because of the darkening sky, the house was plunged into an early twilight and Fiff had already lit the big Aladdin lamp on the dining-room table to lighten the gloom.

The loss of my cardigan and sandals had exasperated her, as my forgetfulness always did. Hoping to placate her, I pointed out that no one would go to the island on a wet night; my cardigan and sandals would still be there tomorrow. I longed to tell her of the adventure on the island, but it seemed a good idea to keep quiet about it, in case I was forbidden to play there again. It was safer to let her think that I had simply forgotten to collect my belongings, but because my forgetfulness was a constant irritant she was not prepared to be mollified.

'I can't understand why you were so scatterbrained as to leave them there in the first place,' she said. 'Really, Fidgie, why can't you keep your wits about you?'

This was a question I'd often asked myself, but always when it was too late. I was still in disgrace when we sat down to supper, but halfway through the meal – hash, made mostly with potatoes and onions and the last slivers off the lamb bone – I remembered I had a trump card and played it.

'There's a sale at Garth Hall in Fairhurst all this week,' I offered hopefully. 'Do you think we could go?'

The effect was gratifying. Fiff brightened up at once. 'Who told you that?'

'It says so on a notice board outside the sale rooms,' I told her, pleased with the effect of my news. 'Oh please, Mummy, can we go?'

Puzzled, because auction sales were her chief diversion, Fiff said wonderingly, 'Are you sure? How did I manage to miss noticing that?'

A sale in a big house was an entertainment almost as pleasurable as going to the pictures. There were holes and crannies to be explored, especially in very old houses, and gardens to race about in, to play hide-and-seek in with all the other children, while their parents, absorbed, followed the auctioneer from room to room indoors. But best of all, there was always a barn set aside, or a marquee on the lawn, where at teatime sandwiches, bread and butter, scones and fairy cakes were served, a measured plateful to each customer, and a cup of tea poured from big enamel teapots. It was every bit as good as the Sunday School outing; better really, because there were no adults to supervise us, to make us do boring and embarrassing things like running the egg-and-spoon race or the wheelbarrow race. And Fiff always came home in a sunny mood, clutching a pair of garden shears or a painting or a cardboard box full of interesting, possibly valuable, odds and ends.

But the pleasant prospect of a day's hunting at the sale did not altogether wipe out the memory of my carelessness. 'You can come with me,' she said sternly, 'but you'll have to go back and find your belongings as soon as the tide is down. And don't come back until you've found them. I can't afford to buy clothes for you to throw away, you young chump.'

Going all the way back to Moravon in the middle of the afternoon meant that I should have to forgo the tea party, unless I could think of a way round it, and I let out a wail of dismay.

'But the tide won't be low enough until teatime,' I protested, to no avail: Fiff was adamant.

'Well?' she said fiercely, daring me to argue.

Going to bed without Tom felt eerily lonely. Even the python seemed to have lost heart. As I lay in bed listening to the rain – real rain now – prickling against the window pane, and watched the curtains shivering in the gap left open, I comforted myself by reviewing the pleasures and excitements of the day and came at last to the worrying things Chaz had told me about the empty house on the marshes. By now, I didn't doubt that he was right, that Mr Guest *had* hidden his car there and made his way back to Holly Hill unseen. It would be easy enough to keep out of sight, following the creeks and inlets in the marshes, hidden from view by the tall rushes. If he had done something so secretive there could only be one reason why. I still preferred to believe that Mrs Guest had shot Teddy Ransom, but even if she hadn't, if Mr Guest had done it, what I'd said to Chaz still held true: I didn't care. It was all her fault anyway, and I hoped that the police wouldn't decide to let her off. If Mr Guest really had gone back secretly to Holly Hill to shoot Teddy, nobody could possibly have seen him, so nobody would ever find out.

With this satisfying conclusion I settled down to sleep, but suddenly a chilling thought woke me up again: *What if Mrs van Gelderen had been watching through her spyglass?*

In the morning we caught the train from the Junction. We'd waited for hours for Cly to come home, but halfway through the morning when she still hadn't appeared Fiff lost patience. 'The sale will be over before we get there,' she said, fretting. 'We may as well go. Clytie is sensible enough to look after herself.'

So she had left the front door on the latch, with a note reading GONE TO GARTH HALL SALE attached with a safety pin to the back of Pipsy's collar in case Cly came home while we were out. Pipsy, shut in the house, watched us in despair, and small broken-hearted sobs followed us from the sitting-room window as we walked to the gate. The safety pin holding the note had slipped round her collar slightly and GONE TO GARTH HALL SALE hung askew now under her ear, giving her a clownish look.

'Couldn't we take her with us?' I begged.

'She'll only be a nuisance,' Fiff said firmly. 'She's got the lamb bone in the kitchen to keep her occupied, and she probably won't be alone long. Clytie should be back from Dolgarran soon. Besides,' she added as an afterthought, 'where else could I put that note so that Clytie would be sure to see it?'

Before that, while we were still expecting Cly to turn up at any moment, Fiff had called me into her bedroom. 'We'll have to do something about those ears,' she said.

'It's all right, Mummy,' I said. 'I've told everyone that it's ink.'

'Hm,' Fiff said. 'That bird won't fly two days in a row. I won't have people thinking I allow my children to go out unwashed.'

So she dabbed vanishing cream into the lobes of my ears and dusted them liberally with face powder. The result was gratifying: my ears were pink again. Nobody would stare at me now. It was a weight off my shoulders. And the scent of the cosmetics was delicious.

But the bruise on my arm was too black to yield to

make-up and the effect was not nearly as successful: even under calamine lotion it still looked like a bruise, thinly disguised, and it hurt however gently Fiff dabbed at it. Standing back and looking at it, she sighed and said, 'Your father must be losing his touch. He doesn't usually leave marks where they can be seen. Just make sure to keep your coat on this time.'

'He won't come back, will he?' I asked, knowing that it was a stupid question – of course he would come back – but hoping for reassurance.

There was a pause before she answered. 'Probably not. He's got what he wants now. At least, for the time being . . .'

For a place usually so deserted, it was surprising to see how many people were making their way along the track from the bridge past River Cottage, heading towards Holly Hill. News about Teddy Ransom must have spread among the holidaymakers, because they were all strangers.

Fiff said, 'Sightseers.' There was an edge of scorn in her voice. 'Hoping to see something gruesome.'

As we emerged from the gate and turned towards the Junction, two men approached us, one carrying a big camera quite different from Fiff's Box Brownie. The other lifted his hat politely and spoke to Fiff.

'We're from the *Daily Sketch*. Could you tell us—' he began, but before he could go on, Fiff cut in sharply.

'It's no use asking me anything,' she said. 'I know no more about that business than you do. Come along, Fidgie, we've got a train to catch.' And she set off firmly towards the Junction.

'But Mummy,' I protested, lowering my voice and hurrying to catch her up. '*I* know about it.'

'No you *don't*,' Fiff said irritably. 'You only *think* you do.'

Behind me, I heard the man say to his companion, 'Wall of silence.'

'The kid knows something.'

'Kids always do.'

As soon as she was sure that we were out of earshot, Fiff stopped and said with startling ferocity, 'I absolutely forbid you to talk to those reporters, Fidgie. Are you listening? Not one word. Do you understand? I'm damned if I'll get involved in someone else's mess. I've got problems enough of my own.'

'But Mummy—'

'*Not one word!* Those men are from the newspapers, and if you talk to them, they'll worm things out of you. And you are such a goofy kid, you could well get someone into serious trouble.'

I thought of Mr Guest, and subsided, but it was frustrating. I wanted to explain to those men that Mr Guest couldn't possibly have shot Teddy Ransom, because he wasn't there. They probably didn't know that. And besides, it wasn't often I got a chance to show off. There were heaps of things I could have told them and I was sure that they would have listened to every word I said, unlike Fiff.

Besides, I resented being called goofy. Scatter-brained, yes; a chatterbox yes. I knew I was both of those things. But I was *not* goofy. I sulked about it and kicked sand all the way to the Junction.

Fairhurst was only the next halt down the coast, but to walk there along the road was out of the question: it was at least three miles, a lot more than that if you counted the walk from River Cottage to the main road. Once on the main road we could have caught a bus, but if Fiff bought things at the sale – and she would have considered it a bitterly disappointing day if she didn't – it would mean carrying them awkwardly, with many stops to rest, all the way back along the track through the marshes to reach home again.

As soon as I'd got out of bed I'd gone to the window in Tom's room and looked out at the river, hoping that by some miracle the tide would still be out, so that I could go back to the island straightaway, but one look at it told me that going back now would be useless: the tide was high and still coming in. The rain had stopped, but not long since, and wreaths of mist draped the shoulders and laps of the mountains like white fur stoles. The day seemed reluctant to begin, the brightness behind the mountains unable to overpower the damp gloom of the valley.

When the train came in, Fiff searched, as she always did, for an empty compartment, and found one at last, but it was an old one, the seats stuffed with horsehair and unpleasant to sit on. 'Where on earth,' Fiff murmured, 'did they dig up this old relic?' Because the horsehair pricked the backs of my legs, I stood at the open window enjoying the damp air in my face and the clean smell of steam from the engine. Sometimes engines threw out steam and sometimes smoke – though there seemed no reason for this difference – and smoke was full of grit and smelled acrid. The marshland was slipping by with its occasional thickets of gorse and bramble and bracken, its spiky tufts of sedge, everything still glittering from the night's rain; and distantly, isolated, there was the empty house – the house where Chaz had seen Mr Guest's car parked – looking emptier and more isolated than ever in this haunted light.

As it slid past the window, I said, 'Did they ever have a sale at that house?'

'I've no idea,' Fiff said without interest. 'It was empty when we came. I tried to buy it at the time, but they wanted over a thousand pounds for it – a ridiculous price to ask! – and they wouldn't come down.' She glanced over at it and nodded with grim satisfaction. 'So now it stands there rotting.'

I looked more closely at its turrets and gables after that, at its graceless mixture of red brick and granite blocks, its air of desolation, this house I might now be living in; and something which was almost a shiver ran through me. 'I don't like it,' I said. 'I'm glad you didn't buy it. It's ugly.'

Fiff laughed as if I'd said something clever. 'Well, River Cottage isn't exactly an architectural gem, you know,' she said, amused.

Fiff never explained difficult words, but I guessed that she was saying that River Cottage too was ugly, something which had never occurred to me. I thought about it.

'All the same,' I said, slightly abashed by her mockery but determined to stick to my point.

Fiff looked at me over the top of her spectacles. I thought she was going to tell me off for arguing, but with a house sale in prospect nothing could dim her pleasure, and all she said was, 'Do try to stop biting your nails, child.'

Fairhurst, with its pretentious, faintly bogus name, was what Fiff dismissively called a mushroom growth. It was an untidy sprawl of summer bungalows and shacks and bathing huts built on flat land at sea level, but hidden from the sea behind a massive shingle bank. From above, here on the railway embankment, we could see over the shingle to the sea beyond. The sky above was black, hung with puffs of white cloud like the smoke from a battle far out at sea. Below this threatening overcast, the sea was a milky pale green, the horizon underlined by a band of dark blue.

We had a quarter of a mile to walk from the railway

halt to the big knoll – a small hill, really, rising abruptly from the flat floor of the valley like all the rest of the knolls here – where Garth Hall stood half-hidden by tall pines, sharing the high ground with the parish church. The sale was already in full swing when we arrived and we found ourselves at the back of a crowd spilling out of one of the downstairs rooms. Most of the people were strangers, holidaymakers to judge by their clothes and their voices, driven from the beaches by the gloomy morning.

I was glad to be out of sight, hidden behind a tall barrier of other people's raincoats. I had been wary of auction rooms ever since the day when I'd very nearly bought a piece of furniture by mistake – or Mr Lloyd-Jones pretended I had – though I'd only been trying to attract Fiff's attention across the room. I had not forgotten the mortifying guffaws of laughter and the grinning faces turning to seek me out when he said, 'Is your little girl bidding for this very fine Dutch marquetry bureau, Mrs Jacques?' After which Fiff, perhaps embarrassed by my gaffe, bid fifty shillings for the bureau, and had to pay another half-crown to have it delivered to River Cottage. But strangely, she didn't seem to mind.

So, to avoid causing similar havoc, I tugged at Fiff's sleeve and whispered, 'Can I go and play?' and she bent down and whispered back, 'Just be careful not to break anything. I can't afford to pay for breakages,' and I made my escape at once. Exploring was, in any case, half the fun of going to house auctions.

I had to decide whether to buy the house or not, so it was necessary to explore it thoroughly first. There were people wandering about in all the downstairs rooms, picking things up to examine them and putting them down again. I made my way round from room to room and floor to floor, starting at the back. The

241

kitchen, the scullery and the pantries were empty, their contents already sold perhaps, though these were usually left to the last. I looked into all of them, but they were bleakly unwelcoming. Cobwebs hung by the windows, cupboard doors stood open looking as cheerless as if no food had ever been stored in them; stone sinks caught drips from crooked taps leaning drunkenly above them. I felt a puzzled contempt for whoever it was who had been content to live like this.

Disappointed, I went upstairs. Here most of the rooms were empty, the floor coverings long since removed, the floors unpolished and gritty from the tramping of feet. From the front windows it was possible to see the sea through the pines, but the ugly bungalows were still there in the distance, ruining the view. The railway line cut across it too. I decided that before I bought the house I would have to wipe them all out, and while I was about it I might as well move the house and its hillock closer to the sea as well. The view was much better after I had done that, and I was pleased with the result, but still uncertain whether to buy the house or not. There was something sad, something dispirited about it. Such an atmosphere would be impossible to dispel and uncomfortable to live with. Things looked even worse up in the attic rooms. Rain had been coming in through the roof. Wet stains spread in patches over the floors, and buckets and bowls had been put out to catch the drips. The whole place was a ruin. I decided against buying it.

Outdoors, the garden was a ruin too. Someone in the house had pushed down the tops of the sash windows to let air into the crowded rooms, and Mr Lloyd-Jones's voice drifted out, asking 'You all done, then? No advance on fifteen shillings? Going once, going twice . . .' followed by the crack of his gavel.

Two or maybe three hours later when the auction

was suspended for the lunch-break Fiff came looking for me in the garden. I was in the middle of a noisy game of Tig with several other children and when I turned to meet Fiff, one of the boys jabbed me in the shoulder and yelled, 'Tig! You're it!' and ran away hooting in triumph.

'That's not fair!' I yelled back. 'I just tigged *you*. You can't tig me back. You've got to tig someone *else*!' But by then he had disappeared into the shrubbery laughing.

'You know I don't like you playing rough games,' Fiff said, frowning, 'especially with boys.'

'It *isn't* a rough game,' I protested, astonished, forgetting in the heat of the moment that contradicting – my besetting sin – always annoyed her. 'And there are girls playing it too.'

This time she let it go, and we sat in the small summer-house I had discovered buried in the shrubbery, and ate the Bovril sandwiches and the maids of honour she had brought with her. The summer house was dank and some of the slats had fallen from its walls, leaving gaps, but the seats were still sound, though green with algae revived by the night's rain. Fiff, who was not fond of washing and ironing, tore up a handful of couch grass from an overgrown flower-bed, beat the soil off its roots, and scrubbed the green film off the seat with it before we sat down. The game had broken up, the other children vanished, called away perhaps by their parents.

In the past two hours I had explored the whole of the house and the outbuildings, and now I reported my findings, or at least those I thought would interest Fiff.

'They've put up the tea tables in one of the barns,' I told her. 'And there's a boxful of kittens in one of the outhouses. Do you think we could take one home with us? There's a grey one just like Mr Channing has.'

It was a mistake. I saw that I'd sprung it on her too suddenly. 'Oh good lord, child!' she said, lowering the sandwich she had been about to bite. 'Couldn't you make do with Mrs Bellamy's cat? Anyway, they're probably too young to leave their mother yet.'

'They're quite big,' I said. 'And no one would know if we took one.'

'Their mother would,' Fiff said drily, and I remembered that the mother cat had hissed at me when I tried to reach into the box.

Nevertheless Fiff allowed me to drag her to the barn to look at the kittens. The skies had been clearing during the morning and now the sun came flooding out through a break in the clouds, filtering through the trees behind the outhouses. Someone had lit a bonfire in a corner of the courtyard and the air was richly scented with the smoke.

'The smell of autumn,' Fiff murmured to herself. Shafts of sunlight were filtering through the blue smoke in just the same way as the light had fallen through the high windows in the church yesterday.

What had once been stables had long ago been converted into storerooms and garages. Cobwebs hung from the rafters and whitewash had flaked off the walls, revealing rough stone. An old car, its back to the world, waited with shabby dignity to be sold, while a petrol pump stood outside, its paint faded, its hose rotting, its tank probably dry long since. I'd never seen a private petrol pump before.

'They must have been awfully rich, the people who lived here,' I said in awe. 'They had their very own petrol pump!'

Fiff said, 'It was just one old lady who lived alone. All her sons were killed in the War.'

Her tone was too elaborately indifferent, as it always was when she said things like that, things she didn't

244

expect me to understand. I glanced up at her, but Fiff made a point of never showing her feelings and her face told me nothing, though I sensed that she meant more than she was saying; so I tried to guess what it must have felt like to live alone day after day and year after year after all your sons had been killed; but I couldn't, and presently I gave up trying. I was sorry, though, that I'd sneered at the ruinous state of her kitchen.

To take my mind off it, I said, 'When I grow up I'll have my very own *paraffin* pump. Oh, Mummy, wouldn't it be *heavenly* not to have to carry cans of paraffin for miles and miles!'

Fiff sighed and said with feeling, 'Wouldn't it just!'

When we got to the storeroom where I had seen the kittens we were too late. The box was still there, half-hidden behind piles of junk, but the cat and the kittens were gone.

'They *were* here, Mummy,' I wailed. 'Honestly.'

I set about looking for them, but Fiff said, 'You won't find them. I expect the mother cat has found a new place to hide them,' and added absently, her mind elsewhere, 'They're probably half-wild.' She had never been interested in the kittens in the first place, and she had already forgotten them, her attention taken now by the rickety junk piled up round the walls, everything labelled with lot numbers ready for the auction. There was nothing, I thought, worth buying, but Fiff was rapt, lost in contemplation. She said nothing but I was sure that something she saw had excited her. It was no use asking, because I knew she wouldn't tell me: she didn't trust me to keep quiet about it. *If you see something you want to buy at an auction*, she had once said to me, *don't let anyone else know you have your eye on it.* All I could see was a mass of garden tools, most of them old and well-used, some with wooden

245

handles riddled with woodworm. We already had garden tools, most of them newer than these. Surely Fiff couldn't be planning to buy the lawn roller, or the ancient motor-mower, or the croquet set?

'Most of this stuff could do with being thrown on that bonfire,' she said drily.

I was still searching for the kittens – though without any real hope now of finding them – and one of the boxes I pulled out was full of Christmas decorations. Tinsel and baubles and paper garlands overlaid Father Christmases, china snowmen, and brown robins with red breasts. The robins' tiny feet still bore traces of icing from long-forgotten Christmas cakes. I felt a vague dismay. Everything now looked sad and shabby, the tinsel tarnished, the whole boxful fit only for the dustbin. Lifting out a faded packet of cake candles, I asked, 'Do you think Auntie Louie will let Tom come home for Christmas?'

When she didn't answer, I looked up. She had turned away and seemed too interested in the junk to be bothered with my question. I thought she hadn't heard it, but when I began to repeat it, she said distantly, 'He'll get better presents if he stays there.'

'Well, I call it a rotten swizz,' I said hotly, though I could see the logic of her argument; and for a moment a picture of all the presents I would like to have for Christmas flashed before my eyes – a big doll with eyes that opened and closed, a long dance dress with puff sleeves in stiff blue watered silk – and I envied Tom with a sudden bitterness I'd never felt before. I blamed Fiff for letting him go away, but when I started to say sulkily that I didn't see why Tom should have all the luck just because he was a boy, Fiff cut me short. Her next words made it clear that I'd annoyed her.

'It must be getting on for two o'clock,' she said. 'Isn't it about time you set off back to look for your clothes?

There's no train so you'll have to walk.'

I had been hoping she'd forgotten, or that, with any luck, she wouldn't remember until after teatime; but Fiff always seemed to remember the things I wanted her to forget.

'But the tide won't be out for hours yet,' I protested.

'It'll take you hours to get there,' Fiff said, and added with brutal candour, 'Knowing you, you'll probably forget where you're going, halfway.'

Then, because I was still reluctant to obey, made desperate by the thought that I would miss the tea party but unable to think up any argument to prevent it, she did something I hated, though it always seemed to amuse her: she raised her hand and wafted her fingers at me as if dismissing a fly. 'Go on, shoo!' she said. 'Before someone finds your things and takes a fancy to them.'

Then, relenting a little, she added as I turned away, 'You can come back, if you want, as soon as you've rescued your trankliments,' but it was small comfort. I knew I'd never be able to get back in time.

As I drew away, mooching grumpily down the road, she remembered something else, and her voice came after me with a grim warning. 'And Fidgie! If I hear that you've been talking to reporters, there'll be a dancing lesson for you, young woman.'

She meant the strap.

What with the unfairness of Tom's good luck and the loss of the kittens and now my summary dismissal and the likelihood of missing the tea party, I set off down the lane past the church in a bad temper, which grew worse as I reached the road from the village. I had secretly intended to walk back the fastest way, along the railway line – something we weren't supposed to do – but as soon as I'd passed the farm at the foot of the hill and the railway line came into view, I could see a gang of railwaymen working on the track and knew that that route was now blocked. The men would stop me and send me back with a flea in my ear. It had happened before, and Mr Morgan the foreman had threatened to tell Fiff if he caught me doing it again. I couldn't risk that, so there was nothing for it but to go back by the road, which would take *hours*. I groaned with frustration as I turned round and broke into a jog-trot, heading for the main road.

Even if a bus had come I had no money for the fare. This thought reminded me with a sudden nervous jolt of the pockey money I'd had on Saturday – twopence and a threepenny bit – and I let out a yelp of dismay and stopped running. What had I done with it? Fiff knew I hadn't gone to the pictures. What if she asked me what I'd done with the ticket money? I'd never dare tell her I'd lost it. And after all this time I'd never be able to find it. Something, perhaps my heart, screwed itself up into a knot inside me. I was having a heart attack, like the one Miss Wragg's mother had died of, and it seemed likely that I would die of it too.

Wild excuses flashed through my mind. Could I say I'd given the money to Tom as a parting present? But if I did, would Fiff believe me? And if she did believe me – knowing that Tom was going to live in the lap of luxury with Auntie Louie and Uncle Frank – she'd probably be just as angry as she would if I owned up to having lost it. And then I thought of Chaz and all the money he carried with him, and wondered if I could ask him to lend me some, just to cover up the deficit. I didn't like the idea much – Chaz, rich Chaz, would despise me – but at least it was a way out.

Cheered by this thought, I started running again, fast this time. Even so, the road, which seemed so short when we went by bus, wound on interminably. The dry-stone walls on either side leaned drunkenly in and out, held together – or weighed down – by thick clumps of ivy. The ivy was in bloom and beset by insects, even though the scent of its small flowers was foul, was utterly disgrumptious. I ran in the middle of the road to get as far away from it as possible.

The empty road slumbered in the sun. Grass and dandelions grew at the edges where the tarmac ended untidily, not quite reaching the walls. The telegraph wires were humming, as they always did, I imagined, when people were making telephone calls. A week ago these lines had been black with swallows gathering, Fiff said, for their journey south to Africa, but they had all gone now until next summer. I was forced to the side only once, when a motorcycle roared past, its driver wearing his cap back-to-front, his eyes hidden behind goggles, his wife and baby huddled together in the sidecar.

The sun had come out strongly now and it was almost unbearably hot running in a coat but I felt honour bound to keep it on as I'd promised. Luckily, it was one of Cly's old coats and I still hadn't quite grown into it, so it was loose and airy, but I still had to keep slowing down to get my breath. Even so, by the time I reached the drive leading to the house on the marshes I had a stitch in my side and had to stop to bend down and hold my ankles.

Except for its roofs the house was invisible from the road, hidden behind overgrown hedges of privet and pussy willow and mountain ash heavy with scarlet berries; the FOR SALE sign half-buried among the leaves. Their exuberant growth, untamed for years, almost hid the entrance to the drive. I had no real interest in the house, but since I was here, it was tempting to sneak a quick look at it while my stitch eased, this house where I might now be living. The gate hung half-open anyway, inviting trespass. Besides, if I took my coat off temporarily to cool down, no one would be able to see my bruises in the privacy behind these high hedges.

But once inside the gate, the silence of the place began to seem oppressive, even sinister, and I found that I was tiptoeing down the weed-grown drive, half-expecting someone to jump out at me in a rage, shouting; perhaps brandishing a pitchfork. It was difficult to believe that the house, when I finally reached it, was really empty. Now that I could see it close up, I disliked it even more than I had from a distance. The windows at the front were too high up for me to see into, which was a good excuse not to try because I had begun to fear that I might see a face, a horrible face, looking back at me. Or there might be a dead body lying on the floor, or worse, a ghost holding a severed head dripping with blood, like the one I'd seen in a book once. But having got this far, pride dictated that I must not give in to cowardice and run away. The Watchers, who didn't usually follow me out of doors, were here, waiting to see if I'd crack, and I was determined not to give them that satisfaction. So I began to walk round the side of the house – though I couldn't quite manage the jaunty air I would have liked – to show them I wasn't scared. Here there was a window I could have reached, but it was filled with stained glass encrusted with salt from the sea winds, and impenetrable; but it occurred to me that the dirt might not stop anyone inside from seeing me, a thought which made my skin crawl. My courage was fast running out, and I was beginning to think that perhaps spying out the house was not, after all, worth the risk of getting caught doing it, when suddenly a noise at the front of the house froze me. Someone was pushing a ghostly bicycle up the drive. The sound was especially creepy because it was a well-bred whisper quite unlike the squeaky, rattling bicycles most people rode around here. It couldn't be a ghost, not in broad daylight, but it might be someone set to guard the house against trespassers; and people like that were always in a bad temper, especially with kids. Too scared for once to worry about the spiders' webs and their fat, golden occupants, I dived behind the nearest bush and held my breath. The whisper stopped and silence fell again, but it was a creepy silence: someone was looking for me, waiting for me to betray my hiding place.

'Come out, Fidgie, I know you're here!'

Chaz's mocking shout was both a relief and an irritation: I'd been caught out, caught hiding in a blue funk, and I resented it. I decided to give him as big a fright as he'd given me, so I crept through the bushes until I was behind him. Then, with hands raised and fingers clawed, I leapt out shrieking.

The effect was disappointing. He turned and said amiably, 'Put a sock in it, Fidgie. I could hear you coming a mile off.'

Accepting defeat – though I thought he might at least have *pretended* to be scared – I asked, 'How did you know I was here?'

'I saw you. I was coming round the bend down the road there and I saw you through the trees.' The sunshine brought out a glint of ginger I'd never noticed before in his hair. 'Why are you mooching around here anyway?' he went on. 'I thought you were supposed to be at Garth Hall, at the sale.'

'I left some things on the island yesterday,' I said economically, 'and I've got to go back and find them.' It seemed shaming to admit that I had to go and collect clothes left sopping wet by a night's rain. I felt sure that if Chaz left *his* clothes behind he would simply forget them and wear something new. I couldn't imagine Mr

251

Channing sending him back to find them. So, to avoid explaining, I said quickly, 'How did you know I was at the sale anyway?'

'Easy,' he said. 'You left a message on your dog's collar. Dead giveaway. You'll have to do better than that if you want to cover your tracks.'

Somewhere in the back of my mind I had been afraid that Cly would have returned by now, lying in wait like a spider, ready to pounce on me when I took my wet clothes home; but if Pipsy was still wearing the message, then Cly couldn't be there yet. I began to feel more cheerful.

'Anyway, I've got to go,' I said. 'I've got to get back to the island when the tide's out or I won't be able to cross.'

Chaz turned his bicycle round and we began to amble back towards the drive. The house had lost its terrors now that he was here with me. As we walked back to the gate, I said, 'My mother says she almost bought this house. So I wanted to see what it would be like living here.'

Chaz said, 'I thought you were looking for clues.'

'Clues?' I had completely forgotten Chaz's reason for snooping round the house.

'You won't find any,' he said. 'The car didn't leave any tracks. I looked.'

Remembering now, I asked anxiously, 'You haven't told anybody? About the car?'

'Of course not!' Chaz was scathing. 'What do you take me for? If the police want to know, they can find out for themselves. That's what they're there for.'

'What about the reporters?'

'Reporters?' Chaz asked, startled. 'Are they here?'

I told him about the two reporters Fiff and I had met this morning, ending grumpily, 'My mother wouldn't let me talk to them.' I still felt disgruntled about it.

252

Chaz said, 'So that's who they were!' He started to laugh. 'Jenkins went after two men hanging around in the shrubbery this morning and saw them off. Good old Jenks!' The idea delighted him, but I felt sorry for the reporters. The two who'd approached Fiff had been perfectly polite – they'd even raised their hats – and I'd been embarrassed by her rudeness to them.

'What's wrong with reporters?' I asked.

Chaz stopped laughing. 'They're worse than the police if you want to keep a secret,' he said. 'The police keep quiet – at least they do while they're investigating – but reporters spill the beans all over the newspapers.'

'Oh,' I said, realizing with dismay how close I'd come to betraying Mr Guest.

'And Uncle Hil doesn't like people much, anyway,' he added.

Now that Chaz was here and I was safe, I began to look around. Through overgrown azaleas I could see the remains of what had once been a well-kept lawn, now patched with moss and sprinkled with rabbit droppings. But what really caught my attention was the clump of mushrooms growing luxuriantly in the grass, and I let out a whoop of delight. I had never quite got over the disappointment of losing the mushrooms I had picked on the knoll. Their mysterious disappearance still rankled.

'Look, Chaz, mushrooms!' I exclaimed. 'Let's pick them.'

Some of them were old and wrinkled, fallen where some small animal had trampled them, but others were fresh and luscious. Propping his bike against a bush, Chaz picked one of them and examined it intently.

'Yes, these are OK,' he said. 'They're field mushrooms. But whatever you do, don't pick any of those things growing under the trees on the moraines –

those hillocks near your house. They're all toadstools, and some of them are deadly.'

'What d'you mean, deadly?' I asked, disbelieving.

'Just that. Especially the greenish-white ones. They're called Death Caps. If you eat one of those, you die.'

A clear picture of the mushrooms I had left lying on the draining board in the kitchen leapt into my mind. Now that I thought about it, they did have a sort of greenish tinge.

'Oh,' I said, and fell silent.

Brown knees bent, Chaz hunkered down and began to pick the mushrooms while I stood staring at them, quaking.

'Well, come on, then,' he said. 'It was your idea.'

I'd suddenly lost my enthusiasm for picking wild mushrooms, but I couldn't tell Chaz that. We collected all but the old, broken ones, and put them in his saddle-bag on top of a layer of couch grass, to cushion them from the spanners and the puncture kit he kept in there.

Watching him, a sudden cheering thought occurred to me. I pictured Fiff, alive and well, enjoying herself at the sale. Even Cly – who wouldn't be missed – must be alive still, or her friends' parents would have sent to tell Fiff by now. I said carefully, 'If you'd eaten poisonous toadstools – say, yesterday – you'd be dead by now, wouldn't you?'

'Not necessarily,' Chaz said, crushing my hopes. 'Depends which ones you ate. If you ate the Death Caps you might not even be feeling ill yet. Uncle Hil has a book about fungi and I read about them. It's really interesting. First of all you're as sick as a dog, then you recover and you think you're all right. And then,' he paused for effect, 'all of a sudden, days later – or even weeks later – you drop down dead.' To illustrate this, he threw his arms up and collapsed on the grass with his tongue hanging out.

I wasn't amused. It was too frightening for that, unless – and here I remembered the other tall stories he'd told me, like the one about the diamond. As he got to his feet again I plucked up the courage and said accusingly, 'You're making it up,' and to myself I muttered, 'It's absolutely dis*grump*tious.' I was hoping he'd give a shout of laughter and admit it, but he didn't; he shrugged. 'Suit yourself,' he said, pushing the bike ahead of him through the gate while I trailed behind, worrying.

I never knew whether to believe him or not. This time, I decided, he was definitely making it up. That silly pantomime of death proved he was just fooling around, showing off. Nobody could fail to die immediately if they swallowed something poisonous. The thought raised my spirits. Fiff, who was knowledgeable about plants, must have known those mushrooms were toadstoools and thrown them away. I pushed the memory of the now sinister greenish things into the back of my mind and, once back on the road, began to skip light-heartedly to help dispel the fright he'd given me.

A few yards further on, he said, 'I've got an idea. Hop up on the handlebars, and I'll give you a ride.'

To my surprise, it worked. Chaz had to stand on the pedals to see over my head, but the road was flat and we made surprisingly good speed. We didn't talk much: I was concentrating hard on keeping my precarious seat and Chaz was too occupied with pedalling and steering. I fell off once, when the bike wobbled a bit as he turned down Blackberry Lane towards the Junction, but after I'd dusted myself down I climbed back on and we set off again, giggling wildly, exhilarated by this new method of travel.

When we got to the Junction we had to get down and walk the bike demurely along the platform, in case there was some railway bye-law forbidding the riding of bicycles along it; and when we reached the end of the platform and descended the ramp to the track again, the path alongside it was so deep in dry sand that it would have been impossible to ride through it. In fact I was glad of the excuse not to climb back on the handlebars because I'd hurt myself – though I wasn't going to admit it to Chaz – when I'd fallen off, catching the bracket where the light was supposed to be. So when we got to the bridge, I said I'd better walk the rest of the way.

'If Mrs van Gelderen saw me riding on your handlebars,' I explained evasively, 'she'd be sure to tell my mother we were doing something dangerous. And then there'd be ructions.'

Chaz, who was probably tired by the effort of pedalling for both of us, didn't argue. Walking gave us the chance to look around and, though it must have been most of a mile away, Chaz spotted the *Slug* almost at once, moored up against the slipway in the harbour.

'Uncle Hil must have brought her,' he said. 'If we can catch him, we can go back with him.'

'To Llwyn-y-eos?' I asked, thinking of the tea party I should miss at Garth Hall if I didn't get back there in time.

'Well, you can go back home if you want to,' Chaz said, catching the note of dismay in my voice. 'But I came to find you because I've got something to show you.'

'What?'

'It's a surprise.'

I loved surprises, but I also wanted to go to the tea party at Garth Hall. 'Can't I come and see it later, after tea? Why can't you tell me what it is? I'm not coming if you won't tell.'

Chaz sighed, his delightful surprise spoiled. 'Oh, well, all right, spoilsport. The tree house is finished. Henderson helped me to build it, and it's really great. I thought you'd like to see it. That's why I came to find you. We could have a feast in there. I've laid stores in, lemonade and stuff, and Mrs Henderson's promised me some scones filled with clotted cream and her superspecial strawberry jam. She's made a sponge cake too, with icing on it.'

I was torn. A feast in the tree house might be almost as good as the tea party at Garth Hall. Meanwhile, Chaz was enlarging on his plans. 'Now that it's finished, I'm going to put my Lilo in it. Uncle Hil says I can sleep in there every night until the hols are over, starting tonight.'

This gave me a sudden startling idea. This, Chaz's tree house, was somewhere I could hide the next time Boko came to stay, and if Chaz was away at school I wouldn't even need to ask anyone's permission. No one would need to know where I was, and Fiff wouldn't be able to accuse me of betraying family secrets. I could pretend I had been invited to stay with . . . well, with someone. Unlike Cly, I didn't have the sort of friends who could ask me to stay the night, so I'd just have to invent someone.

'OK,' I said. 'But I've got to go and collect my things first, and take them home.' This brought an uncomfortable thought. 'Cly may have got home by now,' I said dismally.

Chaz snorted. 'She's there all right,' he said tersely. 'Turned up just as I was leaving. Is she always in such a foul mood? She nearly bit my head off when I asked for you.'

It was obvious that Cly had been as offensive to Chaz

257

as only she knew how. I knew I ought to stick up for her, but a sudden flash brought back the memory of my beautiful shoes, perhaps lost for ever. I thrust it away; it was too painful to remember. I dared not tell Chaz that I'd lost the shoes: he would blame me for not taking care of them. Worse, he might think I was trying to cadge another pair.

'She's as sweet as pie to grown-ups,' I said bitterly, remembering the charm Cly deployed so effortlessly, so entrancingly, so *enviably* in front of adults. 'You just have to steer clear of her.'

'Don't worry, I will,' he said gloomily.

The sun was already tending towards the west. Inland, the foothills leaned forward, their parched flanks the rich gold of apricots against a sky which had remained blue-black all day. In spite of the sunshine, there was a chilly breeze sweeping up the estuary as there so often was, and I was glad of my coat. The estuary acted like a funnel, collecting airs too idle to climb the mountains and whipping them into a breeze. Halfway along the bridge, I stopped to hang over the railing. Below, the tide was still racing out to sea. From here Llwyn-yr-eos was out of sight, but we could see Holly Hill as well as River Cottage and the other two houses, and there was no sign of life in any of them, though a few sightseers were still wandering about.

What little could be seen of the garden of Hill Top House – the bungalow on top of the big knoll – looked less unkempt, as if someone had been tidying it up, and two deck-chairs had been set up. More honeymooners, I supposed, and dismissed it. At Holly Hill the doors of the big shed in the paddock stood open and I imagined that Mr Guest must be in there, working on his improbable machine. High on the hill in the far distance Mrs van Gelderen's great house stood out, staring north, its windows withdrawn and dark. To me they always looked arrogant too, as if they considered the rest of the world beneath their notice.

'Chaz . . . ?' I said slowly, and stopped so long, wondering how to put it, that in the end he prompted me.

'Well, what?'

'Well . . . you know Mrs van Gelderen, the old lady who's always watching through her spyglass in that big house up there?'

'I know what you've told me about her.'

'Well . . . what if she saw Mr Guest sneaking back to Holly Hill, the day Mr Ransom got shot? Would she have to tell the police?'

Chaz thought about it. 'Depends,' he said.

'What on?'

'Whether she felt like it.'

This answer was unsatisfactory: it did nothing to ease my fears for Mr Guest. Seeing the anxiety on my face, Chaz said, 'Cheer up. From what you say, the old girl is a stickler for good behaviour. She'd probably keep quiet. She sounds like the sort of old battleaxe who'd think that Mrs Guest deserves to be hanged anyway, even if she didn't murder anybody.'

This was more reassuring. I thought about it and it sounded right. 'Well, Mrs van Gelderen's the only one who's likely to split,' I said. 'The cook and the maid won't be able to. They'd both gone out. I saw them go, just before I saw you coming in the *Slug*. So that's all right.'

'Anyway,' Chaz went on slowly, as if trying to convince himself, 'we don't *know* that Mr Guest went back to Holly Hill again. Maybe Uncle Hil is right and he went to the empty house just to have a look at it.' It didn't sound convincing but there didn't seem to be anything else to say. A thinking silence fell. We were

259

both certain now that Mr Guest was guilty. The knowledge was a burden, and it was all Chaz's fault for going snooping round that house.

'I wish you'd never gone there,' I said morosely. 'I wish I didn't know.'

We both fell silent. At last Chaz said, 'If we keep our traps shut, nobody can prove anything . . . And maybe Mrs Guest will get off . . .'

We both knew that that wasn't likely, but it was consoling to think that our silence was justified, even noble: we were protecting Mr Guest, who was a nice man.

We began walking again, but as soon as we did, just as if I'd conjured her up, I recognized the distant figure of Miss van Gelderen emerging from the tollbooth, mounting her bike. To me she cut a ridiculous figure, severely dressed in a dark suit and hat in spite of the sunshine, her heavy body supported by slender legs, like a sideboard. She wore her hair in earphones, thin plaits coiled into saucers covering her ears, a style I thought both ugly and silly; but for all that, or perhaps because of it, she was a sight to be dreaded, the harbinger of disapproval and disgrace.

'Quick, pretend you haven't seen her,' I said, turning back to lean over the railing, forgetting that Chaz didn't know her.

'Who? That woman coming?' he said. 'Who is she?'

'It's Miss van Gelderen,' I said, lowering my voice even though she was too far away to hear. 'The one whose mother spies on us. She carries tales.'

But Chaz refused to be cowed. While I climbed up the railing and hung over the top, pretending to be interested in the river below, I noticed out of the corner of my eye that he produced a school cap from his back pocket and crammed it on his head, and when she reached us, he pulled his bicycle aside to make room for her and politely tugged the peak of his cap in salute. She swept past us both, ignoring us.

'Why did you want to do that?' I hissed at him, annoyed that he should have laid himself open to a snub by showing courtesy to someone who deserved rudeness; but Chaz merely shrugged.

'I wanted to get a good look at her,' he said.

'Oh, well,' I said, relenting. 'She'd probably have reported you to your uncle if you *hadn't* lifted your cap.'

He snorted. 'Huh! She'd get short shrift from him if she tried,' he said, and I thought enviously how pleasant, how simple life would be if only Fiff were as dismissive of snitching as Mr Channing was.

I watched her departing back, the disproportionately slender legs sheathed in grey lisle stockings, and longed to insult her. 'I bet she wears great big woolly knickers right down to her knees,' I said acidly, and was rewarded with a burst of laughter from Chaz. A sudden shaft of silliness pierced me, and I went into my imitation of Mae West, putting one hand on my hip and drawling sexily over my shoulder, 'Come up and see me sometime, Big Boy.' It never failed to delight the boys at school, who egged me on to repeat the performance; but Chaz let out a yelp of warning. 'Mrs van Gelderen's watching!' he cried. It gave me a fright until I noticed the grin he wore. It annoyed me.

'You'd be scared of her too, if you lived in our house,' I snapped. 'My mother believes every word she says.' And in spite of knowing that he was fooling, I turned round nervously to check that there was no glint of a lens from the big house on the hill. It was too far away to see any such thing, of course, but I was just in time to see a telegraph boy emerge on his bicycle from between the two knolls. I watched him prop the Post Office bike against the wall outside our house and walk up the path.

261

'Oh, look!' I breathed. 'A telegram!'

To me telegrams were exciting, full of possibilities. One day a telegram might bring amazing news of a fortune left to us by an uncle, unheard-of till now, in Australia. I couldn't understand why grown-ups were frightened of them. Fiff said that it was because of the Great War, when a telegram's arrival meant that someone had been killed, but that was meaningless to me: there wasn't a war on now. But so far the only telegrams we'd received had been disappointing. They came from aunts or cousins to tell us when to expect them, which train to meet. But it might not always be so.

No one opened the door at River Cottage, and the boy pushed the telegram through the letter-box. At least, I supposed that that was what he did: it was too far away to be certain, but presently he left and cycled away again. It was an anti-climax: I had expected someone – Cly probably – to come to the door, tear the orange envelope open and give some sign of ecstasy or woe, throw her hands up or faint – not that Cly ever did either of those things: to show emotion would have been beneath her dignity. Because nothing happened, I decided that the telegram was not interesting, and turned round, disappointed, to continue on my errand.

Chaz, reading my mind said, 'It probably wasn't important. Come on, let's go.'

When we got to the tollbooth at the far end of the bridge, Chaz paid for both of us and the bike without hesitation. His ability to afford things fascinated me. If I'd been on my own, I would have crawled under the turnstile, keeping out of sight, just in case the toll-keeper's wife was on duty. *She* never let us through without paying. It was a rare experience to swank through the turnstile with a clear conscience, and without worrying about the cost.

As we walked away curiosity about his finances got the better of me and I asked, 'How much pocket money do you get?'

'Five shillings,' he said casually.

I was thunderstruck. It was an enormous, an unimaginable sum. *'Five shillings!'* I gasped.

Chaz looked at me, surprised by my reaction. 'Why?'

I was good at sums. Sometimes, borne on a wave of fright, Mr Hughes came surging into the classroom to spring a test on us. He'd call us out to stand quaking in a semi-circle while he tossed questions of mental arithmetic at us; and woe betide the dunce who gave the wrong answer. So now I multiplied five by twelve and divided it by two.

'You could buy *thirty bars* of nut milk chocolate *every week* for that,' I said, shocked and excited beyond words. Even Tom with his extra penny had had to save up for weeks to collect half that sum.

'So what? Who'd want to buy thirty bars of chocolate every week?' he asked, silencing me. I wanted to say *I would*, but I didn't want him to know how greedily I yearned for sweets. I went on thinking about it because the idea of so much money was fascinating. My tuppence a week had to be deployed with skill and cunning, and because I thought in farthings, I multiplied sixty by four. The answer was staggering. I felt dizzy even *imagining* wolfing my way through two hundred and forty liquorice bootlaces, or Mickey Mouse's Eyeballs, or a hundred and twenty paper bags full of dolly mixtures.

It was while Chaz was pushing the bike up the sandy path to the main road that I noticed his wrist-watch again. I had managed to ignore it since our first meeting, when it had seemed such an embarrassing affectation. And when we reached the main road and turned towards the town, there too was the church tower, its clock face staring at me accusingly, a reminder of my fatal backwardness.

Without meaning to, I blurted out, 'I can't tell the time.' The confession was out before I could stop it, and instantly regretted: it sounded like a cry for help, and begging for help was beneath my dignity.

Chaz turned his head to stare at me. 'You can't *what*?' he said, as if he doubted his hearing. I thought I could detect the beginnings of a grin on his face.

I hung my head and scowled at my feet. 'If you're going to be horrible about it, I'm going,' I said sullenly. 'It's not my fault. Nobody ever showed me how.'

I needn't have worried. I had forgotten his passion for collecting and giving out information. He stopped, leaned his bicycle against his hip, and unbuckled the strap of his watch.

16

It was much easier than I'd expected, so easy in fact
that I wondered why I hadn't understood it before. No
wonder Tom thought me such a dunce. But Chaz
insisted on making sure I'd grasped it thoroughly,
turning the hour hands through the hours and the
minute hands through the minutes all over again, and
then trying to catch me out in the same way Boko had,
until I began to get restless. Up here above the river the
air was still, the rock-face giving back the summer's
collected heat. Above the road, the gorse was in full
bloom, its honeyed scent heavy on the air.

We were halfway through his exercises with the
watch when Chaz suddenly stopped speaking. I didn't
notice because at the same time a strange noise across
the river distracted me. It was a whirring, chopping
noise like nothing I'd ever heard before, and seemed to
be coming from up in the sky. Aeroplanes were wildly
exciting, a sight not to be missed, and though this
didn't really sound like an aeroplane, I turned away
and rushed to the wall to look across the river,
forgetting the tedium of the watch. There, over Holly
Hill, I saw Mr Guest's strange contraption rising above
his paddock. It was a long way away but I judged that
it rose about fifty feet, stood still in the air, and sank
back to earth again. Presently it rose again, this time
much higher and hovering longer before it sank again.

'Look, Chaz, look!' I yelled, enthralled. 'He's made
that funny thing fly!'

There was no response, and Chaz was not by my side. I turned and saw, to my dismay, that he was having another of his strange throes. All thought of the autogyro went out of my head instantly. Chaz was still standing where I had left him, holding the watch by its strap, but his face had gone blank and his mouth was working as if he were chewing gum. I looked around, checking to see that there was nobody around to witness this embarrassing performance, but very few people ever came up here, well past the last shop. We were standing on a bend where the road had been cut through the solid rock of the hillside, and the nearest houses were down in the town or higher up the hill behind us, hidden round the bend.

This blackout seemed to go on longer than the ones before. We had been standing almost in the middle of the road, and now to my alarm I heard the familiar *ting-ting* of a bus-conductor's bell, followed by the bus's engine revving up, out of sight behind us.

I didn't think I could drag Chaz out of the way, but surprisingly he moved as meekly as a toy when I took his arm and drew him to the wall. As soon as it lost its support, the bicycle crashed to the road and I dashed back to pick it up just in time. The bus roared round the corner as I hauled the bike out of the way. It had been a near thing: the bus's brakes shrieked briefly and the bus conductor leant out of the door and shook his fist at me as the bus swept past in a green blur.

'Oh Chaz,' I said irritably, 'I do wish you wouldn't keep doing this sort of thing.'

Life began to come back into his eyes. He said vaguely, 'What time is it?'

I pretended not to hear him. I was too annoyed with him for getting me into trouble with the bus conductor, not to mention the driver and the passengers. One or other of them would be sure to tell Fiff that I'd nearly been run over, and she would be angry about it. Sometime tonight, or tomorrow at the latest, I could look forward to a stiff talking-to. Grown-ups always seemed to consider it their duty – one of the more pleasurable ones – to tell our parents how close we'd come to sudden death. 'Come on,' I said, starting to push the bike, 'we've got to get back to the island.'

We were halfway down the hill, almost into the main street, before Chaz realized that I was wheeling his bike, and he took the handlebars from me. I was glad to hand them over: it was a steep hill, and I'd had to squeeze the brakes all the way to stop the machine running away with me.

Even before we left the main street and turned towards the harbour, we could see that something had been attracting everyone's attention, but clearly it was over now, and knots of people were turning away from the edge of the quay like spectators who had been watching a parade, now passed. Small boys, reluctant to leave, were vying with each other to boast about what they'd seen. Arguments broke out between them. I listened in to the nearest one.

'It was just like a grasshopper!'

'Don't be stupid. Grasshoppers have legs. It looked like a dragonfly.'

'Where I live, I seen hundreds of them.'

'I seen *millions*!'

'You never. Don't tell lies. You never seen one before in your life.'

'We've missed something,' Chaz said, slowing down. 'I wonder what it was?'

'I 'spect it was Mr Guest's auto-thing,' I said. 'He's made it fly.'

Chaz was electrified. 'When? Where? Why didn't you tell me?'

Remembering the near-accident with the bus and the

likelihood of having to face Fiff's wrath because of it, I wanted to say nastily *Because you were having one of your stupid blackouts,* but I couldn't quite bring myself to be so brutal. Remembering too Mr Channing's plea to pretend not to notice, I said lamely, 'I thought you'd seen it.'

Sounding puzzled, Chaz said, 'He said it wasn't ready to fly yet. He promised to let me know as soon as he was ready to take it up.'

'I 'spect he couldn't find you,' I said to cheer him up, but he wasn't listening.

'Come on,' he said, beginning to push the bicycle again, urgently now. 'If the *Slug*'s still here, we can get a lift back with Uncle. I've got to get to Holly Hill. I want to see Mr Guest fly the thing. He might let me go up with him.'

The crowds of holidaymakers were much thinner now that August was almost at an end, but with the bike impeding our progress it was still difficult to make our way to the edge of the quay, and long before we reached the steps where the *Slug* had been moored, we saw her already making her way across the harbour, Mr Channing standing at the wheel, his back to us, and Jenkins standing sentinel on the bow. They were already too far away to hear our yells above the noise of the engine.

Chaz let his shoulders drop. 'Damn!' he said feelingly, 'We could have been practically *there* by now.'

'You can go home if you like,' I offered generously. 'You don't *have* to come with me.' The truth was that I didn't want him to come with me: it would be unbearably embarrassing to have him watch me collecting my disreputable clothes from the dunes on the island. After a night's rain, they were sure to look like something out of a dustbin. If I'd been with Ellen or one of the others it wouldn't have mattered; they would have understood that clothes, however battered, were valuable.

But Chaz was not to be shaken off so easily. 'Oh well,' he said philosophically, 'I suppose the autogyro will still be there when we get back. Come on, then, let's hurry.' And he began to push his bike towards the promenade.

Past the big house everyone called the Bath House, the channel narrowed. I threw off my coat, tucked my skirt hastily into my knickers and raced down to the water, trying to get ahead of Chaz. I was wearing a pair of Cly's old gym shoes and I didn't stop to take them off. The water was thigh-deep and slowed me down, and I hoped that, hampered by the bicycle, he would stay behind and wait for me, but he laid the bike down on the sand by my coat and came after me. His legs were longer than mine and he caught me up as I squelched through the loose sand, falling sometimes to my knees in my haste to climb to the top of the dunes. There was nothing for it but to let him witness my humiliating task.

Chaz, unaware that his presence was an embarrassment to me, said as he climbed, 'I expect this island was made by the old sailing ships, dumping ballast before they took on a new cargo. They did that, you know.'

I was too mortified by his presence to listen. The rain had fused the top layer of sand into a thin crust, easily broken, but underneath the crust the sand was as dry and deep as ever and our footsteps were soundless, which must have been the reason why we came upon such an unexpected scene. I was making for the valley – no more than a depression between the dunes – where Ellen and I had been playing. Someone had tossed my cardigan and sandals up to the top of the dune, out of the way, and I pounced on them. But when I stood up I stopped dead. Chaz arrived beside me and together we stood looking down on a man and woman writhing together on the sand, the woman's legs wide, the man, still trousered, on top of her. It was clear, even though I'd never seen it before, that they were *having a spin*.

Neither Chaz nor I spoke. I was studying the tableau, riveted with astonishment and interest, and I think Chaz was too, until the woman looked up and shouted irritably, 'What are *you* staring at? Clear off!'

In my haste to comply I stepped backwards unwarily. One foot plunged into deep sand and I lost my balance, and in flinging my arms out I brought Chaz down with me. Together we barrelled down the slope, ending in a heap at the bottom. Once we'd disentangled ourselves and I'd collected my cardigan and sandals again, I sat down and began to change my shoes. My sandals – Cly's once – were still damp from the night's rain but I preferred them to her old gym shoes, which were now full of water and caked with sand inside as well as out. I was trying to dig wet sand out from between my toes when Chaz, still in thrall to the scene we'd just witnessed, said, 'We could try that; see what it feels like.'

With any of the other boys, I'd have pretended I didn't know what he meant, but Chaz was different. The idea seemed practical and interesting, even exciting. I thought about it.

'Yeah, OK,' I said. 'Where?'

'Well . . . here.'

'Not *here*!' I said, shocked by this lack of forethought. 'The tide's out. People will come.'

And as if to prove my point, excited voices suddenly burst out, quite close, yelling, 'Look! Look! There it is again!'

Alerted now, we could hear it too, the strange

batting sound, like an egg-beater in the sky.

'It's Mr Guest's auto-thing,' I said. 'It's coming this way.'

We scrambled to our feet and raced to the top of the next dune, and there it was again, Mr Guest's weird contraption, heading towards us, brilliantly sunlit against the looming black sky. Chaz started jumping up and down, waving his arms and yelling in an ecstasy of excitement, perhaps hoping that Mr Guest would land and take us for a ride. But the machine swept on, passing overhead and heading out to sea. Together with the small crowd who had waded out to the island, we stood and watched it, fascinated, shading our eyes and turning slowly like sunflowers to follow its passage out to sea.

When it was far out at sea, almost out of sight, it stopped and hovered for a moment.

And then, without warning, it dropped like a stone.

17

After the first collective gasp, we waited in disbelief, half-expecting to see the machine leap up again out of the water. When it didn't, commotion broke out.

Chaz began running to the seaward end of the island, as if by getting closer he could assure himself that he had been mistaken, that the autogyro was still flying. When he saw that it wasn't, a cry of bereavement escaped him and he turned and ran stumbling through the dunes back towards the channel. I followed, splashing into the water behind him, slowed by its depth, unable to catch up.

'Wait for me!' I yelled, but he didn't answer and didn't slow down.

'Where are you *going*?' I shrieked, struggling thigh-deep through the channel, hampered by the clothes I was carrying.

'To get the lifeboat,' he yelled without looking back.

When I finally disentangled myself from the water, I began to race after him. His bicycle was still lying where he had left it on the beach, but he ignored it and ran on, probably reasoning that he could move faster through the crowds without it. I paused only to snatch up my coat and throw it on – the bike was his responsibility, after all, and he didn't seem to care if someone pinched it – but then I suddenly remembered the mushrooms in his saddle-bag and turned back. Just to make sure, I undid the buckles on the saddle-bag. The mushrooms were still there, still undamaged, pale as moons. As I hauled the bike up, two loud bangs, one a few seconds after the other, sounded high in the air above us: the maroons summoning the lifeboatmen.

'Come back!' I shrieked. 'The lifeboat's *coming*!' He *must* have heard the explosions but he took no notice and ran on.

By the time that I'd tied the laces of the gym shoes together and hung them and the cardigan over the handlebars, Chaz was out of sight, lost among the crowds gathering on the promenade, some drifting down the beach to the edge of the tide, drawn like pins to a magnet, all staring out to sea, hungry for drama.

I wasn't really worried about Mr Guest. It wasn't as if he'd crashed on land. He'd get wet, of course, and he'd be annoyed with himself for losing his strange flying machine, but water was a soft and silken thing: falling into it, even from such a height, could be no worse than falling into a heap of feathers. The cry of distress Chaz had given, his race to alert the lifeboat, was explained by the loss of his beloved autogyro. He must have been hoping that the lifeboat would reach it before it sank to the bottom where, of course, it would have to stay. Nobody could haul it up from the bottom of the bay. Probably there were giant octopuses down there who'd wrap their arms round it and refuse to let go.

But all Mr Guest had to do was to swim around – or float if he couldn't swim – until the lifeboat picked him up. I, on the other hand, faced the prospect of having to push Chaz's bike all the way home if I couldn't find him. I couldn't ride it because the saddle was too high: I'd never be able to reach the pedals. And here another, more daunting thought assailed me: I should have to pay the toll on it to cross the bridge – there'd be no possibility of sliding it under the toll-gate – and I had no money.

273

The sand was still damp and firm where the tide had receded. Ticking silkily, the bicycle moved willingly beside me. I pushed it up a slipway to the promenade and from there onto the stone jetty above the deep pool in the harbour. Here even at low water the ferry boats were able to land their passengers. From this vantage point I reasoned that it should be easy to keep watch for Chaz. Instead, to my intense relief, I saw the *Slug* returning, Jenkins at the prow. But Mr Channing was heading towards the deeper channel on the other side of the island. I rang the bell of the bike frantically, but when that produced no effect I leaned the bike against the railing and began jumping up and down, screaming, 'Mr Channing! Mr Chan*ning*!' to attract his attention.

He couldn't have heard me over the noise of the engine, but he must have seen my wild antics because he turned his head at last and once he'd recognized me, he swung the bow of the little boat towards me. His voice came clearly over the water.

'Where's Charles? Have you seen him?' The fierce beard looked fiercer than ever and I began to worry that he was annoyed with me for losing Chaz. The scar had tightened up, pulling his mouth into a snarl. Abandoning good manners I pointed towards the lifeboat station across the harbour.

'He went to get the lifeboat. Mr Guest has crashed into the sea.'

He was closer now, heading for the stone steps leading up to the jetty, and I saw his face relax, anxiety draining out of it. 'I know. That's why I came back. I was afraid the boy had gone up with Guest in that lunatic machine of his.' He was right below me now and seemed to notice the bike for the first time. 'Is that Charles's bicycle?'

I explained that I was guarding it until Chaz came

back. Mr Channing moored the boat to an iron ring in the stonework and mounted the steps, but just as he reached me, my attention was diverted by the sight of the lifeboat racing down its slipway and crashing into the water, sending up a tiara of glittering water round its bows. It was too far away to tell who was aboard it.

'Do you think they'd let Chaz go with them?' I asked.

'Not a chance,' Mr Channing said, watching beside me. 'They wouldn't take a child on a rescue mission.'

Somewhere in the town an ambulance bell started clanging urgently. The sound had a note of panic about it, and for the first time a doubt began to cross my mind.

'Mr Guest will be all right, won't he?' I asked.

Mr Channing didn't answer.

'Mr Channing?'

Instead of replying, he said, 'I think I ought to get you home.'

My heart sank. If he forced me to go home I should miss all the excitement. It wasn't safe to defy an adult, especially a man, but I tried. 'Couldn't we wait till they've rescued Mr Guest?'

'That could take a long time.' The mention of time seemed to act as a reminder. He took a big silver watch out of the breast pocket of his tunic and glanced at it. 'I'll have to be getting home,' he said, 'I'm expecting a guest. She may have arrived already . . .' He glanced down at me. 'And won't your mother be expecting you home for supper?'

The mention of food brought back thoughts of the fairy cakes at the auction and the strawberry scones in the tree house, and I hesitated. I badly wanted to wait until I was sure they'd rescued Mr Guest, but now I realized that I was starving. It seemed a long time since Fiff and I had eaten the Bovril sandwiches in the

275

summer-house at Garth Hall. I wondered if I could devise a sly scheme to persuade Mr Channing to buy me something to eat, but this, I knew, would come under the heading of cadging. While I wrestled with the problem, Mr Channing set about wheeling the bicycle to the top of the steps.

I hurried to catch him up and made one more effort to delay him. 'But what about Chaz?' Without Chaz, there would be no feast in the tree house, and it was probably already too late to go back for tea at Garth Hall.

It didn't work.

'I'll have to come back for him.'

Surprisingly, because it seemed to me that he was such an incredibly old man, he lifted the bicycle easily and began to carry it down the steps to the *Slug*. Jenkins, who had been bidden to stay behind, greeted him as if he'd never expected to see him again.

Still casting about for an excuse to stay, I watched the lifeboat racing past the Point into the open sea; and out of the corner of my eye I saw a distant, familiar movement. It was too far away to distinguish the colours, but it was certainly the beach towel rippling from Fiff's bedroom window, summoning me home.

I suppressed a wail of exasperation. I couldn't ignore the summons, even though I suspected that I was being recalled to greet some unexpected and probably tiresome guests; guests moreover who had no more interest in seeing me than I had in seeing them. But Fiff's decrees were absolute, and obeying them was easier than dredging up excuses later to placate her, so I slopped discontentedly down the stone steps and boarded the boat as soon as Mr Channing had hefted the bicycle and laid it on its side on the cabin roof.

It occurred to me, as he unhitched the mooring rope and started the engine, that it was surprising that Fiff had returned from the auction so soon. Usually she stayed until Mr Lloyd-Jones had sold the very last lot of the day, and that was often quite late, especially if the bidding had been slow.

The strange sky – the same colour as the bruise on my arm – had moved inland as the day wore on. Now it darkened the east and we were heading towards it, the sunshine on the hills ahead incongruously golden against the gloomy backdrop. Boats deserted by the tide lay at an angle on the sandbars in the harbour, the pools around them reflecting the metallic sky. We were halfway to the bridge before Mr Channing said anything. I was used to his silences by now, and they didn't bother me, but what he said did, or rather the way he said it.

'Summer's coming to an end . . .'

Fiff had said the same thing earlier, at Garth Hall, and it wasn't true; it couldn't be. Anyone looking at the brilliant sunshine all around, on the hills, on the water, could see that summer was nowhere near its end; but it would have been bad manners to contradict. All the same, the way he said it – regretfully, as though saying goodbye to someone he might never see again – made me uneasy.

Making things worse, he went on, 'I suppose you'll be back in school again pretty soon.'

'Next Monday,' I said gloomily. I'd managed to put the thought of Mr Hughes and the cane and homework out of my mind ever since the holidays had begun in the middle of July, and the reminder added to my dismay.

'Charles is not due back at school for ten days, but he'll have to go down to London before that, to get kitted out for the autumn term,' he said. And then he stunned me by adding, 'We'll probably motor down on Sunday.'

It came as a shock. I'd known of course that the holidays would end eventually, but not yet, not abruptly like this. Until a moment ago, the summer seemed to stretch pleasurably into the foreseeable future; now all of a sudden it was at an end, everyone was leaving, and there was nothing I could do to stop it. Even the swallows had gone.

'You'll be coming back though, won't you?' I asked anxiously, meaning both of them. It surely couldn't take ten days to buy school uniform?

'I will, but Charles won't. We won't see him again until Christmas. Perhaps not even then, if he elects to spend the holidays with his cousins down there, and he probably will.'

My heart sank. First Tom, now Chaz. I felt as though I had swallowed a stone, sharp-edged and heavy. The pain made me sulky and rude. I said, 'Why can't you keep him here with you?'

He sighed. 'It wouldn't do, Fidgie,' was all he said.

That was when my manners deserted me completely. Without thinking, I said, 'He'd come back if you bought Mr Ransom's boat for him.' As soon as the words were out, I realized how shocking they were. I was cadging again, even though, this time, for Chaz as well as for me. Fiff would have had a fit.

But Mr Channing didn't. All he said was, 'That's quite a thought, Fidgie . . . yes, that's quite a thought.'

Having come so close to disaster, and survived it, I decided that silence would be prudent, and we were nearly home before I remembered something I'd been meaning to ask him.

'Does your cat ever have kittens?' I asked.

'No, never,' Mr Channing said, amused. 'Or none that I know of: he's a tom. Why?'

I'd imagined all cats were shes, but of course – now I thought about it – they couldn't be. Slightly abashed by my mistake, I said, 'I wish I had a cat just like him.'

It was only after Mr Channing had delivered me to the stone steps and I was crossing the gravel to River Cottage that a cheering thought came to me: Cly too would be leaving, going back to boarding school.

Autumn might not be too bad after all.

18

The front door was locked, which was a suprise. Fiff never locked it when she was home. To my dismay, it was Cly who answered my knock.

'At last!' she said when she saw me. 'You took your time answering the signal.'

'I was in *Moravon*!' I protested.

'I know,' she said. 'I saw you flouncing about on the bridge with that stupid boyfriend of yours.'

Using Fiff's signal to summon me home was cheek, and now she had insulted Chaz. I was about to fly into a temper when Cly suddenly softened and smiled. 'Well, now you're here, would you like to be an angel and do something for me?'

The fury I'd felt collapsed at once. If I could get into Cly's good books by doing something for her, I would. I jumped at the chance. 'What do you want me to do?'

'A telegram has arrived. You can take it to Ma. She's at Garth Hall, at an auction.'

She seemed to have called a sudden truce, as she sometimes did, though they never lasted long. As I went to hang my cardigan on the clothes line, it crossed my mind that I could ask her what she'd done with my shoes, and I longed to, but I hesitated. For one thing, I wasn't supposed to have them: they were a secret I'd kept from Fiff. And for another, I knew very well that she'd only laugh and say 'What shoes?' There was nothing for it but to go on pretending that nothing

280

had happened, and hope that she might relent and put them back.

The telegram lay on the dining-room table where Cly had thrown it unopened. I snatched it up and made for the Junction, hoping that the railway gang had moved away, so that I could make use of the short cut along the line; but they were still there, almost at the Junction now, blocking the way. Frustrated, I set off along the railway platform towards Blackberry Lane and the main road. Perhaps, I thought hopefully, they would still be serving teas in the barn at Garth Hall. I broke into a run.

The road, drowsing in the low rays of the evening sun, straightened out after the first few bends, and in the distance a woman who looked remarkably like Fiff was approaching on a bicycle. I stopped, astonished, as she reached me and dismounted, laughing.

'Mummy!' I gasped. 'Where did you get it?'

Fiff, exhilarated by the success of her day at the auction, said, 'At the sale, of course. Didn't you see it in the garage? I bought it. It's almost new. It only needs a drop of oil.'

The bike did indeed look new, though old-fashioned, the sort we called a sit-up-and-beg, with a basket on the handlebars; but under the coating of dust its dark green livery was still shiny, the basket still pristine.

I dug the telegram, now slightly crushed, out of my pocket. 'It came about an hour ago,' I said, though I had no real idea how much time had passed since I'd seen it delivered.

Fiff, standing with one foot on the ground, the other still on one pedal ready to remount, tore open the flimsy envelope and read the message. Her eyebrows rose.

'Who's it from?' I asked, but she didn't seem to be listening.

'Oh . . . only Eric,' she said vaguely. 'He offered to do something for me when he got home. He wants me to telephone.' She remounted the bike. 'You'd better go straight home,' she said over her shoulder as she drew away. 'I'm going to the telephone kiosk in the village. Eric should be home from work by now.'

I had no intention of going back to River Cottage without knowing why Eric had asked Fiff to phone. I trailed after her disappearing figure, dawdling as I reached the turning to Blackberry Lane, pretending to look for blackberries although it was obvious that they weren't ripe enough yet to pick.

An iron plaque bolted to each of the crossing gates read PROPERTY OF THE GREAT WESTERN RAILWAY CO. THESE GATES MUST BE KEPT CLOSED. It threatened a penalty of forty shillings for misuse of railway property, but in spite of this I climbed up to sit astride the nearest gate, and I'd been sitting there for what seemed hours before Fiff reappeared.

'Did you get through?' I asked. Grown-ups never expected to get through on the telephone; getting through was considered a feat, a minor triumph, a source of satisfaction.

The expression on her face was as controlled as ever, but there was suppressed excitement, suppressed laughter, in it. 'It seems your father was taken violently ill this morning,' she said, adding acidly, 'but not ill enough, unfortunately. He's better again now.'

It seemed to me that this was not sufficient grounds for a divorce. While I'd been waiting, I'd been thinking about the conversation I'd overheard on the stairs that night, when Eric had offered to go and spy on Boko. Bearing in mind that I was not supposed to have heard that conversation, I asked cautiously, 'Is that all?'

'No,' she said sombrely, 'not quite all.' Searching her face for clues, it seemed to me that she hardly knew whether to laugh or cry, but all she said was, 'Come along, we'd better get home. It's nearly time for supper.'

We had closed the second of the crossing gates behind us and had set off on the track through the marshes, Fiff pushing the bicycle beside me, before she suddenly started to laugh. It was a harsh, edgy sound, worryingly unlike real laughter.

'What's the matter?' I asked, wanting to join in but unable to see the reason for her merriment.

The question seemed to send her off into fresh paroxysms, until she had to stop walking, tears streaming down her cheeks. Almost sobbing, she pulled a handkerchief from her pocket and took off her glasses to mop her eyes. At last, making an effort to calm down, she said, gasping, 'Oh, dear.'

'But what's so funny?' I persisted, longing to share the joke.

'Oh, nothing,' she said at last. 'It was just something Eric said.' The memory seemed to set her off again, but this time the laughter sounded genuinely merry, but equally uncontrollable. 'Come on,' she gasped between bouts, 'We'd better get home.' And she mounted the bike and set off, much faster than I could run, her laughter beginning to subside at last as she pushed furiously down on the pedals. As she drew away I thought I heard her say, 'Perhaps there is a God, after all . . .' but I may have misheard her.

By the time I reached home, the bicycle was propped against the wall in the back yard and Fiff was in the kitchen talking to Cly. Through the open door I caught part of what she was saying.

'. . . calling herself Mrs Jacques. She didn't know who Eric was, of course; must have thought he was selling something. She must be a fast piece: Eric said she even tried it on with him . . .' She broke off to give a high chime of angry laughter. 'By the time he managed to get away, he knew all about her *husband*, how sick he'd been all morning . . . making herself out to be Florence Nightingale . . . He blames my cooking, of course, not hers . . .'

Cly, fuelling Fiff's rage, said, 'So now we know why he wanted money . . .' and then, incredibly, she added, 'Well, that's what you get for marrying beneath you.'

Silence fell like shattered glass. Could Cly really have said that? I clapped my hand over my mouth and held my breath, waiting for the sound of a slap that would send Cly reeling.

But nothing happened. After several heartbeats, Fiff said grimly, 'Well, let it be a lesson to you.'

They were standing facing each other across the kitchen table when I entered, but the conversation seemed at an end.

The bicycle had given me an idea. While I'd been busy delivering the telegram to Fiff I'd forgotten about Mr Guest, but from where I'd been sitting on top of the railway crossing gate I could see the distant chimneys of the house on the marshes, reminding me. I badly wanted to find out what had happened to him, to make sure that he was all right; and to do that I had to find Chaz, who'd be sure to know. If I could borrow the bike, I could get to Llwyn-yr-eos and back well in time for supper.

'Can I borrow the bike, Mummy?' I asked.

Fiff said automatically, '*May* you borrow the bike. And no, you may not. You'll only fall off it and break something.' She meant something on the bike, an unjustified accusation.

'I never break anything!' I protested hotly.

Fiff wavered, but she was not prepared to give in without a struggle. 'What do you want it for, anyway?' she asked.

I knew that she would disapprove of my going to Llwyn-yr-eos without an invitation, so I said vaguely, 'Oh . . . just to ride around a bit . . . to see if I still remember how.'

'Oh, let her have it, Ma,' Cly said irritably. 'She's only in the way here.'

Fiff gave in. 'Ten minutes, then,' she said, and immediately undermined herself by adding, 'Supper in half an hour. See that you're back before then.' As I made a dash into the yard, her voice followed me out. 'And I want that machine back in one piece, remember!'

The seat of the bicycle was not as high as Chaz's – he rode with his bottom in the air – but even so I could only reach the pedals with my toes. After a few false starts when I kept falling off, I managed to pedal standing up, though it meant that the bike swayed from side to side as I trod first on one pedal then the other. It was gratifying to find that I hadn't forgotten how to do it. Avoiding the ruts, I kept to the grass strip running down in the middle of the track where the going was smoother. Elongated in the setting sun, tall and tapering as Blackpool Tower, my shadow ran beside me, copying everything I did.

There was no sign of the reporters, and the last few sightseers were trailing back towards Moravon and supper. I had almost reached Holly Hill before I felt confident enough to look up. Vaguely at the back of my mind while I toiled with the bike I had been aware of the distant sound of a boat's engine, and now I saw the *Slug* below, making its way upriver, Chaz at the wheel and Mr Channing sitting in the cockpit. I jumped off the bike and yelled, but they were well ahead and both had their backs to me; and almost immediately they disappeared behind Holly Hill's rocky outcrop.

On the gravel drive outside Holly Hill itself a black police car was parked, but there was no one in it. I supposed that the police must be down by the river, looking for more clues, and I hoped that they wouldn't find any, or none anyway which would get Mr Guest into trouble. As I struggled to remount, I became aware of another engine, behind me this time, and turning, I saw a car approaching – an open tourer driven by a woman. I pulled the bicycle to the side of the track and waited for it to pass, but it stopped beside me and the driver leaned over towards me. It was unusual to see a woman driver and I stared, fascinated.

'Do you speak English?' she asked with a disarming smile.

But for that smile I would have pretended not to understand. It would have been fun to rattle away in something that sounded like Welsh, and watch her expression turn to despair. But I'd have been sure to burst out laughing and give the game away, so I nodded.

'Sometimes,' I said.

'I seem to be lost,' she said. 'I'm looking for a house called Llwyn-yr-eos.'

She mispronounced it so badly that I didn't recognize the name, and I shook my head. 'I've never heard of it,' I said apologetically. 'There's nowhere called Linny-rose around here. This road only leads to Llwyn-yr-eos. That's where Mr Channing lives.'

'That's it! I think I must have missed the turning off the main road. How silly of me. Thanks.' She bathed me in another sunny smile and drove off with a parting wave.

I liked her, and I liked her even more when it occurred to me that Chaz and Mr Channing would have to stay now that she had arrived. She must be the guest Mr Channing had been expecting, and he and

Chaz couldn't very well go away and leave a guest behind, could they? No, of course not: that would be bad manners. So that was all right: they would have to stay.

When I arrived at Llwyn-yr-eos, I paused at the twin stone pillars marking the entrance and peered through the shrubbery. In the distance the tourer was standing abandoned outside the front door while Henderson unloaded luggage. Even at this distance I could see that the suitcases – heavy yellow cowhide, like one Fiff had – were covered with the travel labels of steamship companies. I waited until, laden with luggage, Henderson disappeared into the house. Distantly, from the direction of the river, I could hear Chaz and Mr Channing talking as they approached.

Uncertain of my welcome now that there was a stranger here, I inched further up the drive, and through the bushes I just had time to notice that someone had been using a scythe to mow the lawn, leaving the grass to dry in rows, before Jenkins arrived with a furious challenge and planted himself before me, ready to attack.

'It's all right, Jenkins, it's only me,' I said hastily, but the big dog only relaxed when Chaz arrived a moment later pushing his bicycle.

'Don't tell me,' he said with a grin which looked sarcastic to me, 'You forgot the mushrooms.'

'Mushrooms?' I said, baffled.

'In my saddle-bag,' he said. 'They fell out on the deck of the boat. I must have forgotten to buckle the straps.'

Annoyed that he should think I'd come cadging, and irritated by the familiar accusation that I'd forgotten something, I said coldly, 'I came because I wanted to know if Mr Guest was all right.'

The grin vanished. 'Oh, that,' he said. 'I don't know. Nobody would tell me anything, and Uncle Hil wouldn't let me hang around any longer.' He bent to unbuckle the straps of the saddle-bag, adding wistfully, 'Damn shame about the autogyro, though. Mr Guest'd promised me – well, *half*-promised me – a ride in it. It would have been something to tell them about when I get back to school.'

I could sympathize with this. I well understood the importance of having something to swank about at school; and perhaps Mr Guest had managed to swim ashore. I willed him to do it.

I said haltingly, 'You don't suppose he did it on purpose, do you?' This idea had come to me while I was sitting on top of the railway gate, looking at the chimneys of the house on the marshes. I wanted to discuss it.

But Chaz was appalled. 'Crashed the autogyro, you mean? Why on earth should he?'

I backed down in face of his disbelief, and mumbled, 'Well . . . because of Teddy Ransom . . . and all that . . .'

Chaz didn't answer. He had undone the straps of the saddle-bag and lifted the flap. Across the meadow that had once been a lawn, Mr Channing was heading straight for the house with Jenkins at his heels.

To change the subject, I said, 'Someone's come to see you.'

'My Aunt Lois,' Chaz said with a glance towards the car outside the front door. 'She's been touring Scotland. She dropped in to see Uncle Hil on her way back to London.'

As he loaded the mushrooms into the basket on Fiff's bike, he said, 'Tell you what. I've got to go in now that my aunt has arrived, to pay my respects, but we can still have our feast in the tree house if you come out later. Have you got a torch?'

I was startled. 'You mean *after* dark? My mother'd never allow me.'

'Can't you sneak out without being seen?' he asked. 'Go on, I dare you.'

I thought about it with mounting dread and excitement all through supper. As far as I knew, Fiff never entered my bedroom after I'd gone to bed, unless I was ill. She stayed up reading, or listening to the wireless and sewing, until late – I knew that because I'd sometimes gone downstairs after a bad dream – and I was pretty sure that she didn't lock up until just before she went to bed herself.

The thought of failing to accept a dare was almost more than I could bear, but to go out alone after dark was to break Fiff's sternest rule. I was so engrossed with the problem of whether or not to risk it that I hardly heard a word of the conversation – which was desultory anyway – between Fiff and Cly. We were all preoccupied with our own private problems. Cly was probably thinking excited thoughts about Dougie Parrish or some other boy, and Fiff was still absorbed, though more sombrely now, by the memory of Eric's phone call, and neither of them noticed my silence. Fiff, who had intended to make Welsh rarebit, changed her mind when she saw the mushrooms I'd brought, and we were eating creamed mushrooms on toast to the accompaniment of a dance band on the wireless.

By bedtime, I had scared myself so much with the thought of the consequences of getting caught that I had reluctantly made up my mind not to keep the date with Chaz at the tree house. Cly's ears were sharper than Fiff's, and it was too risky to creep downstairs and sneak out through the back door.

But Chaz had dared me, and I had my reputation to consider: I was famous for my daring. Even if the other kids never found out that I'd refused a dare, *I'd* know it, and it would rankle. Besides, I was haunted by the thought of strawberry scones and cream, and just out of interest – just to see what the night looked like – I pushed my bedroom window wide open and hung out over the window-sill.

I liked the dark. Owls were hooting and the occasional cry of a nightjar hung like a question mark in the darkness, but none of it was frightening – certainly not as chilling as the night sounds from the jungle in Ceylon. The moon had not yet risen, and when it did, it would be little more than half the size of the brilliant full moon which had sailed the night sky a week ago. Even with her spyglass, Mrs van Gelderen wouldn't be able to see anything.

But the yard wall below and the wash-house roof were illuminated by the light from Mrs Bellamy's kitchen window, and all of a sudden, on shaky legs, I found myself climbing out.

Walking alone and unseen in the dark, losing myself in it, becoming a part of the night, was even more pleasurable than I had thought it would be. The sense of freedom went to my head: I wanted to laugh and dance. There were glow-worms here and there, tiny illuminations to celebrate my escape. They reminded me with a pang of Ceylon and the times when the Festival of Lights turned the tropical night into fairyland. One day, I thought fervently, one day I'll go back . . .

But even though I began to jog as soon as my eyes got used to the dark, it seemed to be taking a long time to get to Llwyn-yr-eos, and it would take even longer to reach the tree house. Once I had savoured the thrill of freedom, I began to have doubts about the wisdom of this adventure. I pictured Fiff going into my bedroom and finding my bed empty, and the thought was so scary that I might have turned back if Chaz hadn't come to meet me with a torch.

'I wasn't sure you'd come,' he said.

I remembered that I was supposed to be a daredevil, and said carelessly, 'You dared me, so I did it. Why not? It wasn't much of a dare.'

'I thought you'd be scared of the dark,' he explained.

'*Here?*' I scoffed. 'I used to walk around at night in the *jungle* in Ceylon.' He probably knew this wasn't true, but he didn't challenge it.

Now that the grass had been cut, it was easy to run down the meadow at Llwyn-yr-eos without tripping over a tussock. We climbed into the tree house in high glee to find the feast laid out on a chequered tablecloth, lit by the candle he'd stuck in a jam jar.

We had been sitting on the floor, wolfing strawberry scones and sponge cake for quite some time when Chaz suddenly spoiled everything.

He had selected a bottle of ginger ale from his store of pop. 'Oh, by the way, I meant to tell you,' he said, shaking the bottle to make sure the pop would burst out when he opened it, 'They found Mr Guest. He was still alive, but only just. They've taken him off to hospital somewhere, but they think he's broken his back. If that's right he'll never walk again. He'll be crippled for life; probably have to be pushed around in a bath chair.'

I'd been licking cream from my fingers and planning to begin on the chocolate marshmallows, but this news put all thought of food out of my head.

'That's horrible,' I said, offended. 'How can you say things like that?' Chaz was making this up to shock me. It was worse even than the rubbish he'd told me about the toadstools. 'He only fell into the sea. I've jumped into the sea hundreds of times. *Thousands.*'

'From a hundred feet up?' he asked, and when I

didn't answer, he added, 'It would be like hitting a brick wall.'

I still didn't want to believe it. If I argued enough he might change his mind and admit that Mr Guest was all right after all. 'But how do you know? Mr Channing brought you home before they found him. You said so.'

'Uncle Hil knows the harbour-master,' he said. 'He phoned him.'

'You don't even care!' I burst out. 'How can you be so . . . so disgrumptious?' I began to scramble to my feet, afraid that I was going to cry. 'I'm going home,' I said. 'You've spoilt it now.'

'You can't go yet,' he protested. 'We were going to try our experiment. Like those people on the island. Remember?'

I did remember. I hesitated.

'Come on,' he said persuasively, 'you haven't had any pop yet.'

If I'd known at the time how long it would be before I saw Chaz again, I'd have been nicer to him – or at least less ungracious – especially when he gave me his watch.

'But I don't need a watch,' I said. 'And what if they think you've lost it?' I knew what Fiff would say if I lost something as valuable as a watch.

'That's OK,' he explained. 'I've got another.'

19

I didn't see the second telegram arrive. I had been back
at school for days by then. Cly too had gone, back to
her boarding school, and the house seemed strangely,
almost eerily, peaceful. Pipsy mooched about at a
loose end, getting under our feet until Fiff lured her out
into the yard with home-made dog biscuits and
quickly shut the door on her.

As soon as Cly had gone I'd been into her bedroom
just to see if I had the courage to pinch her bottles of
scent, but all her cosmetics – the Pond's vanishing
cream, the Coty powder, the Tangee lipstick as well as
the scent – had vanished, taken back with her to
school. I'd searched the room for my shoes, but of
course I couldn't find them: I hadn't really expected to.
But she'd hidden them somewhere, I was sure of that.
In growing despair I'd searched the wash-house,
the coal house, Pipsy's bedding, the outside dubby, the
kennel and the meat safe, all the places where Cly
might have hidden them. I'd even stood on the seat
of the dubby to feel on top of the cistern. I'd climbed
into the attic, but the stacks of steel trunks – most of
them locked – were too daunting to attack, and the tea
chests held only straw and screwed-up newspaper.
Increasingly disheartened, I'd cast about hopelessly
among the hollyhocks and Michaelmas daisies in the
garden, all to no avail; but I couldn't bear to think that
I'd never see my beloved shoes again, and I went on
looking.

The day after the feast in the tree house had been almost unnaturally quiet. Because of a guilty conscience, I wanted to avoid Chaz. I'd gone to Garth Hall again with Fiff, and this time there had been no reason to leave early, and the tea party in the afternoon had been as satisfying as it always was, not because there was so much to eat – there wasn't – but because it was a treat. Going out for a meal was rare, and Fiff never served afternoon tea unless we had visitors. We trailed home from the Junction in the evening empty-handed but for the bearskin rug she'd bought, and I was relieved to see that there was no sign of Chaz.

But by the end of the next day, when he had still not appeared, I began to miss him, and while Fiff prepared supper, I borrowed the bike again and cycled to Llwyn-yr-eos in the slanting evening light.

This time there was no challenge from Jenkins, and as I pushed the bike through the shrubbery and out into the open, it seemed to me that there was an unnatural silence about the place, as though everybody had suddenly been wiped out by a disaster. The rows of mown grass were still lying roughly where I had last seen them, though they had been turned and tossed, and now the grass had dried into hay and the air was sweet with its scent. But the place looked – and felt – deserted. The uncurtained windows of the house stared out across the fields towards the river with the bleak emptiness of dead eyes. I had long since lost my terror of the place, but now, faced with silence, with desertion, it threatened to come back.

It had begun to dawn on me the day Mr Channing had taken us to lunch in the Golden Lion that Jacko – or someone – must have made up the story about the mad old man. The whole thing was a myth – of course it was – but it was such a good myth that I was reluctant to part with it. Looking at the ancient house, I was sure the story must have been true once, perhaps hundreds of years ago; and all houses as old as this had ghosts. Something dreadful might have happened since I'd last been here. I might even have imagined Chaz and Mr Channing.

While I was trying to make up my mind whether I could raise the courage to approach further, I heard a distant door open, and a voice said something I was too far away to hear, but I was sure it was Mrs Henderson, and relief flooded through me. And presently Henderson appeared from the back of the house pushing a wheelbarrow, a hay rake lying across it. He saw me and raised a hand in greeting as he made for the lawn.

'I'm afraid you've missed them, Miss Fidgie,' he called over. 'They all left for London this morning.'

I trailed after him. 'But Mr Channing said they wouldn't be going till Sunday,' I protested, as if he could somehow reverse their decision and magic them back.

'Ah,' he said, beginning to toss the hay. 'Changed their minds. Decided to go along with young Mrs Channing in her car.' And as an afterthought, he added, 'Took that young tutor with 'em an' all, so there's nobody here at all now . . .'

That had been the last day of summer. Lashing rain laden with salt swept in from the sea that night, carried on the first autumnal gale. The wind roared in the chimney and rattled the windows, trying to get in. It was an oddly comforting sound, and I fell asleep to its lullaby.

But for the next few days I couldn't think of anything I wanted to do. I still went with Fiff to the auction in Fairhurst, dashing through the rain to the Junction, but I had lost interest in Garth Hall and I went mostly to avoid being left alone in the house with Cly. Losing Chaz and Tom had taken the heart out of everything.

I was glad when school started again, even though I'd been moved up a class to a different teacher. My ears had turned pink again by then, and even the big bruise on my arm was fading, turning yellow at the edges and green in the middle. The visitors, the people from away, had disappeared as if a trapdoor had opened and swallowed them as soon as September had started. They had vanished in packed trains, the children waving a last dispirited farewell from the carriage windows as the trains pulled out of Moravon station. And suddenly the beaches were deserted, the seagulls' cries disconsolate.

Ellen and Ruthie and Dilys and I slipped back into the familiar rituals in the playground, the hopscotch and Tig and Wallflowers and skipping, as if the holidays had never interrupted them. Fiff had made me a new gymslip and I was proud of it, though I made up my mind that once I finished school – if I ever did – I'd never wear navy blue again. *Ever. Or* black woollen stockings. It was too warm yet, but I knew I'd have to wear those again – *and* itchy woollen combinations – when it got colder. Cly wore a liberty bodice, which was much more sophisticated.

Ellen had forgiven me for getting her into that scrape on the island. At least, I supposed she must have, because she didn't say anything about it when I called for her on my way to school. She didn't twit me about Chaz either. If she had, I was going to impress her by telling her that he'd gone to school in London. I might do that anyway, to show off. London was a fabulous place: only the boldest, the most sophisticated people ever dared to go there.

This was the first day of the autumn term, and we walked to school together, but as we neared the gates I saw Jacko ahead and broke into a run to catch up with him.

'I've got a bone to pick with you, Jacko Jones,' I said sternly, poking him in the back.

He swung round, his small monkey face screwed up. 'You talkin' to me or chewin' a brick?'

This was the very latest in smart repartee. I'd been trying to find an opportunity to use it myself, and I was furious that Jacko had beaten me to it.

'You *fibber*!' I said accusingly. 'You made up all that stuff about the old man at Llwyn-yr-eos. It was all lies. I found out.'

I was half-hoping that he'd stand by his story; tell me I'd got the wrong house, the wrong old man, but he opened his mouth in a wide grin of triumph. 'Aah . . . ha . . . ha . . . !' he brayed, pointing a mocking finger at me. 'And you believed it!' He broke into a run, chanting, 'Sucker! Sucker!'

I chased him, shouting 'Fibber, fibber, *fibber*!' until he escaped round the corner into the boys' playground, where girls weren't allowed. It was infuriating. He had been a bit spiteful ever since I'd refused to go up the mountain with him.

Ellen wouldn't eat school dinners any more. They were always the same – a pudding-bowl half-full of thick meat and potato soup, dished up from a big cauldron in the dark basement under the school – and Ellen swore that she'd once found a dead spider in hers. Ever since then we'd gone across the road at dinner time to buy a ha'penny bag of chips from the fish-and-chip shop opposite the school gates.

For ages now, the poster outside the newspaper shop next door had carried the headline HUSBAND OF MURDER SUSPECT IN AIR ACCIDENT. I'd tried not to look at it because I felt like bursting into tears or flying into a temper every time I thought of Mr Guest. Chaz had said

297

that he would never be able to walk again, and remembering how we'd walked to Holly Hill together, I couldn't bear to think of it. But the local paper only came out once a week and the poster stayed up. People stood around talking about it, excited by Moravon's sudden fame.

We were sitting on the school wall eating our chips when I noticed a new poster outside the newsagent's. Now it read LOCAL WOMAN CHARGED WITH MURDER; and below that, MISSING SHOTGUN.

I pointed it out to Ellen; but Ellen, knowing as always, sighed and said impatiently, 'That's *old*! Wake up, Fidgie! That was in all the papers days ago. They say she's going to be tried at the Assizes in Dolgarran.'

'Well, I hope she gets hung,' I said savagely. 'It's all her fault Mr Guest is nearly dead. He wouldn't have crashed but for her shenanigans.' That was the word Fiff had used.

'What you talking about?' Ellen asked. 'She didn't have nothing to do with him crashing. She wasn't there.'

I looked round to make sure there was nobody within earshot. Then, to make doubly sure, I cupped my hand round her ear and whispered, 'I *told* you. She was *having a spin* with Mr Ransom.'

I thought she must have forgotten this titbit. I expected a gasp of astonishment, a round-eyed *Oooh . . . !* but she drew back and looked at me with disdain. 'Everybody knows *that*,' she said crushingly. 'That's no secret.' She dug hungrily into her bag of chips. 'What's more, everybody thinks it was Mr Guest shot Teddy Ransom, even if he *was* supposed to be in Manchester.' She pointed a chip towards a group of people gossiping on the pavement outside the newspaper shop. 'They say he tried to do 'imself in so's not to give evidence at her trial.'

It was alarming to find that everybody – perhaps

298

even the police – had jumped to the same conclusion as Chaz and I had. To cover up for Mr Guest, I said what Chaz would have said. 'That's *cock!*' But I knew it wasn't enough to convince her.

It was not until two days after school had started that I saw the *Slug* again. Swinging my satchel, I had just pushed my way through the turnstile on the bridge when I saw the little boat below, puttering placidly downriver, Mr Channing at the wheel, his pipe clamped between his teeth. There was no sign of Chaz, of course, but I climbed up the railing and waved wildly all the same, delighted that Mr Channing at least had come back, even without Chaz. He looked up and raised a hand casually in acknowledgement as the *Slug* disappeared underneath the bridge. It had been raining on and off all morning, but all of a sudden the sun came out like a burst of applause. I started to dance along, convinced that – any moment now – something good was going to happen.

Perhaps that was why I suddenly looked up and noticed movement at Hill Top House. The bungalow, half-hidden among the oaks on the crest of the knoll, had come to life. A woman was moving about in the garden, hanging washing – curtains, by the look of them – spreading them over the bushes to dry. And presently a girl about my size came out to join her.

It was possible, of course, that this was just someone who'd come to clean the house. It was too far away to be certain, but this woman looked quite different from the little plump woman who usually came to do that. She didn't look like a honeymooner either, though I wasn't quite sure what honeymooners looked like. I began to run, eager to ask Fiff if we had new neighbours. If we had, and if they weren't honeymooners, I might go up there and ask that girl if she wanted to come out to play. But first I'd have to hang around and make sure that she looked OK. She might be stuck up, like Cly; or worse, she might be a cry-baby. I couldn't stand cry-babies.

When I hurtled into the kitchen, Fiff was ironing, a harassed expression on her face. She hated ironing. The irons – always two, so that one could be switched for the other when the first had cooled – had to be heated on the oil stove in the summer when the range was out, and if the wicks were turned up too high – as sometimes happened – they smoked, and soot built up unnoticed on the irons. A moment's inattention left black streaks on the clean laundry, which was more than Fiff could bear.

Because of this, it was wise to avoid the kitchen when she was ironing, and her mood was perilous when I burst in. Before I could get my breath back, she said icily, 'Have you been on the cadge again, young woman?'

Startled, I said, 'No, I *haven't*!' and added guiltily, '. . . At least, I don't think so.'

'I've just received a note from your friend up the river,' she said. Fiff had a curious dislike of putting names to people she had never met. I supposed she meant Mr Channing, now that Chaz had gone. She went on, 'He says he's got a kitten for you – a tom like the one you wanted – and asks if I will agree to let you have it.'

I was thrilled. 'Oh, Mummy, *please* say yes.'

But Fiff refused to give in easily. 'I'll think about it,' she said. 'Now go and get washed.'

Nothing happened for days after that. Fiff stamped on my pleas and ignored my soulful looks, but she must have written to Mr Channing because, a few days later, Henderson arrived in the Rolls and carried a wicker hamper to our door.

When Fiff saw the kitten she said, 'It looks to me like a pedigree.' There was a note of disapproval in her voice, as if a pedigree was going to impose a needless worry on her. 'You'll have to take extra special care of him.'

I didn't care. The kitten's fur was the same blue-grey as Mr Channing's cat. He was beautiful and I fell in love with him at once.

'I'll call him Uncle,' I said, 'after Mr Channing.'

'You'll have to write a thank-you letter,' Fiff said sternly. 'Straight away. In your very best handwriting.'

But before that, before Henderson came with the hamper, the telegram arrived. When I got back from school that afternoon, I could hear Fiff laughing in the sitting-room. I thought she must have someone with her – Mrs Bellamy perhaps, though she and Fiff never entered each other's houses – and I was going into the kitchen for a drink when it occurred to me that I couldn't hear any other voice in the sitting-room, and the laughter sounded exactly like the strange merriment which had overcome her the night she phoned Eric. The Ewbank was standing abandoned in the hall as if she had been interrupted in the middle of sweeping the carpet.

She stood up when I entered. She was trying to wipe the laughter out of her face and appear brisk and businesslike. 'I'll have to go out and make a telephone call, child,' she said. 'So stay here and don't get up to any mischief while I'm out.'

I followed her out of the sitting-room and watched while she took her raincoat from the row of hooks in the hall.

'Oh, and while I'm out, make yourself useful,' she said. 'Take the Ewbank out and empty it for me.'

Halfway through the door she suddenly turned and

said, 'Were you fond of your father?'

Thunderstruck by this idea, I said, 'Fond of *Daddy*?' I was afraid that she was having some sort of attack, perhaps like those Chaz had, only worse.

'Because you won't be seeing him again,' she said.

'Are you going to divorce him?' I asked.

Laughter began to come back into her face. She struggled to straighten her mouth again. 'It seems there won't be any need for that now,' she said, and went out.

After she'd gone I carried the Ewbank out to the rubbish tip behind the hydrangeas. Until then, I'd forgotten about the box of cream cakes, and now I wondered if they'd still be there, deliciously awaiting my return; but as soon as I'd pushed my way through leaves heavy with the day's rain, I could see that I was too late; much too late. The box was still there, but rain-sodden and torn open long since – probably by a fox – and a fat black slug was busy tidying up the last vestiges of meringue and puff pastry and cream. In a fit of spite, I emptied the Ewbank over it.

'You can eat that too while you're about it,' I told the slug vengefully.

It was when I turned to go that I caught the dull gleam of something familiar under the hydrangeas, and with a gasp of excitement I pulled it out: one of my dancing shoes. A frantic search under the bushes yielded the other. Cly must have thrown them out of my bedroom window when she'd heard me coming that evening. Miraculously they were almost as good as new, a little dusty but perfectly dry, protected from the rain by the spreading shrubs. From long habit I looked inside the toes to check for scorpions, and then I bore them home in triumph.

It didn't matter now that Fiff might return and question me about them. Nothing mattered now that

I'd got them back. After I'd blown the dust out of the rosettes and polished the leather lovingly with a duster, I put them on and began to dance from room to room around the house. That was when I noticed the telegram lying on the table in the dining-room, and paused to pick it up. The strips of paper stuck across it read:

TERRIBLE NEWS JUST RECEIVED STOP THORP
PASSED AWAY LAST NIGHT STOP MORE
FOLLOWS STOP LOUISA STOP

I put it back on the table and wandered into the drawing-room, thinking. I knew that people said 'passed away' when they meant dead. They thought it sounded more polite. But Boko was too big, too loud and too frightening to have passed away: it just wasn't the sort of thing he'd do. I must have misunderstood, or else Auntie Louie had made a mistake. That must be the reason why Fiff had been laughing.

But gradually I allowed myself to imagine what it would be like if it really were true, if Boko never did come back, if he had mysteriously *passed away* and couldn't come back. I'd never again have to stand in that huge, menacing presence, watch his face contort with rage, see him raise that heavy hand across his chest.

Fleetingly, it occurred to me too that there would be no more mauve fondants either, no more pink and white coconut ice, no more sixpenny bits.

But that seemed a small price to pay. I'd never again have to listen, not knowing what to do, outside a door, to Boko's voice roaring, and the crashing and the gasps of pain inside; afraid that this time, this time, he really would kill Fiff. I could bear my own beatings, but I couldn't bear Fiff's.

The records he had brought were still lying beside

the gramophone in their brown-paper sleeves. He must have forgotten to take them back with him. I wound up the gramophone and lifted its lid. There was already a record on the turntable. I switched on and placed the needle carefully on the first groove. The mellow sound of a big dance band flooded out. A man's voice began to sing *When day is done* . . .

I remembered hearing it drifting upstairs while I was cowering on my bed in the dark the last time Boko had been here. Remembering that, I listened uneasily at first. But it was a big, swinging tune, and in the end my feet couldn't resist it.

It was, after all, what my dancing shoes were made for.

Tomorrow, I thought happily, I'll sneak up to Hill Top House and hang around a bit – pretend I'm looking for mushrooms or a lost ball perhaps – and see if I liked the look of that little girl up there. It would be fun to have someone nearby who could come out to play. I'd think about it: it was something to look forward to.

And perhaps too – now that I'd given him the idea – Mr Channing would buy Teddy's boat, and then Chaz would come back. I looked down at my beautiful bronze dancing shoes and suddenly I was walking on air.

The tune and the beat were entrancing but the words were sad. I tried to make my heart sink in response to them, but it refused to be quelled. It rose irresistibly on the tide of music.

Dreamily, I raised my arms and began to dance.

Indescribable, I thought, was a nice word, and I was pretty sure that it was a real one. From now on, everything would be indescribable.

THE END